Rachel's  to His Le...

"I didn't expect you to play the martyr, sacrificing your virginity in abject fear and trembling of your master."

His teasing stung her to a spirited response. "I am not afraid, sir, simply—inexperienced and . . ."

"That can be simply remedied." He sat up and took her chin between his thumb and forefinger, turning her face toward the firelight. "You are angry with me. That's better. I like a show of spirit. I knew you had it and it governed my choice."

"That—and my dower."

"A sharp tongue, too." He chuckled. "I'm not unappreciative of that either, at the right time and place—and this is neither, wife." His hard kiss silenced her as he drew her chilled, rigid form into his arms.

His fingers, feather-light on her throat, breasts and waist, roused her to a wild ecstasy of desire, so that she accepted his heavy weight—hard on her body— without further resistance, biting her lips hard to prevent herself from crying out. . . .

Dear Reader:

We trust you will enjoy this Richard Gallen romance. We plan to bring you more of the best in both contemporary and historical romantic fiction with four exciting new titles each month.

We'd like your help.

We value your suggestions and opinions. They will help us to publish the kind of romances you want to read. Please send us your comments, or just let us know which Richard Gallen romances you have especially enjoyed. Write to the address below. We're looking forward to hearing from you!

Happy reading!

The Editors of
Richard Gallen Books
8-10 West 36th St.
New York, N.Y. 10018

Temptation's Triumph

JOANNA MAKEPEACE

PUBLISHED BY RICHARD GALLEN BOOKS
Distributed by POCKET BOOKS

This novel is a work of historical fiction. Names, characters, places and incidents relating to non-historical figures are either the product of the author's imagination or are used fictitiously. Any resemblance of such non-historical incidents, places or figures to actual events or locales or persons, living or dead, is entirely coincidental.

 A RICHARD GALLEN BOOKS *Original* publication

Distributed by
POCKET BOOKS, a Simon & Schuster division of
GULF & WESTERN CORPORATION
1230 Avenue of the Americas, New York, N.Y. 10020

Published by arrangement with Futura Publications Ltd.

ISBN: 0-671-44694-0

First Pocket Books printing April, 1982

10 9 8 7 6 5 4 3 2 1

RICHARD GALLEN and colophon are trademarks of Simon & Schuster and Richard Gallen & Co., Inc.

Printed in the U.S.A.

For Edith Ellen York, my mother,
my most respected and beloved critic

"Now death rides triumphantly on his pale horse through our streets and breaks into every house . . ."

Dr. Vincent, August 1665,
Writing of the Plague in London

Chapter 1

October 1664

The gardens were shrouded in a gray veil of misery in keeping with her own brooding resentment, thought Rachel, as she pushed wide the casement and felt the mist fall on her hair and face. The fog made it almost impossible to distinguish the red brick walling of the formal garden or the thatch on the stable roof.

As if only dimly aware of the abrupt drop in the room's warmth, Phoebe stirred in the big oaken bed and murmured sleepily in remonstrance, then turned over again and was immediately asleep. Rachel smiled wryly and quietly drew to the casement, but, despite the chill in the room, she continued to sit in the window embrasure, unwilling to return to the bed where she had tossed wakefully through most of the night.

How could Phoebe sleep on like that, today of all days? Strands of her sister's soft fair hair had escaped from her linen nightcap and shone brightly against the pillow. She still seemed so much a child.

Phoebe was sixteen only last month and today was her betrothal day. Still she slept on, dreamlessly oblivious of the momentous change so soon to affect her, just as she had sailed through those sixteen years of girlhood, apparently unaware of the strains and stresses life imposed on those around her.

"How can I resent it?" Rachel thought tiredly. "I love her so dearly." Rachel knew it was dread of being alone once Phoebe left and her fear of her father's new alliance with Mistress Burnell that made her less than generous. She castigated herself for failing to give Phoebe the whole of her heart when, Heaven knows, she might find the thorns on the stems of the roses very soon now.

Even so, Rachel was afraid. Roger was perceptive, astute, a promising newcomer to the magistrates' bench. Phoebe's loving, gentle immaturity might pall on him soon after the early pleasures of the marriage bed.

It had been decided years ago between the two gentlemen farmers that Roger Talbot should wed one of the Nashe girls and there had been little doubt that his choice would fall upon Phoebe. For the past three years Roger had been studying law at Cambridge and had recently ridden over to Glebe once or twice between terms. He was no Cavalier, but a sturdy brown man of twenty-two summers, attractively featured, of average height. Phoebe, shamefaced, confessed to regarding him as somewhat dull.

"He's so stern, Rachel. I shall always be afraid of displeasing him." She had sighed, then brightening, grinned at her sister impishly. "But for all that, he's a proper man, and it will be good to live so near to you all at Barrow. I should have hated it if I could not see you almost every day." The smile had faded then, the blue eyes clouded with doubt. "I wish I could have waited just a few months more, or even a year. I shall make such a bad housewife, Rachel. I'm so dreadfully forgetful and inefficient."

Rachel rose from the window seat. Her leg was beginning to ache a little and it would stiffen if she didn't move soon. She must dress and go out now, before the household stirred. She needed to be alone for a while. Already the fog was beginning to disperse. It augured a fine day to come. There was no point in lying any longer in bed. She had stood too long yesterday in the kitchen, supervising the preparation of all the jellies, tarts, pies and syllabubs for today's feasting. She always paid the price after long hours of standing.

She dressed quietly so as not to wake Phoebe. It would be cold out and she chose her warmest blue gown, the one she usually wore when working in the herb plot. She tied the strings of her brown frieze cloak tightly and pulled up the hood over her plain linen cap. Her soft brown hair was smoothed back decorously, well out of sight.

Leah was already overseeing the two kitchen maids, as they struggled with bellows to start the sulky kitchen fire. She looked up in surprise at Rachel's cloaked form.

"I thought you'd be resting up this morning, Mistress Rachel," she said.

"It's my duty to see to all the arrangements, Leah. Father will expect it of me. I'd not have the household disgraced. It's true Glebe is not famed for its hospitality. All the more need now we've a reason for celebration that we make a good showing. Mistress Talbot, though she's ailed lately, has always had the reputation of being such a careful housewife. She will be looking to us for signs that Phoebe has been well trained."

"She does well enough when she's a mind to it, but she's a mortal one for daydreaming, Mistress Phoebe."

"But very gentle and biddable. Mistress Talbot will soon instruct her to her own satisfaction."

Leah Ashley had been wet nurse to both Rachel and Phoebe. After their mother had died giving birth to Phoebe, Leah had taken her place and devoted herself to the girls.

"My head has ached since I woke, Leah," Rachel said now. "I'm going to walk for half an hour or so. Did you see that Barnaby went to old Diggory's cottage as I

3

asked, and chopped enough wood for the next couple of days?"

"Aye, he did, Mistress Rachel." The old woman snorted. "And got little thanks for his pains. The old fool had only himself to blame that he fell from the stable roof. If he'd taken less ale, it wouldn't have happened."

"It's his one consolation since Charity died. We'll have to be patient with him for a while. The doctor says the leg is badly broken. He won't be able to look after himself for a time yet. I'll try to get to see him tomorrow. There should be some little delicacy or other to take over."

"You spoil him, Mistress Rachel. The old man's crotchety and stubborn to boot, and not worth your trouble."

Diggory Whatsize was their head gardener and the frequent spates of temper between the old man and Leah were a source of amusement to the Nashe girls. It was a common morning entertainment to see Diggory stump out of the kitchen, spitting sourly onto the cobbles of the yard, after high words with Leah about which vegetables were required for table. It seemed that whatever Leah demanded was, somehow, never available. Rachel concluded that it was the one way the old rapscallion found of getting back at her for insisting that he remove his boots before setting foot in hall and kitchen, and for her plundering of his beloved flower garden.

Rachel turned with her hand on the latch of the kitchen door.

"It's a great pity this betrothal feast is late in the year. We're so short of flowers. There are still some of those tall yellow daisies and the purple Michaelmas near the back wall, very bedraggled, I'm afraid. Tell Prue to pick any that are not half dead. I'll gather some ivy and I remember seeing some pink valerian growing in the angle of the walls at Hetherington."

"Don't you go a' climbing, Mistress Rachel."

"I'll take care."

She escaped into the chilly dampness of the herb garden. Swirls of mist enveloped her and the coach-house loomed eerily through the eddies of trailing whiteness. It was a foolish notion to walk in this. The hems of both cloak and gown would be soaked if she ventured across the deerpark to Hetherington, yet, for the moment, she could not bear to face the hectic bustle which would surround her in kitchen, dairy, dining and drawing room. Everywhere there would be chatter about the betrothal.

Phoebe and the servants would gossip incessantly about the guests. No, time enough to bear all that when she must. . . .

Once free of the muck-strewn courtyard she struck out for the neglected, half-ruined pile of Hetherington Manor. The estate had always been a favorite haunt of the two Nashe sisters. It was a fifteenth-century moated manor, constructed in red brick. Unfortunately, only the stout gatehouse and west wing were still standing. The great hall was a gaunt, blackened shell and the east wing a total ruin. After the manor had been sacked and fired by the Parliamentary forces, the present owner, Sir Nicholas Hetherington, had fled to the continent in the steps of his young sovereign, Charles II, having fought gallantly at his side at the fatal battle of Worcester.

Four years ago, in 1660, that same Sir Nicholas had accompanied his King back from exile, but, apparently, had made no attempt to occupy the house or begin rebuilding, to the relief of the villagers at Hetherington. Over the years the property had been plundered of brick, stone and lead, and many of them were guiltily

5

aware that it was public knowledge that they'd been present on the night Colonel Nashe's detachment of Ironsides had ridden over the moat bridge to order torches set to the building. Retribution had not yet struck. Sir Nicholas, they heard, had been appointed gentleman of the King's bedchamber, and neither he nor his younger brother, Christopher, had made so much as a fleeting visit to the village. The widowed Lady Hetherington had accompanied the Dowager Queen, Henrietta Maria, to France after her husband, Sir William, had been killed at Naseby.

Now the loneliness of the place seemed inviting to Rachel, and there would be ivy in plenty straggling over the crumbling walls. The great house appealed to the romantic side of her nature, a side rigidly withheld from her father and revealed only to her beloved grandmamma. As a child she'd imagined the manor as it had been soon after it was built: the enormous kitchens, presided over by the sturdy male cook with his huge wooden ladle, the stables and dairy, brewhouse and buttery. She'd visualized the knights and their ladies clad in velvets and brocades with the bright bannerets floating in the breeze as the retainers of visiting lords, perhaps even the King himself, rode over the bridge.

How could the present owner allow the lovely old house to fall into further decay? She looked up longingly at the two sturdy towers which guarded the surviving wing. The fabric of the structure was basically good here. It could be made habitable, even comfortable, but it would take ample funds.

A sudden movement behind her caused her to turn so suddenly that she stumbled and almost fell. A figure rose from a kneeling position near the board-covered rim of the old courtyard well. A wave of relief swept over Rachel as the woman approached.

"Zillah, you startled me!"

Had she not known Zillah Lee from childhood, she might have been further alarmed by her eccentric appearance. Long tangles of dark hair fell forward in elf-locks, almost obscuring the woman's face. She pushed the hair aside with a brown, work-worn hand. For as long as Rachel could remember, Zillah and Old Salome had occupied a tumbledown hovel a mile or so from the northern end of the village. Leah had told how, years ago, Salome had appeared in the district in the wake of one of the armies carrying Zillah, then a babe in arms. There had been no man with them and the nurse had remarked tartly that she'd thought Salome a camp follower. Both women were so swarthily featured that Rachel guessed they were originally of the old "Egyptian" itinerant community which traveled the length and breadth of the country, dealing in horses or mending iron pots and cooking vessels. Why Salome had left her tribal band was not known. More than likely her child, Zillah, had been fathered by a man outside the tribe. Salome had a reputation among the villagers for dark dealings with Satan, and her cottage was shunned by most, with the exception of one or two brave or desperate souls who stole away to visit her under cover of darkness, anxious to buy ointments and salves, for Salome was recognized, though somewhat grudgingly, as wise in herbal lore. Rachel suspected the purchaser occasionally also requested some potion or charm to stir desire in male or female loins.

Rachel pitied Zillah, knowing the woman's pride to be as fierce as her own. Leah had surmised that the gypsy must now be nineteen or twenty, so they were much of an age.

Zillah indicated a rush basket she'd left near the wellhead.

"I gather herbs when there's few people about, it's easier that way."

Rachel did not need explanations. "I wanted some

7

greenery to decorate the table for my sister's betrothal feast, ivy and valerian, if there's still any on the walls."

"There's still some over there." Zillah indicated a spot high up where the angle of wall from the ruined east tower met that of the great hall. "I'll get it for you."

Rachel flushed darkly, but the gypsy did not wait for her answer, simply gathered her skirts, showing bare-footed, long brown legs, and clambered nimbly on to a ledge where she dislodged the bright pink flowers.

"There's autumn crocus to the south of the gate-house and yellow toadflax in the park if you look carefully. They'll make a brave show." She bent and uncovered her own basket. "I've fumitory." She held out the herb with its feathery, delicate foliage. "Corn mayweed and chicory roots." She looked at Rachel questioningly. "Your leg aches?"

Rachel inclined her head stiffly.

"Mother will make you a potion. You'll sleep sound-ly then. I'll bring it to the house, unless you'd rather fetch it yourself." A grim smile twitched the chapped lips. "Perhaps you fear the works of the devil and would rather not accept our assistance?"

"Of course I do not."

Zillah laughed and Rachel marveled as the flash of large, strong teeth relaxed the raw-boned, severe fea-tures, so that the woman looked almost handsome.

"Wise of you, Mistress Rachel. There are worse devils on the earth than off it, as we all know to our cost. So your sister plights her troth today without need of old Salome's potions."

Rachel did not answer, though, surprisingly, she was not angered by the other woman's overt insolence.

"Perhaps we could help you, Mistress Rachel, or even your father," Zillah said mockingly, "if you were both to trust us."

"I think not," Rachel replied curtly, "and you should be cautious these days that you are not seen collecting herbs by moonlight or any other such nonsense, Zillah. It's not long to All Hallows."

Again the snakelike tresses were tossed derisively. "So stupidly superstitious, your true Puritan, self-righteous and condemning until help is needed to ease tight breathing when the fog and rains come, or skilled hands at a long, hard birthing and, of course," the hard laugh sounded again, "special, secret knowledge that only *we* can give. It's as well we've close mouths, my mother and I."

"Is she well?" Rachel said gently. "The men say they expect a hard winter. You'll need help with the wood store. I could send Barnaby . . ."

Zillah turned abruptly and faced Rachel, her eyes glittering. "We'll not need it."

"But . . ."

The woman shook her head, smiling secretively. "Truly, I know it, but you're kind to offer, and it's so rare it won't be forgotten. I'll bring the potion discreetly, never fear."

Before Rachel could prevent her or ask the meaning of the odd comment, she had lifted the basket, jumped up on the ruined wall and was clear away across the deerpark with a fleetness Rachel envied.

What *had* Zillah meant by that mention of her father? It had been plain enough what she was offering to Rachel and her cheeks burned at the thought that Zillah Lee pitied her. It was humiliating.

Rachel knew that the villagers were as aware as she of the reason why Simon Nashe had not insisted on the betrothal of his elder daughter first.

The affliction had not been noticed until after Rachel had begun to walk. One leg was slightly shorter than the other and it caused Rachel to limp. It was a noticeable limp, albeit a slight one, and the leg did not bother her unless she stood or walked for long periods. Then it would ache until she got some rest. But Rachel had many blessings for which she should thank God. She ailed rarely, was not even subject to the winter coughs and chills which plagued Phoebe. She was efficient in household management, had a good head for accounts. The servants respected her. There was simply no sense in bemoaning her lot. There was always so much to be done at Glebe and she loved the rambling, Elizabethan house.

The heat from the kitchen met her as she pushed open the door. Dinah Brown, the waif from the poorhouse, struggled from the courtyard with the heavy pail of water for the iron cooking pot suspended above the hearth. Leah and Prue Whitney were already red with exertion, their foreheads greasy from sweating over the fire. The air was redolent with the smell of roasting meat and herbs and the yeasty, familiar scent of new-baked bread. Rachel nodded approvingly.

"Put this greenery somewhere cool until we're ready to lay out the tables, Prue. I'll change and help with the sauces and custards. Has Phoebe breakfasted? And father? Has grandmamma come down?"

Leah wiped her forearm over a shining brow. "There's cold meats and ale set out in the dining room, Mistress Rachel. Your sister's with your grandmother in her bedchamber. The colonel has ridden over to Mountsorrel. He's to escort Mistress Burnell personally."

Rachel hesitated in mid-stride. So Judith Burnell had been invited to today's feast . . . Simon Nashe had served with her husband, Josiah Burnell, on the justices' bench until he died almost a year ago. Judith was a plump, attractive widow of some thirty summers.

For a split second Zillah's mocking words flashed across her mind. Had the woman seen them together?

Hard upon the realization that Phoebe was to leave Glebe, it was still more difficult to accept the possibility that Judith Burnell might soon take her place as mistress of this household.

Chapter 2

Sir Nicholas Hetherington drew rein outside The Sun Inn. Throughout their intolerable journey north, Kit had questioned his brother concerning Hetherington. Nick had shrugged it off, since Kit had previously shown little enthusiasm about returning home and he himself had undertaken this expedition for one reason only: His mother had required it of him. She'd been blunt and direct.

"It's time you saw how things stand at the manor. Nearly four years and you've not so much as cast eyes on the place. For your father's sake I'd have thought you'd force yourself to withdraw from the delights of town, if only temporarily."

He'd received her at his lodgings in Pall Mall, surprised by her visit. She rarely left her rooms at Somerset House these days, where she waited devotedly on the Dowager Queen whose consumptive cough worsened daily in the smoke-grimed air of the capital.

He'd risen immediately to seat her in the one comfortable chair his rooms boasted. "I'm honored, mother. You rarely come to see me."

She was still beautiful, regally tall, carrying that elegantly coiffured head superbly. Her honey-gold locks had whitened prematurely after the loss of his father, but her face remained unlined. Her expression bore its habitually severe frown as she settled her green silk skirts to her satisfaction.

"Now that Kit is down from Oxford, I'd not have him idle away his time as you do, Nicholas."

He smiled wryly. "Hardly that, mother. I do serve His Majesty . . ."

"Handing your sovereign his satin drawers is hardly work I consider suitable for either of my sons," she rapped out tartly. "There's real work to be done—at Hetherington."

"Hetherington is in ruins, mother," he reminded her steadily, "and beyond the limits of my purse to repair."

"Your steward reported that the west wing was habitable. I've a mind to spend Christmas there. Can it be arranged?"

He shrugged. "It's unlikely to be very comfortable. Why the sudden whim?"

"Hetherington is—was my home. Who knows how long I'll have to spend in it? I've been too long away."

"Are you ill?" he said sharply.

"Not that I'm aware of, but Her Majesty's worsening condition reminds us all we are but mortal." Her blue eyes skimmed over his tall figure in the heavy brocade dressing robe. In appearance he resembled her closely; the same haughty, hawklike features, eyes bluer than her own, greenish-turquoise in some lights—or on the rare occasions when he was aroused. In defiance of Court fashion he continued to wear his own fair hair in long curls to his shoulders, but he'd given way to the current mode to ape His Majesty and cultivated a thin golden moustache. His easy, languorous movements as he seated himself on the tall-backed chair opposite irritated her. Was there nothing of William's strength and enthusiasm in him?

Life had been hard for them all after Worcester; a degrading hand-to-mouth existence in Holland and France. Nicholas had seen service with the French

12

King; but now that Charles had returned to Whitehall and Nicholas had been granted a position at Court, his mode of living followed the pattern set by his sovereign —the late rising, the easy saunter in the Park, the hard gambling and drinking, the frequent visits to the coffee-house and theater with its accompanying pleasures of actresses and orange girls. Her heart ached for the waste of it all—and was Kit to follow his example?

So far her younger son had escaped the attitude of bitter cynicism Nicholas had assumed after Worcester. At the restoration of the monarchy four years ago Nicholas had placed his brother at Magdalen College, Oxford. Now Kit was down and already savoring the delights London offered. If she could not see him safely established in Leicestershire, she would lose him as she'd lost her elder son.

"Then you've no intention of taking your place on the justices' bench in the county?" she asked curtly.

"If you've a desire to go to Hetherington, I must ask the King's leave for absence from Court. It will be more sensible if Kit and I precede you and do what we can to make the house presentable. I have funds enough for that." He shrugged. "Kit may well enjoy the hunting. I'll send to inform you when we're ready to receive you, then either Kit or myself can ride south to escort you home."

She'd been mollified and her glacial stare relaxed a trifle as he bent his golden head to kiss the tips of her fingers.

Kit had exuded enthusiasm for the new venture. He'd even enjoyed the grueling ride north through mud-caked lanes and lowering pewter skies. Now, praise God, the sun was out again and they had reached The Sun Inn, where they could rest for a while and linger over ale.

The host received them unctuously. As they stepped into the taproom, Kit glanced around appreciatively at

13

the clean-scrubbed tables, rush-strewn tiled floor and gleaming copper and brass ware in the inglenook.

"We have about a mile further to go," Nick said. "I've a notion to push on now and see the worst."

Kit looked up at him sharply. "You're really dreading it? I'd not thought you so concerned about the manor."

"And how could you judge the matter, since we've not discussed it above a couple of times and then in mother's hearing? I'd no desire to distress her further."

"No offense meant, Nick." Kit shifted uneasily. "I'd simply thought you settled at Court."

"Since there was no help for it, it was as well I was. We were fortunate the property was not sequestered. The point is we're unlikely to be able to afford to live there. While the King keeps me by him, I have some hope of a grant or pension which would go some way to stopping the rot to the remaining fabric."

"It's perhaps as well mother didn't voice her usual advice that you find some lady suitably dowered to see you out of your difficulties."

"She didn't need to voice them. I was fully aware of what was in her mind."

"You're thirty, Nick. It's likely she'd look to the inheritance. Come now, are you telling me you encountered no wealthy, eligible ladies at Whitehall to suit our purposes?"

"Wealthy yes, eligible to suit *my* purposes, no." Sir Nicholas drained his tankard. "Now, if you please, we'll take a stroll outside after paying our score. Have a word with the landlord, Kit. It may be necessary for us to put up here for a night or two."

Sir Nicholas sauntered into the sunshine. A coach had drawn up by the inn door and Master Gilpin was leaning his head in to confer with the traveler. He straightened as Sir Nicholas approached.

"Here's the gentleman now, sir."

14

"Ah." The person addressed pushed open the vehicle's door and stepped down into the roadway. There was no mistaking that tall, slightly stooping figure, and Sir Nicholas stiffened as the man turned to face him. Color suffused the pale, stern features as recognition was mutual.

"Sir Nicholas Hetherington?" Simon Nashe acknowledged him coldly.

"Your servant, sir." The frosty note was just as noticeable in Sir Nicholas's reply.

"Home at last. You're journeying to the manor, I take it?"

"Indeed I am, sir."

The colonel turned toward the shaded interior of the coach. "Allow me to introduce the squire, Mistress Burnell. You'll not have met Sir Nicholas Hetherington."

The lady inclined her head at the window as Sir Nicholas bowed.

"Charmed, sir. We've wondered long about you and we trust you'll remain enough time with us to make yourself known in county circles."

"That may be so," he returned gravely.

She was comely, though not in the first flush of youth. Perhaps his own age or a little older, elegantly dressed, he could see, without ostentation. A widow, doubtless. Sir Nicholas's lips twitched slightly as he could not fail to observe Simon Nashe's proprietorial glance in her direction.

"I'm escorting Mistress Burnell to Glebe for my daughter's betrothal feast. I'd be honored if you'd eat with us." He cleared his throat deliberately. "I trust, sir, that we can put behind us past differences and, following the example of His Majesty, work together in the best interests of our tenants."

There was a short silence. Sir Nicholas continued to smile, but he made no move to take the other's hand or reply. It was then that Kit burst from the doorway and hesitated, somewhat discomfited at the sight of his brother in conversation with a stranger. He was no fool and hastily perceived the embarrassingly chilled atmosphere.

"My brother, Mr. Christopher Hetherington. Mr. Simon Nashe, Mistress Burnell."

Kit gave a sharp intake of breath but, at a nod from his brother, acknowledged the introduction, bowing a little awkwardly.

"Mr. Nashe, hearing of our difficulties, has invited us to drink a toast at his daughter's betrothal feast. A neighborly gesture, I think you will agree, and one we'd be churlish to reject."

"Then I look forward to receiving you later. Good morning, Sir Nicholas." Nashe took his seat in the coach by Mistress Burnell's side and both Sir Nicholas and Kit doffed their beavers as the vehicle lumbered off toward Glebe House.

Meeting Kit's wide-eyed stare, Sir Nicholas gave his habitual shrug. "You'd not have me so soon at odds with my neighbors, would you, Kit?"

The sun shone out fully as the two brothers rode across the moat bridge, revealing, in all its stark ugliness, the ravages of the sack of the building and intervening years of neglect. The water, choked with weed, was brown and dull. Somewhere a shutter banged disconsolately.

Sir Nicholas dismounted and stared over the weed-grown gravel to the blackened shell of the great hall. "It seems the one wing is solid enough. Hawkins informs me he put what furniture remained whole after the looters had gone under wraps."

"Mother must not be allowed to see this. She cannot have known . . ."

"Oh, yes, she knows well enough. Don't doubt it

and, aware as I am of her indomitable determination, she will insist on holding Christmas here, so you and I have work in plenty. A hasty look around is called for, I think, and then back to the inn."

It took the combined weight of both their shoulders to shift the main door. Their riding boots echoed over the dust-grimed flagged corridors as they walked into room after room. Everywhere was darkened and what furniture had survived was shrouded in holland covers.

Sir Nicholas surveyed the ruin of his mother's cherished drawing room.

"The fireplace is intact, and two of these windows. We'll have the glaziers over first. Hawkins must still hold last quarter day's rents and the sum should suffice to restock our larders, make this room and three bedrooms reasonably comfortable and allow us to engage a skeleton staff. We'll get the local joiner to furnish the required stools, chairs and beds for the servants. And firing for the winter. It will be a start. And now, Kit, we'll go groom ourselves to meet our neighbors."

Chapter 3

Phoebe's new gown enhanced her youthful loveliness, with its tightly fitted laced bodice, lace-edged hem and the modest deep collar with its three priceless tiers of Mechlin lace carefully unpicked from an old gown of their mother's and stitched onto fine new cambric by Rachel.

Grandmamma twitched Phoebe's collar and cuffs into place. "Can you manage now, Rachel? Prudence is

17

to help me. I think I should begin to change, everything takes me so long these days." The old woman turned, giving the preening Phoebe an amused glance.

Rachel donned her best burgundy velvet gown, pleased that its subtle shading brought out the reddish gleams in her brown hair, emphasizing the dark rim around the iris of her tawny gold eyes. She had none of Phoebe's fresh-complexioned prettiness, but her features were regular, the bone structure well modeled. Both her nose and mouth were too large for true beauty and, she thought ruefully, I frown far too often and will be lined as an ape before I'm thirty. But her appearance was not displeasing, and seemly enough to satisfy her father's rigid demands of decorum.

She was proud of the results of all their handiwork. The whole house glowed from attic to cellars. Ivy trailed on the damask cloths and Leah had surpassed herself in the kitchens. The table groaned under the weight of venison and mutton pasties, fowls, cold meats, jellies, candied fruits and custards and the great silver punch bowls. Glebe had not seen such an occasion for twenty years, and was unlikely after the wedding itself to see another for as long again, unless . . . She thrust aside the probe of doubt. Was her father besotted by the handsome Burnell widow? He was twenty years her senior, but what of that?

Phoebe came excitedly to her side. "Will you wear any jewelry? I have so little of value . . ."

"I don't think I will. The lace is sufficient." She regarded Phoebe's anxious face in the mirror. "What is it?"

"I—I don't know. Rachel, I wish Roger were not so serious-minded."

"You don't want to marry a fool, surely?"

"Of course I don't." For once Phoebe's answer was sharp. "But I'm not clever, Rachel. I want to run his home efficiently. I'm willing to learn. I want

18

babies . . ." She blushed, lowering her head. "But I want some gaiety, too. Is it so vain and stupid to want pretty gowns and to entertain and be received in the county?"

"Of course not. Roger will want and expect you to play your proper part in county society. Phoebe, this is your great opportunity to escape . . ." Rachel drew a deep, heavy breath. "When you're married, you will have the right to make your own decisions in household matters and you must not allow Mistress Talbot to dominate your life. Promise me that."

"I don't know if I can." Phoebe blinked unhappily. "I fear Roger will be as strict with me as father has always been, and he does defer to his mother. A dutiful son should, I know, but, Rachel, I never know what to say to him."

"That's natural enough at first."

"I cannot imagine why it was not decided that you . . ." Her voice trailed off. "You don't hate me, Rachel, do you?"

"How could I ever do that?"

"You would have liked to have been the first to marry, wouldn't you?"

"What ever put such an idea into your head?" Rachel rose briskly. "Oh, come now, Phoebe, we both know I am unlikely to marry."

"But it's so unfair."

"Life is rarely fair. I'm afraid you'll soon recognize that. Don't be upset. I enjoy running Glebe." She laughed shakily. "The situation has its compensations. I'm unlikely to be pressed into a disastrous marriage."

"But—just suppose someone old or—repellent to you asked. Wouldn't you feel that you must because . . ."

"No, Phoebe. Recognizing my duty to father and respecting his opinions, I will not allow myself to be sold into some shameful arrangement. He won't want that of me." She kissed her sister's forehead lightly. "I'd not stand by and see you pushed into this marriage if you were truly afraid. You don't actually dislike Roger, do you?"

"No, of course not. I know him well and like him. But at the back of my mind I keep thinking I shall disappoint him."

"I don't think so. Roger is too strong-minded to be pressed into this. I've seen him looking at you, Phoebe. He loves you. You'll deal very well together, truly."

Her words were borne out when she saw Roger's eyes linger on his betrothed. Rachel stood beside her father with Phoebe to greet their guests, the Talbots from Barrow, the Stainers from Quorn, Master Illingworth, the rector, the Baxters from Belgrave and Mistress Burnell from Mountsorrel. Rachel found herself staring at the woman. She was tiny, shorter than Phoebe, and the top of her head scarcely reached Simon's shoulder. Rachel was not the only woman who regarded her with scant warmth. Mistress Talbot eyed the widow with that frigid stare habitual with her.

Dressed becomingly in dove-gray, her dark hair showing demurely under the lace-trimmed cap, Mistress Judith Burnell formed the perfect image of the fragile little woman so tragically left unprotected by the untimely death of her husband. Rachel could not bring herself to believe the woman as helpless as she appeared, nor did she fall victim to the soulful appeal of those pansy-dark eyes.

Rachel was dumbfounded when her father withdrew from his other guests some half an hour later to greet two late arrivals. Both were dressed in the height of fashion, the taller resplendent in a beribboned short jacket and petticoat breeches of tawny velvet, white satin bows at waist and shoulder and even decorating his red-heeled shoes. Entering the hall, he doffed a broad-brimmed beaver trimmed with a curling ostrich plume. Behind him, similarly though less strikingly attired in dark blue velvet, followed a smaller, darker companion. The two resembled those gaudy, flamboyant birds from the Indies, surrounded as they were by the decorous, conservatively attired guests from the neighborhood, most of whom had espoused the Parliamentary cause during the late wars.

"Gentlemen, may I present Sir Nicholas Hetherington," her father drew the pair into the dining room, "and his brother, Mr. Christopher Hetherington. Welcome to the county, sirs, and please join us at table and drink to my daughter's happiness."

Sir Nicholas pressed his lips to the tips of Rachel's fingers as her father presented his elder daughter first.

"Mistress Nashe, I am sure your betrothed finds himself today a proud and fortunate man."

To her distress, Rachel found herself staring into his blue-green eyes. Hastily, she yanked her hand away as she heard her father say quietly, "It is my younger daughter, Mistress Phoebe, who is to wed Mr. Roger Talbot, sir."

Sir Nicholas murmured an apology, noting the heightened color on Mistress Rachel's cheekbones. He kissed Phoebe's hand, confusing her utterly, and allowed himself to be drawn to a seat and introduced to one after the other of his neighbors. They received him courteously, though warily. Kit soon found himself pleasurable company. Later, when recorders and fiddles began their gay country music, Sir Nicholas stationed himself at Mistress Wilson's side to watch the company.

He wondered why the brown-haired girl with the beautiful eyes was not today's betrothed bride. The little fair child was lovely and would doubtless prove biddable. The puritanical young swain clearly doted on her. His early speculation as to his host's interest in the attractive widow was borne out. Sir Nicholas watched

Mistress Rachel through narrowed eyes as she talked and laughed with her father's guests. How would she fare when her position in the household was usurped? He found himself next to her as the company withdrew to the hall to dance.

"I trust you have eaten and drunk well, Sir Nicholas," Rachel said, conscious of her manners. "My father informs me that you have only this morning arrived at the manor. You must have found the house in considerable disorder."

He smiled a trifle sardonically. Was she aware that her father was responsible for the greater part of the ruin of his property?

"Thank you. I've been overwhelmed by the hospitality I've received. Mistress Wilson here has been regaling me with information about some of my tenants."

"I hope she is not scaring you off, sir. We have looked to your arrival here for some time."

"Nothing alarms me, Mistress Rachel, certainly nothing in Leicestershire."

"Forgive me. I had no wish to offend you . . ."

"You haven't. I am touched by your apparent interest."

Unused to the facile flattery of Court circles, she lowered her gaze a little uncertainly. "Naturally, the arrival of the squire is bound to attract attention. Do you intend to stay long at Hetherington?"

"Not long, the place is hardly comfortable. My mother has a mind to spend Christmas here."

"You will be welcome at the houses of the gentry, I'm sure, and will perhaps ride to the New Year meet."

The mouth with its narrow golden moustache relaxed into a thin smile. "You think I shall be popular then?"

Her tawny eyes regarded him directly. "It is too long after the wars, sir, to hold grudges."

Was that a comment on county opinion, he wondered, or a warning?

"Do you dance, mistress?"

It was her turn to give a slight gasp of surprise and then she nodded. "Certainly, sir."

He was pleased to find that she managed the lively, complicated movements of the country jig without any apparent difficulty.

Roger came to claim her as the dance finished, but she drew him toward one of the cushioned benches.

"Let me catch my breath."

"Shall I fetch you wine?"

"No, thank you, I've had sufficient."

His eyes followed the form of the squire, now in talk with the rector. "So, he's home at last."

"But unlikely to remain long. He has a position at Court to uphold."

At Roger's half-scornful snort of derision, she asked, "Do you envy him the gold which puts satins and velvets on his back?"

"I do not. The man is a veritable peacock and his brother scarcely less so. I despise such fripperies and warrant he has scarce enough to keep him afloat after Christmas. These courtiers live from hand to mouth and do not shame to continue to owe their tailors and vintners. Surely you are not impressed by fine feathers, Rachel?"

"No more than you are, Roger," she riposted lightly, her gaze following his to where Phoebe was dancing joyously with the younger of Mr. Baxter's sons. "She is very lovely, isn't she? Don't expect matronly behavior of her too soon."

His face reddened with pleasure. "I could not be happier at the match."

The company began to disperse at last, and Prue Whitney helped a weary Mistress Wilson to her chamber. Phoebe was tired, but rosy with happiness.

"Oh, Rachel, it was all so exciting and the dancing such fun. We *will* dance again at my wedding, won't we? Mistress Talbot sat in the drawing room looking very forbidding, but she did admire my new gown, and said it was 'decorous and seemly.'"

"I don't think she will deny you such an innocent pleasure as dancing. The days of the Commonwealth are over. Though some regret their passing, the new regime does not frown on merrymaking. Father is not such a fanatic. Now take off that gown or you'll crumple it sadly. I shan't be sorry when I'm in bed beside you."

"Does your leg ache?"

"I'm afraid it does, horribly."

"I'll rub it with warmed oil. That has sometimes helped."

"I'll need to check first that everything is secure. A last word with Leah and I'll be up."

"Rachel?" Phoebe pleated the blue satin of her skirt nervously in her fingers. "Do you know what Samuel Baxter said tonight?"

"Something foolish I've no doubt."

"He said father might well be wed before me—to Mistress Burnell."

"Did he, indeed?"

"Did you know? Has father spoken to you? Do you think there is anything behind the talk?"

"I don't know and haven't the wish to speculate. In all events, if father decides to marry again, it cannot affect your future."

"But what of yours, Rachel? How would you feel if she . . . ?"

"Phoebe, I'm too tired to consider the matter." She turned hurriedly as Simon Nashe came in on them. His brows drew toghether as he noted Phoebe's flushed embarrassment and divined the cause.

"I shall escort Mistress Burnell to Mountsorrel, Rachel. You will see the house secure?"

"Of course, father."

His thin, stern face relaxed. "I must give praise where it's due. You have done excellently, child."

"Thank you, father."

"You must be very wearied. Sonetimes we forget and put too much on you."

"No. Anyway, I'm soon for my bed."

"Aye." His gaze softened as he looked at his younger child. "When on your knees tonight, do not forget to thank the Lord God that he has seen fit to grant you so fine a man as Roger Talbot."

"I will not, father."

"Then goodnight."

A few moments later Rachel heard him giving orders to Job Paskell and to their young groom, Barnaby. The boy would wait up for him and Job must come armed with a blunderbuss. His return would be late and fraught with dangers from highwaymen.

Leah and the maids were exhausted and Rachel ordered them to bed. She was about to go up herself, when an abrupt knock came on the kitchen door. Leah was already halfway to the back staircase and the two girls stared at Rachel round-eyed.

"Well, find out who it is. Quickly," she said impatiently.

"But, Mistress Rachel, it's so late," Dinah said timidly.

"Really, child, you start at shadows." Rachel moved swiftly to the back door and undid the bolts. Despite her brave words, she opened the heavy door with caution, regarding the dark cloaked form waiting on the doorstep suspiciously.

"Who is it?"

"Zillah Lee, Mistress Rachel. I said I would come. I waited till your guests had all gone."

"Zillah, of course, come in."

Rachel ignored the deliberate way both Prue and Dinah edged away from the gypsy.

"I've brought the potion. Three drops in wine should ease your pain and let you sleep soundly."

Rachel gingerly took the phial from Zillah's brown hand. The woman gave a harsh yelp of a laugh.

"It's harmless unless you exceed the dose."

"I'll fetch coin and pay you."

"I'd prefer payment in kind." Zillah looked hungrily at a ham still uncovered on the table awaiting the master's late return.

"Of course. Prue, fetch a basket for Mistress Lee, and Dinah, there's fresh-baked bread in the pantry, some ham, broken meats and some tarts. Sit down and eat something now."

Zillah sank strong white teeth into a venison pasty. The girls packed up the food and Rachel dismissed them.

"I saw your father drive off with the widow."

Rachel chose to ignore the comment. She poured ale for the gypsy.

"And the squire's home at last. There's many'll regret that."

"Perhaps."

"Your father among them."

"I think not. Their differences are long behind them."

"Who knows?" Zillah rose from her stool. She moved superbly. "I can see you'd welcome my absence more than my company."

It was true. Zillah Lee disturbed her and she did not know why. She certainly did not hold the woman or her mother in the superstitious dread of the villagers, yet Zillah had the ability to alarm her as if she were, indeed, able to divine the future and know little comfort from it.

"I'm tired," Rachel said quietly, "and grateful."

Zillah nodded, picked up her basket, sketched a somewhat mocking curtsey and took her leave.

Chapter 4

Phoebe spent a restless night, though she had tried to lie very still for fear of waking Rachel. Zillah's potion appeared to have worked well, for Rachel was fast off when Phoebe crept carefully out of bed into the chilly morning air. She shivered as she dressed and her fingers longingly caressed the satin of the gown she had worn the day before. It had been laid out carefully by Prue to allow the creases to fall out before being put away in lavender-scented linen wrappings. Phoebe sighed as she struggled into her sober gray gown with its high, severe linen collar. There would be few occasions when she would again be allowed to flaunt such finery. Mistress Talbot would see to that.

It had been pleasurable to be the center of attention yesterday, to receive the congratulations and admiration of their neighbors, but, looming closer by the hour was the threat of life at Barrow under the gimletlike gaze of Mistress Talbot. Phoebe felt unprepared, worried that she knew too little of household management, and increasingly found herself gazing at Roger with apprehension. What would it be like to lie by his side, submit to his caresses? Phoebe could not imagine Roger caressing anyone. He was always so dignified and restrained.

After prayers with her father and grandmamma, Phoebe joined them for breakfast. Immediately afterwards grandmamma sent for Leah to discuss the heavy task of putting the house to rights. What precious plate that remained to them after the war, the linen and glassware, must be cleaned, wrapped and laid away against her coming wedding feast. Phoebe thrust that thought aside as she offered her assistance.

"No, go up to Rachel and see she has had breakfast and is thoroughly rested. Don't allow her to fuss over the work. We can manage. Dinah shall put up a basket of delicacies for Diggory. See if you can persuade Rachel to go with you. She needs a respite from household duties and it will do you good, puss, stop you worrying about what lies ahead."

"Grandmamma, I *am* fond of Roger, truly, it's just that the ceremony yesterday made me realize that I'm no longer a child. I don't know that I like the notion."

"We all go through it. You'll adapt; we all do."

Rachel was already dressing when she went upstairs and had breakfasted from the tray Prue had taken up.

"Phoebe, you should have awakened me. Father will be displeased and I want to see that the girls remember to deal with the winestains on the napery and . . ."

"It is all in hand and father accepted your need to rest. Grandmamma says you are to come with me to visit Diggory."

"Phoebe, I can't."

"Yes, you can. Leah is coping efficiently and, Rachel, I have to get out of the house. I feel stifled."

Rachel glanced at her shrewdly, but made no comment.

Diggory was pleased to see them, but attempted to hide the fact beneath his usual growled, half-respectful greeting. He seemed to be in less pain. Phoebe saw a small glass phial near his truckle bed and wondered if Salome Lee had provided a drug for the old man, as she had for Rachel.

Coming out again into the autumnal sunshine, they

saw Sir Nicholas and Mr. Hetherington riding toward The Sun. The men reined in beside the women's mounts and courteously doffed their hats.

"Good morning to you, Mistress Nashe, and to you, Mistress Phoebe." Sir Nicholas bowed in the saddle. "I trust you both are not exhausted from the rigors of yesterday's glorious feast."

Rachel looked up to find Sir Nicholas's piercing blue-green eyes straight on hers. To her annoyance she flushed slightly and said tartly, "We are used to hard work, thrive on it," and cast her eyes down to avoid his gaze. Suddenly, she wished she were not dressed in her plain linsey woolsey gown and black cloak. Both men were dressed extravagantly in lace-trimmed velvet.

Kit Hetherington addressed Phoebe. "And how does Mistress Phoebe face the prospect of soon becoming a bride?"

Phoebe felt the blood rush to her cheeks. "I—I have not had the time to think too closely."

"He seems a very worthy man, Mr. Talbot."

"We have known each other all our lives," she stammered. "My father could not have arranged a better match, sir."

"Ah, I wish some pretty maid would speak so well of me."

"I'm sure they do, sir." She broke off in confusion. Her mare sidled and he put a steadying hand on hers, gripping her reins.

"I fear not, Mistress Phoebe. My mother says I'm a sad rake, and I confess the charge is too near the truth for comfort."

Phoebe had no way of countering such obvious teasing. She urged her mount closer to Rachel, who was advising Sir Nicholas of the coming hiring fair.

"There's one in Leicester next week. I imagine you'll need servants if you intend to remain at the manor."

"We'll move in when the windows are glassed and the floorboards sound. Till then we'll rely on Mistress Gilpin at The Sun for our comfort. We have just been over the house with our steward. I've given instructions about which work must take precedence."

A sudden scuffle and a whoop of laughter made them all look up sharply as two village boys jumped the churchyard stile, one falling, helpless with mirth, the other yelling to him to "mind out where he was a' going." They scrambled into line hastily at the sight of the squire and ladies. The taller boy, who'd fallen, muttered some incoherent remark, touched his forelock and tugged the other away.

"Wat Potter," Rachel said reprovingly. "I wonder what devilry he's been up to this afternoon. Poor Tom Bates is constantly getting a beating for being involved in some prank of Wat's devising. Tom's wits are sometimes lacking. He's easily led."

"Then you'd not advise me to employ those two?" Sir Nicholas's lips twitched.

"Not if you want to sleep safe in your bed at nights. Wat might easily take it into his head to fire your rick or put a burr under your saddle for the pleasure of seeing you cope."

"I don't think he means serious harm," Phoebe said gently.

"Wat Potter's a cruel devil," Rachel said sharply. "I'd trust him with no beast of mine."

Phoebe's eyes caught a blur of red by the church wall as Zillah Lee jumped the stile, then made a quick bobbed curtsey. There was a cut on her cheek and mud on her shoulder.

"Zillah, you're hurt. Did those boys . . . ?"

"No, no, I'm just clumsy, Mistress Phoebe, caught my cheek against the church porch, slipped on some mud. Good day to you, Mistress Rachel."

"Zillah Lee is a wonder with herbs, if you've need of

her, Sir Nicholas." For once the depth of Zillah's curtsey implied respect as she faced the squire.

The gypsy scanned Rachel's form closely. "So my drops worked. I'm glad." She was off down the village before Rachel could thank her.

Sir Nicholas said, "You think the boys attacked her?"

Rachel nodded. "I'm sure of it. She and her mother are fair game. Salome is getting frail now and needs protection. What alarms me is neither of them will ask for it, nor the constable give it."

His eyes narrowed. "I'll speak to the man." The brothers then took their leave.

As she and Phoebe rode home, Rachel spoke of Roger's intention to call on them that afternoon.

Phoebe nodded. "He's off to Cambridge tomorrow. He did tell me what business he had there, but I've forgotten. His mother looked most unwell, didn't you think so?"

"She's looked pale and drawn for as long as I can remember. I don't think this recent illness was too serious."

"I hope not," Phoebe said doubtfully. "I can't bear to see people in pain."

When they entered the hall, they were glad of the warmth from the logs glowing in the large old firegrate, for the afternoon had turned chill now that the sun had gone down.

Roger had already arrived, and his eyes lit up at the sight of them. Phoebe inquired after his mother and was relieved to hear that she seemed better. The talk centered on the coming of the Hetheringtons to the district and the conversation the girls had had with them.

"So it's true that they intend to winter at the manor?" Roger was clearly none too pleased by the news.

Rachel shrugged. "Sir Nicholas tells me Lady

Hetherington has expressed a wish to celebrate Christmas at the manor, but the prospect looks bleak. The place seems a total ruin."

"I imagine he will hardly be pleased that he must withdraw from the more appealing attractions of town."

Rachel glanced thoughtfully into the dancing firelight. "I think perhaps Sir Nicholas is more adaptable than we imagine."

Roger spoke of the plans being made at Barrow to receive Phoebe. "I need to vacate my lodging in Cambridge and should be back in Leicestershire for the second or third week in November. The banns can be read then and our marriage will take place in the second week of December. We'll celebrate Christmas in your new home, Phoebe. Keep the thought in your mind over the weeks we are parted." He kissed her gently and they watched from the window as he strode across the courtyard to call for his horse.

The days turned colder and damper toward the end of the month and grandmamma developed a chesty cough. Though it did not appear serious enough to send for a physician from Barrow, Rachel advised her to keep to her bed. Phoebe was unusually restless and often found excuses to ride into the village to see Diggory, with Prue in attendance. Colonel Nashe was often away from home and the girls began to wonder if he were making more frequent visits to Mistress Burnell in Mountsorrel. Phoebe was, however, grateful that he appeared too occupied at present to make many inquiries as to how she spent her time. Rachel was busy nursing grandmamma, so Phoebe was thrown back onto her own resources. It seemed providential that whenever she rode into the village or about the estate, she frequently found Mr. Hetherington similarly bent on exercise.

She was passing The Sun with Prue in attendance on her latest errand of mercy to Diggory's cottage, when the squire's brother rode out of the inn courtyard. He reined in his horse on catching sight of her and doffed his hat in greeting. Her heart fluttered unaccountably.

"Mr. Hetherington, I had thought you and your brother had taken up residence at the manor."

He acknowledged Prue with a friendly grin. The maid responded with a cheerful smile and drew her horse back apace, so that Mr. Hetherington and Phoebe could ride on side by side.

"We moved in yesterday, but it's vastly uncomfortable. Mistress Gilpin is a very good cook, however, and the company is entertaining."

She gave a little bubble of laughter. "Oh, Mr. Hetherington, how can the talk of our country bumpkins compare with your Court wits?"

"Their humor appeals to my sense of the ridiculous, and their general chat is well salted with an earthy but pointed jocularity concerning their near neighbors."

She looked away from him down at her horse's satiny coat.

"My father does not approve of bawdy talk or malicious gossip. He considers a sharp tongue an instrument of the devil. Our servants are usually rather quiet in our presence."

His brown eyes twinkled. "Yes, I can appreciate that he keeps a tight rein on his servants' behavior."

"He is not unkind, Mr. Hetherington," she said hastily. "My father is a good master. He looks to all their needs but he does expect very high standards of conduct from—from all of us." The last words were added in a little rush. She looked up at him anxiously and her horse sidled, bumping awkwardly into his so that she was startled and he put a strong brown hand protectively over hers to reassure her.

His touch sent a rush of warmth through her and,

though she knew she should instantly disengage her fingers from his hold, she allowed them to stay there, hoping that the wild excitement which raced through her being did not reveal itself in heightened color nor the over-loud pounding of her heart.

As if aware that he had embarrassed her, he withdrew his hand and passed on to talk easily of work at the manor, amusing her with an impromptu imitation of the works foreman.

"He's a great burly man, with a chest like a barrel, and he has a decided lisp. You cannot imagine how odd it is to hear a voice like that come from such a body. It is all I can do to keep my face straight when he is issuing orders. Mind you, the fellow must have a fist like an ox, for no one dares argue with him and they rush back to the job if he comes on the scene, even if they've only paused for a moment or two."

His spirited performance brought tears of laughter to her eyes. It was so good to be in such pleasant company, where she did not fear to show ignorance. With Roger she always found herself weighing her words carefully, wondering if he compared her conversation with that of his mother, whom Phoebe could never believe guilty of uttering one single idle comment.

Kit Hetherington was dressed dashingly as usual in green velvet, and the sun glinted on his brown hair. Phoebe's eyes passed admiringly from the ribboned knots on his shoulders to his lace-trimmed boot hose. Her father had already spoken slightly of the sinful extravagance which both brothers lavished on their persons when they were known to be in need of ready gold for the house repairs. Even if the lace on Kit's collar was frayed and the leather of his gauntlet gloves and bucket riding boots somewhat worn, he made a strikingly handsome figure.

They had reached the crossroads and she knew she

must tear herself away. Phoebe felt her lips tremble as she framed her words of farewell and held out her hand to him.

"I must be getting home, Mr. Hetherington. Please convey my regards to the squire."

They had exchanged so few words, yet it was a wrench to leave him. Only in his presence did she feel that she came fully alive. Whenever she came to the village now, it was with the desperate hope that she would see him. Soon these hurried meetings must end, for Diggory would be perfectly well and stumping about his duties at Glebe again. The squire and his brother would leave the county and return to the rumbustious pleasures of the capital. The thought pierced her to the core.

Roger would soon be home.

She swallowed salt tears as she thrust back the vivid picture of herself married, living at Barrow under Mistress Talbot's severe gaze.

Kit Hetherington's merry eyes had softened. His lips lingered caressingly on her gloved palm.

"But you *will* come again to see your servant—soon?"

The fingers trembled convulsively and he took her hand firmly in his and squeezed it demandingly. Her blue eyes met his in puzzled wonder.

"I—I think I need to, and there are two, perhaps more, villagers I should visit for Rachel."

"Tomorrow, you'll come tomorrow, about this time?"

Phoebe glanced fearfully behind her to where Prue sat her fat pony, her face impassive.

"I . . . I think . . . Yes, I will try, tomorrow."

His eyes lit up again, twinkling delightfully. "Then I shall find a need to come to The Sun."

She bowed her head in acknowledgment as he rode slightly away from her, turning his horse expertly, his plumed hat saluting her as he swept it low to the stirrup.

Calling to Prue, she found it hard not to look back as she urged her mount toward Glebe.

The next afternoon Mistress Phoebe was emerging from Diggory Whatsize's cottage when Kit rode up to the village green. He saw she had with her the scrawny, frightened little maid he'd seen only once before, scuttling from the village on some errand. Mistress Gilpin had clucked her tongue at the sight of the girl.

"Found badly beaten and half starved outside the poorhouse she was, about a year ago. Nobody could get much out of her as to where she came from or who'd mistreated her. Either she couldn't remember, poor lass, or wasn't prepared to say. Leah Ashley, up at Glebe, has taken her under her wing and she has a good place there. For all Colonel Nashe's a stern man, he's just and kindly to his servants, provided they behave sensibly. 'Tis to be hoped she regains her wits in time. As it is, no man's like to ask her in marriage. She still shies away from everybody who tries to get near her."

The maid appeared more nervous today than ever. As Kit dismounted, sweeping off his ostrich-trimmed beaver, Phoebe was reproving the girl.

"I'm ashamed of you, Dinah, taking account of such rubbish. Hobgoblins at your window, indeed, it was more than likely a branch of the old elm. You mustn't heed the teasing of the other girls."

"But it is All Hallows, Mistress Phoebe, evil spirits and witches are abroad today. We should take care."

"Do not let my father hear such talk. He'll instantly forbid you to attend the feasting tonight."

She was looking remarkably lovely this morning. Her blue woolen gown was severely cut as usual, but her cloak strings were loosely tied and he saw that her linen collar was lace-trimmed. The wind had whipped tendrils of curling hair from the confinement of her plain linen cap and brought color to her cheeks, a color which deepened when she saw Kit approach.

"Good afternoon, Mr. Hetherington. I trust you and your brother are well."

"In excellent health, Mistress Phoebe." He assisted her to mount, cupping his two hands for her to step up. "You are looking quite enchanting today."

"You must not flatter me so shamelessly, Mr. Hetherington," she said, laughing. "I'm no Court lady, to be so easily cozened."

"No Court lady possesses such flawless skin or such brightness of eye. The grime of London's new industries soon destroys such freshness of beauty. They would all envy you, mistress, I assure you."

"If that were so, they would all be abandoning the Court for the country." Her expression became wistful. "I think I would risk my rustic charm for an opportunity to see Whitehall and St. James's, catch a glimpse of Their Majesties promenading the park."

"Why not, indeed?" Kit assisted Dinah to mount her pony and returned to Phoebe's side. "Cannot you persuade your betrothed to take you to view the sights?"

"The Talbots are not worldly. They'd think poorly of me for wishing to see such vanities." Her fingers tightened on the reins, and in her confusion on seeing him, she'd dropped her riding gloves. He stooped and retrieved them, pushing them unobtrusively into the deep pocket of his riding coat.

Excusing his action, he said, "I had thought your girth strap loose, but it seems correctly buckled." He mounted his chestnut. "May I escort you at least part of the way home, Mistress Phoebe? I'd deem it an honor."

She nodded, flushing. They ambled their horses through the village street, acknowledging respectful salutes from the village folk. Kit turned briefly to see that the maid was well behind them.

"Will Lady Hetherington be arriving soon? I hear the work is going smoothly at the manor."

He grimaced comically. "Such a cacophony of hammering and sawing that I find myself frequently eager to ride out. Yes, the west wing is now habitable, just. It's to be hoped mother will have the foresight to bring some small comforts with her. Of course, she is not accustomed to luxury. Palaces, Mistress Phoebe, are vastly overcrowded and chilly, even in summer. My mother's apartment at Somerset House is scarcely larger than a closet."

Phoebe's blue eyes widened at such a disclosure.

"The Dowager Queen is a gentle and virtuous lady. My mother considers it a great honor to serve her and gladly accepts the discomforts involved."

"I am sure she must. Is there feasting at Somerset House and masques as there are at Whitehall?"

"Hardly. The Dowager Queen is deeply religious, as I hear the late King was, and since his untimely death she has lived largely in seclusion."

They had left the village now and were skirting Malkin Copse. Phoebe gave a little dismayed exclamation. "My riding gloves! How odd that I had not noticed I wasn't wearing them. I was intent on your talk, Mr. Hetherington."

"I imagine you left them in the village."

"In Diggory's cottage, most likely." She frowned uncertainly. "They were a betrothal gift from Mistress Talbot."

"Then you will be upset to lose them. Could you not send your maid back? You will be safe enough under my escort."

Phoebe hesitated and he said reluctantly, "I could go back."

"No, why should you be inconvenienced for my carelessness?" She made up her mind quickly. "Dinah!"

The girl rode up anxiously.

"Ride back to Diggory's and bring me my gloves. You must find them. Mistress Talbot would take it amiss if I couldn't produce them when we next meet."

"Mistress, it's right through the village, past the churchyard."

"You are not still harping on that 'spirits' nonsense, are you?" Phoebe's tone was sharp and Dinah's eyes filled with tears. "It's broad daylight, Dinah, and there are villagers about in plenty. Now do hurry, girl, and catch us up. We must be home before dusk."

Reluctantly, the girl turned her pony and jogged off. When she was hidden from view by a thicket of bramble, Kit leaned across and struck the rump of Phoebe's mount smartly with his riding crop. Unused to such treatment, the beast galloped off at a sharp pace, the startled Phoebe struggling to stay in the saddle.

Kit's horse swept alongside; he seized her bridle and pulled the animal to a halt. Dismounting, he ran to her side and lifted her down. She clung to him breathless and terrified.

"Forgive me, that was foolish. I needed to touch you, hold you. It was a dangerous ruse and could have harmed you. I thought you a more experienced rider."

Dark color suffused Phoebe's face and throat and, holding her close, he could feel the wild thudding of her heart. Her hair had torn loose and fallen to her shoulders in a silken cloud. The sweet freshness of her warm, young body teased his senses and he stooped and kissed her hard on the lips.

She struggled ineffectually against his hold.

"No, we mustn't. It's sinful. I'm betrothed. Roger . . ."

39

"Do you love Roger, little Phoebe?" His voice had thickened oddly and she found it both alarming and exciting.

"I respect him, admire him."

He kissed her again, cutting short her reply. Through the trees he had glimpsed the long-deserted old charcoal burners' hut. He'd come upon the place when walking the woods with Hawkins, the steward. His grip tightened on her arm, urgently leading her toward it. She was like a bird, half fearful of being caught, half anxious to be tamed, dragging a little, then allowing herself to be led. At the hut's entrance she started around wildly.

"What of Dinah?"

"She'll be gone for a while."

"It is not so far to Diggory's."

"But the gloves are not there. She will have to spend some time searching for them." He produced them, laughing, drawing her further into the shaded interior.

"You should not have done it." Her eyes widened as she strove to accustom herself to the dimness. Surprisingly, after long neglect, the place smelt only of earth and fallen leaves which had drifted in through the broken shutter.

"Are you afraid of me, Phoebe?"

She gave a despairing little sob, shaking her head. From the first moment she had set eyes on him at Glebe, he had stirred her senses. Under his gentle teasing that first time they'd met in the village, she had experienced a wild longing to see him again, made excuses to ride out on errands. They had always kept within the bounds of propriety. Prue had always remained close, but now Phoebe could not deny that her need to be with this man alone, far from prying eyes, was as necessary to her as breathing. As he drew her close, her arms stole around his neck and she gave little gusty sighs when his lips pressed on her hair, her throat, slid lower, to where the linen of her collar concealed the budding glory of her young breasts.

He tempered his passion to her growing alarm as his touch aroused her, whispered endearments till she quietened and only then did he draw her down onto the carpet of leaves. He was very gentle with her and she made no objection when his fingers at last stole to the lacing of her bodice.

She gave a little gasp as his hand cupped her breast and squeezed it gently. He bent and kissed the firm white flesh and she moaned softly under his hold, her body arching to his in swift response.

It was the work of mere moments to complete the necessary undressing of himself and her. He was an expert and she made no further remonstrance when he pushed aside her drab, heavy woolen skirts, revealing the slender white thrust of her young limbs.

The light filtered down through the ill-fitting slats of the shutter, dappling them in golden rays as they lay sprawled in artless abandon. Her mouth parted sweetly under his and her arms tightened viselike behind his head as he drew her close to his heart.

Her surrender was so trusting and complete that afterwards he felt a pang of disgust for his own duplicity. This child loved him, offered her body to him as freely as she gave her heart. He sensed that demonstrations of affection had been few in that dour household at Glebe. She had been totally unprepared for the surge of ecstasy which had consumed her utterly. She had given one sharp cry at his taking of her, then her body had responded joyfully to his. It had been sweet, overmastering, deeply satisfying.

He lay with her head against his heart, then bent to kiss her eyes when he saw slow tears course down her cheeks.

"Hush, sweeting, don't cry. I didn't hurt you, did I?"

"It is not that. Oh, Kit, what have we done? I shall

be completely damned." It came out in a despairing little wail.

He chuckled low in his throat.

"No, sweeting, God meant us to take joy in our coupling. Why else should he have fashioned us so?"

"But I have betrayed Roger." Her guilty, tearful whisper stirred his pity. "I cannot absolve myself from blame. I guessed what would happen if I allowed myself to be alone with you. I wanted you to love me like that. I'm a harlot like Rahab, shameless."

"No, my love."

"Kit, please tell me you love me. It will not be so terrible if I hear you say it."

"I *do* love you, little Phoebe."

"Kiss me, kiss me again."

He complied, this time gently, without passion, for already he could see she was deliberately restraining her own longing.

She sat up, firmly putting aside his hand from her breast.

"I must go. If my father even imagined . . ." A great shudder ran through her. He saw that now realization had come, she was stricken with remorse and horror. Climbing to his feet, he turned from her as she attempted to put to rights her disheveled clothing.

"I'll get the horses."

"We should have tethered them." Her voice was shrill with alarm.

"Be easy, I looped the reins to a low branch."

They heard the commotion as he lifted her into the saddle, a confusion of hoarse shouts and cries. Phoebe turned her head sharply.

"It sounds as if it's coming from the north end of the village near the Lees' cottage."

He frowned, recalling the sight of the unusually large gathering near the church. "The gypsy girl's?"

"Yes." Phoebe pointed urgently. "Smoke rising, over there. The villagers have fired the cottage."

"It could be simply a bonfire of leaves." While he sought to reassure her, they both heard the screams and the bawling and shouting intensify, coming closer.

"It's All Hallows. Those cowardly villagers have always threatened the old woman and Zillah, now they've been roused into action. We should try to help them."

"Your father is on the magistrates' bench?"

"Yes."

"Then he could prevent violence. I'll ride for the manor and fetch Nick and Gaston. We'll need pistols and muskets. There are some to hand. Are you afraid to ride home alone? If you skirt the copse, you will be safe. Keep well clear."

"I will, yes. Please go, Kit, quickly. They'll make for Hetherington Pool, I think, over there. It sounds as if they're moving that way. It feeds the manor moat. The Potters have often threatened to swim the Lees."

"Trust me. Now ride fast and don't stop to let any of those louts catch you, use your whip if need be."

She dug spurs into her mount and was off toward Glebe, riding as furiously as she dared. He waited no more, but turned for the manor.

Rachel was coming from the dairy when Phoebe rode into the yard. She checked, horrified at the sight of her sister, hair flowing wildly, cap dangling from her neck by its strings, cloak flapping uselessly behind her. She hurried to the mounting block as Job Paskell came to the stable door with the colonel.

"Phoebe, what is it? You're white as death! Where's Dinah?"

"Dinah?" Phoebe had momentarily forgotten her maid in her urgency. "I—I don't know. Back in the

43

village. Father, you must go at once to Hetherington Pool. Tod Potter's aroused the villagers against the Lees, and I think they've fired their cottage. There's a crowd, men mostly, but some women. I saw them from the copse." She drew great shuddering breaths. "They were dragging along the two women. I think Salome's hurt, she could hardly stand. Wat Potter was bawling that they're going to swim them as witches. You have to stop it. Rough handling could kill old Salome."

Rachel was greatly alarmed. It was All Hallows' Eve and the superstitious dread of the villagers had been given full rein. She'd warned Zillah to be careful.

"Yes, father, you should go, exercise your authority till this matter can be properly examined by the vicar."

Simon Nashe's raised brows expressed distaste for his younger daughter's unseemly dishevelment.

"I think not. Let matters take their course. These foolish and godless women have defied the authority of the Church for years. Now that the villagers have at last turned on them, they have no one to blame but themselves."

"They do no harm, father," Rachel said quietly. "Salome has helped many with her herbal brews."

"Do no harm, when that beldame dispenses love charms and amulets, encouraging lewd behavior among the village louts and wenches? I think I am the better judge of what harm is caused by this pandering to heathen practices."

"Father, they'll hang them," Phoebe pleaded. "Zillah doesn't deserve to die, nor the old woman either. Please. Mr. Hetherington was nearby . . . he—he went for the squire, but we are nearer. There's no time to waste . . ."

"I'll not be instructed by my own child on my moral duties," the colonel snapped. "Go to your room, miss, calm yourself and pray God grant you the attitude of mind in which to address your father."

Phoebe had been helped down by Job. She stood uncertainly. For the first time in her life she considered disobeying her father and riding back to the pool herself, but she was in no state to think clearly.

Rachel took the initiative. She snatched the reins of Phoebe's horse from Job and pulled herself into the saddle while the groom stood bemused.

"If you will not act, father, I must. I hold some degree of respect in the village. They may listen to me. I can delay them from harming those unfortunate women till some help arrives. Job, send Barnaby for the constable. Phoebe, you're in no state to be helpful. You're trembling where you stand. Do as father says."

Without stopping to hear her father's furious rejoinder, she dug spurs to her mount and rode toward the Hetherington deerpark.

The scene which met her eyes as she topped a small rise to view the pool etched itself on her memory. The sun was beginning to sink and bathed the landscape in an ominous red glow. Rachel kicked her feet free of the saddle and jumped clear. The old woman lay trussed like an oven-dressed fowl at the water's edge, a pitiful bundle of drab cloth, guarded by the older village women. Some yards distant, Zillah struggled in the arms of two burly youths. Rachel thought one was Wat Potter. Her black hair streamed to below her waist, writhing tendrils, Medusa-like. A man removed himself from the jeering, gesticulating mob behind the old woman and pointed to the boys. Another man stooped in obedience to his unspoken command and began to pull Salome to the water.

"Stop it, stop it, I say," Rachel furiously commanded them.

"Here, Mistress Rachel, don't you let your soft heart deceive you and stand in the way of rightful punishment. These 'ere women are spawn of the devil. We've known it for years and now we're going to swim 'em,

45

prove their wickedness, make them justices try 'em and hang 'em. Jacob Newby's dead, poisoned by that evil bag of bones there."

"You're talking arrant rubbish, Tod Potter, and you know it. If Jacob has died, I'm sorry to hear it, but he died from natural causes and not as a result of any action of either Zillah or Salome. Your own good sense tells you that."

"She's been giving 'em potions and now he's dead. What killed him if they didn't? Ask Dame Alice there."

"If Zillah administered medicine brewed by her mother, it must have been at Dame Alice's request."

Alice Newby's spiteful voice cut in. "I *had* to summon her. How else was I to clear the spell she'd cast on my Jacob? Hale he was, straight as a die till Friday last, then took all of a sudden, fell down in the house, stricken as if by a lightning flash and his mouth all twisted and no word 'as he spoke since."

"Dame Alice, you know very well people are taken so, even young people. You cannot hold Zillah or Salome responsible for what was, sadly, the will of God."

"Aye, it is so sometimes," Tod Potter agreed. "I've known cases like that in my time, but that's not all. We've been to that cottage and there was familiars."

Rachel's cheeks blanched. She knew well enough the commonly held belief that Satan gave familiar spirits to his minions, in the guise of animals or birds to work their spells for them, familiars which must be fed by the witch herself from some hidden teat on her body. Did Zillah possess some mole or blemish which could damn her? Rachel shuddered. It would please the likes of Tod and Wat Potter to strip both women now, before them all.

"Zillah has always been fond of wild creatures. What more natural than you should find some tame ones in her cottage?"

46

"Aye, but black they were, both black and deformed, agents of the devil, a great flapping raven and a cat with a twisted left foreleg."

"The raven had a broken wing," Zillah put in wearily, "and Sukie was caught in a trap, more than likely one of yours, Tod Potter, set on the squire's land."

"You slut!" He dealt her a brutal blow and her head snapped back so that it was all her captors could do to hold her upright.

"Aye, aye, brave you are all, when dealing with helpless women." To Rachel's surprise the old woman gave a cackle of windy laughter. "I've not found it so when you've come to me with pains in your guts that doubled you up, Tod Potter, or when that wife of yours had taken risks to rid herself of the child she carried. Needed us then, you did, or she'd have fair bled to death."

"Throw the old beldame in the water." Tod Potter fairly danced with rage. "Still her evil tongue. Accuse us of child murder, would she?"

Before he could be obeyed, a coldly uttered warning halted the men in their tracks.

"Release both women. Stay still, the pack of you. I'm holding a cocked pistol at your head, Master Potter, I believe you're named, although I've not the privilege of your acquaintance. My brother and servant have others of you covered. Since you are trespassing on my land and, it would seem, have destroyed one of my cottages, I'm within my rights to defend my property."

Rachel half stumbled in her relief at the sight of Sir Nicholas, Mr. Hetherington and an elderly servant armed with a musket. Sir Nicholas wore drab cloth breeches, a buff coat, and his shirtsleeves were rolled to his elbows. But there was an undeniable air of command about him.

"Sir Nicholas, these women have been seized and ill-used without one shred of evidence. A man has died suddenly, but from natural causes. In all probability, a seizure or from apoplexy," Rachel explained.

"Begging your pardon, squire," Tod said sullenly, "I can't see as how you can judge this accusation fairly, since you don't know the Lees. Mistress Rachel here has always had too gentle a heart."

"I don't know you either, Master Potter, but I do know you are overreaching yourself, arrogating power which can be dispensed only by a justice."

"But it's All Hallows . . ."

"Are you a parcel of children to be frightened by tales of evil spirits and hobgoblins? Where's your sense, man?"

"It's not a matter of sense, but of conviction," Potter growled. "I've seen matters judged like this before . . ."

"Before our Kingdom's rulers came to their senses again, instead of allowing fools and canting despots to terrorize the countryside, seizing on any helpless old man or woman judged to be different from the rest of us. Pah, the very stench of your fanaticism and your puritanical whine make me sick to my stomach. Get off my land. If you've intention to bring charges against these women, do it before magistrates tomorrow. Be very sure you've undeniable proof, for, understand this, I'll bring counter-charges of damage to my property."

The murmurings grew to a crescendo, then subsided suddenly. One or two villagers on the fringe of the group turned away. Zillah's captors still held firmly to her arms, their eyes seeking Potter's for orders. Sir Nicholas snapped out a command and the man on the rise trained his musket on Wat Potter. His father gave ground with ill grace.

"Let her go, or there'll be blood spilt."

Potter's reaction would have been comic under less tragic circumstances. He blustered his way through the crowd.

"I'm no warlock. Every man here knows I'm a true son of the Church. I call on God to strike . . ."

"Don't work yourself into a fit, man. If you have a seizure, it might well bring the rest of your family under suspicion. Now, off with you all. I give you two minutes to clear my land, then I shall give my servant here leave to fire on trespassers."

Zillah had immediately gone to her mother. Mr. Hetherington was struggling with the old woman's bonds. He gave a half-choked gasp. "Mistress Nashe, I fear the old woman is dead."

The eerie red glow had paled now to greenish half-light. Rachel saw that Salome's head lolled awkwardly and there were dark bluish shadows around her lips. Sir Nicholas gestured to his manservant.

"We'll need a litter. Get the help of the workmen at the manor." He stooped and assisted Rachel to her feet where she knelt by the gypsy's body. "I regret this, Mistress Nashe. Your efforts to save the old woman have proved vain. I imagine the shock has been too great for her heart. You must be exhausted. Leave the lass with her mother."

Rachel turned pityingly to where Zillah sat, tearless, her mother's head cradled on her lap. "She has nowhere to go. I doubt if my father would allow me to take her in."

"I'll find work for her at Hetherington. She'll be protected there from further abuse, certainly until the dead woman is buried. They are my tenants, I'll see to the old woman's bestowal."

He assisted her to where Phoebe's horse stood docilely waiting. Reaction had set in and she found herself trembling. "Thank you, sir. My father holds fanatical views akin to Potter's."

He nodded.

Rachel said wonderingly, "She knew. Zillah knew her mother would die."

"I don't understand."

"Some weeks ago I offered to send our stableboy to help stack firing for the winter. She said, and I thought it strange then, that they wouldn't need it," Rachel said and lurched against him. The incident had taken its toll. Her eyes blurred and she was afraid she would break down. Her tears, she knew, were not solely for Salome's death nor Zillah's loss, but a mark of her acknowledgment of the brutish stupidity of decent folk who'd allowed themselves to be roused to such violence by fear. Guiltily, she recognized the fact that she herself was fearful of Zillah's strangeness.

As if he read her thoughts, Sir Nicholas said quietly, "Don't blame them too much. They've been bred on such foolish whims, taken them in with their mothers' milk. They live such dull lives. Many will be deeply shamed in the cold light of day when All Hallows, with its sinister menace, is well behind them." He lifted her easily into the saddle. "Kit will see you safe. I must do what I can for that poor girl."

Shakily, she said, "It was good for the village that you were here, Sir Nicholas."

"I am glad you should think so, Mistress Nashe." Nicholas looked at her keenly, and watched as she mounted her horse.

Dusk shadowed the deerpark as Rachel and Kit made their way along the path. Rachel's lips tightened at the thought of the coming reckoning with her father. This latest affair would not engender better relations between the squire and the colonel, who would see in Sir Nicholas's flouting of village opinion a challenge to his authority. But at least while the Hetheringtons remained at the manor, Zillah Lee would be safe.

Chapter 5

All Hallows dawned in thick fog and both sisters descended to morning prayers dreading retribution for their temerity in challenging their father's authority. He greeted them coldly but, surprisingly, made no reference to the Lees, not even inquiring of Rachel as to the outcome of the affair. He had flatly refused to receive her last night, a mark of his severe displeasure. Clearly, he had decided to wash his hands of the matter. He continued to act coldly distant to them both over the following days, but to Phoebe's profound relief, her own part in the day's happening seemed forgotten in the excitement over the squire's stand, Salome's tragic death, the funeral of Jacob Newby and the news that Zillah was now in service at the manor.

The fog persisted for days and was followed by a period of cold, rainy weather which depressed all their spirits. Not even the arrival of Phoebe's wedding gown from the dressmaker and tailor in Leicester could dispel her guilt-ridden misery.

Her love for Christopher Hetherington had proved both a delight and a torment. She longed to see him again. The thought of that wild joy they had shared in the charcoal burners' hut made her pulses race, but she was perversely relieved that the inclement weather made it impossible to make further attempts at meeting him. He had said he loved her; surely she could not have imagined the fervor of his caresses—but he was the squire's brother, a Hetherington, and one who had suffered in the War from her father's over-zealous destruction of Royalist property. Even were she to be freed from her betrothal, and she knew well enough she hadn't the courage to speak of her doubts to her father, she could see no prospect of future happiness with Kit. His brother would look for a wealthy bride, a nobly born dame whose background and training were akin to those of the Hetheringtons.

News came from Barrow that Mistress Talbot had taken to her bed. Roger's mother had fought encroaching illness with dogged tenacity, so it was obvious that her condition was now grave.

Phoebe drove to Barrow with her father and Rachel. She swallowed hard when they entered the sickroom. Mistress Talbot looked waxen-pale, her cheekbones sharply accentuated. There was a stale, sickly smell overhanging the chamber. When Phoebe curtseyed and approached the bed timidly, the sick woman opened her eyes and caught the girl's hand in a clawlike grip.

"Promise me you will care for my son, be industrious, obedient."

"I promise." Phoebe's whisper was husky with tears. She had never before recognized the nearness of death, and could think of nothing to do or say.

Downstairs, later, Rachel gravely questioned Roger.

"What does the physician say? She seems deadly pale and has no strength."

"She coughed up blood the day they sent for me and has continued to spit blood since. The physician hedges, but I'm afraid it is the wasting sickness and I fear for her recovery."

"Is your father prepared for the worst?"

"I believe he is, Rachel. I thank God his great faith will sustain him."

Rachel left to join her father and Mr. Talbot. Phoebe picked at the stuff of her gown uncertainly.

"Roger, I am so sorry. I shall pray for your mother's recovery."

He forced a smile. "I am grateful for your gentle sympathy and good sense, Phoebe." He hesitated. "If—if the worst happens, it will, of necessity, postpone our wedding. I shall regret that but . . ."

"That cannot be helped, Roger. I understand. This will be a house in mourning."

She tried to subdue the little tingle of relief that went through her. It was wicked, unseemly, while Roger grieved so for his mother. He turned from her, his voice hoarse. "She is a good woman, Phoebe, dutiful if sometimes unbending. I love her deeply."

Mistress Talbot died two days later and the Nashes attended her burial at Barrow Church. Phoebe watched Roger's black-garbed shoulders bowed in grief as he stood by the graveside and sighed at her own inability to find suitable expressions of comfort.

"I didn't know what to say to him, Rachel," she confided afterwards. "Mr. Talbot bears up well, but Roger is deeply affected. He has decided to return to Cambridge for a further term, since it will be impossible for us to marry before next spring. Mr. Talbot is to stay there with him at least until after Christmas."

Preparations for Christmas now occupied them all. On the few occasions Phoebe had ventured into the village, she had not spoken one word with Kit Hetherington. She had seen him, of course, resplendently dressed, in the Hetherington pew each Sunday by his brother's side. Once, when he had deferred to her courteously in the church aisle as they prepared to leave after matins, she had caught an amused twinkle of those lively brown eyes and her heart had missed a beat as she made a bobbed curtsey in answer.

The following Sunday the squire's mother was in The Hetherington pew. She had apparently been escorted by a Cavalier friend of Mr. Hetherington, since Kit walked today beside a dark young man with whom he was obviously well acquainted. Phoebe and Rachel were not alone in their curiosity to view Lady Hetherington. Heads craned toward the pew, and poor Mr. Illingworth must have been patently aware that his sermon was receiving less than its customary attention. Lady Hetherington's fine blue velvet gown, set off by a short ermine cape and muff, and her fashionable low-crowned beaver with its curling blue feathers were seen to full effect when she emerged from the church porch on her son's arm at the close of the service.

"I think you are acquainted with my mother, Colonel Nashe." Sir Nicholas paused to introduce his guests.

Phoebe eyed Rachel uneasily. This meeting between her father and the woman whose home he had put to the torch could not be easy for either of them.

Simon Nashe bowed and Lady Hetherington inclined her head stiffly. Phoebe saw she was a handsome woman, carrying herself superbly, and with the haughty, aquiline features of her son.

"Mother, you will, I think, know Mistress Wilson, but not the colonel's daughters. May I present Mistress Rachel and Mistress Phoebe."

Lady Hetherington's glacial blue eyes passed from Rachel to Phoebe and, in that single moment of greeting, Phoebe was aware of something akin to hatred directed full at her. It was so strong that she drew back as if to avoid a physical blow, meeting that venomous glance with an utterly bewildered one of her own. What could Kit's mother hold against her? They had never met.

"Welcome back to Hetherington, my lady." Simon's tone was tinged with just a trace of embarrassment.

"Mistress Wilson, I trust you keep well." Lady Hetherington held his gaze with her own. "You are blessed in your daughters, Colonel. Mistress Rachel, Mistress Phoebe." Both girls curtseyed and Lady Hetherington addressed her elder son curtly. "It is icy here in the church drive. Will you hand me into the coach, Nick?"

The assembled villagers doffed their hats and bobbed their curtseys as the Hetheringtons moved toward their coach. A thin-faced maid was handed up to sit beside her mistress. Sir Nicholas beckoned to the two younger men, who lingered in talk near the porch. Kit moved hurriedly to brush Phoebe's elbow. "All happiness to you over the coming Holy Season, Mistress Phoebe," he murmured.

She colored and stammered at the warmth of feeling she read in his eyes. His bow to the ladies was so low that the ostrich plume of his hat swept the church path. "I—I thank you, sir."

He hastened to the lich gate to join the family gathered in the coach. Phoebe's eyes strained for a final glimpse of him as the vehicle lumbered off. Instead, she again met the icy blast of Lady Hetherington's stare and shivered under it. How strange and frightening! Anger directed at their father would have been understandable. Kit's mother had received none of the Nashes graciously, but it had been at her, Phoebe, that the flash of pure hatred had been directed. Why? Did she suspect Phoebe's involvement with Kit?

Colonel Nashe was silent throughout the short ride home, and grandmamma seemed wrapped in her own thoughts. There was a suspicion of a tremble to the older woman's lips. Had this inauspicious meeting with Lady Hetherington recalled her grandmamma's grief for her daughter's passing? The encounter had aroused unpleasant memories both in her and her son-in-law. Phoebe sighed inwardly. Past enmity could never be completely erased. She saw that now, and the gulf between herself and Kit Hetherington had widened and deepened.

Rachel was more than a little startled when her father announced that he had invited Mistress Burnell to spend Christmas Day at Glebe.

"There need be no undue fuss. Mistress Burnell is a practical housewife, no spendthrift."

"It will be pleasant to have company," Rachel agreed. "Phoebe will enjoy it. She's feeling low, understandably, since she'd expected to be a bride and spending her first Christmas at Barrow."

Grandmamma was not so delighted. "For all your father will expect no extra expenditure, he'll find the lady used to more liberal entertaining. I noted her excellent taste in wines when she attended Phoebe's betrothal feast."

"I think father has been visiting her frequently." Rachel hesitated, her eyes troubled. "Phoebe thinks he is courting her. Has he spoken to you yet?"

"No." The old woman's tone was guarded. "But I've a feeling in my bones Glebe will have a new mistress by the summer, or even earlier."

"Her period of mourning Josiah will soon be over."

"M'm. I think your father will wish Phoebe to be already married before he brings his new wife home."

Rachel lowered her head abruptly over a lawn shift she was embroidering at the hem as Phoebe's Christmas gift. Judith Burnell could not be expected to view with pleasure the prospect of a sixteen-year-old unmarried stepdaughter continually under her feet, and an older girl already accepted by the household as mistress of Glebe.

"I'll have words with Leah. Something more elaborate than our usual Christmas fare will be called for, I think."

Though Simon Nashe did not approve of overindulgence and roistering over the Holy Season, Christmas was celebrated quietly but pleasantly at Glebe. No "heathen practices" were tolerated, such as the dragging in of the Yule log or the visits of the local mummers, whose traditional plays had been revived now that the Commonwealth strictures had been relaxed. Simon Nashe regarded them as lewd and unseemly. The household looked forward eagerly to the seasonal rich food and simple exchanges of gifts.

On Christmas Day Simon Nashe hastened his family from the chilled church, anxious to welcome Mistress Burnell to Glebe. Roger had sent gifts, new collars of fine cambric trimmed with deep lace, for the girls. Simon had presented his daughters and Mistress Wilson with new gowns, plain cut, certainly, but of excellent quality. Phoebe's was in light blue velvet, neckline, hem and sleeves edged in lace, and Rachel's was in heavy gold and brown brocade, which pleased her, for the coloring accentuated the tawny-gold of her eyes and flattered the reddish glints in her hair.

Dinner was excellent and expertly served. Leah had done well. Mistress Burnell had now emerged from mourning and was resplendent in a gown of wine brocade, the neck cut lower than Rachel considered her father would approve. He appeared genial, taking pleasure in his guest's company, inviting Rachel to display her skill on the virginals and even dancing a measure with Mistress Judith. It was when he returned the blushing lady to her chair that he ordered Prue to refill their glasses and then dismissed her.

Rising to his feet with calm deliberation, he eyed his womenfolk thoughtfully and cleared his throat.

"It seems the appropriate time for me to make the announcement and I cannot believe it will be any great surprise for you to hear. Mistress Judith has done me

57

the honor of granting me her hand in marriage. You may kiss your stepmother-to-be, girls, for we intend to publish the banns shortly."

Rachel obeyed him immediately while Phoebe gathered her wits.

"Now, Simon, you promised me you'd not rush matters. I am, only this month, out of mourning for poor Josiah, and we agreed that Phoebe here should wed first."

"Well, poor Roger cannot be blamed for the delay, but I see no reason why we should suffer for it." He beamed down at her in excellent humor.

Playfully, she tapped him with her painted fan.

"I can see you are going to be as masterful as Josiah was, but I'll not object to that. A man should be undoubted master in his own home, don't you agree with me, Rachel?"

"If there's love in the home, ma'am, I see no conflict of interests," Rachel replied quietly.

"I never saw the need to put my man on a pedestal," Mistress Wilson put in dryly.

"He was very wealthy, I understand, did uncommonly well during the late war."

"He owned two ships and yes, he certainly left me more than adequately provided for. As you put it so aptly, both sides found a need for provisions and good cloth."

Colonel Nashe kicked at a log. Aware of a sudden tension within the room, he muttered some comment about seeing Mistress Burnell's coachman and ensuring her comfort on the return journey to Mountsorrel.

"I'll get one of the girls to provide a footwarmer, Judith, it's freezing hard."

Left alone the women trod warily in their conversation, until Mistress Judith said directly, "It must mean a great deal to you to know these girls are well provided with dowers, Phoebe so soon to be settled. Let us hope Rachel will soon follow her example."

"You are knowledgeable indeed, Mistress Burnell. My granddaughters will both receive from me considerable portions which, added to those provided by their father, should give them admirable marriage prospects. I'm sure, however, it was not Mr. Talbot's sole consideration in seeking Phoebe's hand, since he has known and admired both girls since they were children."

Judith Burnell's dark eyes darted to Phoebe's expression of embarrassment.

"Such a pretty child, and Rachel, too. You are quite lovely, my dear, and so practiced in the management of a household. I cannot believe that you will remain long unmarried despite—your misfortune."

Rachel moved determinedly back to the virginals. "Sing for us, Phoebe, Mr. Purcell's song about the shepherdess. I'm sure Mistress Judith would enjoy hearing that." Despite her battle to remain calm, her fingers were trembling so that they had to be forced to fulfill their function and she feared the performance was ill-done.

She assisted her grandmother to bed while her father escorted Mistress Burnell to her carriage. Lying back on her pillows, the older woman surveyed Rachel after Prue had been dismissed with the warming pan.

"You must face the inevitable. Life won't be easy with Mistress Burnell ensconced here."

"I've little choice but to remain."

"Don't be too sure, my girl. You'll be a wealthy woman, especially after my death." She put up a hand to trace her granddaughter's loved features. "She didn't flatter you. You are quite lovely. Don't despair."

"But . . ."

"Rachel, my dear, any man worth his salt is unlikely to take too much account of this lame leg of yours.

Besides, I've noticed you greatly exaggerate its importance."

Rachel rose from her stool by the bedside. "And how shall I know how worthy he is, when you are so ready to bribe him for me? Bless you, grandmother. Phoebe is fortunate. Roger loves her. I'm sure of it."

The old woman sighed. "Oh, yes, he does. I wish I didn't think that his particular misfortune."

Chapter 6

Rachel rose early on New Year's Day to see her father off to join the hunt. She handed him and Mr. Stone the customary stirrup cups of mulled spiced wine.

Tom Stone was in good spirits and raring to be off.

"It's cold but sunny. We should have excellent sport. The squire's to join us this morning, but I understood young Master Hetherington escorted his mother back to London last night."

Rachel caught a startled gasp behind her and turned to see a white-faced Phoebe catch the doorpost for support. She hastened to put an arm around her sister. Colonel Nashe and Tom Stone had already gone off down the drive.

"What is it? Are you in pain?"

Phoebe pulled herself free, shaking her head, and hurried off above stairs. Rachel was left staring after her, the wine cups in her hand. Obviously, Phoebe was not ready to be fussed over; better to leave her to herself; woman's trouble, likely enough. Phoebe was subject to considerable pain during her monthly courses. Rachel turned into the kitchen to confer with Leah about the morning's work.

When Rachel *did* have occasion to go up to their chamber, she was alarmed to find her sister lying full length upon the bed, her face buried in the pillows, weeping as if her heart would break.

"Phoebe?" Rachel closed and fastened the door. "Tell me, Phoebe. Something's terribly wrong. I've been conscious of it for a week or more now."

"No one can help me, not now."

"Nothing is so bad it cannot be helped. Phoebe, don't cry like that, you'll break my heart. What is it? Have you had word from Roger again, postponing the wedding?"

Phoebe sat up abruptly, her usually gentle mouth set in a bitter grimace. "Roger? Postpone the marriage? That would be funny, if it were not so—terrible."

"You don't love Roger. I know that, but . . ."

"Can't you guess what's wrong? Can't you? It feels to me as if it shouts itself to the rooftops. I'm going to have a child—Kit Hetherington's child."

The blood drained from Rachel's face. She felt her whole body go cold, her facial muscles harden and tense. Phoebe knelt against the pillows, her body withdrawn into a tight, forlorn ball. Rachel ignored her apparent hostility and drew near, sinking down on the bed and reaching out her arms. For a moment Phoebe continued to hold back, then she threw her arms round Rachel's shoulders and they rocked backwards and forwards together while the younger girl sobbed out the bitterness of her suffering.

"Hush, hush, now. You mustn't. Oh, Phoebe, my darling, why, *why* didn't you trust me before? How long have you known?"

"About a month ðr more. I feared—I missed my monthly course and—and I sent for Zillah. I dared not ask you or grandmother, I was so ashamed. I thought Zillah would know—or could help me. I'd heard snippets of talk from the maids about—about girls who were in—in my position and went to old Salome."

"What did she say?"

"That it was too early to be sure and that—in any case, she wouldn't help me, that it was dangerous and she hadn't her mother's skill." Phoebe's mouth twisted. "She told me I was not alone. She is to have a child—about the same time, I think. I'm sure now. I have been very sick today, was yesterday and a day or two before that. Oh, Rachel. What can I do? Father will kill me—the disgrace—and Roger . . ."

"Does he know—Mr. Hetherington?"

"No. I haven't seen him since his mother came to the manor and before that only from a distance. It was difficult to find excuses to ride out, the weather was so bad . . ."

"When—when do you think this happened? Can you be sure?"

Phoebe nodded, swallowing back further sobs. "It—it was the day Zillah and her mother were taken. We—Kit and I—were coming back from the woods when—when we heard the commotion. Don't—don't despise me, Rachel. I couldn't bear that. I love him so."

"Phoebe, I'm sure that you do."

"It—it was so beautiful, not sordid and nasty like the girls say. We had met and been riding, then he lifted me down and we walked. His hand touched mine and we looked at each other . . . Oh, it sounds so childish and silly. You would never have succumbed, you're so sensible, but I was so unhappy, Rachel, about the marriage, frightened of Mistress Talbot and Roger, and Kit was so kind and gentle. I loved him that first time I saw him at the betrothal feast. We danced and even then, his hands touching mine excited and thrilled me . . ." She put a tired hand up to push back the mass of her golden hair, free for once of its cap. "There was a little hut, for the charcoal burners, and we went in there out of the cold. He put back my hood and ran his hands through my hair. He—he spread his cloak and we . . . Rachel," it was a cry from the heart, "I never meant it to happen, I . . . I swear it. I'm not a wanton. It was for Kit—only for Kit."

"Of course you are not a wanton, Phoebe. What can you think of me, that I would not understand, am incapable of realizing how easily . . . Let us talk sensibly for one moment. Mr. Hetherington is away from the manor, as we heard this morning. He must be told when he returns."

"But he may not."

"Phoebe, did he tell you he loved you?"

"He said he—we kissed . . ." Phoebe's blue eyes regarded her, as bewildered as a child's. "I believed that he did. Oh, Rachel. Will he abandon me? He couldn't. He would not be so cruel."

"Did you speak of breaking your betrothal?"

"No, we never talked of Roger at all." Phoebe gazed bleakly beyond Rachel to the window. "You are thinking Kit Hetherington is used to encounters like this—many girls like me, some of them—less innocent. That he expects me to marry Roger, dismiss that occasion as just . . . He does not think of a child. If you think that the case, I wouldn't tell him, wouldn't try to force him to stand by me."

"That's nonsense, Phoebe. Of course he must be told. Who knows? You've a considerable dower. I cannot believe that Sir Nicholas would put insuperable objections to this marriage. He will see that it is necessary."

"But I couldn't go to him—tell him. What will father do . . . and Roger . . ." She shuddered, plucking at the sheets.

"Then I must."

"You? No, Rachel, you mustn't. It's all impossible, I can't believe it's happening to me."

"It is happening to you." Rachel made her tone purposefully stern. "A child is growing within you. It has to be faced. It is Kit Hetherington's child and he must acknowledge it as such. There may be some talk, but that will pass. Now you must think of yourself and the child."

"Suppose—suppose he should deny—that it is his?"

"You say you love him, Phoebe. Do you believe that of him?"

Phoebe drew a hard breath. "No, no. I don't think he is cruel, but his life has been so different with his brother on the continent, then at Oxford and—and they say the Court is licentious . . ."

Rachel thought quickly. "Grandmamma must be told."

"No!"

"It is necessary. If father disowns you—and he could abandon you to the cruelty of the Church fanatics—you will need money. *We* shall need money, for, of course, I would take you away from here."

"But, Rachel, where would we go? How could we live?"

"Grandmamma would not see us destitute. We could take a small cottage some miles away, perhaps. It is possible she would come with us. She has no wish to live here with Judith Burnell."

"Oh," Phoebe whispered brokenly, "I had forgotten about Mistress Burnell. I would kill myself rather than live here under her."

"Do not talk such wicked nonsense. Pull yourself together, Phoebe. There are ways out of this and we must find them. Bathe your eyes. Take to your bed for now. You have been sick. We'll say something disagreed with you. There has been so much rich food over Christmas. The excuse will serve."

"But the girls will guess. Prue's eyes miss nothing."

"Not yet a while if we are careful. Now trust me."

Phoebe's eyes closed wearily and she forced a smile. "You are always so good to me, Rachel."

"I love you, little goose." She paused with her hand on the door handle to glance back at Phoebe. This bitter experience had forced maturity. Already Phoebe had put off childhood. The rounded lines of her face were subtly altered, despite the redness and puffiness of swollen eyes. Rachel frowned. Soon the change in her sister would be apparent. Not the betraying heaviness of the coming child, not for months yet. But the bittersweet experience in the charcoal burners' hut had affected her beyond doubt. In some indefinable way, she was already growing beyond Rachel's own experience, yet she needed help, desperately. Before anything further could be decided, grandmamma must be told.

It was some hours before Rachel managed to get herself closeted with Mistress Wilson in her bedchamber. The older woman was not as stunned as Rachel had expected.

"You've been aware that she was meeting this man?"

"Some man, I had no idea who."

"Advise me, grandmamma. What must be done? Roger needs to be told and father . . ." Rachel bit her lip uncertainly. "How can we protect Phoebe? I know she's been foolish, but not wicked. She says she loves young Hetherington."

"This must be kept from your father until we have worked out some course of action. Just now, any breath of scandal might endanger this match with Judith Burnell."

"But Phoebe cannot marry Roger without confessing. This thing has gone too far. Even if I were to countenance deception, and I could not, Roger would know soon enough. Roger is a stern man. He could denounce her, set aside the marriage. The disgrace would kill her."

"No, I agree. The betrothal must be broken."

"She sent for Zillah. I think she was desperate enough to . . ."

Mistress Wilson shuddered. "No, I've known girls to die horribly that way, and whatever the circumstances, I cannot believe that child-murder is acceptable before God. Phoebe must bear this child. She is young and strong. The baby must be placed with reliable foster folk. It can be arranged. In the meantime we must think up some way of putting aside the coming marriage plans and taking Phoebe off somewhere with us until she's delivered. I thank my dear husband's foresight in providing for me so I've money in plenty to see us through this."

"You spoke of our portions to Mistress Burnell. You remember?"

"Certainly."

"How much could each of us expect to take to our husbands?"

"Five thousand pounds. I could perhaps manage six."

Rachel's eyes rounded. "As much as that? The child of an earl would expect little more."

"Less. The child of an earl has her nobility to make her acceptable."

"Then I shall go to Sir Nicholas, point out his responsibilities in this matter, and the advantages to be gained by such a match."

"Rachel, that is out of the question!"

"It's necessary. You have already agreed that father must not be told. I know that he should be the one to demand marriage for Phoebe, but I'm afraid he would not."

"A match with the Hetheringtons?" Mistress Wilson pursed her lips thoughtfully. "Sir Nicholas is gentleman to the King's bedchamber. He'll aim high for his brother."

"Yet he needs money more than he needs noble blood."

"Even six thousand pounds might not be considered sufficient inducement."

"With some of my portion added, it should prove sufficient. It is the only way, grandmamma, that Phoebe has any chance of happiness."

"And *your* needs? I had laid by such a sum . . ."

"We have talked of that before. I'll manage."

"I should go with you."

"No, you aren't well. I'll take Prue as chaperone, but if it's improper for us to talk alone, then it must be. Circumstances require it."

"You do not know this man. Suppose he insults you, threatens to reveal Phoebe's shame. We have no rights in this matter."

Rachel laid a gentle hand on her grandmother's arm. Then she looked away. "Perhaps Nicholas Hetherington is worldly, but I believe he will listen to me. He may even weigh the advantages in our favor."

"But he cannot command his brother to marry Phoebe."

"No, but I think he has considerable influence over him. What other choice have we, unless we try to conceal this birth and farm out of the child? Phoebe would break her heart if she is forced to lose it."

"You think so?" The old woman's tone was grim. "Phoebe is made of sterner stuff than you imagine, Rachel. In considering your futures, I fear far more for you than for her."

"I don't understand."

"I know you don't. But there—you'll go your own way whatever I say." She compressed her lips. "I hope your trust in the squire's discretion is not ill-placed. When will you go?"

Once committed, Rachel found herself less anxious to proceed. "Soon. I must try to find him alone and when father is absent from home."

"It mustn't be delayed. Sir Nicholas may leave for London at any time. Tomorrow your father will be at Mountsorrel."

"Then that must be the time."

"You will not tell Phoebe?"

"Best not, lest it come to nothing. Poor child, she has lived in torment for weeks. I'll see she sleeps well tonight. If I fail to convince Sir Nicholas, we must make plans. What a blessing Roger is from home." Rachel frowned. "It seems dreadful to be thankful that poor Mistress Talbot's death has delayed this marriage. It could have been disastrous for Phoebe—and for Roger."

That night, as she lay beside Phoebe, Rachel wondered how she would bring herself to tell Sir Nicholas of Phoebe's condition. She was at least relieved to see that Phoebe was sleeping peacefully, Zillah's potion having done its work.

Rachel decided to call on Sir Nicholas Hetherington alone. It seemed purposeless to take Prudence along. She could not be present during the interview and could not be relied upon to keep the visit a secret should it prove abortive, as Mistress Wilson feared. She told Phoebe she was going into the village to see one of the tenants who had been unwell. Fortunately, Phoebe did not press to accompany her. She looked distinctly unwell at breakfast and Rachel blessed the fact that their father was so wrapped up with thoughts of Judith Burnell that he failed to notice anything amiss.

She called first at the village and then returned home by way of Hetherington. As she rode across the moat bridge, she saw the workmen's trestles and platforms in position against the west wing. Shutters had already been repaired and the windows facing her were freshly glazed. Sir Nicholas's manservant, Gaston LeFarge, came to the stable door as she led her horse to the mounting block.

"Good morning, Gaston. Is Sir Nicholas at home? Would he receive me?"

The Frenchman assisted her to dismount.

"He is, mademoiselle, and I'm sure will be pleased to receive you."

The door was opened abruptly by Zillah, who immediately escorted Rachel into the hall and indicated two solid riding chairs for the convenience of callers.

"Will you sit, Mistress Nashe, while I inform the master that you're here?"

Rachel avoided looking at the gypsy too closely. Was it true? *Was* she carrying a child? The thought crossed Rachel's mind that if so, it might well be Sir Nicholas's. He had been quick to offer Zillah assistance when she was in distress.

Zillah returned soft-footed.

"Sir Nicholas will receive you now, Mistress Nashe."

"Thank you, Zillah. You are well—and happy?"

Dark eyes darted over Rachel's tense form as if she read how nervous she was, dreading this coming interview.

"Very well settled, Mistress Nashe. I hope all are well at Glebe."

"Mistress Wilson's cough troubles her, otherwise we are all in good spirits."

The drawing room, to which Zillah escorted her, was still sparsely furnished, but a bright fire burned in the grate and loving care had been lavished on the heavy oak court cupboard. The velvet curtains had been skillfully darned, but the material had been of the finest and would keep out the worst of the draughts. Sir Nicholas had been reading. His long-stemmed clay pipe was laid by as he rose to greet her, bowing.

"An unexpected pleasure. Please come to the fire." He plumped up two cushions on the old, high-backed Elizabethan settle. "You must be chilled. Zillah will bring you wine or mulled ale."

"Ale, please." Rachel concentrated on removing her riding gloves and settling her skirts to her satisfaction. She had dressed without ostentation in a well-cut riding dress of blue wool. When Zillah brought the ale, Rachel sipped it gratefully while gathering the courage necessary to come to the point of her visit. Over the rim of the pewter tankard she considered Sir Nicholas doubtfully. He was dressed simply this morning in green velvet breeches and a short, silver-buttoned jacket, revealing his fine, lace-trimmed shirt. His fair curls were touched with reddish gleams from the fire-light and Rachel was conscious of the two heavy gold rings on his fingers, one enameled, one set with a huge green stone. Now, while he lolled easily opposite her, they seemed worlds apart. Hetherington might lack comfortable furnishings, Sir Nicholas himself be impoverished, but the man was a gentleman, no well-to-do yeoman farmer like her father. Mistress Wilson's forebodings were uppermost in her mind: "He will aim high for his brother."

He did not press her to come to the reason for her call, nor did he make idle conversation. He merely waited her convenience.

At last she put down the tankard. Quietly, a little haltingly, she explained. He listened to the end without comment and without any movement or frown of disapproval.

"Were you aware of your brother's association with my sister, sir?" she concluded a little shakily. "She had been foolishly trusting, but I beg you to believe she is no wanton."

"I knew of Kit's interest." His brows grew together in thought rather than anger. "Your father has not been told?"

"No, sir, not as yet—my grandmother and I dared not tell him. His fury will be terrible. He does not easily accept the failings of others, especially weakness such as this. I dread to think how he will deal with Phoebe."

"She has not told Kit—about the child?"

"No, she has not seen him—since she was sure. Did he speak of his special regard for her?"

Those strange green-blue eyes regarded her piercingly.

"You ask if he loves her? That I do not know, Mistress Nashe. Kit and I have not been close of late. I am not his keeper. He would not mean to be cruel, but I doubt if he has thought seriously of any particular responsibility toward Mistress Phoebe." He shrugged. "We knew, naturally, of her betrothal. They are both young, in love with life. What has occurred is not to be unduly castigated."

"But you must see that what may be of little moment to your brother is disastrous for my sister, sir."

"What have you in mind?"

"Will he return soon?"

"No. He has received an enthusiastic letter from a friend of his at Oxford. Both are looking for adventure. Our victories in Guinea and the capture of Cape Verde have fired them with a thirst to set sail. Tom Spicer has been offered a commission at sea by the Duke of York, who, as you know, is Admiral of the Fleet. Kit has escorted our mother to Somerset House and will lodge with Tom in London. Who knows when they'll leave for Chatham or Southampton?"

"Then he may soon set sail?"

"Indeed, I'm afraid so."

"And could be at sea for months?"

"Certainly. The Dutch will not take our naval actions lying down. Already their ambassador has complained to our King. We are virtually at war."

"I had hoped . . ."

"Yes?"

"Sir Nicholas, I will be frank. My sister and I will receive marriage portions from my grandmother," she hesitated, avoiding his direct gaze, "as well as from my father. I would be prepared to forego a considerable part of my dower in Phoebe's favor if your brother could be persuaded to marry her."

It was out and she found herself trembling violently. There was a little silence.

He said a trifle sardonically, "How much would be your dot, Mistress Nashe, since we are speaking so frankly?"

"Some six thousand pounds from my grandmother alone. My grandfather was a wealthy merchant. I have some jewelry—father might refuse to furnish Phoebe's dower since—but she would not be an encumbrance on your brother, sir, I think you will agree."

"Certainly. I must send immediately to Kit and inform him of his good fortune, but, as I explained, I cannot be sure of my letter reaching him before he sails."

"You would raise no objections to the match?"

"By no means."

Rachel thought desperately. Even if Christopher Hetherington would agree to marry Phoebe, how could he be reached in time, before the need to face Roger and the imminent marriage? Her throat was thickening with the emotional stress of this embarrassing conversation and she fought back foolish tears.

"It seems you cannot help us, sir. I'm sorry I

troubled you. We, grandmother and I, must think how best we can shield Phoebe from the worst of this. The news will be a terrible blow. I don't know how she will bear it. She's such a child and she loves your brother deeply."

"You will take your sister away from Glebe?"

"I think we must. Soon Phoebe will have to confess to Roger Talbot."

"And he, like a good Puritan, would shame her publicly before the Church congregation?"

Rachel went white to the lips. "I cannot believe he would be so cruel, but his family hold rigid convictions. My father is soon to be married. He is very vulnerable to scandal just now."

"I could offer a solution, one you might consider carefully."

"Sir?"

"I could marry you."

She stared at him and saw that he was watching her closely. "I don't understand."

"It's simple enough. A lady with six thousand pounds to offer is quite a prize. I would make you a considerate husband. The plan has its merits. Think about it carefully."

She blinked rapidly, struggling to make sense of this sudden change of attitude. He was lolling back against the cushions of the daybed, his head tilted slightly, as if to assess her reaction.

Hot blood flooded her cheeks. He was mocking her, reminding her that a Hetherington was not to be bought, certainly not by some upstart chit whose father had grown fat on the misfortunes of better men. So Kit Hetherington had taken his pleasure with one of his neighbor's daughters. Unfortunate that she had conceived, but whose fault was that but her own?

Rachel rose abruptly, stumbling awkwardly in her haste. "I see, sir, that you have been vastly amused by this interview. I thought you a gentleman who would not take advantage of my desperate need. Of course I should not have come. Please forgive me."

"I think you misunderstand, Mistress Rachel."

"No, sir," she replied cuttingly, "*you* misunderstand. I had hoped there had been some trace of affection for my sister which caused your brother to use her so badly. She is a child, had not known that men could prove so heartless. She will learn very soon in a hard school. I have no experience of the ways of Court, had thought that to speak to you openly without the restraint of formality, you would advise, even be able to help me. I see I am wrong. Now, please ring for your maid. I would like to leave."

He rose and jerked the bell pull. She curtseyed, coldly, caught up her riding gloves, and turned away from him. Zillah came to the door.

Behind Rachel came Sir Nicholas's urbane tones.

"Mistress Nashe wishes to leave. Has her horse been tended?"

"Yes, Sir Nicholas. Gaston has it ready."

Rachel did not turn as he bade her "good day." Her eyes were smarting with tears of frustrated anger. Head high, she walked into the hall trying desperately not to limp ahead of Zillah and out into the courtyard as the Frenchman led her horse to the mounting block.

She mounted and turned out through the gatehouse.

Chapter 7

Rachel was struggling from her muddied riding gown when grandmamma came to her chamber.

"Phoebe is in the kitchen. I was anxious. Did you see Sir Nicholas?"

"Yes." Viciously, Rachel snapped her bodice lacing and frantically searched for another. "Oh, yes, I saw him. He cannot help us."

"And Mr. Hetherington?"

"Is bound for the Indies. He and a Mr. Spicer, presumably the man we saw with them at church, are off adventuring."

"Dear God, what is Phoebe to do?"

"I don't know, grandmamma, I cannot think clearly."

"Will Sir Nicholas try to contact his brother?"

"He believes he will already have set sail from Chatham, but, in all events, I doubt if Kit Hetherington would consider Phoebe's plight a matter to disturb his conscience, let alone cause him to alter his plans."

"Did you speak of the dower?"

Rachel averted her gaze. Even now she could not bring herself to speak of the studied insult she'd received. A pulse beat angrily in her throat.

"I—I did, but Sir Nicholas made it plain that my ill-bred suggestion that a Hetherington would stoop to wed an upstart Nashe, even for ready gold, was a matter for levity."

"My poor Rachel. I should not have allowed you to

subject yourself to such an interview. It is just that we are desperate . . ."

"I know, grandmamma, I know." Rachel touched the older woman's hand gently. "Please do not distress yourself. We'll find a way."

Rachel was relieved to find her father absent from the dinner table. Her hand shook as she raised her ale cup and Phoebe looked at her wonderingly. No one ate much. Leah grumbled as the girls cleared away the congealing dishes.

Worrying about the coming sweeping changes in the household when Mistress Burnell arrived at Glebe, *that* was what was bothering the ladies. Well, little Mistress Phoebe would soon be out of it, but Leah's heart ached for Mistress Rachel. The colonel had shown little enough affection for his older daughter over the years, now he would consider her merely an encumbrance.

Rachel was summoned to her father's study later that afternoon. She went in trepidation. Was he aware that she had gone to the manor alone? How dared she answer for her blatant flouting of the proprieties?

She stood, frozen with horror, in the doorway, as Sir Nicholas rose from his chair. His fine eyes flickered with a trace of amusement over her tense form, as he made her an extravagant bow. She swallowed painfully and advanced into the room.

Her father cleared his throat, a habit he only employed in moments of bewilderment or stress.

"Rachel, I have sent for you to impart the most unexpected and joyous news. I trust you will regard it so. Sir Nicholas has come to ask your hand in marriage. He tells me he has held you in the highest regard since your first meeting in October and has waited only his opportunity to express himself."

"My admiration for Mistress Rachel knew no bounds when I saw how bravely she tackled the villagers over the matter of the Lee women, nor could I be ignorant from then on of the high esteem in which she is held in the village."

Rachel's eyes avoided those of both men. She had the suspicion that their visitor was mocking her father and had no wish to see that faintly satirical smile which she knew could linger around the long-lipped mouth beneath its fashionable thin moustache.

"Father, I—I would like to talk with you alone on this matter." Rachel heard herself speak the words, though without conscious volition.

"Naturally. I'll conduct you to the drawing room, sir. I'd be honored if later you'd sup with us."

Rachel's limbs were trembling and she seated herself while her father left the study with their visitor.

It was not possible. Sir Nicholas could not have been serious. Had she read her father's wishes correctly? He was welcoming the proposed match? It made no sense. When he returned, latching the door firmly against possible interruption, she looked up at him, troubled.

"Do you really wish me to marry this man, father?"

Simon Nashe prowled to the window, his back to her. His voice was brusque, but she read in the tone a tinge of half-shamed embarrassment.

"There are considerable advantages to the match, Rachel," he said shortly.

"Nicholas Hetherington is a Royalist, a member of the Court, your former enemy."

"Ah, you put your finger squarely on the point at issue. Your marriage with the squire would put an end, once and for all, to the resentment which lies here between the former warring factions. I think Sir Nicholas recognizes that; it's one of the reasons why he chooses to ask for you."

"The other being that I'm suitably dowered."

Though he didn't turn, Rachel saw that her father's neck had blushed fiery red.

"That is never an inconsiderable factor, Rachel, in

77

any match. Even the Talbots saw the advantages and . . ." He sought for words which would not wound. "Dower or no, I cannot see you receiving a wealth of offers, my child. I think you know that well enough."

"You mean few of our neighbors want a crippled bride for their sons!"

"You put the matter harshly. I know the thought is humiliating, but it has to be faced. God saw fit to burden you with this disability and now we must offer him thanks that he has also seen fit to provide for you a husband of whom you can be justly proud. The man is personable. You'll be 'my lady.' I could not have hoped for so much."

"And Mistress Burnell will not want me at Glebe when she comes here as a bride." He said nothing and she pressed the point inexorably. "You are commanding me to accept Sir Nicholas?"

"He is disposed to wait a day or so for your answer. I think when you've carefully considered, you will not be foolish enough to refuse."

"Would it be proper for me to speak with him before I decide?"

"Under the circumstances, I think I can give my permission."

He turned and faced her, his habitually severe expression softening. "I am convinced an acceptance would be in your best interests, child."

She shook her head, knowing if she attempted to answer she would break down and weep. She curtseyed and left the study.

Sir Nicholas was surveying the garden from the latticed window of the drawing room. A log in the grate spluttered and subsided into gray ash. He turned as the door clicked open. He looked startled at seeing her, then smiled at her with unexpected warmth.

"You left me over-hastily this morning. I felt it

necessary to make my meaning clear to you immediately."

"Did you tell my father I had discussed with you the amount of my dot?"

"That would hardly have been to my advantage," he said shortly. "We did discuss the matter of the marriage settlement after I had put forward my reasons for proposing such a match. I was relieved. I'd thought he might be decidedly unwilling to accept me as a son-in-law."

"He wants to be rid of me."

"Ah." He waited courteously until she had seated herself. "I think you do him an injustice. He is anxious to assure your welfare."

She looked up at him gravely. "I cannot see why you should want this match, sir."

"I need a wife. You were at pains to inform me you are not ill-dowered. You are young, strong, quite lovely . . ."

"And crippled."

"I think you are oversensitive on that score. I see by the excellence of arrangements here at Glebe that you would make a fine chatelaine of Hetherington." He seated himself opposite, leaning forward in his effort to convince her. "There is another, distinct advantage to our early marriage. Naturally, I am prepared to accept responsibility for my brother's coming child. Your sister could come to Hetherington under my protection. I think your father would make few objections to that in view of his own plans to establish a new mistress at Glebe. We can take her away somewhere secluded. Once the child is born, we can consider how best to arrange for its future care, suitable foster parents, perhaps."

What he said made sense. She saw herself at Glebe living under the rule of Judith Burnell, growing older, shabbier, or in some cottage with grandmamma and Phoebe, withdrawn from society.

As if he read what was passing through her mind, he said quietly, "Please understand me. I want sons. This marriage will be a true one in every sense of the word. I expect from you respect, discretion and obedience." The last word was put in with a faintly amused, sideways tilt of the head. "We are no verbal fencers, you and I. Our cards on the table, each clear about what is offered to the other. Will you take me?"

She had no choice. Her father had made his wishes plain. She drew a hard breath. "I shall be honored to become your wife, Sir Nicholas."

He stooped, took her hand, turned it and kissed the palm gallantly. "I am the one to be honored. Now, can I press you to haste?"

"Whenever it pleases you, sir, if it does my father."

"Then we'll publish the banns immediately and marry at the end of the month, which gives us some time at Hetherington before I'm likely to be recalled to London. Shall we inform your father?"

Simon Nashe expressed himself delighted with Rachel's good sense. For once he embraced her with some warmth.

"Now, off to your chamber, change your gown since Sir Nicholas is to sup with us. This will prove an excellent opportunity to inform your sister and grandmamma of your good fortune."

Rachel stood before the small traveling mirror on the chest in her room and stared at herself distractedly. She had chosen to wear the burgundy velvet gown in which Sir Nicholas had first seen her.

What had Sir Nicholas said? She was lovely? Her features looked back at her, totally unremarkable. Her skin was good, her eyes unusual, but she'd none of Phoebe's exquisite fragility. He had recognized her strength, determination, chosen her above some patrician Court beauty. For her dower alone? His reasons were incomprehensible to her.

She would be mistress of Hetherington. A little thrill of pleasurable anticipation shot through her. How would she cope with his prodigal extravagance? Her dower must be put to good use, to rebuild Hetherington Manor and not squandered on lascivious pleasures of Court life.

She tried to assess her own response to him. He aroused some feeling in her that she dared not analyze. She found his bantering manner and blatant flaunting of his handsome masculinity utterly overwhelming.

She had no opportunity to speak with either Phoebe or grandmamma, since both had already descended before her to the dining room. Her father's jubilant announcement stunned them both. Phoebe stared at Sir Nicholas in blank astonishment, while grandmamma regarded Rachel intently.

Sir Nicholas congratulated his host on the comfortable appointments at Glebe. "As you've doubtless heard, we have made the west wing of the manor tolerably habitable. Everything which remained whole of the furniture is solid enough, but sadly outmoded. Mistress Rachel will find conditions at Hetherington somewhat Spartan, I'm afraid, but that should soon be remedied."

"Will you continue in service with His Majesty?" Colonel Nashe inquired.

"For as long as he has need of me, naturally. I feel my mother's term of duty waiting attendance on the Dowager Queen is likely to end soon. The poor lady is quite ill. When the time comes for my mother to relinquish her duties at Somerset House, she will wish to retire to Hetherington."

Rachel considered the fact and found it disagreeable.

In that first icy encounter in the churchyard, Lady Hetherington's feelings toward the Nashes had been made blatantly plain.

As Sir Nicholas took his leave, he kissed Rachel's hand again. She found his affected gallantry unnerving and her fingers trembled in his grasp. "I shall write to my mother immediately," he said.

Rachel said soberly, "I fear she will not approve. The War made our families enemies." They were some distance from the others. She had not wished her father to overhear the comment.

"You said yourself how foolish it was to dwell on past hates. She will receive you gladly. She's been pressing me to marry these last nine years. She may not find it possible to attend the ceremony. If the weather closes in, journeying will be difficult."

Rachel nodded. She could not reply that she would be vastly relieved if Lady Hetherington were prevented from attending.

After Sir Nicholas had taken his leave, Agnes Wilson kissed Rachel gently on the forehead. "God grant you contentment, my child."

Within their room Phoebe clung to her tearfully. "Rachel, I'm so glad for you. He's so handsome and grand. Surely you will learn to love him."

"I don't have such romantic notions, goose," Rachel said, laughing shakily.

"I'm to lose you soon. Rachel, how shall I bear it . . . ?"

"You mustn't be frightened. I told Sir Nicholas." Quietly, she informed Phoebe of Kit's departure for the Indies. "Sir Nicholas has promised you shall stay with us for a while, till the child is born. He'll be able to protect you. Between us, we'll consider how best to tell Roger, and, of course, father . . ." Her voice trailed off uncertainly.

"I'm beginning to think Kit will never come back, that he never really loved me."

"Try not to think of it. If need be, we'll face up to that—if he refuses to help you."

The next weeks were a flurry of activity, for Rachel's wedding day was set for January 30th. Phoebe insisted on helping Leah in the kitchen with the preparations and baking for the wedding feast, which left grandmamma and Rachel free to concentrate on Rachel's inadequate wardrobe. Simon Nashe did not begrudge her funds for materials and sewing thread and sent them into Leicester to do the buying. Rachel was determined that most of the money should be spent on household linen for Hetherington.

"It's much too late to have a wedding gown made," she said, when grandmamma protested. "I'll buy lace to refurbish my newer gowns and I'll wear the gold brocade for the ceremony unless it is really too icy, and if so, the burgundy velvet will have to do. I'll want flannel and cambric for nightwear and underclothing." She laughed at her grandmother's air of comic dismay. "I'm unlikely to need formal gowns, and Sir Nicholas isn't marrying me to show me off in company. It's far more important that Hetherington should be made comfortable than to squander funds on finery which might only be worn once or twice."

Whenever she rode in the village, Rachel was aware of the curious eyes surveying her. Sir Nicholas's tenants greeted her respectfully and with some warmth, since they'd known her all her life, but she read in their eyes their bewilderment at this hasty and unexpected marriage. It was common knowledge that the Nashe girls were well dowered and the squire in need of money. She determined to ignore the speculation. She'd grown a thicker skin over the years.

Phoebe pressed gifts upon her. "I wish you'd let me have my gown altered for you. It seems so unlikely now that I'll ever wear it."

"No, Phoebe, you *will* wear it one day, if not for your wedding. You'll look so lovely in it. I won't let you set it aside. I'll do very well with what I have. Father has given me two feather mattresses for Hetherington and fine new bed hangings. I'm delighted with them."

A few days before the wedding Gaston rode over from Hetherington with an oilskin-wrapped package for Rachel.

"From Monsieur Nicholas, with his compliments."

Excitedly, the women carried the bulky package to Rachel's bedchamber and snipped impatiently at the cords which held the cover tight.

There was a great gasp from Phoebe as the contents were revealed and they all stood back, staring in wonder. Grandmamma lifted out the gown and placed it carefully on the bed.

It was made in the new style of heavy white velvet frosted on the bodice with tiny droplets of crystal. Sleeves and bodice were slashed to reveal the under-petticoat of gold silk and a froth of Mechlin lace bordered the wide-puffed, elbow-length sleeves.

"You must try it on. Rachel, how could Sir Nicholas be sure of the fit? Perhaps he consulted the tailor in Leicester. He would know," Phoebe said.

Grandmamma and Phoebe persuaded Rachel to step into the gown and they laced up the back of the bodice.

"We'll have to stitch the wedding knots on the skirt very lightly," grandmamma said, "so as not to crush the pile."

Rachel stared at herself in horror. "Grandmamma, I cannot wear this." She wrenched at the stiffened corsage, cut so low that it scarcely concealed the swell of her breasts. "It's immodest."

"It's beautiful," Phoebe whispered enviously. "I

think the fashion at Court is to wear gowns cut even lower, Rachel."

"That may be, but I am to wear this in church before our Godfearing neighbors. Father would never approve."

Agnes Wilson touched the soft pile tenderly. The girls were too young to remember the days before the Commonwealth forced women to hide their beauty under drab clothes of shapeless cut. She had worn such gowns, though perhaps never so daring as this current fashion apparently demanded.

"Since your father has given you in marriage to Sir Nicholas, I cannot see how he can object to you wearing the gown your husband-to-be has chosen."

"It's crass foolishness to squander money so," Rachel said wrathfully, "when we need every penny we possess for Hetherington. I'll speak to him, suggest it be returned to the tailor."

She raised the matter with her betrothed on his next visit to Glebe.

"Our neighbors are used to simplicity. Even our feasting will be regarded with disapproval in some quarters. Had we been married in London—"

"Wherever you are married, you will soon be a Hetherington," he said coldly. "I'll take no Puritan bride to the altar. I've no taste for this hypocritical concealment of the beauty God Himself fashioned." His eyes went disapprovingly to the plain linen cap which hid her hair from him.

She flushed hotly. "Then it must be as you wish, sir."

"I *do* wish. As to the celebrations, I leave the arrangements to your father. I would not subject you to the ordeal of public bedding."

He grinned wickedly at her dismayed expression. "I promise you, sweeting, I'll accustom you to our Cavalier ways by degrees. As to the extravagance, allow me my wish in this. You shall hold the greater part of my pursestrings once we are wed. I shall leave matters of household management and expenditure entirely in your hands. I'll not attempt to entertain lavishly at Hetherington, not yet a while, I assure you."

Rachel confided her defeat to grandmamma. "I can see he wishes me to wear my hair free like a hoyden. Grandmamma, can we ever live together without stress, do you think? Our attitudes to life are so different."

"I'm inclined to agree with him. Much of this psalm-singing and plainness of dress is hypocrisy. Many a man garbed in Puritan black has had all he can do to hide his lascivious thoughts, I'll warrant. Rachel, the world is changing again. There'll be little chance of happiness for you if you fight your husband in these matters."

She went to her own room and returned with a leather-covered jewel case. "I wore this rope of pearls at my own wedding, your grandfather's gift. We shall wind it amid your hair, my dear. It will complement the gown superbly."

So, after all, Rachel went splendidly attired to her wedding. It was cold but sunny when the Nashe coach lumbered to the lich gate where two young boys, laced with ribbons, cousins of the Paskells, waited to escort her. Young Barnaby himself carried before her the traditional bride cup with its branches of rosemary, gilded and garlanded with white silk ribbons. Job played his fiddle, and behind him came Phoebe, rosily pretty in her blue satin gown, then the maids in their best attire carrying the bride cakes and decorated garlands of wheat, the symbols of fertility.

The bridal feast took place at Glebe, since there was not yet a room at Hetherington large or comfortable enough to contain all their guests. It was a joyous gathering and the fiddle played merrily. Colonel Nashe had not stinted on the wine. Sir Nicholas sat beside her, handsome in his elegant suit of scarlet velvet. Rachel ate and drank sparingly. She had gone through the ceremony in a state of suppressed dismay, numbed by the speed with which all this had caught up with her. She pledged her husband in the bride cup and he reached out and squeezed her fingers as she restlessly crumbled her manchet of bread. He bent toward her, concerned.

"You are exhausted? Ready to retire?"

She nodded, scarlet color mounting to her face and throat. Only now she was dry-mouthed with alarm.

Sir Nicholas summoned Gaston to his side, ordering him to bring around the hired coach, for he had insisted that he carry his bride to the manor for their wedding night.

Rachel rose and nodded to Phoebe. The guests scrambled toward the bridal couple, squealing and laughing. Sir Nicholas steadied Rachel while they caught at the bride knots, the women kissing her and wishing her well, the men uttering bawdy, encouraging comments to the bridegroom, which would not have been tolerated six years ago, before the King's restoration. She endured it all. Finally came her father's grave injunction to be a good and dutiful wife and then Prue came with her warm cloak and hood and her husband led her to the waiting coach. Within its gloomy interior she watched the brightly lit windows of Glebe fade into the distance until the horses thundered across the wooden moat bridge and she was home, at Hetherington.

Sir Nicholas insisted on lifting her from the vehicle into the house. He put her down in the corridor at her husky request. Two strange maids waited to greet her, bobbing respectful curtseys, and Zillah Lee waited at the foot of the stairs, a silver candlestick held high to light her way to their chamber.

Sir Nicholas stood back, smiling. "I'll take a glass of

brandy before coming up. You'll find the girls have prepared everything for your comfort."

The great bedchamber appeared huge and shadowy. She swallowed hard, longing for the comforting familiarity of the room at Glebe which she had shared with Phoebe since childhood. There was a great, heavy oaken bed, its posts elaborately carved in the fashion of King James's day. Before it was placed ready her bridal chest, conveyed only this morning from Glebe. A bright fire spluttered in the hearth and she was glad of it, for she was shivering violently. The bed hangings were those in blue brocade on which she and grandmamma had worked so lovingly. The bedcovers were turned down and her lace-trimmed nightgown laid ready.

Zillah introduced the girls. "Tabitha and Sarah Sharman, my lady." The form of address was alien, reminding her of her new station. "They come from Birstall. Tabitha is sixteen and Sarah fourteen. You'll find them sensible and willing."

"I'm sure I will." Oh, for Leah and the well-known faces of Prue and Dinah!

Tabitha withdrew the warming pan from the high bed while Sarah made up the fire. Zillah dismissed them as she moved to divest her mistress of her wedding finery.

"I've done all that's needful, be sure of that."

Rachel glanced at her hurriedly and Zillah returned her that slow, secretive smile Rachel always found disturbing. The sweet, haunting scent of herbs, rosemary and lavender and others she could not recognize, teased her nostrils as she slipped between the sheets and Zillah's remark was made clear. The gypsy girl had omitted none of the pagan customs to ensure fertility in these marriage rites. As the girl bent close, Rachel was aware of Zillah's swelling breasts, proclaiming the girl's own fecundity, and was faintly nauseated, though, as ever, Zillah's body smelt fresher than any of the maids' had done at Glebe.

"Is there anything further you want, my lady?"

"Nothing, Zillah. You have done everything beautifully."

"The night cup is by your bed. I wish you all happiness, my lady."

Rachel fought back the ridiculous desire to call her back as the door closed softly on her retreating form. She reached out for the wine cup and sipped to give herself courage for the ordeal ahead. The wine was subtly spiced. Rachel could not identify its unusual flavor, but was glad of its warming afterglow as it coursed through her veins.

She sat up abruptly as the door opened and Sir Nicholas, dressed in a heavy brocade bedgown, was framed in the opening. He put down his candlestick on the bedtable and, walking to the fireplace, kicked the logs into soaring flame.

"I thank God frequently the manor isn't built of stone. Brick is so much warmer. Are you cold?"

She shook her head, aware that she'd self-consciously pulled up the sheets to her chin.

She looked away while he removed his slippers, threw off his robe and slipped into bed beside her. Anxious to cover her rising alarm, she said hastily, "Zillah and the girls have done excellently." She was aware that he was naked beside her and shivered.

"They seem good girls."

He reached out and touched the heavy brown mane of hair spread loose to her shoulders, the firelight picking up and brightening the reddish glints within it.

"I was right. You looked very lovely in the gown and," he chuckled soft in his throat, "very dignified, too. I was proud of my bride."

"Thank you, sir." She suffered his caress in silence,

aware of a tingling within her body, strange, frightening, but also exhilarating.

He firmly drew aside the bedcovering and she made a helpless little attempt to cover herself. He shook his head, smiling.

"They have made you ashamed of your own loveliness. You will not need this nightgown, pretty as it is. I'm your husband, mistress, I've the right to look at you."

She submitted, scarlet-faced, as he deftly disrobed her, then sat miserably huddled, starting when his hand cupped her high, rounded young breast, and slid down her tense-held form to the molded splendor of her thigh. She made an instinctive withdrawal and he checked. His brows twitched sharply together.

"They have made you ashamed of that, too. I told you before, this slight halt of yours is nothing to me. It was barely noticeable as you walked down the church aisle."

"That isn't true."

"It is true. Dismiss it from your mind."

He drew her into his arms then, his lips pressing hard on hers. Grandmamma had not left her in ignorance. She was prepared to endure, but she was deeply afraid. He would know it, she thought despairingly, my heart is beating so fast it seems it will start from my breast.

Her eyes were drawn inexorably to his lean, hard-muscled body. A jagged scar ran from beneath his breastbone to his right armpit. He had been fortunate to survive that butchery at Worcester. How had he escaped the field, wounded so badly? Panic engulfed her as she was reminded starkly of the injury her father had done him. She was now his chattel, at his mercy. Would it amuse him to make her suffer? She tried to control the trembling of her body, but her limbs refused to obey her and he laughed again softly.

"I didn't expect you to play the martyr, sacrificing

your virginity on Hymen's altar in abject fear and trembling of your master."

His teasing stung her to a spirited response.

"I am not afraid, sir, simply—inexperienced and . . ."

"That can be simply remedied." He sat up and took her chin between his thumb and first finger, turning her face toward the firelight. "You are angry with me. That's better. I like a show of spirit. I knew you had it and it governed my choice."

"That and my dower."

"A sharp tongue, too." He chuckled. "I'm not unappreciative of that, too, at the right time and place, and this is neither, wife." His hard kiss silenced her as he drew her chilled, rigid form into his arms.

His fingers, feather-light on her throat, breasts and waist, aroused her to a wild ecstasy of desire so that she accepted his heavy weight hard on her body without further resistance, expecting the agony of first penetration, biting her lips hard to prevent herself crying out.

As she lay quiet afterwards, her body burned with a sense of mingled shame and delight. He slept soundly at her side, the rose-tinged glow of the fire gilding the curling hairs on his chest and playing upon the tautness of belly and thigh muscles, for he had moved impatiently in sleep, thrusting aside the bedcoverings, and she had not dared try to replace them.

She was alarmed at her own response to his lovemaking. There *had* been pain, but ecstasy, too; a consuming fire, mounting to match his passion, which brought a hot flush of shame to her cheeks. He was her husband and she had been taught to honor him, submit to him in all obedience, as Holy Scripture commanded. She was unprepared for the arousal of her own senses, which even now caused her breasts and loins to ache with longing.

Had she disappointed him? It must be so, since

surely he had pleasured many women more passionate and experienced, skilled in the arts of delighting men.

Even in sleep he had kept one arm tight around her waist, a symbol of his complete possession of her.

She moved cautiously in an effort to ease her exhausted body and stiffened limbs. He stirred awake instantly, drowsily drawing her close again, so that her head was pillowed comfortably against his shoulder. She gave a little sigh of contentment, allowing herself at last to relax into sleep.

The flames soared up to a final, dying spasm and subsided into a pile of gray ash as white spears of daylight pierced their half-drawn bed curtains.

Chapter 8

When Rachel awoke, the sun was making patterns of light and shade across her bedcoverings. Wonderingly, she looked up to find the bed curtains fully drawn back. A second, hurried glance sideways told her that Nicholas had already risen. A soft indentation where his head had lain on the pillow beside her reminded her of their lovemaking and made her catch her breath. Her body felt over-heavy and languorous, a slight soreness between her thighs confirming the fact that she was no longer a virgin.

Zillah came to the bedside. Self-consciously, Rachel avoided the gaze of those piercing dark eyes.

"Good morning, my lady, I hope you slept well. I've brought up a pot of chocolate and rolls fresh from the oven. Shall I shake up your pillows so that you can sit comfortably to eat?"

Hectic spots of color burned in Rachel's cheeks. Why was it Zillah was always so aware of her special needs? It was difficult for her to sit without firm back support but, since she was rarely indulged at Glebe by being allowed to remain in bed for meals, even when ill, it had not proved necessary for Prue or Dinah to help her.

"I should come immediately down to the kitchens. Sir Nicholas . . ."

"Was up over an hour ago. He breakfasted and was off riding about the estate. He wished me to see that you rested this morning, ordered me to bring up your tray. Yesterday's ceremony and the feasting must have tired you."

Zillah put down the tray on the bedtable and came closer. Rachel's nightgown, discarded and thrown across the room last night by Nicholas, and her bedgown were laid ready over her arm.

"If you will allow me, my lady."

Shamefaced, Rachel accepted her help as she donned the garments.

What *did* she look like? Surely her eyes must reveal to the world how those hours in Nicholas's arms had changed her. Yet Zillah showed no sign of noticing anything unusual in her mistress's manner or appearance as she deftly shook up the pillows and brushed Rachel's tangled hair into some semblance of order. Rachel hoped fervently that the gypsy would not notice the trembling of her fingers as she took the mirror from her.

Did her expression appear subtly altered, or was she the only one aware of the change within herself? Nicholas had said she was lovely. She saw in the mirror a pale, oval face in which the tawny brown eyes appeared over-bright and large this morning. The faint flush of embarrassed color on the cheekbones merely enhanced the fine-drawn lines of her features. While

Zillah turned away for a moment, Rachel touched her lips experimentally. They were fuller today, redder, yet showing little visible sign of the ardent kisses Nicholas had pressed upon them; nor were there marks of purple bruising on the soft flesh of her throat and shoulders. She let out her breath in a little sigh of relief. Her hair hung in a silken cloud. He had stroked it caressingly, run his fingers through its heavy brown tresses. She had always considered the color insignificant, had guiltily envied Phoebe those golden locks which curled so delightfully from beneath her sister's linen cap. Now the sun glinted on her own brown mane, highlighting bronze and golden shades she had previously overlooked.

Zillah placed the tray across her knees, bent solicitously to pour out the steaming chocolate.

"Lady Hetherington's favorite, my lady. I'll see the girls bring up hot water for your tub."

Rachel bit her lip doubtfully. A hot tub. That *was* an extravagance. Her father would have frowned upon such pandering to the flesh. Phoebe and Rachel always washed from head to foot in cold water at Glebe, even on the sharpest of icy days. Zillah had rekindled the fire and it burned cheerfully in the hearth. How good it would be to submerge herself in the hot water, indulge herself utterly.

Zillah gave her no time to countermand the suggestion. Already she was at the door, calling to Sarah to get Gaston to help her carry up the heavy wooden tub. Rachel sat in her shadowed refuge listening to the panted breathing as the tub was sited before the hearth, then to the light pattering of Tabitha's feet as she came in with a great copper ewer of water. The girls made several more journeys with water before Zillah assisted Rachel into the scented water which lapped her aching body in silken-smooth bliss. Rachel basked in voluptu-

kept her eyes lowered to her plate, managing to avoid his gaze throughout most of the meal.

He rose finally and went to his piperack.

"Have you any objection if I smoke? I've fallen into the bachelor habit, found it strangely comforting."

"No, no, of course not."

She was unwilling to leave the table and come closer to him, but he waited courteously, until she had seated herself on the cushioned settle nearer the fire. He stretched himself on the cane daybed opposite, puffing contentedly at the long clay stem of his pipe.

Even in his plain country clothes he was quite magnificent, his cambric shirt and buff coat unfastened, his legs crossed easily in arrogant repose. He watched her lazily, his blue-green eyes narrowed over the rising blue smoke wreaths.

She found it hard to begin a conversation, clearing her throat awkwardly, a mannerism she found irritating in her own father. What could she find to say to this man who, in one sense, was almost a stranger to her, yet who had caressed her so intimately last night in the privacy of their chamber? Why did he not begin? She sensed that he was deliberately baiting her, aware of her decided unease in his presence.

"I trust you had a pleasant ride, sir." It was a foolish, vapid observation. Did he think her a simpleton?

"Perfectly satisfying. I was inspecting the woodland. We shall need more timber cutting."

"Yes, I was wanting to speak to you about—about the dining room. It should be restored." She rushed on now in her eagerness to fasten on to a suitably engaging subject. "You will wish to entertain the neighbors, fellow justices, some of your friends perhaps from London."

"You think so?"

There it was again, that subtle note of raillery she found so unnerving.

"Why, yes, I think you will, don't you agree?"

"If we must." He tamped down the tobacco in his pipe bowl. "Rachel, take off that hideous cap."

"Sir?" Her tone was frigid, incredulous.

"You heard me. Take off that cap."

"My father and friends would think I was—"

"I do not care a fig for the opinion of any psalm-singing Puritan. I demand that my wife refrain from wearing such a monstrosity. God gave you a glory of nut-brown hair. Give me the pleasure of viewing it whenever and wherever I please."

Obediently, she untied the strings, tangling them in her awkward haste. He nodded, satisfied, as she ran an anxious hand over her hair in an effort to smooth it.

"That's better. Oblige me by disposing of that article to one of the maids."

She pushed the offending cap beneath a cushion behind her and waited for him to return to their discussion of the dining room but, irritatingly, he refrained, his eyes coolly appraising her, so that she moved restlessly, discomfited by his scrutiny.

At last she returned doggedly to the subject at issue. "Do you not think, sir, that we should call in plasterers and carpenters to begin the work?"

"My baptismal name is Nicholas. Please use it. I'll have no servility from you, Rachel, in this household."

She hesitated, her eyes widening uncertainly. "As you wish, sir, my pardon, Nicholas."

He considered, then nodded. "Very well, I'll give Hawkins the necessary orders."

While he appeared to be in a more conciliatory mood, she chose to remind him of his promise regarding Phoebe and grandmamma.

"If they are to come here, as we planned, we shall need a second bedroom put at their disposal."

He sighed. "It would seem so. I'm beginning to fear

the house will never be free of this constant hammering and sawing, but since I intend to establish myself here for part of the year, at least now, the sooner the house is put into some semblance of order, the better.''

To Rachel's relief Hawkins, the steward, called later with more documents which demanded Nicholas's attention. This necessitated a courteous invitation to the man to sup with them and she was glad of a temporary respite from striving to entertain her husband. She had suddenly become tongue-tied when left alone with him.

They retired early, and this time Rachel made very sure she did not drink from the night cup left on her bedtable.

If Nicholas sensed an undue restraint in her, he made no comment, nor did he try to force a response. She gave herself dutifully, but doubts concerning her previous joyful participation tortured her and she lay wakeful for hours afterwards, staring up at the canopied bed tester. She slept raggedly at last, and awoke late to find herself alone.

Refusing to pander to her longing this morning to linger in her chamber over breakfast, she pulled the bell pull to summon a maid. Zillah entered, efficient and deft as usual, to help dress her and receive her orders for the day.

"I want to make a complete inventory of all household linen and plate remaining and, if there's time, we'll take a walk in the park. We must have a garden, Zillah, an herb plot first, then a vegetable patch and, possibly, a small sheltered pleasance. I must consult with Sir Nicholas about procuring more servants at the next hiring fair.''

She spent an energetic morning with Zillah exploring the dusty, neglected rooms, peering into cupboards, unearthing trestles, shrouded tapestries in sore need of repair and one or two paintings—portraits of Nicholas's grandparents and one extremely fine one of Lady Hetherington as a young bride. How beautiful she had been, and still was, and Nicholas so like her! Rachel sighed. She wondered if she could ever aspire to satisfy her aristocratic mother-in-law.

Nicholas had ridden into Leicester, so she took dinner alone, then settled by the fire to begin work on the largest of the tapestries. The manor was still very drafty and the hangings were sorely needed.

When Sarah tapped on the door, Rachel looked up sharply. "Has Sir Nicholas returned?"

"No, my lady. It's the tailor from Leicester."

"Tailor, for me?"

"There's a woman with him, the dressmaker, my lady. He insists they were sent for."

"Send him in. I'll explain the mistake."

Rachel recognized Master Shaw. His establishment in Leicester's High Street was held in high esteem and he charged excessively high prices for the new, elaborate gowns he contrived for the gentry.

Master Shaw bowed obsequiously. He was small and birdlike, a trifle stooped, bright eyes set in his wizened face twinkling with good humor.

"Master Shaw, I cannot imagine how you can have thought I had sent for you. I regret you and Mistress Cleaver made this journey needlessly, but I've no need of your services."

Doll Cleaver was a huge woman who towered over her business colleague. She stopped short in the doorway, her bovine features registering bewilderment till she was nudged from behind by Gaston, who came in laden with several bales of cloth shrouded in coarse holland wrapping. Tailor and dressmaker exchanged puzzled glances.

"My lady, Sir Nicholas himself dispatched us this very morning. I explained we were busy, but he insisted that the commission of several gowns would more than compensate us for the late hours we must work."

"Several gowns, Master Shaw?" Rachel's voice expressed horror at such wanton extravagance.

"Several gowns."

She turned hurriedly as Nicholas himself entered. His repetition of her words was mildly spoken, but his eyes held hers and she gave a little helpless shrug.

"Gaston, take Master Shaw and Mistress Cleaver to my chamber. I'll come up shortly. Sarah, help him with those bundles."

"*Oui*, madame." The Frenchman led the way and Sarah ran to help him, while the little tailor could be heard chattering away as he climbed the stairs.

Nicholas sauntered to the fire, carelessly dropped his gauntlets on the settle and held out chilled hands to the blaze.

"I cannot have you dressed like a farmer's wife. It is an affront to my sensibilities, smacking of the canting hypocrisy which cost the late King his life and brought wholesale ruin to all I hold dear. You spoke of our entertaining here. Well and good; then you must be fittingly gowned to receive my friends."

"But the exorbitant cost . . ."

"It is necessary, an investment for the future. You must understand that my position as gentleman of the bedchamber imposes certain standards. What may seem prodigality to you is blatant necessity to me. I suggest you order four gowns and the necessary mantles. The styles should be your choice, but allow Master Shaw to advise you."

The implied suggestion that she would not know what was required of her in polite circles distressed and shamed her. It was pointless to argue and she went upstairs.

She could not repress a little gasp of delight at the

101

sight which met her eyes. The bales had been undone and the folds shaken out over her bed coverlet. There were rich browns, greens and blues in heavy velvet and the softer shimmer of silks and satins, paler blues and rose, golds and apricots. Such finery would undoubtedly cause heads to turn at Hetherington Church, but how would her father view such vain peacocking?

The tailor drew out for her approval a length of apricot velvet.

"Sir Nicholas declared his fancy for this cloth, Lady Rachel. He said it would bring out the golden glints in your eyes and hair. He is truly observant and an excellent judge of what would most enhance your beauty."

Mistress Cleaver draped the rich-piled cloth across Rachel's shoulder, deftly adding gilded ribbons and creamy lengths of Mechlin lace. It would be her task to provide the fine cambric chemises with their ruched, lace-trimmed sleeves and to add the finishing touches to Master Shaw's expert cutting and draping of boned bodices and skirts.

Sudden tears misted Rachel's eyes. Nicholas could not have chosen better for her.

"Yes, Master Shaw, that will do excellently. I leave you to decide the style, provided it is not indecorously cut at the neck, you understand."

His eyes twinkled mischievously. "Oh, certainly, Lady Rachel. You can trust me implicitly to know what is fitting."

She chose a further length of sapphire-blue velvet with matching cloak and hood and two lengths for the later seasons, one in soft green satin and another in shimmering rose silk. They spent a further hour measuring and examining Mistress Cleaver's book of styles.

"The gowns will be ready within the specified two weeks," the tailor assured Sir Nicholas, and the two finally departed with many protestations of gratitude for the squire's distinguished patronage. Nicholas's slow smile showed her he recognized her reluctant delight in the promised finery.

Over the next few days the house was flung into a state of frenzied activity as, once more, carpenters, joiners and plasterers descended on them to begin work on the new dining room. Nicholas insisted the new room be truly splendid and imposing. Paneling must be skillfully repaired, floorboards and ceilings replastered, cornices and paintwork picked out in gold leaf. One last extravagance he insisted on: two silver gilt candlesticks in which Rachel could not but take special pride when she saw their reflections in the lovingly polished surface of the restored tabletop.

The second bedroom in the north tower had been replastered and painted and furnished with one of the beds from store. Rachel stitched bedcoverings and curtains herself, with Zillah's and the girls' assistance.

When the workmen finally withdrew, it was with immense satisfaction that Rachel reviewed the completed dining room. The portraits of Nicholas's grandparents showed to advantage against the dark paneling and the especially fine one of Lady Isabel took pride of place over the fireplace.

When Simon Nashe married Judith Burnell in the last week of February, Phoebe and grandmamma were installed at the manor. Rachel had begged her father that they should keep her company for a while, and no objection was made to the move. Judith obviously viewed this suggestion as an opportune one. Rachel had greeted their arrival with a mixture of regret and relief. Their presence eased the tension which was growing up between herself and Nicholas, yet she castigated herself inwardly for a certain resentment against a shattering of that domestic intimacy which was also developing.

Once over the early discomfort of pregnancy, Phoebe seemed very well and delighted to be away from her father's eye and in the more pleasurable atmosphere of the manor. Life here was easier for all of them under Nicholas's less despotic rule. Though he insisted on good service from all the household, there were no restrictions on laughter and talk, and both grandmamma and Phoebe were able to take advantage of the opportunity to sleep late in their chamber if either felt tired or unwell. Rachel had asked Nicholas timidly if morning prayers were to be instituted at the manor, as at Glebe.

He shrugged. "By all means, if you wish it, but none of my people are to be pressed to attend, certainly not Gaston."

Rachel presided over a simple service each morning, which as it happened all the servants attended, with the exception of Gaston, whom Rachel presumed must be a Papist.

Phoebe exclaimed over the splendor of Rachel's new gowns.

"I really envy you." Phoebe stroked the rich blue velvet pile as Rachel prepared to change for supper, for Nicholas expected her to preside at table superbly gowned.

"Is—is Nicholas demanding?" Phoebe's embarrassed whisper brought a sudden surge of color to Rachel's cheeks. It was hard, even now, to accept the fact that her younger sister was no longer a virgin. "Can you love him, Rachel, as I—I love Kit?"

"Of course I admire and respect my husband." Rachel briskly straightened the toilet articles on her bedtable.

Phoebe gave a little sigh. Her question, it seemed, was answered by her sister's very evasiveness.

"You're not too frightened about the coming arrangements?" Rachel's tawny eyes regarded Phoebe anxiously.

"Strangely not as much as I thought I would be; certainly not now that I am away from Glebe. You have been so good to me, Rachel. Of course, I hope—always, that there will be some word from Kit, that he will want me—and the child." Her lip trembled. "You have no sign yet that you—"

"No," Rachel said curtly, "I am certainly not expecting a child." Phoebe's question disturbed her. It was very early yet, but she knew many of her neighbors conceived almost immediately after marriage, and Nicholas wanted an heir. Deep within her was a growing resentment toward Zillah's approaching motherhood, becoming more evident now since the gypsy made no attempt to hide her condition from public view.

Her anger against Zillah crystallized sharply one day in late March. Nicholas had made Rachel another lavish gift of an exceptionally fine chestnut mare, Damaris. Rachel's pleasure in the animal overbore any guilty feelings she might have felt at accepting an unnecessary addition to their stables. She had always loved to ride, and it pleased Nicholas to have her accompany him as he made inspections of the estate.

On this occasion it was a fine spring day and Nicholas had gone out without her. Grandmamma encouraged her to ride to meet him. Rachel set off toward the Blore farm, where Nicholas had expressed his intention of stopping. She was approaching Malkin Wood when she heard Nicholas's voice raised in anger. "Don't dare take that tone with me, boy. I'll take my whip to your hide."

Rachel reigned in, thoroughly alarmed, on a small rise. Rachel's eyes widened as she saw that the gypsy was again the subject of the dispute between him and the Potter boy, Wat. Zillah was clearly distressed, breathing heavily as if she had been running hard, leaning against a tree trunk for support, her basket of herbs scattered.

Young Wat faced the squire truculently, his hands thrust disrespectfully deep into the pockets of his working smock. His sneering tone reached Rachel's ears clearly enough.

"Us in the village want the witch away. It's no good you going on protecting her, squire, cos us'll have her yet. Now she's a brat to bring into the world to plague us. Her ought to be whipped at the cart's tail like all drabs. That's what she is, whoever her brat's father may be, and I tell you, squire . . ."

He got no further, for Nicholas, who had dismounted to go to Zillah's aid, turned on him in a fury. He brought his riding whip down hard across the boy's leering young face. Rachel turned away with a little cry. She could almost feel the searing cut which laid open the boy's cheek. She could see the dark blood plainly even from this distance. Wat uttered a hoarse, animal cry and made as if he would lunge at his attacker, then, apparently, thought better of it.

"You'll be sorry as you done that, squire," he shouted defiantly, "and so will she as you're so anxious to help."

The inference was obvious and again Nicholas raised his whip menacingly. The boy cowered back, lifting his arm to protect his wounded face. Nicholas leaned toward him, his tone icy and clear. "Listen to me, Wat Potter. You have molested this girl for the last time. If I find you once more on my land or attempting to harm her anywhere else, for that matter, I'll strip your hide to the bone. I'm squire of this land and I'll have you remember it. The times are gone since louts like you could terrify helpless old people and maids. Now get off."

The boy gave a muffled curse, turned and set off at a stumbling run for the village. Rachel was about to ride down to help Nicholas attend to Zillah, when the gypsy turned from the tree and went to him. To Rachel's utter astonishment she stooped low in the dust of the roadway and pressed her lips against Nicholas's hand. He bent his head to speak to her.

Zillah, of all women, whose practice it was to show servility toward no one, behaving so with Sir Nicholas! Rachel burned with anger. *Was* Zillah Nicholas's mistress? Wat Potter's sneer had implied as much and, if so, it had been well discussed in the village. How dared they shame her openly! Rachel waited only to see Nicholas lift Zillah to his saddle bow, then she turned Damaris and galloped hard for the manor.

Grandmamma greeted her curiously as she swept into the kitchen.

"Is anything wrong? The mare didn't throw you?"

"No, I'm tired. I think I must have strained my hip reaching up to the bed tester. I thought it best not to ride very far. I'll go up and rest."

"Shall I bring up your dinner, my lady? Zillah's out gathering herbs."

Angry tears pricked at Rachel's lashes. "No, Sarah, I need nothing, only to rest."

She bolted the door against intrusion and sat on the bed, weakly allowing herself, for once, the solace of tears. She had prepared herself to accept Nicholas's infidelities, but had assumed he would do her the courtesy of indulging in his affairs well away from Hetherington. It was humiliating to think her father's friends would be aware of her shame. More than once she had detected a marked lack of respect in Zillah's attitude. Much as she pitied the girl, she could not be allowed to remain in service at the manor for much longer. She faced the problem soberly. Nicholas would not easily be persuaded to dismiss the gypsy. Rachel must await her opportunity. She would do her best to ensure that Zillah did not suffer unduly. The woman could hardly be blamed for yielding to a master so forceful and demanding as Sir Nicholas Hetherington.

"My lady."

Rachel looked up as the knock came at her door. "Sarah, I told you I did not wish to be disturbed."

"I'm right sorry, my lady, but there's a messenger arrived, from Court, he says."

"Is Sir Nicholas not back?"

"Not yet, my lady. The man says he needs to see him urgently."

"Very well. I shall have to come down. See the man is offered ale and food and that his horse is watered and well tended."

"Yes, my lady. Young Jem Paskell's rubbing him down now."

Hastily splashing water on her reddened eyelids, Rachel hurried down to greet the visitor.

The man wore royal livery.

"Lady Hetherington? I have a letter for Sir Nicholas."

"He is expected, sir. Do you leave straight away? We can offer you a bed for the night."

"Thank you, no, Lady Hetherington. I have other errands and will leave immediately for Leicester the moment my letter is handed over."

Nicholas's voice resounded in the courtyard, followed by Zillah's answer, too softly spoken for Rachel to catch what was said. He stamped mud from his riding boots before entering the kitchen, pausing, his eyebrows raised in surprise, at the sight of the liveried courier.

"You have dealings with me?"

"Sir Nicholas?" The man bowed. "I have instructions to hand the King's letter directly to you."

Nicholas took the letter and waved the man to a stool at the table. "Eat your fill, man. I know you've ridden hard." He broke the seal and read the contents. "There's no written reply. I shall travel to Whitehall myself as soon as possible. Assure His Majesty of that."

The man nodded and Nicholas drew Rachel into the drawing room.

She said quietly, "I've ordered the maids to see to the man's comfort."

"Yes, he'll be off the moment he's eaten and his horse sufficiently rested."

She avoided his eyes. "So you leave soon for London?"

"By the beginning of next week, Monday, if possible. I'll send Gaston ahead to find us accommodation. My old lodging in Pall Mall will prove much too cramped."

"Us?" Her chin jerked in astonishment. "You wish me to go with you?"

"Certainly. You must be presented and it seems a golden opportunity for Phoebe and grandmamma to accompany us. It will give us the excuse we need to take your sister from your father's sight for a while. There are places near the capital where she can be confined, no questions asked. Zillah can wait on you all. Tell her to keep the baggage to a minimum. I'll instruct Gaston to send back a hired carriage for us from Leicester. There should be ample room. I shall ride."

"Zillah?" Rachel's tone was sharp. "Surely that would not be wise. Tabitha's a good girl."

"But not nearly so practical and reliable as Zillah."

"But Zillah is not far off her time," Rachel hedged, hoping that the deep resentment she was feeling did not reveal itself in her tone.

"Exactly, and will prove a suitable wet nurse for

Phoebe's child. Zillah's strong and healthy. She should take no harm from this journey. Speak to her on the matter. See that Phoebe packs only necessities. I need to travel fast." The moustached mouth parted in an amused smile. "Though that must not prevent you from taking your newest gowns. You will need them at Court."

He excused himself and went to his study, which he now used when interviewing tenants.

"Ask Tabitha to serve my dinner in there and send Gaston in to me. There are urgent matters which demand my attention before we leave."

Rachel was left a trifle bewildered at the speed events had overtaken them. She *had* expected Nicholas to be summoned back to the capital to resume his duties, but not that he would wish to take her with him.

Phoebe was wildly excited at the prospect. "Oh, Rachel, I may see Kit soon—"

Grandmamma exchanged glances with Rachel over Phoebe's bent head. "Kit is at sea, child. It may be some time yet, months, before he is home. Don't raise your hopes too high."

But nothing could dampen Phoebe's enthusiasm. She had never before traveled further afield than Leicester, and London was a golden lure which for the moment blotted out all fears she had about her coming lying-in.

"Grandmamma, help me to choose what to take. I shall look so dowdy compared with Rachel."

Nicholas was amused over supper by Phoebe's unbounded delight in the coming adventure. Phoebe's chatter gave Rachel a breathing spell in which to consider the implications. She had fully expected to remain rusticated in Leicestershire while Nicholas was at Court, and had resigned herself to the situation. Now it seemed he wished her to be presented. A fierce little glow of pride ran through her. Surely he could not be so ashamed of her as she had feared.

Later, in her bedchamber, with Zillah in attendance, Rachel felt a sudden revulsion against the gypsy's touch.

"That will do," she said curtly, as Zillah unpinned her hair and began to brush it.

"My lady?"

"I—I have a headache."

"I'm sorry, my lady. I can fetch you a tisane which will help you to sleep."

Yes, Zillah would prefer that, Rachel thought mutinously.

"That will not be necessary. Sir Nicholas wishes you to accompany us to London next week."

"Yes, my lady."

"I thought . . . Perhaps since you are getting near your time, you might prefer one of the younger girls to take your place."

"Oh, no, my lady, there is still time yet, and I shall take due care." She gave a little secret smile which infuriated Rachel. "This baby is very special. I will see to the packing first thing tomorrow."

"Very well. That will be all."

Zillah turned, her hand on the door latch. "Mistress Phoebe will be needing me when the time comes. You can trust me, my lady. Goodnight."

Rachel found herself watching Nicholas covertly when he came to bed. Perhaps, after all, it would be advantageous for all of them to be away from the village for a while. When they returned, gossip would surely have died down and Phoebe's child would have been born. The magnitude of that problem was more than Rachel could face at the moment.

When Nicholas swept her into his arms, she set herself to lay aside her misgivings. He checked and sat up, putting out a long, beringed finger to tilt her chin. "You are icy cold tonight. What is it? Tabitha told me earlier you were not well. Are you in pain?"

"No." In spite of herself she felt her body stiffening within his arms. "I strained my hip reaching to hang the bed curtains."

"See that the girls do the heavy work. Remember, you are Lady Hetherington now. At least while we are in London, there'll be a respite from all this bustling about the house."

His kisses were hard on her mouth, his body lithe, firm against hers. She closed her eyes, repressing a little sob of despair.

Please, God, let me conceive soon, give him an heir, she pleaded silently.

This, only, she could do for him.

On Sunday, after church, Simon Nashe received the news of their intended departure without undue displeasure. Rachel was thankful he made no objection to Phoebe and grandmamma accompanying her. His eyes went to Phoebe where she stood with Nicholas near the church porch.

"Your sister doesn't look well. This delay in her marriage plans is bound to depress her spirits. A new interest should prove beneficial. Roger should be home at Barrow by now. Though his year of mourning isn't over yet, there would be no general disapproval of a quiet ceremony. I'm anxious to see Phoebe settled."

Rachel looked toward her stepmother, deep in talk with the vicar. "I understand from Roger's last letter that his uncle has now fallen ill. There are legal matters which keep him occupied in Cambridge."

"H'm. His legal training should stand him in good stead should the old man die. See that you do not overtire your grandmother and don't forget your upbringing. Hold fast to the Lord's commandments in respect of loose, lewd conduct. The Court is a sink of iniquity. Keep yourself aloof from such wickedness."

Rachel received his cool kiss and drew away hurriedly as Judith rejoined him. She was anxious to keep Phoebe from their stepmother's shrewdly calculating gaze. As yet, no one could guess Phoebe's secret, well concealed beneath the careful lacing of her corset and her skirt's voluminous folds, but Rachel knew her sister was always in a state of panic whenever Judith approached her.

The journey south was pleasanter than Rachel had expected, though tiring. The roads were still muddy but not yet hard-rutted, so their discomfort was not heightened by too much jolting. Rachel found the bustle of Stamford on the Great North Road quite fascinating, though she found it hard to sleep because of the clanking and clatter of the wheels.

But by the time the capital was in sight, even Rachel's interest in each new place along the road had been taxed to the uttermost. Cramped by too long sitting, she was thankful when Nicholas rode to the side of the coach to point ahead with his whip.

"See the church spires on the horizon. You'll sleep tonight in your own bed." He grinned ruefully as Phoebe's head emerged from the window aperture.

"It is pleasant enought for the moment, but when we get closer in, you'll see the heavy pall of smoke which constantly shrouds the city from the workshops of the brewers, soap boilers and dyers and this new sea coal is polluting the air, covering the buildings and churches with soot." He smiled reassuringly. "Gaston has obtained the lease of a house in Russell Street, part of the Earl of Bedford's development round the new square of Covent Garden. I'm sure you'll be delighted with it. It's by no means so fashionable as the newest houses by St. James's Park, but it's well west of the stinking hovels of the inner city, and convenient for the shops and market."

Soon the dirt road gave way to cobbles and the

women found themselves jolted unmercifully. Once Rachel and Phoebe were flung across the coach as the coachman drew up short, cursing as a hackney cut straight across his path.

Nicholas leaned in as Rachel drew herself ruefully back into her place and put an arm around the frightened and tearful Phoebe.

"You're not hurt? Hold the hand grips now we're in the town. The traffic is heavy—carts, hackneys and sedan chairs, all fighting for a right of way."

Rachel wrinkled her nose against the stinks from the open kennel running down the middle of the street.

"Dear Heaven, Nicholas, is that a dead cat?"

"I fear so. The town ditch is far worse choked, with bloated bodies of animals, even babies and those set on by footpads, but preparations are now in hand to fill that in. The stench you noted earlier was when we passed one of the laystalls where the filth of the city is deposited daily by the paid scavengers."

"How can the people bear to live in such close proximity?" Rachel said as they proceeded along enclosed streets where the overhang of the upper storeys blocked out the light.

Nicholas grinned. "The delights of London outweigh its inconveniences for those who enjoy the fashionable life of Court. When you get used to the smell, the noise and confusion, I think you will be fascinated by the scope of entertainment offered to divert you. When I can get leave from Whitehall, I'll introduce you to the splendors of the theater and, more to your taste, I believe, the beauty of St. James's and Vauxhall."

With a kerchief soaked in rosewater pressed to her nose, Rachel hoped she would come to agree with him. She did, however, give a little cry of pleasure as the coach drew up in a much wider thoroughfare lined with elegant rows of houses built of fine red brick and stuccoed in the Italian style the King's architect, Mr. Inigo Jones, had brought to England, from abroad.

"We are home. Fourteen Russell Street, and Gaston here to greet you."

Rachel was assisted down first, and Gaston smilingly gestured toward the front steps.

"I sincerely hope you will approve, madame."

"It is quite beautiful, Gaston."

"Cramped, madame, I regret, but all accommodation in London is so expensive."

"We shall do excellently." She turned as Nicholas offered his arm to Mistress Wilson and Phoebe fell in behind. Zillah remained by the baggage.

To Rachel's unsophisticated eyes the house appeared quite overwhelming—tiny by comparison with the manor, but splendidly appointed. They passed through a small entrance hall into an elegant drawing room. The walls were plastered and painted mint-green, the ceiling elaborately molded, the furniture much lighter than that at Hetherington, painted white, and picked out in gold in the French style, prettily upholstered.

"I have engaged a cook and maid for the rough kitchen work, madame. We have stabling for the horses at the rear." Gaston smiled deprecatingly. "You'll not find the need for so great a staff, as so much can be purchased here so simply, *oui?*"

"Yes." She smiled at him tiredly. "I'm so much a provincial housewife, you'll need to instruct me. Thank you, Gaston. Will you see that the baggage is carried up, and tell Zillah she must rest for an hour or so."

Supper was a pleasant meal, the food somewhat overspiced for Rachel's taste, but served in the small paneled dining room with its shining walnut table.

The bedroom seemed close and overpowering, used as she was to the cold, clear air of the Hetherington deerpark, but the bed hangings and coverings looked clean, and she was thankful at last to accept Zillah's assistance and climb into bed. Nicholas excused himself.

"It's essential I pay my respects at Whitehall. The King's message appeared urgent."

She pictured him among the painted, elegantly gowned ladies of the Court, that bawdy, rowdy, licentious Court where he would be hailed familiarly and welcomed, a world in which she could have no part. She was not surprised that he did not return until well after dawn.

She was awakened early by the clattering and clanking of carts in the street and the raucous cries of the sellers of fish and fruit and the milkmaids. She had slept raggedly and blinked drowsily, not expecting to find her husband already up and dressed.

"You'll become accustomed to sleeping through that." He was trimming the fine golden moustache carefully. "I'll take you to see some of the sights, if you've a mind for it, and I think we should make a duty call on my mother at Somerset House."

Rachel smothered a feeling of rising panic. So far she had been spared Lady Hetherington's chilling reception of her daughter-in-law.

Rachel pleaded first to see St. Paul's, but was vastly disappointed. The spire had fallen long ago and the interior was dark, in some places quite ruined, and used more as a place of assignation by gaudily dressed painted women than as a place of worship. She shuddered at her first sight of the Tower, decayed heads displayed above its turrets. The river traffic was unbelievably busy, crowded with sea-going ships and barges laden with sea coal, smelted iron, soap and dyes. Nicholas was forced to hold her close as they were jostled by the swearing, vociferous boatmen. He hired a hackney to convey them to Somerset House to wait attendance on the Dowager Lady Hetherington.

Nicholas's mother swept into the tiny room assigned to her use with a rustle of heavy silk skirts.

"Ah, Nick, so you're here at last. Gaston told me you were expected. So," she offered a cold cheek for Rachel to kiss, "you present your bride to me after all these months. You look well, child. I trust the winter hasn't been too extreme at Hetherington. It's been a torment here, the river frozen over for weeks at a time. The damp affected Queen Henrietta's lungs. I hope she will leave the city soon. Even at Windsor or Richmond she'd benefit from the clearer air, but I think her heart longs for France now that all she loved here has been taken from her."

It was a tacit reminder of the King's death at the hands of the Parliamentary party. Lady Hetherington was not prepared to let her forget her father's allegiance to that cause.

"Mother, is it necessary for you to continue to live here under such cramped conditions?" Nicholas protested. "There's room for you at Russell Street if you decide to take a leave of absence from your service."

"I shall remain with the Queen while she has need of me, but if she removes to Court, I'll ask to be excused." Lady Hetherington's haughty face expressed rigid disapproval. "It is bad enough that she, as the Queen Mother, should be forced to witness the excesses of her sons. I have no wish to accompany her."

Rachel knew that Queen Henrietta had been devoted to the martyred King, whose private life had been moral if not austere. From neither parent had Charles inherited the sensual, pleasure-loving nature which made "The Black Boy" so popular with his less religiously fanatical subjects.

"The King was anxious to have me near him. De Ruyter, the Dutch commander, is a man to be reckoned with, but His Majesty appeared to be in excellent spirits when I presented myself last night."

"When is he not?" Lady Hetherington's sniff was distinctly audible.

"He requested that I present my wife to him tomorrow."

"Indeed." Rachel had the feeling that Lady Hetherington was relieved that her daughter-in-law would be unlikely to attract the attentions of the monarch. "I hope you have prepared Rachel for the outspoken and outrageous behavior she is likely to find at Court."

"I'm aware that malicious gossip and tale-bearing is rife," Rachel said quietly. "I hope I shall give Nicholas no cause to be ashamed of me." Her eyes met those of her mother-in-law challengingly.

"Have you word of Kit?" Nicholas asked curtly.

"A letter reached me a month ago from Dunkirk, where the ship put in for fresh water and supplies. He appears to have survived the horrors of seasickness."

"I think you should know that Rachel's sister Phoebe is expecting Kit's child in July. We'd hoped he might be home by then and able to shoulder his responsibilities."

There was a flash of chilly distaste from Lady Hetherington's blue eyes. "I take it he does not know?"

Nicholas shrugged. "It seems unlikely."

"I understood the lady was to be married."

Rachel checked her rising anger with an effort. Her mother-in-law showed remarkably little disapproval of her younger son's action in seducing a respectable girl, nor any sympathy for Phoebe, though *that* she had never really expected. "My sister is betrothed to Mr. Roger Talbot of Barrow. His mother died last autumn, which delayed matters. The marriage cannot go forward now."

"That is markedly impossible. What's to be done, Nick? Mistress Phoebe is very young. As I recall, she features her mother strongly."

"I shall make arrangements for her to retire from

society soon now. I've been making inquiries. I hear there is a suitable place at Islington." He shrugged again. "Naturally, I shall assume responsibility for the child's welfare."

"You'll find suitable foster parents?"

"That does seem to be the most acceptable solution, though there's the question of Mr. Talbot."

"I see your problem, but I can hardly see what Kit could do. He is not sufficiently set up for marriage, even were he to sail for home before July. Since Mistress Phoebe was foolish enough to get into this mess, it would seem that it is up to her to confess and face the consequences."

"I think you are unduly hard on my sister, my lady," Rachel said icily. "As you yourself said, she was very young. Mr. Hetherington, it seems to me, was well aware what he was about, and should bear the blame for what occurred. Not that any of this is to the point. Our principal concern is to extricate Phoebe from this coil as painlessly as possible. She is already being adequately punished. She's frightened and ashamed. There is not the slightest need for anyone else to add to her distress by telling her how stupid she was to trust Kit."

Nicholas looked from his wife to his mother with an amused lift of his brows. Before his mother could add fuel to the fire already kindled in Rachel's breast, he rose and bowed. "We should take our leave now, if you please, mother. Rachel must be fatigued by the journey yesterday and the exertion of walking around town with me today. I want her fresh for the presentation at Whitehall."

Rachel curtseyed in icy politeness. Lady Hetherington unbent sufficiently to again offer her cheek in parting. Rachel kissed her mutinously, but aware of her duty.

Their journey home was made in an atmosphere of cool restraint.

Nicholas left for Whitehall and Rachel told her grandmother quietly what had occurred between herself and Lady Hetherington.

"I can't see any prospect now of Kit arriving home before the birth of the child or any way out of her difficulties if he did so."

"Would it be best to write to Roger?"

Rachel frowned. "On a matter so delicate? I'm hoping the confinement will be safely over before we find it necessary to inform him. He mustn't be allowed to see Phoebe in her present state. My principal dread is that he might follow us here."

"And your father?"

"The thought of telling him terrifies me more. I have the feeling the news will come as no surprise to Judith."

As they sat together quietly in the drawing room, she regaled her grandmother with the account of their sightseeing, in an attempt to thrust from her mind thoughts of what was entertaining Nicholas in Whitehall.

Nicholas hurried Rachel, who was magnificently dressed in her white velvet wedding gown, to the King's Presence Chamber, where Nicholas, as gentleman of the bedchamber, was privileged to enter. The room was packed with silk-clad courtiers and ladies, talking overloudly to Rachel's country-bred ears and sensibilities. They drew aside, good-humoredly, to allow the couple passage, several gentlemen acknowledging Nicholas's acquaintance with exaggerated bows. Rachel was conscious of the avidly curious gaze of both women and men. She walked slowly, as Nicholas had encouraged, still nervously aware of her limp.

Nicholas led her into one of the galleries overlooking

the banqueting hall where the King could be observed dining in public as custom demanded.

A table was laid before the fireplace. Rachel thought it looked somewhat forlorn in that vast, tiled hall, with just one place laid, linen crispy white, glassware and gold gleaming in the subdued light. Liveried servants waited like statues until there was a light pattering and scrambling sound, excited yelping, and the chatter of the waiting courtiers died as King Charles entered the hall preceded by two or three boisterous, small brown and white spaniels.

"Now, now, children, less noise. We shall all have better digestions if we eat with greater dignity." He faced the spectators, sweeping off his feathered beaver in greeting and sitting with particular ease and grace in the highbacked chair.

He was tall, taller than she had expected, and dressed in black velvet, gold frogged and trimmed, crossed by the bright blue band of the Garter. The heavy mane of black curls which framed his face under his beaver was touched with gray.

A page knelt with rosewater in a golden bowl and proffered the royal napkin. As King Charles began the meal, the talk and chatter resumed behind Rachel. The spaniels added to the general confusion by uttering shrilly demanding barks for tidbits offered from the royal, bejeweled fingers.

Afterwards Sir Nicholas was summoned with his lady wife to the Privy Chamber. Rachel arose from her deep curtsey to meet the genuinely kindly smile from the long-lipped, good-humored mouth. He was dark-skinned and heavily lined, but it was a handsome, sensitive face, and she was totally overwhelmed when he rose to lift her to her feet and kissed her hand gallantly.

"Welcome to Whitehall, Lady Rachel. I've waited

impatiently to greet Nick's bride since he wrote informing me of his betrothal. I can see I am not to be disappointed. You are as lovely and gentle-natured as he has described you." He waved a slender brown hand toward a chair nearby. "Please sit."

"Your Majesty—"

"I insist. I would be at ease, and how can I sit in the presence of such beauty unless she pays me the compliment of being easy in my company?"

It was fulsome but kindly meant, not facile, Rachel believed, and she sat down, though in some confusion. Her embarrassment was lessened by the fact that one of the spaniels immediately took the opportunity to jump on her lap. Instinctively, she fondled the silky ears, and the little creature rolled onto its back, slobbering in complacent delight.

"I see you are as stupidly fond as I am. Petronelle, down, you will crush Lady Rachel's splendid gown, and mark the pile with greasy paws. Down at once, I say."

The bitch rubbed her head affectionately against Rachel's arm and reluctantly obeyed the command of her master, rolling on her back before him in the servile gesture of trusting surrender.

He rubbed her belly affectionately with a toe of his rosetted silk shoe.

"And how do you find the air of our capital, Lady Rachel; too strong for your nostrils, I vow?"

"Russell Street is well appointed, Your Majesty, but I confess I was overwhelmed by the bustle and confusion of our journey yesterday to St. Paul's and the River Quay."

"We need more bridges. Traffic delays there are becoming intolerable, worse as the weather becomes warmer." He smiled, large teeth white against the dark-moustached upper lip. "For all its inconveniences and disagreeable stinks, I still find London the most exciting and exhilarating place in the world, and I've traveled widely and not always in state."

She smiled, acknowledging the good-humored reference to his ill-fated venture at Worcester and the alarums and escapades which had followed it. Nicholas had played some part in the King's dangerous exploits and she recognized that he would always be welcomed in Charles's company; indeed, the King's easy acceptance of her was a measure of the esteem in which her husband was held.

After her pleasant audience with the King, she and Nicholas emerged into the Presence Chamber to be again eyed speculatively by those who were waiting for a like honor. Nicholas introduced her to some of the courtiers and they were kept in talk for a few minutes by a lanky, pale-faced individual with a lugubrious expression and a ready wit which belied it—Sir Richard Summers, whom Nicholas acknowledged as a boon companion both after Worcester and during the days of penury following it.

"We shared rooms in various hovels." Nicholas grinned. "He snores atrociously."

"He makes no mention of the fact that he saved my life after Worcester," the other drawled. "La, when I think of the risk, my whole being shakes. He dragged me clear of some Roundhead trooper who'd had the temerity to die after thrusting his pike through my shoulder and fallen so that he nearly crushed what life was left from me. Then this golden-haired devil of yours heaved me across his blown nag and got me somehow clear of the shambles. I'll never know how."

"Every time you tell the tale, it gains somewhat." Nicholas grinned.

"Like those of His Majesty, still, we all continue to listen to them avidly."

Sir Richard Summers's brown eyes had darted over

her and summed her up and Rachel knew he approved Nicholas's choice. She acknowledged his approbation with warmth, recognizing instinctively that there was genuine affection between the two men and that she could turn to Sir Richard for help in a crisis.

"By the way, Nick," he drawled, "did you know that Baxter's back in England? I saw him in St. James's yesterday."

Nicholas's brows swept up and he was about to reply when Sir Richard added, "Speak of the devil and 'tis said he appears. Here he is, now, with the fair Lettice."

Rachel turned to the door as she saw her husband's attention was entirely taken by the couple who had entered. The woman was astonishingly lovely, dark, statuesque, in a daringly cut gown of apricot satin. Her escort was no less distinctive. He was a big man, heavily moustached, and florid-featured but with a twinkle in the eye which Rachel found engaging. The pair swept across the antechamber as if both had more right to be there than His Majesty himself. The woman hailed Nicholas as they approached, vigorously plying her fan of painted chicken skin.

"Nick Hetherington, la, sir, I'd no notion you were back in civilization."

He bowed. "Lettice, your servant, I rejoice to see you well. So you're home, Arthur. Dick was about to tell me about your meeting yesterday. May I present my lady wife, Rachel, Lady Lettice Ryall and another boon companion from my days in exile, Sir Arthur Baxter."

Rachel curtseyed. She felt Lady Lettice's dark eyes fixed on her intently as Sir Arthur gallantly kissed her hand. As they stood chatting with Sir Richard, Rachel found herself watching Lady Lettice covertly. The lady was obviously well acquainted with Nicholas. Her attitude could almost be described as proprietorial. Sir

Arthur was flattering Rachel shamelessly and she felt unable to cope, awkward, gauche, especially when she found Lady Lettice smiling at her as if the situation appealed to her sense of the ridiculous.

Rachel was relieved when Nicholas made his excuses and they left the palace environs by the water steps.

She was silent as the boatmen pulled for home, glad of the cool river breeze after the scented oppressiveness of the crowded anteroom. Nicholas pointed out to her some of the well-known landmarks along the banks and she listened attentively. Once she glanced up at him sharply as if to gauge the effect the meeting with his former acquaintances had had on him. Nicholas rarely showed the slightest sign of embarrassment, but Rachel was sure that while he had been delighted to acknowledge Sir Richard Summers, he was by no means pleased to have encountered Baxter and the beautiful Lady Lettice, certainly not when she, Rachel, was with him.

Chapter 9

Rachel enjoyed her new life in Russell Street despite the noise, the smells and the unseasonable warmth of April. Nicholas saw to it that the womenfolk visited most of the sights of the city. By the end of the month Phoebe was becoming more and more depressed by the lack of news from Kit, though Simon Nashe wrote that now, at last, Roger had returned to Barrow and he wrote affectionate letters to Phoebe hoping that she would soon return to Glebe.

The first rainstorm in weeks relieved the dustiness of the streets and Nicholas proposed an excursion to St. James's Park.

"The King will more than likely be playing pell-mell today, since the air is fresher. The outing will do Phoebe and Mistress Wilson good. Dick Summers mentioned last night he would take his wife for a stroll there."

Rachel had met Sir Richard Summers's wife on a drive in Mulberry Gardens and had taken as great a liking to the buxom, auburn-haired woman as to her husband. Magdelin Summers was eight years Rachel's senior, the daughter of a wealthy goldsmith. The two had much in common and Rachel welcomed the advice the older woman was able to offer her, particularly about fashionable society.

Mistress Wilson agreed to accompany Rachel and Sir Nicholas to the Park, which Charles had replanted with fruit trees and restocked with deer, and in which he had made the famous lake around which he walked his beloved spaniels regularly to feed the ducks.

It was a merry throng grouped around the King, who was chatting with Lady Frances Stewart. Sir Richard and Magdelin Summers greeted the newcomers warmly and Magdelin complimented Rachel on her newest blue taffeta gown. A familiar husky voice made her look up sharply to one of the ladies attendant on the King's favorite. Though she was masked, Rachel could not mistake the magnificent form of Lady Lettice Ryall. Baxter, her constant companion, hailed Nicholas, who strolled off with Dick Summers to greet the King.

Magdelin, Mistress Wilson and Rachel seated themselves on one of the marble benches placed for the convenience of the guests. Rachel smiled as the King's vociferous companions barked and skipped about as excitedly as ever. Magdelin smoothed her silk skirts appreciatively.

"Thank God for yesterday's rain. The stinks in the city are growing worse, I swear. I never stir these days without my pouncet box. Had you heard there were rumors of more plague deaths?"

"Nicholas was saying there'd been trouble in Yarmouth, houses and inns boarded up lest plague was carried from the Dutch sailors by our men who'd been in contact with prisoners." Rachel eyed her wonderingly. "There have been outbreaks within the oldest areas of the city most years, I understand. I suppose the early hot weather will increase the risks."

Magdelin nodded. "Dick has been at me to leave London." She laughed ruefully. "He'd like to be rid of me, I don't doubt, but it's true many of the elderly people are leaving already. Some of them remember the bad outbreak of 1625 and some others, even older, the one in 1603 in King James's time. There are always plague scares every year, and the fanatics contend it's a warning visited on us by God for our lust and covetousness."

Mistress Wilson put in quietly, "But I understand the justices last month gave instructions for the building of new pesthouses and the provision of roads to be kept clear leading to them. Surely that is an indication they've been receiving disquieting news concerning the sickness?"

Magdelin sighed. "Possibly so. Certainly, if it gets any hotter, I shall obey Dick and go north for a month or two. Will you go home to Leicestershire?"

Rachel shook her head. "Nick has made arrangements for us to stay in Islington for a week or two from the beginning of June. We shall be well out of the crowded thoroughfares."

Magdelin's blue eyes darted to her as if in inquiry. It was well known that Islington and Doddington were favorite retreats of Court ladies who had become pregnant and wished to conceal the fact from society, and Rachel reddened. The Summerses had been to supper with them at Russell Street. Phoebe's condition could not have escaped their notice.

Lettice Ryall had challenged Nicholas to a game of croquet. Rachel watched them intently. It was surely no accident that the woman brushed against him so closely. He threw up his arms in mock surrender and the King called some derisory comment on Nick's ineptness. Dick clapped him on the back and they were about to rejoin their ladies when an equerry summoned both to the King's side. He walked off down the avenue in close talk with them. Rachel was puzzled. What private business could the King have with her husband? She blushed as she recalled gossip about Will Chiffinch, the King's trusted secretary, whose employment lay chiefly in ushering female visitors to and from the King's bedchamber by way of the backstairs. Nicholas and Dick had talked openly of the King's outrageous affairs and his neglect of the gentle Queen.

As gentleman of the bedchamber, was her husband accustomed to perform favors for the King similar to Chiffinch's? Nicholas had intimated that the King had need of him. Why had he been summoned to Whitehall, since for over a month now he appeared to have been waiting attendance idly at Court?

Rachel's gaze hardened as she saw that Lady Lettice Ryall had joined the two men with the King. Charles bent gallantly to kiss the tips of her fingers and to whisper in her ear. Lady Ryall nodded in answer and swept him a deep curtsey, then Sir Nicholas returned her to Baxter while Dick strolled back to the bench. He made no comment about Lady Ryall or about what had passed between the three men.

Phoebe greeted them hysterically as they arrived home.

"It's Zillah, I think her baby's coming. The girls have both run out on me and I didn't know what to do." She burst into tears and Rachel drew her to the sofa.

"There now, it's natural you should be frightened, but calm yourself. Where is Zillah?"

"In her own room. She stayed with me for quite a while. She was so brave, Rachel, biting her lip till it bled. Gaston wanted to get a midwife but she wouldn't have it. Then, suddenly, she said she must go upstairs."

"I'll go to her." Grandmamma smiled reassuringly. "Don't worry about Zillah. She's young and strong and she's seen birth often enough. No, you stay with Phoebe, Rachel. Better still, see if you can find those idiot girls to get hot water and towels, torn sheets in plenty."

Rachel was relieved that for the moment she did not need to go up to the stifling attic below the eaves where Zillah struggled to give birth. She was ashamed of her reaction. She gave a hurried glance at Nicholas, but other than being genuinely concerned for the gypsy girl's suffering, he seemed unperturbed. To Mistress Wilson he said quietly, "For all Zillah's objections, let me know at once if you think she needs professional help."

Rachel hurried Phoebe to the kitchen to give her something to do. She could see that the sight of Zillah's pain had unnerved her.

"Grandmamma is right. Zillah's a country girl. There's no danger."

But she knew there was. So many girls died bearing their first babies and many, too, of milk fever following delivery. At home, at Hetherington, there would have been older, experienced farm women to turn to, yet, in Zillah's case, she recalled, there would have been some reluctance to attend the girl. She had always been regarded with a sense of nervous awe and, since

Salome's death and the attempt to swim the Lees, Rachel was sure the village folk had become downright afraid of her.

She found one of the girls skulking in the pantry and briskly set her to work.

"Now," Rachel told her sternly, "you take that jug of hot water to Mistress Wilson in Zillah's room . . ."

"I'm afeared, my lady."

"Nonsense, it won't be long before you have a child of your own, particularly," she added waspishly, "if you carry on the way I've seen you recently with every scullion and pot boy in the vicinity." Rachel turned and mounted the stair to the attic.

Zillah's swollen body arched in a sudden spasm as Rachel pressed against her grandmother into the tiny room. The gypsy's lips were badly bitten, her hair sweat-soaked, but she smiled gamely.

"Little Miss Phoebe's frightened. She needn't be. Everything is going normally. I can tell."

Agnes Wilson wiped her forehead with a cloth soaked in vinegar and water.

Rachel said, "We can send Gaston for a midwife, Zillah. Don't be a stoic. If you need one, we must send at once. Don't you think you'd better?"

"Not me, Lady Rachel. Me, want one of those drink-sodden, stinking hulks I've seen about in the city?" She gave a harsh laugh which turned to a choked cry. "Nay, I'll do well enough. Hard work to bring forth. That's what my mother used to say, so long as the babe's lying right, nature should take its course. I'm certain my babe's placed right. It's a matter of time. They don't come easy, first babes."

"Let me sit with her a while," Rachel said to Mistress Wilson. "You'll be of greater assistance later. I've no experience in birthing."

"Very well, I'll relieve you in an hour or so. Call me if there's need."

Rachel sat down on the stool near the truckle bed and resoaked the cloth.

"Best if Mistress Wilson rests until she's needed."

"Aye." Zillah's face contorted and she gripped the rough wooden side of the truckle bed.

To divert the girl's mind from the pain Rachel talked of St. James's and the Park. She was unsure if Zillah was attending. She never found it easy to converse with the gypsy, yet she felt a sincere desire to assure herself of Zillah's safety. There was some need each felt for the other. Rachel could never explain it, even to herself. She was ashamed now of her inexplicable anger against the girl. If Zillah were bearing Nicholas's child, could she be blamed? What more natural enough? He had saved her, taken her under his protection. She was well formed, lusty, doubtless. Not once had Rachel questioned her about the father of the child, and Zillah rarely referred to her condition. She bore all adversities without complaint, from the lack of help in the kitchen, if the maids were incompetent, to the terrible death of her mother. Once, when Rachel had tried to express her regret for what had happened, Zillah's dark eyes had flashed oddly, compelling her to silence, and she had never again broached the matter. But she had not forgotten the strange prophecy the girl had made concerning their need for firing for the winter: "We'll not need it."

Had she known? Seen in some vision or flash of insight what was to come? It was a chilling thought. Rachel had the uncomfortable feeling that this girl could read her innermost doubts and fears, and it was uncanny and frightening to think she might know the future . . . for all of them.

"Lady Rachel," Zillah's breathing was coming fast, harsh, "I think, if you will, you should ask Mistress Wilson to come now."

Rachel hurried below stairs, grateful when her

131

grandmother took her place. She had sat cramped and stood now in the hall, easing her aching back. There were some choked cries from above them. Phoebe ran to the door of the salon, her blue eyes pits of dark terror. Nicholas drew her back.

"Come, I'm still trying to teach you the intricacies of chess. You're sadly behind Rachel. She can even beat me on occasions."

Rachel's eyes met his over Phoebe's golden head. Those green-blue eyes of his were troubled. Did he wait impatiently to know if he'd fathered a son?

They were not kept long in doubt. Mistress Wilson called down to Rachel.

"Zillah's delivered of a fine boy. More hot water, please. Come up now, if you've a mind to see him."

Rachel turned abruptly to the kitchen to call for more hot water as Nicholas mounted the stairs, a natural reaction from master to maid to see her child and know she was well after the ordeal. Rachel followed less enthusiastically, unwilling to lay eyes on the baby.

Zillah looked exhausted, yet more herself, a flannel-wrapped bundle close-held in the crook of her arm. Nicholas was already preparing to leave.

"A fine boy, Zillah. Try to sleep now."

"Thank you kindly, sir."

Rachel passed him in the doorway, unable to read his expression.

Zillah put back the covering from the baby's face for Rachel to view him. He was brick-red, eyes fast shut, head crowned with soft black down. Rachel found Zillah's eyes viewing her intently.

"What will you call him?"

"Bart, my lady." There was no hesitation.

"He must be baptized soon at the new church in the square."

"As you please, my lady."

132

Zillah recovered quickly. She was soon up and about supervising the kitchen staff. Little Bart was a good child, appearing to make few demands on his mother. Once fed, he lay contentedly in a deep wooden box in her attic, thumb pressed into his mouth. The servant girls clucked over him, as did Mistress Wilson. Rachel watched Nicholas covertly for sign of undue partiality.

The weather became unbearably hot, and soon it was apparent that more and more people were deserting the capital. Nicholas brought news from the navy office that instances of plague had been reported among the fleet. The townsfolk of Southampton and Portsmouth had become thoroughly alarmed and threatened to close brothels and inns to crewmen. It was well known now that the sickness had raged throughout Holland, spreading from Amsterdam to the Hague and Leyden. Merchantmen from Spain, Portugal and England, as far back as the winter before hostilities had begun, had refused to call at Dutch ports.

"I would by now have packed you all off to Hetherington," Nicholas said, "except that circumstances forbid it. Magdelin Summers is to drive to Yorkshire tomorrow. By next week the four of you will be safely established in Islington, at Mistress Smart's."

"Is there real danger of contagion?" Rachel asked quietly, as they lay together that night. "Is Dick afraid for Magdelin? I know the astrologers have been printing a great deal of rubbish over these last weeks. The shops are full of predictions and amulets, charms and such like, but have the King's advisers real grounds for alarm?"

"It's difficult to tell the true facts. Fourteen deaths from plague were reported last week, but it's likely there were far more. It's easy to bribe the women searchers who examine the corpses. Relatives are not anxious to be confined within a house where one has

133

died with the sickness. A groat or even a bottle of wine will buy discretion. Mourners hold cloths to the faces of corpses to disguise the plague tokens, the reddish-purple blotches and swellings behind the ear and under the chin."

Rachel had only just returned from the market the next morning with Zillah, when a King's messenger was admitted to the house asking urgently for Sir Nicholas. He'd arrived in a hackney, which surprised Rachel till she saw that he was carrying a large wicker basket which he placed down before her, bowing.

"A present to you, Lady Hetherington, from His Majesty, hoping it will give you as much pleasure as he believes from watching your behavior over these past weeks."

Mystified, Rachel knelt to undo the hasp and put back the lid. The sounds from inside had prepared her for the contents. She lifted out the silky brown and white spaniel as Nicholas strode into the salon. The messenger explained. "His Majesty has noted how, on several occasions, you have nursed and fondled his pets. He is sure you will lavish care and affection on this one."

The puppy licked her frantically and she rose to sit on the sofa and nurse it, quieting its fears. "Thank His Majesty. He could not have given me anything I would treasure more."

The man bowed again and held out a sealed letter for Nicholas's attention.

The puppy gazed at her trustingly out of its protruding eyes and she pulled gently at his ears while she waited for Nick's reaction. He straightened, nodding to the messenger.

"Tell His Majesty I shall leave first thing in the morning."

He placed the letter carefully into the deep pocket of

ous content while Zillah gently soaped her hair and skin, pouring in hotter water as that in the tub cooled. Afterwards Rachel sat by the fire enveloped in a soft, warm towel as the gypsy combed out her hair, damp little tendrils curling childishly onto her forehead.

She should insist on dressing and hastening down to take over the reins of household management, but she snuggled happily under her towel as she thought how disapproving her father would be at her surrender to sybaritic enjoyment.

Zillah was busy about the bed. Rachel's eyes passed to the bedtable and caught the gleaming rim of the cup from which she had drunk last night. A pulse raced in Rachel's throat. Had the cup been spiced with some love potion? If so, that might explain the easy abandon with which she had surrendered to Nicholas's consummate skill, a surrender which now deeply disturbed her.

How dared she face him in the full glare of daylight? Here, in the cloistered enclosure of their curtained bed, she had lain naked in his arms, breast to breast, thigh to thigh, his passion-heated body bringing warmth and life to hers. What had passed between them now seemed shameful to her in the light of the stern teaching she had received from her father and the rector. Her duty, she knew, was to humbly grant her husband the pleasure of her body, but was it not sinful to experience such wild joy from the mating as she had done last night?

Abruptly, she called Zillah to her.

"It must be almost noon. I should go down. Sir Nicholas will soon be home and requiring dinner, and neighbors may call to wish us well."

"They would be thoughtless, indeed, to do that today, my lady."

Rachel was about to utter a sharp rebuke for Zillah's wanton insolence, then thought better of the notion.

The woman appeared to have the ability to look into her innermost thoughts and doubts.

"Nevertheless, I will dress now."

She deliberately chose her severest gray gown, with its plain linen collar and matching cap. Her traitorous body well concealed beneath its heavy folds, she descended to the kitchen to supervise preparations for dinner.

The two serving girls cast her curious glances which made her cheeks flame and she moved briskly to the fire to check the contents of the cooking pot and then to the large table to ascertain if the great copper pans had been cleaned and scoured to her satisfaction.

There was so much to be done here at Hetherington. Nicholas was accustomed to eating breakfast in the kitchen and dinner and supper in the drawing room. This arrangement could not go on. The old dining room must be refurbished as a first priority. She would tackle Nicholas on the matter when he returned.

He swept in half an hour later, putting his head around the kitchen door to inform Zillah and the maids that he was back.

Her heart beating fast, Rachel found it hard to greet him without embarrassment. His riding whip tapped impatiently against his thigh-length riding boots as he regarded her, one eyebrow raised slightly.

"Dinner will be ready in a few moments, sir," she said quietly, striving to keep her tone level before the servant girls while her pulses raced wickedly again at his nearness.

"Good. I've worked up quite an appetite. It's sunny but still very cold out. Gaston," he called, "help me off with these muddied boots, man."

He made a good dinner, though drinking ale sparingly. Surprised, she noted he refused wine. She found it unaccountably hard to talk with him naturally while Zillah and Tabitha hovered close by in attendance. She his jacket and strode to the window looking out toward Covent Garden Square.

"I had hoped to go with you to Islington, but, unfortunately, the King has entrusted me with an errand and I need to leave tomorrow."

Rachel stroked the soft fur of her new pet. Why Nicholas? Why not a King's messenger? Obviously, the errand demanded extreme discretion and, more than likely, involved some lady. As if by some strange premonition, she gave a sudden start when he said, "His Majesty wishes me to escort Lady Ryall to her home in Southwold and then report to him at Court."

"I see." Feeling her tone somewhat chilly, she forced herself to smile. "I understand. It will be no problem to get Phoebe settled in Islington. Do you leave Gaston with us?"

"Yes. I must."

"Well, you had not intended to stay in Islington. It would be incredibly boring for you. We'll keep you aware of events." She was conscious that her tone was brittle, but continued to make idle conversation. "You'll get some fresh sea air, which should do you good, while we are enjoying the pleasanter atmosphere of Islington. How kind of the King to send me the puppy! You will thank him again when you report. You know I have always longed for a special pet. My father had hounds, of course, but thought it foolishness to lavish affection on lapdogs."

"You're highly honored. The King treasures his spaniels above rubies. Lady Castlemaine has said he thinks more of them than he does her."

"Would he be offended if I called him Charley?"

"Amused and delighted, I would think."

"I'll instruct Gaston to pack your valise. Will you be gone long?"

"Some days. I'll see Gaston knows just what I'll
135

need. I must travel light." He bent to fondle the spaniel and left her to complete his arrangements.

Rachel was surprised when Nicholas came to their chamber as Zillah was undressing her. He dismissed the gypsy and peeled off his elegant satin short coat.

She had expected that he would wish to spend this last night in the town, since the pleasures of the theaters and coffeehouses would soon be denied him.

She delayed moving to the bed, aware that he was lying back against the pillows watching her. Abruptly, he reached out and drew her to him. She detected wine fumes on his breath and instinctively flinched. He put back his head and laughed.

"Still you pull up that ridiculous nightgown so tight around your throat. Court ladies display more of their charms in public than my wife is prepared to do in the privacy of our bed."

She flushed dully at the contemptuous tone of his rebuke. Obediently, she stripped and climbed into bed, leaving the silken covers turned back in open invitation. As always, before their lovemaking, she could feel the hot blood pounding in her veins and it was hard to prevent her limbs from trembling.

Pride forbade her to comment tartly that if she displeased him, doubtless he would find Lady Ryall more accommodating.

As he loomed over her, she attempted to avert her gaze from the splendor of his naked form. He was a god, broad-shouldered, slim-hipped, not an ounce of spare flesh on his frame, despite his apparent predilection for the fleshpots of Court life. The scar served only to emphasize the beauty of his masculinity. She was excited, aroused, despite her determination to keep herself pure in thought.

His hands descended upon her shoulders, and his lips caressed the tip of her ear, moving lower to her throat, breasts and most secret, private places.

"My virginal wife." His breath teased her ear. "Can you not give yourself freely tonight? So soon you'll be rid of me for a while."

"I—I have no wish to be separated from you, Nicholas," she whispered uncertainly. "You—you wrong me."

He cut off her protest by a lingering kiss hard on her mouth. "Do I? Wrong you? Prove to me that you want me."

"I—I have never denied you, sir."

"Never denied me your body. Your inner self you hold back. Don't you think I know when I hold a chilled shell of a woman in my arms?"

Tears pricked at her lashes. "I'm sorry—sorry."

He laughed again and there was less bitterness in the sound now. "Come, my wife. Don't cry. I demand too much, it seems. Grant me your body at least in these short hours before we must part."

She was tempted to give herself completely. How could she hold him when he was so soon to go from her into Lettice Ryall's arms? She lay back, docile, receptive, yet, even now, she found herself unable to mount with him to the ecstasy of perfect fusion.

Later, as she lay by his side, she was conscious that yet again she had failed him and she turned away, her tears soaking into the fine cambric of the pillow covering.

He said curtly, "Gaston has explicit instructions for his care of you, especially on the journey to Islington. You may find him a trifle sullen. He wants to come with me, but that's impossible. The moment Phoebe is fit to travel, I want you to go to Hetherington."

"Surely you will be back by then."

"I expect to be." He was silent for a moment, staring up at the bed's tester. "The King has charged me with Lettice Ryall's safety. There are reasons why he has sent me. You understand?"

"I understand that you cannot question the King's command, certainly."

"I would be grateful if you would keep in touch with my mother. I know there is a constraint between you, but I think you will make allowances for that."

Rachel wondered silently if Lady Hetherington could ever be persuaded to forget the differences between the families.

"I'll call on her the moment we get back from Islington."

He was up at first light, Gaston hovering in attendance. From a drawer he withdrew two silver and ivory mounted pistols together with a quantity of powder and shot. He also buckled on a more serviceable rapier.

"A precaution. There's been trouble recently on roads out of the city. Country folk aren't anxious to receive travelers from London. I've warned Gaston to expect something of the kind on the way to Islington. Trust him. He's to take you early tomorrow."

"So soon?"

"Better you go immediately."

Kate knocked on the door of their chamber. "The traveling carriage has arrived, Sir Nicholas, and your valise is already strapped on."

He drew Rachel abruptly into his arms. She smelt the unfamiliar sharp scent of leather and metal oil from his newly cleaned pistols.

Peering through the curtains she glimpsed a woman's white beringed hand on the woodwork of the window aperture and, briefly, the masked features of Lettice Ryall as Nicholas took his seat in the carriage.

The hackney to take them to Islington arrived early. Gaston saw to the valises and Phoebe climbed in awkwardly.

"The straw stinks. I feel sick. Oh, do get in quickly, Zillah, and let the driver get off."

Grandmamma frowned at her peevishness. In fact, the vehicle was tolerably clean by London standards. Gaston had done well to hire the man.

Soon they were heading north, rolling along the Strand, past Lincoln's Inn toward Clerkenwell and Islington. Once clear of the narrow streets and the stinking laystalls, Rachel let down the window and drew in the scent of newly scythed grass and hay.

The road was hard-rutted and grandmamma held Phoebe close to cushion her against the bone-shaking jolts. Rachel was relieved when the village, with its thatched black and white cottages and gray stone church, came in sight; then the hackney drew up so suddenly that the women were abruptly thrown together onto the floor.

Angrily, Rachel thrust her head through the curtains.

"Gaston, what it it? Are we there?"

He leaned down from the box beside the driver.

"*Oui,* madame, close now. But there is trouble, men and women in the roadway. Our coachman, he had to pull up short." His eyes were wary as he leaned toward her. "*Excusez moi,* madame, I go to see what is wrong."

Rachel craned her head through the window opening, but could not see clearly.

Zillah said, "Let me get out, Lady Rachel, if one of you would hold Bart—"

"Certainly not. You stay with the child. I'm in charge here. I'll deal with it." Rachel dumped Charley, struggled with the door and then jumped down.

Gaston was gesticulating, pointing ahead, then back toward the carriage. A hefty, red-faced man in a countryman's smock was jabbing the Frenchman angrily in the chest with a dirty thumb. He turned to regard Rachel truculently.

"What is all this, Gaston?" she demanded.

"Ye're not coming further," the red-faced man said flatly.

"I don't understand." She deliberately made her tone haughty.

"If ye're from London, ye're not staying here."

"Nonsense. Our rooms are bespoken, Mistress Smart is expecting us. My sister has need soon of a midwife's services."

"It's no use you arguing. We're all of one mind. Nobody is coming in the village, not now."

"But your livelihoods . . ."

"No use no livelihood when life's at stake. Get back to the city, lady, you and all your plague-stricken brood."

"There is no sickness among us."

"Who knows?" He was stubbornly determined. "You've men there and we've all heard. More and more deaths last month. Houses boarded up, folk a-dying in the street. We'll not have it here. Turn the carriage and get back."

"I can't do that. I tell you, my sister will soon need help."

"We'll *all* need help if we harbor you." The man had moved from his position near Gaston and was menacing Rachel, looming over her. She could feel his foul breath on her cheek. Gaston made a warning mutter, his hand flying to his rapier. Rachel hurriedly checked him before matters got out of hand. In a fight with this man, Gaston could not win. Four women against at least twenty sturdy countrymen and women on the fringe of the group a little behind, no less determined to oust the newcomers, and the coachman could not be relied on to help.

"We must do as they say, Gaston. There would be no point in remaining here with the villagers so hostile. Tell the coachman to turn the horses. We'll go back to Russell Street."

"Madame—"

"Obey me, please. We have Phoebe to think of and Zillah's child."

"*Oui*, madame."

She addressed the village spokesman. "If you are all so cowardly, I can only give way to your wishes." Her voice was cold with contempt. "God help any one of your number who falls victim to this." Rachel turned her back on the crowd and went to Phoebe.

"We have to go back. They will not accept us here. They are afraid of the contagion."

"But my baby . . ."

"We'll find an accoucheur in London. Don't worry."

"Don't worry?" Phoebe's blue eyes blazed. "Of course I worry. If the sickness spreads, what hope have we? The child? People will know."

Rachel forced her tone to remain level. She was growing frightened and determined not to give way. "We've no choice. As for the disgrace, there is too much disruption in London for gossip to carry. And anyway, it cannot be helped."

She was standing close to the door when a sharp pain in her shoulder caused her to stagger. Turning, she saw one of the men in the act of throwing a second stone.

"Get further in," she said tersely to Phoebe. "Gaston, let us hurry."

"*Oui*, madame, these men, they are getting—how do you say—ugly."

She thrust Phoebe back from the door and scrambled in, pulling it to and latching it, jerking the leather curtain across to shield them further. She was shaking with a mixture of terror and fury.

There was a scramble of frightened horses. Then they were off, the carriage swaying wildly as the driver whipped up his horses in an effort to quickly draw clear of the shower of stones and missiles. Rachel could hear Gaston's string of French oaths as he commented, bitterly, on his inability to take reprisals. Then they were in open country again and the frantic pace slackened.

Rachel stared ahead dully as Phoebe continued to sob brokenly, until the jolting of the vehicle's iron wheels over cobbles told her they were once more in the streets of the capital.

Chapter 10

A round-eyed Kate opened the door to them.

"We weren't expecting you, my lady—"

"I'm aware of that," Rachel snapped. "See that warm water is brought to our bedchambers. We shall all be staying here in Russell Street until Sir Nicholas returns. Our plans are changed."

"Yes, my lady." The girl bobbed a curtsey. She was clearly bewildered. "There's a visitor inquiring for you. He's in the salon. I was about to give him your address in Islington. Shall I ask him to wait till you can receive him now or is he to come back?"

"A visitor?"

Agnes Wilson stopped abruptly at Rachel's sharp tone as she was about to lead the distressed Phoebe up the stairs.

"A Mr. Talbot, my lady, from Leicestershire." Phoebe gave a strangled cry and clawed at her grandmother's arm. "Roger? Oh, no, he mustn't see me . . ."

The door of the salon jerked open as if their visitor was aware of some altercation in the hall. Roger Talbot's sturdy figure, austere in his mourning suit, was silhouetted against the white and gilded paintwork of the door. He stood stock-still, his eyes drawn like a lodestone to Phoebe's swollen figure as she crouched awkwardly at the foot of the stairs. She gave a low moan of despair and Agnes Wilson directed one warning glance at him and drew the girl to her room. Roger and Rachel stood facing each other, silent, as the door slammed decisively above their heads. Rachel sighed and moved woodenly forward.

"You are entitled to an explanation, Roger. Shall we go into the salon?"

She waved him to a seat, noting how out-of-place he appeared in this elegant room. Kate hovered anxiously.

"Would you care for wine?"

Roger shook his head and she dismissed the girl. He waited, shoulders held stiff, till they were alone, then he said, his voice tight with contempt, "I left your father only four days ago. He should, in honor, have told me."

"He does not know," Rachel explained quietly. "We've been at pains to keep it from him. Phoebe has been with us at Hetherington and here, in Russell Street, since my father's marriage."

"Who is the man?"

She hesitated.

"Hetherington? Then, why in God's name did he marry you?"

"Sir Nicholas is not the father."

"Ah, then it's the younger whelp. And he's abandoned her? Does he know?"

"He's privateering. We've had no word of him since Christmas."

Roger's grim expression broke and he averted his gaze from Rachel.

"I love her, God help me. If she'd confessed . . ."

"You have had your own problems, Roger." Rachel's mild tone implied no blame, but reminded him he had neglected his betrothed. "Since you have not been to Glebe since the funeral . . ."

"What will she do?"

Rachel gave a little helpless shrug. "Nicholas made arrangements for the confinement in Islington. We have just returned from there. We were refused accommodation in the village."

"Fear of the sickness?"

She nodded.

"It's for this I came to take Phoebe back to Glebe. We're hearing disquieting rumors in Leicestershire. I'd hoped to persuade Hetherington to bring you home. I hear he's away."

"On the east coast on an errand for His Majesty."

"He leaves you alone at such a time? The city is breaking into chaos. I saw windows boarded and doors daubed with the red cross," he shuddered, "bloated bodies of dogs and cats lying in the streets, conduits fouled. You must leave, Rachel, immediately."

"Nicholas had no choice. He is employed in His Majesty's household. We should be safe enough here in Russell Street, well away from the crowded hamlets near St. Paul's and the Tower. I cannot take Phoebe home—not yet. It is too near her time for her to travel so far north."

"Then get her out of the capital, to St. Albans or Barnet."

"We might well have the same problems as in Islington and here we have a refuge."

"If I escort you . . ."

"That is kind, under the circumstances." She straightened a statue deliberately, while she strove to think clearly. "Lady Hetherington, Nicholas's mother, is still in attendance on the Dowager Queen at Somerset House. I promised Nicholas I would see she is protected if the Court leaves the city."

"What about the child?"

"I don't know, Roger. All this time we have hoped Kit would return and—then make plans. Zillah is with us. If the child continues without a father—I should wish to adopt, but it must be for Nicholas to decide that. Naturally, he has assured us that he will make financial provisions. I cannot tell what Phoebe will wish to do. She is so distressed and incoherent. She may well refuse to be parted from the child."

"But Hetherington will offer no objections to the match with his brother?"

"None."

"Provided I release her from the betrothal. Has she . . ." he ground out the question, "has she affection for young Hetherington?"

"I believe she has."

He stood up and prowled the room.

"I still think it criminal folly to remain here."

"Phoebe is desperate for news of Kit. Now war is declared, we should have definite information soon."

"I cannot see her," he said harshly, "not yet, but if you've need, send to me. I've lodgings in Holborn. Your maid has details, but don't delay, Rachel. This outbreak of the sickness threatens to be more serious than any previous one, even the visitation in the old Queen's time."

She nodded as he gripped both her hands tightly in his. "Thank you, Roger. Believe me, I'm deeply distressed that you have been so badly hurt. I know how deep your convictions go, but—" she swallowed, a thickening in her throat, "try to forgive. Phoebe is no wanton. This is no arrant wickedness. She is so young and loving, unprepared for the strength of her feelings. The betrothal was too soon, I think. She was frightened by the prospect of such responsibility."

"I shall pray for her." His brown eyes glinted with tears. "For both of you."

She stood uncertainly, rubbing a hand over her aching brows after he left, then abruptly went upstairs to grandmamma and Phoebe.

Phoebe had sobbed herself into a frenzy. She reached out to clutch at the silk of Rachel's bodice, tearing away lace and ribbons.

"I can never go home to Glebe now, never, never. Roger will proclaim my shame."

"I'm sure he will not." Rachel sat on the bedside and looked gravely across at her grandmother. This would not do. Phoebe would make herself ill, bring on the birth too early.

Zillah, at her elbow, entering soft-footed as ever, said quietly, "I have a tisane for Mistress Phoebe, my lady. After such a distressing experience at Islington, she needs a good rest."

"I think we are all in need of your tisane, Zillah," Rachel said shakily. She rose. "Roger is very anxious for us all. You can rest easy on that score, Phoebe. Hurt he may be, angry, but I cannot believe he would do anything to deliberately harm you."

"Leave her to me, Lady Rachel. You are both in need of rest yourselves."

In the salon Rachel briefly told her grandmother what had occurred between herself and Roger Talbot.

"He is deeply concerned and painted a ghastly picture of some of the streets, but we cannot travel with Phoebe in this state."

"Most unwise." Mistress Wilson sighed heavily. "We must hope we are spared and that your husband comes back soon.

Rachel shook her head wearily. She could not trust in that.

They were awakened early by an urgent knocking on the front door. Rachel hastily slipped on her bedgown, hoping against hope that Nicholas had indeed returned.

Chastity, her cap awry, bodice unbuttoned, burst into her room on her call. "Come in."

"Lady Hetherington, my lady, that is—"

"Yes, I understand. Conduct her ladyship into the salon. Ask if she has taken breakfast. Send Kate or Zillah to help me dress."

"I'm here, Lady Rachel." Zillah hastily hooked her into the first available gown and she descended the stair, anxious to know what calamitous news had brought Nicholas's mother so early to Russell Street.

Chastity had provided chocolate and rolls for the visitor, but Rachel sensed her agitation as she crumbled the bread nervously and turned her cold blue eyes on her daughter-in-law.

"I had expected Nicholas to be here."

Charley scampered to greet his mistress, rolling playfully in front of her feet. Quickly, she snatched him up and sat down.

"He is on an errand for the King, escorting Lady Ryall to Southwold." Rachel smiled ruefully when Lady Hetherington regarded the antics of the spaniel puppy doubtfully, as it squirmed under her hand. "A present from His Majesty."

Lady Hetherington sniffed audibly. "It would be like Charles to remove your husband from you at so critical a time and offer an extra responsibility."

"I'm sure His Majesty meant the gift kindly."

"I suppose so." Lady Hetherington's gaze passed bleakly to the chocolate now chilling. "Is young Phoebe still sleeping?"

"Yes, we had a frightening experience yesterday." Rachel explained. "So you see, we shall have to remain here for her confinement."

"Yes." There was a telling silence, then, "I have news of Kit. Tom Spicer came to see me yesterday."

"Kit's friend?"

"Yes. His ship, *The Yorkshire Rose,* came to harbor in Bristol a week ago."

"Kit was not with him?"

"No." The single word was calmly spoken, almost without emotion, but Rachel waited, fearing what was to follow.

"Kit was sailing on the sister vessel, *The Royal Stuart.* The two engaged a Dutch ship off Jamaica. There was a running battle. *The Royal Stuart* was holed below the waterline and sank. Tom says he saw some of what happened from the deck of *The Rose.* Masts and rigging were ablaze and he feared . . ." She broke off abruptly as they both heard the patter of slippers on the stair and Phoebe thrust the salon door open.

"I thought I heard the bell pull and wondered if there was news of Nicholas or Roger. Oh." She looked in blank astonishment at Lady Hetherington, then down self-consciously at her own swollen body. It was the first time they had met since that unpleasant episode in Hetherington churchyard. She had sensed then Lady Hetherington's open animosity, but how much worse matters were now. She stammered uncertainly and made a clumsy half-curtsey.

"Oh, forgive me, Lady Hetherington. I—I was not told you were here."

In the intense heat which had prevailed in the city, Phoebe had taken to wearing a loose silk bedrobe about the house and was guiltily aware that she was not suitably attired to greet Kit's mother.

Lady Hetherington inclined her head a trifle stiffly. There was an awkward silence while Phoebe looked from her to Rachel. Her face paled as she read the older woman's distraught expression.

"Nicholas? No, it's Kit, isn't it? He's been hurt, captured? Please, Lady Hetherington, I must know. Is Kit—dead?" The final words were low and Rachel hastened to support her as she swayed on her feet.

"Come and sit down, Phoebe. Lady Hetherington has had news that—" she swallowed as Phoebe gazed at her imploringly, "that Kit's ship has been sunk. She was about to tell us what Kit's friend, Mr. Spicer, saw from his vessel, which was in the same engagement."

"Kit's ship was burning fast and listing. Mr. Spicer feared there would be few survivors, indeed he thought the Dutch man-of-war would be unlikely to stop and pick up any of the swimmers. He could not be sure, of course. *The Yorkshire Rose* made off soon after, and managed to limp into Bristol a week ago." She paused and Rachel thought she detected a gleam of tears in those fine blue eyes. "I wish I could believe there was some hope, but—but I fear my son was drowned with the others."

Phoebe gave a choking cry and clawed at her sister's hands.

"No, it can't be true, not Kit, please, dear God, not Kit."

Rachel hugged her sister tight to her heart, her own tears falling on the bright gold hair.

"Be brave, Phoebe. We cannot be sure that all were lost. We must hope and pray for Kit and all those men with him."

But Phoebe was beyond comfort. She sobbed brokenly. Rachel rocked her as she would a child. If only Nicholas were here.

"Come, Phoebe," she said at last, gently, "let me help you to your chamber."

Lady Hetherington nodded, tight-lipped, as Rachel led away her sister. Hurriedly, Rachel told her grandmother the gist of Lady Hetherington's news.

"Oh, poor child, how will she bear this? And her ladyship has had troubles enough, her husband killed at Naseby, now her son . . ."

"I must go down to her. Try to comfort Phoebe. I'm afraid for her in this state."

Rachel returned to their visitor. She would have liked to take the older woman's tight-clenched hands in her own, offer some words of comfort, however vain, but she sensed Lady Isabel would bitterly resent such an overture.

"I'm sorry. Phoebe is terribly upset. She—she loved Kit deeply."

Lady Isabel blinked back angry tears. "This news comes at a bad time for all of us." Then, more briskly, "All who can are deserting the city. I can see that for you that is impossible. Queen Henrietta is to go to Hampton, and has relieved me of my duties in attendance. You will need help here, if only to control the servants, who are very likely to panic. I'll come to you here. I've some experience of coping in a crisis."

"You would be most welcome." Rachel meant it. Any resentment she had felt for her mother-in-law had vanished, and now she only felt an intense relief that she might rely on Lady Isabel's inner reserve of strength and courage. During those terrible War years, Lady Hetherington had learned in a hard school.

"I'll return to Somerset House and pack. I'll bring Louise, the French maid, though much use she will be. All she is good for is pressing my gowns and arranging my hair, though I'll grant you she does both exquisitely."

Lady Isabel arrived during the late afternoon, attended by a thin individual with a quantity of red hair and a waspish tongue, who alienated Rachel's two maids from the moment she came. Lady Isabel tartly forbade further complaints.

"Hold your tongue, Louise, or take yourself off. There can be no hardship in your being required to share your sleeping quarters. Heaven knows, there were at least six of you crowded into that small cubicle at Somerset House, and three to a bed."

"*Mais, oui,* madame, but Somerset House was a palace."

"If that's your argument, go seek employment at Whitehall." Lady Isabel waved her off testily. "Unpack my bags and make yourself useful in the kitchen." She turned to Rachel. "The stupid creature knows well enough how fortunate she is. The wealthy are leaving St. James's by the carriageful. Many of the houses are boarded up and the servants left to their own devices."

"Poor souls. How will they manage?"

"They won't, more's the pity. They'll loot and rob. Tell your man to keep a tight watch that all's bolted and barred by nightfall."

Rachel escorted her mother-in-law upstairs. "The guestchamber isn't large. I could move out of my room—"

"You'll do no such thing. Nicholas, it's to be hoped, will soon return. This will do excellently."

She settled in quickly and with less fuss than Rachel could have expected, making few demands upon the servants. Indeed, she soon became a tower of strength, ordering the domestic arrangements, freeing Mistress Wilson, who soon tired, to give complete attention to Phoebe.

Rachel and Zillah undertook the shopping for the household. Food soared in price due to the difficulties of procuring supplies, and it was on these excursions to Covent Garden market and into the city that they saw the ravages that the sickness was making on London.

Sewers overflowed so it was impossible to venture out without a pomander at one's nose. As Roger had warned, the bloated corpses of dogs, cats, pigs, even sheep, left unattended and covered with hordes of flies, abounded. Many shops were already deserted and the apothecaries were crowded with customers demanding specifics against the sickness.

More and more houses were now daubed with the dread symbol of the red cross and the scrawled words

"Lord have mercy on all within." Watchmen, armed with halberds, mounted guard to restrain those within from venturing out.

"How will they obtain supplies?" Rachel asked.

"The watchmen and searchers will provide—at a price. Money is placed within vessels of vinegar and lowered out from the upper windows, food drawn up in baskets afterwards."

"Is vinegar really a safeguard?"

Zillah shrugged. "I think there's little one can do for victims except try to ease their sufferings, sponge the body to bring down fever and lance the buboes if they are agonizing, to let out the pus. Give soothing draughts to appease the mounting thirst and encourage sleep. Either the fever will break or it won't."

Rachel shivered. How terrible to be walled up living with the dead without hope! How the mothers would suffer, seeing their children sicken and die one by one.

June 7th was the hottest day Rachel could remember, the air so still it seemed solid. Since the news of Kit's death, Phoebe had become sullen, withdrawn, less irritable, and lay all day stretched on her bed. A letter was received from Roger, delivered by a young ragamuffin in ragged breeches. It read:

> *Lady Rachel,*
> *Since I have received no word from you regarding your intention to leave the city, I feel it would be wise if I took the opportunity to set out today for Leicestershire. There is need of my presence at Barrow. Naturally, I shall speak no word of your difficulties, at Glebe. I pray God to keep you safe from pestilence and bring Phoebe a good delivery. My best regards to your grandmother.*
> > *Your obedient servant and friend,*
> > *Roger Talbot*

It was what she had expected, but she felt a terrible sense of loss on receipt of it.

First Nicholas had left them unprotected, and now Roger was deserting them. Silently, she handed the note to her grandmother.

"He feels betrayed. He can do nothing here, but I would have felt safer with a man within call. There are such terrible stories of wild looting and attacks on property."

Rachel nodded. Hurt and dismayed though Roger was by Phoebe's conduct, she felt it was terror of the sickness that had driven him so hastily from London, and Lady Isabel agreed with her.

"Men are ever so. They'll face a cavalry charge or pike thrusts, even a pistol ball with equanimity, but a debilitating illness puts them into a sweat of panic."

The following day it was forbidden to leave the city without a certificate of health provided by a justice. No one could remain unaware of the closeness of death as the bells around Covent Garden and the neighboring parishes tolled for the dead.

Rachel had received no word from Nicholas, and late in June the King moved his Court to Hampton, after first escorting his mother to the coast where she was to sail for France. Would Nicholas resume his duties in the King's household without contacting her?

Phoebe could not now be moved and Rachel was thankful that Lady Isabel had arranged for the services of a noted accoucheur.

July dawned as humid as ever. Rachel was lying supine, hating to drag herself out of bed, when a piercing scream rang through the house. Before she could reach for a bedgown, Kate was running down the stairs, sobbing incoherently.

"My lady, my lady, come quick. Oh, come quick. It's the Frenchwoman."

Rachel reached for her slippers, thrust her arms into her bedgown sleeves and jerked open her door. Lady Isabel was already on the landing and shaking the girl hard.

"What is it? Why are you making this abominable noise?"

"It's your maid, my lady. She's taken sick." Kate's voice rose to a half-shriek. "She's got the plague. We'll all die. We will."

"Be quiet. I'll come at once. Be quiet, I say. You'll upset Mistress Nashe."

Lady Isabel hastened to the attic, Rachel close on her heels. Chastity Pogson, the younger maid, crouched on the top step. Even in the dim light Rachel could see the girl was shaking with terror.

They were halted in the doorway by the appalling stink of stale vomit.

"Stay back, Rachel. There's Phoebe to think of, and don't let Zillah near."

"But if the girl is really ill—"

"Get back, I say. Here, you girl, Kate, fetch me some water and clean up this mess."

"I daren't, my lady."

Lady Isabel administered a sharp slap on the girl's cheek which set her blubbering. "Do it now. Tell Gaston I want him." She turned on Rachel. "Neither you nor Mistress Wilson are to set foot in that room. If you do, you'll not be able to go near Phoebe."

"But you?"

"I'm the girl's mistress."

Kate scuttled below stairs, still sobbing. Rachel looked anxiously toward the attic room, but Lady Isabel barred her way.

"Rachel, I'm ordering you to leave this business to me. Nicholas would wish it. Keep those stupid girls from screaming it out to the neighborhood. If it's even

154

suspected we've plague here, we shall be confined in the house for the prescribed forty days, and no midwife will come near us."

Rachel went cold with fear.

"Keep Phoebe in her room. If I call, come to the foot of the stairs, no nearer. Zillah will know what I need. She's to put fumigatory herbs and a jar of vinegar on the bottom step."

Rachel hesitated, then, reading the urgency in the older woman's eyes, she went down to Phoebe's room. She hastily called a warning to the two in the bed.

"Stay where you are for the moment. Lady Isabel's maid is taken sick. We'll know the worst soon enough." Checking her own panic, she said sharply, as Phoebe's frightened wail reached her, "You must keep calm, Phoebe, for the child's sake."

Isabel Hetherington forced herself to approach the girl on the bed. The room reeked of vomit and blood. The coarse sheeting was slimy with it. Louise lay half out of bed, her hair tangled and sweat-streaked. Lady Isabel thrust her kerchief to her nose as Gaston came up behind her.

"If you're afraid of the pestilence, Gaston, I shall understand. Where are the girls?"

"Locked in the large pantry, madame. I wait to know what is wrong. There is such crying and wailing." He approached the bed as the maid's body arched convulsively.

"*Mordieu,* it is the plague sickness, *non?*"

"I'm afraid so." Lady Isabel stripped off the befouled sheet.

"Will you help me lift her?"

"*Mais certainement,* madame. I think it best, *non,* if we tie her down. I hear victims can become mad with the pain."

155

Lady Hetherington nodded, tore off a cleaner strip, then another, and tied them together into a thickish rope, while Gaston strove to hold down the thrashing body. Between them they managed to get the improvised rope around the girl's waist and knotted beneath the bed.

Zillah's voice called from below. "Water, Lady Isabel, and the herbs you asked for. I'll leave them here."

"Good. Don't come up. You have your own babe to think of and Mistress Phoebe will need you soon. See if one of the maids is calm enough to help us. Let none of them out into the square. It would certainly doom us all."

Gaston was staring, horror-stricken, at the purplish blotches on the pale skin of the maid's breast.

"The plague tokens, madame. I see no buboes. They say without them there is no hope."

"None at all," Lady Hetherington said shortly. "The onset was so sudden. She's in delirium. Did you see her last night? Had she any sign of this then?"

"No, madame, I did not see her. She has been staying out very late, the girls say, but she seemed well enough in the morning when she crossed the yard."

Kate Pogson came tiredly into the room, lugging the heavy wooden water pail. Her eyes were red-rimmed, but she looked much calmer. "She said she was tired, my lady, complained of a bad headache. We thought it was just the heat. She hasn't been eating. Oh, my lady, is she going to die?" She caught her breath sharply and backed against the wall as the maid's body heaved against the rope sheeting.

"Can you be brave, Kate? I think she *will* die, there's no point in trying to hearten you with false hope. You both shared her bed, as usual?"

Kate gave a horrified nod. "I woke up to find her retching, and there was blood in it. It's so terrible—"

"If we summon the parish clerk and ask for a nurse or physician, we shall all be locked up here. Since you were so close to her, you would not be allowed to leave this room. You understand that?"

"Yes, my lady."

"What is Chastity doing now?"

"I—I don't know. She's not said a word, just scrambled out of bed when I screamed and stood staring, then downstairs she started to scream. Gaston slapped her. She's terrible afraid."

"We all are, Kate. Get a cloth and mop up that vomit." Lady Isabel soaked a pad of sheeting in the water and wiped down the sufferer's face, throat and breast. Though the hair was soaked in sweat, the flesh was hot and dry. Louise was burning up with fever.

Pitifully, she pleaded in French for water. Gaston found a cup on the bedchest and filled it. The French girl gulped at it thirstily, but in moments she was sick again.

There was little they could do. The girl was dying before their eyes and in dreadful agony. Her delirious muttering became wild raving and convulsions followed. She frothed at the mouth, bloodied spittle dribbling from the corner, there was a rattle in the throat, and she fell back, eyes staring to the roof rafters.

Gaston drew a hard breath. *"Elle est morte,* madame." He crossed himself.

"I pray God she is, no one should endure such suffering and go on living. Cover the poor girl, Gaston." Lady Isabel staggered and the manservant supported her to a stool.

"We must consider what to do," she said at last, shakily.

157

His troubled brown eyes met hers and he gave a little decisive jerk of his chin. "Madame, the officials, they must be told."

"Can you—can you dispose of the body?"

He considered, rubbing his chin. "*Oui*, madame."

"It will be dangerous. If she is found, later . . ."

"Madame, people will not concern themselves about those who disappear. Things are now bad, very bad. But you, madame, and the girls—"

"We are all likely to develop the sickness, that's very plain."

Kate stifled a sharp cry by thrusting her knuckles hard against her mouth.

"There was some man, my lady. She used to meet him at a tavern in Luckenor Lane."

"Foolish chit, he was more than likely a seaman. Hadn't she the sense to know that the sickness began among the crewmen of the fleet? The poor girl paid hard for her stupidity. What's to be done, Gaston?"

"I will bury her beneath the stable next door, madame; there are no horses there, the house has been deserted some weeks."

"So it's empty?" Lady Hetherington's head jerked up as she thought hard. "It would make sense for me to move there with you and the girls. None of us wishes to end in a pesthouse and we must avoid contact with Lady Rachel and her sister. The gypsy girl must not come near us, either. Kate?" She fixed the girl with a hard stare.

The girl swallowed. "Yes, my lady, I can see it's best. Even if we tried to run, we'd starve, better we stay together. I'll talk to Chastity, only—" her teeth chattered as she strove to harness her failing courage, "I'm so frightened after what I just seen . . ."

"Yes." Lady Hetherington nodded toward the bed. "We'll need to help you get her downstairs, Gaston. Disagreeable as the task will be, it has to be faced as soon as possible. In this heat we risk greater danger to all in the house if she isn't buried soon."

"*Non*, madame, I will do that." He averted his eyes from the huddled form on the truckle bed, covered with the blood-spotted sheet. "She should first be wrapped—"

"We'll deal with that. Everything in this room must be destroyed and fumigatory herbs burned in the grate. Get below, Gaston, and make your arrangements. Call to Lady Rachel to come to the stair foot as you go."

"*Oui*, madame."

Lady Isabel waved to Kate to follow him. "Go and try to pacify your sister. Make her see that we've no choice but to stay together."

"Yes, my lady." Kate looked to the sheeted corpse and shuddered. "You'll need help to lift—that."

"Can you help me?"

Kate's frightened eyes dilated, but she nodded. "Yes, my lady, I'll come straight back."

"Good girl."

Rachel called to her mother-in-law from the stair foot.

"Lady Isabel, how is Louise? Has she truly developed the plague? Is she . . .?"

"Dead, and we should thank the good God for it. Listen, Rachel, and see you obey me to the letter. Even now we cannot tell if it is too late." Brusquely, she hastened on. "Gaston and I, with the girls, will move next door, a necessary precaution since we have all been in close contact with the dead girl."

"But if *you* become ill?"

"We'll make shift for ourselves, as you must do." She lowered her voice slightly. "Gaston is to dispose of the body. We'll get rid of everything in here. I want all of you to strip and bathe, then wipe yourselves all over with cloths soaked in vinegar, board up this room, or avoid it, fumigate all your other rooms. Zillah will get

159

the necessary herbs. One of you must do your own marketing. I don't want you even to touch coin or food we have handled. Gaston will serve us. If—if he can't, I'll call from the stables and you must leave food for us in the courtyard. Rachel?" As there was no answer, she called again imperatively.

"Yes, Lady Isabel, I hear you," The words were muffled, tearful. "I'll do exactly as you say, because I must."

"Good. Necessary and practical. Now go into the salon, all of you, and stay clear of the kitchens until we have left. Tell Zillah to cleanse all the cooking vessels." There was a pause, and then she added, a trifle hoarsely, "Kit is lost to me. I want to hear his child has been safely delivered."

"I understand."

Kate had come up to the attic pulling a reluctant Chastity with her.

"We must help ourselves," she said fiercely. "I'll help Lady Isabel with—with Louise. You get the floor scrubbed. We shall all need to change and burn our dirtied gowns and shifts down there."

Lady Isabel closed the dead girl's staring eyes and, with Kate's help, managed to wrap the body in sheeting.

Gaston took in the sight from the doorway. "I am ready now, madame, if one of the girls will keep watch for me by the door."

She nodded, tight-lipped. The girls pattered downstairs. Chastity called up that all was clear and Gaston shouldered his heavy burden. Now the most horrible task was behind her, Lady Isabel swaye on her feet. A sudden pain clawed down her arms and across her breast. She gasped with the severity of it, then forced herself to stand up as Kate hastened up again with a bundle of clothing.

"It was put ready on the stairs, my lady."

"Chastity?"

"She's coming now, bringing us some hot water. Will you go to your own room, my lady?"

"No, I'll strip down here, better if I don't go any nearer to the others. Don't be afraid to strip yourself here in front of me, Kate. We shall all need to tend each other if the worst happens. Shyness and pride won't help."

Methodically, they stripped the truckle bed, bundling straw mattress and soiled coverings out of the window to where Gaston waited below. He would burn them in the courtyard, where he was unlikely to be overlooked. Lady Isabel had had some experience of nursing smallpox victims during the war, and had learned then the necessity of burning all the sufferers' clothing and bedding. She would take no chances now. If cleanliness could help them fight this horror, she'd stand over the girls and forcibly make them obey her.

Such determination proved unnecessary. As if they believed she possessed some power to ward off the pestilence, the girls trusted her completely, and worked with a will under her direction.

Lady Isabel shivered, despite the heat, as she scrubbed her body with a cloth soaked in vinegar after bathing herself and then re-dressed in a shift, busk and gown of Mistress Wilson's. Zillah had provided clothes for the girls.

It was well past noon when Gaston called that he was ready for them.

"I break down the shutters of number twelve, madame, and opened the back door from inside. We should go now. There is food taken there for us."

The room had been scrubbed and scoured; noxious-smelling herbs pervaded the house. Lady Isabel looked around and sighed. "Go, girls, hurry."

She stopped in the kitchen. "Rachel, we are leaving now. God protect you all."

"And you." Rachel's voice was clear but tense.

Lady Isabel stepped into the yard, turned toward the darkened interior of the stables, and then she followed Gaston into the deserted hallway of number twelve.

Gaston swore and struggled to his feet. Even in the darkened stable interior the heat was appalling. He had decided to install himself here, leaving the womenfolk in complete possession of the empty house. He grunted and turned into the Hetherington stable. It was time to feed and water the one horse they still kept there for his use.

Lady Rachel came to the kitchen door as he was drawing water from the well.

"Zillah thinks the accoucheur should be summoned. We are not sure, but Mistress Nashe seems very restless this morning, though the pains haven't begun."

"I will go immediately to Drury Lane, madame. The man will soon be here. Do not be afraid." He carried the water to his horse and fed it, then washed himself at the horse trough. He called to Kate where he was going and took a basket to bring food from the market.

There was little to be had at market, since the countrymen had ceased to be allowed in; coarse bread, which would not please madame, limp vegetables, wine, more vinegar.

As he moved east, the streets showed further signs of the ravages of pestilence. Grass grew between the cobbles, and the open kennels stank to the heavens, choked with refuse and slops. Scavengers whose work it was to carry off the waste to the laystalls outside the town had long since given up their tasks.

Gaston started as he heard a tolling bell, and saw the waiting death cart ahead before one of the houses. The attendants were about to leave their grisly charges to enter and the guard on duty exchanged some bawdy jest with them and two blowsily dressed females, nurses sent by the parish clerk to attend the sufferers inside.

Gaston crossed himself at the sight of the bloated corpses heaped one upon another: men, women with bodices and skirts indecently ripped in the search for jewels hidden on their persons, some stripped of all garments by the rapacious searchers. It was more usual for collections to be made by night and, despite himself, Gaston was unnerved. He edged by, thrusting his hand tight against nose and mouth, for the stink of that rotting flesh was unbearable.

Gaston peered around for the house numbers. A window was jerked open above him. "What do you want?" The old woman's peevish tone was marked with suspicion. "The master's not at home."

"Milady Hetherington in Russell Street has urgent need of Monsieur Howard."

The head, crowned with a ridiculous yellowed cap, lace-trimmed, beneath which greasy straggles of hair were escaping, leaned closer to peer down at him. "Monsieur Howard is not available. He has left the city like all the rest."

"The lady is gently born. She is in sore need . . ."

"Then she'll have to learn to make shift like the rest of us. Comes to all women, the same in the end, don't it, the curse of Eve? You tell 'er I said so."

The casement was banged to.

He leaned against the door wearily. It was useless. The man would not come, nor any other midwife.

Phoebe sat near the window in the salon to get what faint breeze there was, clutching her grandmother's hand for comfort.

Rachel caught her grandmother's eye.

163

"Yes, the pains are about to begin, I think. Is your back paining you, Phoebe?"

Phoebe nodded. "I couldn't sleep, and it's so hard to get comfortable."

Zillah and Rachel tackled the work in the kitchen.

"She's becoming very frightened."

Zillah nodded. "Her progress is what I'd expect at this stage. Best not to put her to bed yet a while, she'll only fret."

When Gaston reported that Monsieur Howard was not available, Zillah snorted and said, "If all goes well, we'll not need this male midwife." From the first she'd been doubtful about this latest fashion of employing such experienced men to attend the confinements of the wealthy.

Phoebe's pains had begun and were rapidly increasing in intensity. They did not inform her immediately of the refusal of the accoucheur to come to her assistance, and, later, as the depth of suffering overcame her, she was in no state to care. Zillah took charge and Rachel felt strangely helpless.

At nightfall she drew Zillah from the chamber. Phoebe's moans and cries were now more frequent.

"Is this normal, Zillah?"

The gypsy shook her head. "You remember what I said when my own child was born? The babe should come head first. If it is lying badly, there could be problems. We really do need a midwife's skill. This stage of labor seems to be taking much too long, but Mistress Phoebe is slim-hipped and it is her first. Sometimes it is like this. My mother would have known what to do."

A scream of agony caused Rachel's knuckles to glisten whitely as she clung to the banister rail. "Can't we do something to ease her pain?"

"No, Lady Rachel, that would only slow up labor. She must endure."

"But it is taxing her strength."

"I know," Zillah sighed. "Go to her, Lady Rachel. Encourage her. Mistress Wilson should rest and eat and I must feed Bart."

Phoebe's pretty face was almost unrecognizable, her fair hair dark with the sweat of exhaustion. Someone had tied a strip of torn sheeting across the bed and her fingers clutched at it convulsively. She did not turn her head as Rachel took her place on the stool by the bedside.

"Phoebe, my darling, have courage, just a little longer and the child will be in your arms soon, soon now."

Sweat streamed down Phoebe's face, throat and shoulders. Rachel reached for the cloth and basin placed ready, sponged her sister down and dried her gently on a linen napkin.

"I'm—going—to die." The words were jerked out.

"No, darling, of course not. Remember how quickly Zillah recovered?"

Rachel knew she was mouthing platitudes. Phoebe was frailer, smaller—but suppose Zillah was right in her assumption that there was something radically wrong?

Phoebe did not speak again. Rachel sat on, talking, encouraging, bathing her sister's forehead and breast, her own throat tightly constricted. When her grandmother murmured behind her, she looked up, blinking into the light of a candle and realized it was full dark.

"I'll take over now. You go down now and eat something."

"I couldn't eat. She can't go on like this, can she?"

"She should be nearer delivery now by the frequency of the contractions, but it's often bad with a first child."

"Suppose something's wrong—" She caught a sudden gleam of concern in her grandmother's eye.

"It's possible. I don't think so. She has carried the child without undue distress."

"Zillah says if the child isn't placed right . . ."

Grandmamma nodded, her gaze troubled. "We are at a disadvantage without a trained accoucheur, who would know, but—she is tiny and it is the first."

Rachel went to the kitchen, and forced herself to swallow some buttermilk and a slice of bread, then settled in the armchair to wait.

She woke with a start as her grandmother shook her shoulders gently.

"I can't have gone to sleep—"

"You were exhausted."

"Is she—is the child—"

"No." Her grandmother sank down on a stool by the chair. "She's becoming more and more exhausted. The contractions are too fierce and there's no sign of the child's head appearing. I want you to come and talk to Zillah."

"I don't understand."

"Her mother knew how to cope with emergencies such as this, and Zillah must have some skill. She must try. She's frightened of harming her, but unless something is done . . ." Her voice trailed off.

Rachel hurried above stairs. She was appalled at the sight of Phoebe. She was too weakened now to scream, simply writhed on the bed, sweat-soaked.

Zillah came to the landing and Rachel drew the chamber door to.

"Mistress Wilson says there is something you should try, Zillah, for the love of God."

"I—have never attempted it with a child—animals maybe. The babe should be turned, but—"

"Zillah, only you have a chance of saving her now—"

"I could endanger her further—"

"Zillah, nothing could."

The gypsy drew a hard breath. "Very well. Have sheets ready. I'll come down and scrub my hands. Mother always did."

She looked quickly at the little knot of women before reentering the room. "I'll need light—held just so. Lady Rachel, your hands are steady. Mistress Wilson will help when the child comes."

Rachel moved with leaden limbs to the bedside. Despite Zillah's assertion that her hands were the steadiest, the hot wax spilt onto her fingers as she held the candlestick high for Zillah's examination.

Phoebe whimpered as the gypsy bent close. Her features looked like those of an old woman.

Zillah gave the ghost of a smile. "I think I know just what has to be done—provided—"

Rachel forced herself to hold the light still while Phoebe thrashed under her grandmother's grip. There was a sudden sweet, sickening smell of blood in the fetid room.

"It's almost over."

Rachel averted her gaze from Zillah's bloodied hands, but the gypsy's voice was stronger, more confident. "Push down for me again, Mistress Phoebe. Soon now, rest again, easy, breathe easy—now again, push down hard. I can see the baby's head and shoulder. Very soon now—"

The gurgled, choked scream was cut off short and Zillah had something slimy and bloodstained in her hands.

Rachel stared horrified at the spreading bloodstains on the sheets.

"She's hemorrhaging."

"No, Lady Rachel. It's not exceptional."

Behind them a wailed cry, mewing like a kitten. Grandmamma said crisply, "You've a daughter, Phoebe, a lovely child."

But Phoebe was in no state to hear them. The ordeal over, unconsciousness had claimed her.

Rachel helped strip the bed, bathe and make Phoebe comfortable, and raise the bed foot. Zillah nodded, tight-lipped, as she stopped to listen to her patient's breathing.

"We can do nothing more now. Only rest can mend the torn body."

"If the bleeding goes on—" Rachel shuddered.

"The curse of childbed, hemorrhage and milk fever. But the worst is over."

Instinctively, Rachel bent and gripped the gypsy's brown hands. "Thank you, Zillah."

Zillah withdrew her fingers with her customary restraint. "Bart needs me, Lady Rachel. Call me if she seems worse or the bleeding remains unchecked. I'll prepare some poppyseed in case she wakes."

Rachel sat by Phoebe until the sun was again fully up, drenching the room with waves of fierce yellow heat. She pulled to the shutters. As she did so, Phoebe moved, her eyes flickered and she smiled weakly.

"It's all over, darling, you have a daughter."

Rachel had taken her sister's hand, but it went slack in hers. The eyes closed again and Phoebe slept.

Chapter 11

When Rachel took Phoebe's baby from Zillah the next morning, its tiny fingers clung possessively to hers. It had a crown of soft fair hair and was remarkably beautiful after the long struggle for existence. The baby was smaller than Bart had been, but Zillah pronounced it lusty enough. Rachel felt a surge of tenderness sweep over her. She handed the baby back.

"Zillah, will Mistress Phoebe recover? She seems weak and languid."

"I see no reason why not." Zillah was cautious. "Provided there's no fever, she should soon get back her strength."

After breakfast Rachel sallied out with Charley. It was not yet suffocatingly hot and the little spaniel skipped about excitedly before her. She released him from his leash and relished what breeze there was. Turning into the now-deserted Covent Garden Square, she strolled at leisure.

She called Charley to heel, but the dog had run off on his own pursuits. There was no sign of him. She retraced her steps to the Square and, as she turned the corner, heard his pathetic whimpering cries as he struggled in the arms of a half-naked boy.

Furiously, she called across the brown grass, "Put my dog down at once. What are you doing?"

"He's a spreading of the sickness. All stray dogs to be killed. There's a notice out, lady. Tuppence I'll get for his hide."

"No." Rachel was thoroughly alarmed, for she saw the boy was armed with a butcher's knife. "Charley's no stray, and in touch with no contagion. He was the King's gift."

The dog squirmed and bit at his persecutor, but the boy held on strongly.

"No matter, lady. He's fairly caught and mine. Tuppence is hard earned these days. Most of the cats and dogs are already dead . . ."

Rachel halted several yards from him, her heart pounding. "I tell you Charley's no stray," she said quietly. "Never fear that you'll lose out on this. I'll give you a silver groat and food, too, if you'll release him."

The boy gave a muffled oath as the dog bit on his

hand and let his prize go. Rachel stooped to leash the spaniel and then threw the boy a silver coin. She was trembling as, laughing and crying with relief, she made her way back to Russell Street.

The boy was still shadowing her as she made to enter the house.

"What's your name?"

"Toby—Toby Nabb."

"Come around to the kitchen. I'll put food up for you. Where do you live?"

"Where I can, mistress."

"Your people?"

He shrugged. "Ain't got no people. Me mother's dead."

"Of the sickness?"

"Ner—years ago. Ain't never had no dad. I sleep where I can, used to get work from the big houses sometimes. The lords and such, they've all packed up and gone."

"So you starve?"

"Unless I gets an odd job or two—or," he eyed her doubtfully, "I loots a bit. Not much left now though."

Rachel hesitated. The boy showed no sign of the deadly sickness. They needed help in the stable and yard, fetching water, running errands.

"I could find you work here. You can sleep in the stable next door. It's deserted. Our neighbors left. I'll provide you with blankets."

"No need, mistress."

"You shall have what comforts I can manage and food daily. Can I trust you with Charley?"

He put his head on one side and grinned. "If it warn't for need, I like dogs. This one's a rare beauty."

"Toby, I'm very attached to Charley."

He digested this confidence and nodded again. "I'll walk 'im and keep 'im safe."

Zillah took out blankets and food to the new arrival and insisted he strip and wash himself in the horse trough, despite his protests. An old shirt and breeches of Gaston's which she handed him looked ridiculously large on the stunted body.

"There's no marks of the sickness on him," she reported, "and he looks healthy enough considering he's half-starved."

Rachel wondered if she had further endangered the household, yet she was sure, in any case, that Toby would have hovered near to the house, sensing her sympathy and hoping for future handouts.

Phoebe allowed herself to be fed like a child. Her eyes were purple-shadowed and she moved listlessly, but said she had no fever and was in no pain. She stared, wide-eyed, at the swaddled babe when Zillah brought her in later. Wonderingly, she took the child into her arms as if she was fearful of breaking her.

"Rachel, how small she is and so beautiful." There was a catch to her voice. "But not like Kit at all."

"Babies change, Phoebe. What shall we call her? A pretty name it must be, she's so delicate and flower-like."

"I don't know. A fancy name will be against her when—when she's fostered."

Rachel said gently, "Shall it be Corinna? You know, Phoebe, after the poem you loved so much, about the 'maying.'"

"It's a lovely name." Phoebe clutched the baby close, tears falling onto the tight swaddling bands. "Oh, Rachel, I cannot bear to part with her."

Phoebe surrendered the baby reluctantly, dropping a kiss on the tiny forehead. As Rachel carried her to the kitchen to Zillah, she considered the possible fate which shadowed Corinna's future.

There could only be one way. She, Rachel, must

adopt Corinna. But would Nicholas allow it? There would be difficulties, gossip. It might be supposed that the child was her husband's. She sighed as she set about preparing for supper. If only Nicholas were here.

Rachel saw the worsening situation when she ventured out with Zillah or grandmamma to do the marketing. Thousands were now dying of the sickness each week. They encountered old men and children running mad in the streets, corpses left to lie where they fell, and each night they heard the ominous rumbling of the death cart. Its attendant's call, "Bring out your dead," sent a chill of horror through all of them.

Gaston received the news that young Toby Nabb was to join the household with a grunt, half of relief that the boy could assume his duties at number fourteen, half of concern that the urchin would steal whatever he could lay hands on and make off with it. When, later, his worst fears remained unrealized, he set about training the boy.

Gaston had been in service with Sir Nicholas Hetherington since January 1651, when Sir Nicholas was in the Faubourg St. Antoine, waiting attendance on the young King Charles II at his cousin's Court. Gaston considered his loyalty as essential to his master's service as breathing, and this naturally extended to his care for Lady Rachel, Lady Isabel and Monsieur Kit. Just now it seemed that the Dowager Lady Isabel had greatest need of him.

He had just returned from Covent Garden market when Kate met him, white-faced, in the hallway.

"Her ladyship ain't at all well. I'm terribly worried about her. I think we should have a doctor."

The sickness? His heart plummeted. After all this time, could Lady Isabel have taken the contagion from her maid?

"She's not sick, but she's sweating something terrible

and finding it hard to catch her breath. I'm sure she's in bad pain, though she won't admit it."

He hurried up to the chamber where Lady Isabel had established herself. Fortunately, the former owners had not entirely stripped the house, and the bed and mattress had remained intact. Gaston had transferred sheets and blankets from number fourteen and they were all tolerably comfortable.

Madame was sitting well propped up. He was alarmed by her pallor and the bluish tinge of her lips. Her breathing was indeed labored, as Kate had said.

"What is it, madame? Have you fever?"

"No, Gaston." Her words were jerked out with effort. "I have been so before. I cannot believe that I have the sickness, but we must take precautions. Leave me food and water and stay well clear."

"I should summon a physician, madame."

"Certainly not," she snapped. "The fool would immediately assume the worst and we should all be mewed up to no purpose. Get Zillah to bring me some brew for the pain. It's all we can do."

"*Oui*, madame." He moved uneasily to the door.

"I know, Gaston," she said, more gently, "you feel it your duty to wait on me for Sir Nicholas, but we have to consider your mistress. We cannot endanger her, nor Mistress Nashe's child. You've not seen it as yet, I suppose?"

He caught the gruffness of her tone and glanced at her curiously. Was it as he had thought? The child was either the offspring of Sir Nicholas or Monsieur Kit. Lady Isabel's interest in the babe could not be ignored. He could not believe his master would have seduced *la jeune mademoiselle* and married her sister. That was not his way. So the child was Monsieur Kit's, *le bon Dieu* rest his soul.

"*Non*, madame, but Zillah says it is a lusty babe."

"Good. Try not to alarm Lady Rachel. I've known

173

for long enough now—my heart is failing. The Queen's doctor warned me over a year ago. Off with you, man. I shall get over this or—I shan't."

Gaston gave the Pogson girls their mistress's orders. "I do not believe it to be the plague. We should not despair."

"But, Gaston, her ladyship should have a woman by her to—" Kate faltered.

"*Oui,* I know it. I go now to inform Milady Rachel."

Zillah received Gaston's news at the kitchen door. She questioned him carefully as to the exact nature of Lady Isabel's symptoms.

"It *does* appear to be a bad heart attack," she admitted. "My mother died of it. She suffered pain down the arms and across the chest and her breathing was bad. I'll prepare a draught of foxglove leaves steeped in wine as well as poppyseed for the pain."

"She will recover, *oui?*"

"She may." Zillah shrugged. "I'll tell Lady Rachel."

"I shall nurse her myself." For once Rachel was adamant. "Grandmamma, you and Zillah can give Phoebe all the care she needs. I *must* do what I can for Nicholas's mother. There is little danger of this being the plague. I cannot leave her in Gaston's charge. There are intimate tasks to be performed for her, and naturally the girls are still afraid."

Agnes Wilson's expression was grim. "Rachel, we cannot be sure. If Sir Nicholas were here—and he ought to be—even he would harbor doubts as to the wisdom of you sacrificing yourself." It was the first time her grandmother had uttered a criticism of Nicholas's behavior.

Rachel knew only extreme concern had driven her to so express herself now. She occupied herself in getting together what she would need.

"Lady Isabel was willing to risk her life for us. Now we can be reasonably certain there is no risk, I cannot, in honor, fail to go to her."

Phoebe, surprisingly, did not attempt to dissuade her. She clung a little tearfully in parting and Rachel was conscious of how frail she still seemed. Bending, Rachel kissed the tiny fist, careful not to wake the child.

Lady Isabel greeted her ungraciously. "God's teeth, I thought you would have more sense." Her face contorted with pain and Rachel hurried to the bedside.

"Hush, you need a woman's care and Zillah cannot be spared, as she must suckle the babes. But she gave me explicit instructions." Rachel wiped the sweat from her mother-in-law's forehead.

"No word from Nicholas?"

"None." Rachel could not keep the acidity from her voice.

"What can he be about to desert us at such a time? The babe and her mother are well?"

"Excellently so, though Phoebe is still listless. Zillah says that is to be expected. Don't try to talk. I'll get Kate to prepare your medicine."

The potion afforded Lady Isabel some relief, for she slept later, though fitfully. Rachel was comforted by the knowledge that there appeared to be no fever developing and the breathing was becoming less labored. She sat down by the bed to keep watch.

Lady Isabel muttered in her sleep and tossed about, displacing the bedcoverings. Rachel rose to replace them and, bending close, heard the fretful murmur, "Like her mother. Like Dorcas Wilson. Cannot forgive. Never."

A sudden vivid picture of their first meeting in Hetherington churchyard flashed across Rachel's mind. She had felt the chill of Lady Hetherington's displeasure, had thought it due to past enmity, but now there appeared to be a private cause.

Why could not Lady Isabel forgive her, Rachel's mother? For what? Surely she could not hold Dorcas Nashe responsible for her husband's vicious destruction of Hetherington Manor. She had spoken of Rachel's mother as Dorcas *Wilson*. So she had known her before her marriage to Simon Nashe.

Lady Isabel turned again in the bed, her head rolling weakly against the pillows. "Again. Fate turning. Turning full circle. Kit so like William. And the girl—"

Rachel's lips tightened. Phoebe. Phoebe, so like her mother. So it was *Phoebe* toward whom Lady Isabel's venom had been directed.

Quietly, Rachel took her seat near the opened window and dozed in the heat, lulled by the monotonous drone of flies and moths against the casement. She was startled awake by Charley's shrill barking and, leaning out to see the cause, almost fell out of the window in the shock of seeing Nicholas ride into the courtyard.

He silenced the dog with a sharp word and, unused to such harsh treatment, Charley slunk away. As Gaston told him the news, he looked upwards to the window. Within minutes he had hurried upstairs, his riding coat and boots still gray with the dust of the highway. Rachel met him on the landing.

"I imagine Gaston told you your mother was ill. I don't think you should waken her just yet. She is breathing more easily now."

He hurried in to his mother and, bending close over the bed, stooped and brushed her forehead with his lips. Rachel left them together. Later he joined her below stairs.

"She's still sleeping. You are sure it's not the plague?"

"Not sure, of course, but she says she'd had attacks like this before; her heart, the doctors told her."

"Yes, I wondered—her anxiety to see the manor at Christmas, have me settled . . . She must be worried sick about Kit."

Rachel called to Kate to bring refreshment for the master, and then quietly told him what she knew.

He stalked to the empty grate, booted leg on the dusty fire dog, one arm on the elaborately carved overmantel. "So there's little hope? We must presume him dead."

"It seems so."

"And you are all well despite the contagion sweeping the town? And Phoebe?"

"Gave birth to a healthy daughter on July 2nd. We were not admitted into Islington. The villagers were in panic after what they'd heard. The birth was difficult, but the child is thriving and Phoebe is recovering, albeit slowly."

"I'm sorry I was forced to leave you at such a time." His apology was stiff.

"You were on the King's business. How is Lady Ryall?"

He glanced down at her sharply. "Oh, in excellent health. The sickness has not reached Suffolk."

She was about to comment, but Kate entered with a platter of meat and a tankard of ale.

"Will you stay here or go next door? You must be tired after the journey. Zillah will cook you supper. It won't be as palatable as you are used to, I fear. Food is in short supply in the city."

"Naturally. You've had a difficult time. I'll stay here tonight, to see how mother fares in the morning."

"I'll ask Gaston to make up a bed for you."

"That daybed will do well enough. And you?"

"I shall sit up tonight with your mother." She shook

her head as he was about to protest. "I never sleep well in this heat. Zillah has been a tower of strength. I've managed to get rest enough."

She thought, later, as dusk shadowed the bedchamber, that he'd told her nothing of what had kept him in Suffolk, nor what had now brought him home. He was as much a stranger to her at this moment as he had been when he'd asked her to dance with him at Phoebe's betrothal, yet as she thought of the intimacy between them during those nights at Hetherington, color suffused her cheeks.

After midnight Lady Isabel's condition worsened. She woke and gasped for breath. Hurriedly, Rachel sat her up, packing the pillows to support her. She poured Zillah's drops into wine. Lady Isabel swallowed, though with effort.

"Nicholas is back," Rachel said. "I'll call him."

"Nick here?" The blue lips writhed over the words.

Nicholas came immediately. His shirt was a pale blur in the dimness as he put an arm around his mother's shoulders.

"Don't talk. Just lie back. I won't leave you. I know about Kit."

"It's so very dark."

Hands shaking, Rachel kindled two candles and brought them closer to the bed. Lady Isabel's color was gray, her breathing labored.

"Nick—promise me—Hetherington—"

"Yes, I swear I'll rebuild when I can. I'll send Gaston for a doctor."

"No . . ." His mother's fingers clawed at his free hand. "Kit's child—keep her safe. Haven't seen her—because—because I feared—the sickness and—and—the mother is so like—" She turned and looked at Rachel. "Your wife, Nick. Sensible, loyal. Be—good—to her."

Rachel turned away. She had no place here. She

went from them onto the landing and stood, crying quietly, her hand clutching the banister. It seemed a long time before Nicholas joined her.

"She's gone."

"Oh, Nicholas, I'm so sorry after—after . . ." She broke down and sobbed. He smoothed her hair caressingly.

"I think she knew months ago—before Christmas. I'm grateful I was here in time. At least she had the comfort of one son by her." He swallowed painfully and she understood how hard it was for a man, unable to display his grief openly.

"I'll send Gaston to make the burial arrangements. She must be laid to rest in the churchyard of the new church in the Square."

The hawklike face was set hard with the strongly etched lines of grief. "When all is done, I shall take you from the city."

"Nicholas, we shall not be allowed. It is essential—"

"I will deal with it. I come from Hampton."

"There is Phoebe's child to be considered. If we go home—"

"I shall adopt Kit's daughter."

She gazed at him wonderingly—such a simple statement, solving their most urgent need. "Yes, Nicholas," she said thankfully.

Chapter 12

On a bright October afternoon Nicholas's new carriage trundled its way through the village toward the manor. The four weary women sat silent. Zillah cradled her son. Corinna's fair down of hair lay comfortably in Rachel's arms. Phoebe smiled tremulously opposite. She had been pathetically grateful when Rachel told her of Nicholas's decision.

"It will be as if she is our daughter. You will be able to see her often. But will you be able to bear that you are unable to acknowledge her as yours?"

"I must. Oh, Rachel, I could not have expected so much for her, but won't there be talk? Will father suspect? Suppose Roger has already—"

"Nicholas intends to call on Roger as soon as we arrive in Leicestershire to find out exactly what has passed between him and our father regarding the betrothal. I cannot believe Roger would divulge what has happened. His last letter was not couched in bitter terms. I think he loves you still, Phoebe. We can perhaps find some convincing reason for breaking the betrothal which would not be damning to either of you. Roger would be badly humiliated if the truth were known. It's in all our interests to keep this quiet."

"But father will be very angry if the marriage doesn't go forward."

"Possibly," Rachel said guardedly. "You may have to face that." She did not add that Phoebe could scarcely expect to escape all blame. "There will always be a refuge for you with us, you know that."

"But how will you and Nicholas account for your guardianship of Corinna?"

"Nicholas will say that the child was brought to Russell Street by his mother and, since her death, we have naturally decided to adopt her."

"But won't people think—"

"That she is his? Yes, I imagine that will be very likely. Talk will soon die down."

"Rachel, won't this hurt you?"

"I can accept it. Members of the Court do not consider such behavior reprehensible. Since it will be assumed the affair took place before our marriage, it can bring no disrepute on me."

Once again at Hetherington and in her own chamber, Rachel looked at the large bed somewhat nervously. Nicholas had made no demands on her since his return from Suffolk. Only once had Lady Lettice's name been mentioned. Rachel had said, "I shall be so glad to be home, but I imagine Hetherington will grate on you, Nicholas, after the excitement of Court life and the comforts of Lady Ryall's well-appointed household."

Those fierce green-blue eyes had found and held hers for moments, then he had lowered his and said, equally coldly, "Lettice is an excellent hostess, certainly, but Hetherington requires my attention. There's still much to be done before the winter, and I have obtained extended leave of absence from Whitehall."

He had gone into the courtyard for a final stroll.

Sarah came up with the warming pan. "It's turned a bit chilly, after all them dreadful hot days, my lady. I can see you're feeling the change, shivering like."

"What? Oh, yes, it's good to be here in Leicestershire again. The air is so fresh. It was decidedly oppressive in the city."

"I 'spect it was frightening, all them people dying of the sickness. There's talk in Leicester that there's a village in Derbyshire took sudden with the plague, whole families stricken at once. They've shut themselves off. It makes you think how lucky you are, my lady, to be safe here. Shall I help you undress?"

"Thank you."

Gratefully, Rachel stretched out between lavender-scented sheets. She dismissed Sarah and lay listening to the curious plopping noises which came from the moat. What of Nicholas? He would want an heir. She longed for a child of her own. Yet now she stared resentfully up at the bed tester. The thought of her husband's continued interest in Lettice Ryall was humiliating.

She tensed as he came into the room and, in spite of her misgivings, her heart stirred at the sight of his naked form as he stepped to the bed. The nearness of her husband's body in such intimate moments always produced this result.

He lay back for a while, his head resting on folded arms. "How quiet it is, peaceful."

"Yes, instead of that ghastly death cart approaching the house, it's possible to hear all the little animal sounds from outside."

"I wish I could afford to restock the deerpark, but that won't be possible."

"Was Lady Ryall's home untouched by the War?" She was angry with herself for mentioning the name.

"It was never besieged. They were forced to pledge their plate and tapestries. Timber was plundered, but the house remains comfortable enough. Sir George was killed at Marston Moor."

"Your mother wanted the manor whole again."

"She did—her last request to me," then, leaning toward her, "she also wanted an heir for Hetherington."

As he drew her close, despite her longing to surrender, something within her forced her to hold back. She was aware of his irritation, for after taking her he withdrew from her in the bed. He made no comment, but she turned from him, tears scalding her cheeks.

"Forgive me, I am more tired than I thought."

"Of course." His tone was coldly courteous. "This separation has been too long. You've endured too much this summer to let the thought of it go lightly. Sleep now."

But she couldn't. Thoughts crowded her tired mind and would not be dismissed. Phoebe and Roger: Rachel's heart ached for them both. Corinna: how would she face her father's curious eyes, when he saw how the child already resembled the Hetheringtons? There was still so much unresolved.

Nicholas had left Lettice Ryall's side, but for how long? And now he was back near Zillah again. Fiercely, she reminded herself of her resolve to accept his subsequent neglect with patience. She did not truly love Nicholas, did she? The marriage was convenient for both of them, that was all. Once autumn wore on, there would be too much for her to do about the manor to allow her time to brood.

She rose early and after breakfast she went up into the attic with grandmamma, where much of the furniture had been stored, to consider what could be useful for the new nursery. Though she had discovered portraits of Nicholas's grandparents under holland sheeting, they had not come across one of his father.

"Did you know Sir William, grandmamma? Was he a handsome man? Nicholas appears to resemble his mother."

"Kit was more like Sir William. The squire was a pleasant-faced man: big, square, brown-haired, nothing so striking as Sir Nicholas."

Rachel sorted through some linen, her head lowered so that grandmamma would not be able to read her expression. "I understand Lady Isabel was acquainted with my mother."

Agnes Wilson dropped some heavy fire irons with a clatter. Looking up, Rachel saw her grandmamma's face was ashen. She drew the older woman to the dusty window seat and put a gentle hand on her knee.

"What is it, grandmamma? I asked because Lady Isabel spoke of my mother just before she died."

"Just what did she tell you?" Rachel paled at her grandmamma's tortured expression.

"I couldn't grasp the meaning. It was jerked out and she was rambling but she said she could not 'forgive.' What was between them? I'd thought Lady Isabel despised me because of my father's stand against the Hetheringtons in the War, but there was more to it than that, wasn't there?"

Agnes Wilson nodded slowly. "I should have told you the truth before you married Nicholas Hetherington. Lady Hetherington found your mother and Sir William together in Malkin Wood. It was only weeks before Naseby, not long after Dorcas's marriage."

"You mean they were lovers?" Rachel's whisper sounded over-loud in the dusty, neglected room.

"Do not blame her too much, Rachel. She was so young and loving, very like Phoebe, and little older. The country was in a state of chaos. Robert and I wanted to see her settled. Simon Nashe had always admired her. He was a fine, steady young man, high-principled. I'm afraid now, looking back, that we pressed her too hard to accept him."

"But when did she meet Sir William Hetherington? Was she attracted to him before the marriage with my father? I don't understand. Wasn't she always escorted?"

"I don't know how many times they met, Rachel. There was one occasion when we were buying bridal clothes, Christmas 1644, that must have been. We saw

Sir William with Lady Isabel in the High Street in Leicester. I think I saw then, in his eyes, something more than courtesy, for, like Nicholas, even in those days of deep divisions between men of Puritan and Royalist persuasion, he was always gallant. I remember he swept off his plumed hat and kissed Dorcas's fingers. She was quite overcome, so young and shy, and he the Cavalier to his fingertips, and our squire. She married your father soon after, and Sir William was fighting with the King's forces near Taunton. Then he was wounded in some skirmish and we heard he was home at the manor. Spring it was, a fine golden May."

"She told you what happened?"

"She came to me in Leicester. She'd Leah Ashley with her, but I saw at once she was frantic. I took her up to my chamber. Fortunately, your grandfather was not in the house and she told me. She was so ashamed and frightened."

"And Lady Isabel actually saw them?"

"In a hut in Malkin Wood. And Leah was always fiercely loyal to your mother. Dorcas told me that Lady Isabel said not one word, but went riding off so madly that she and Sir William thought she'd break her neck. Of course, I was shocked that my Dorcas could do such a thing. I should have known how it would be between her and Simon Nashe. He was always such a stern, upright man, though fanaticism and bitterness came later."

"Then he discovered my mother's betrayal of him? That was why—"

"He burned the manor? I always believed so, though, to be fair, it was a legitimate act of war."

"But how? How did he know? Did my mother confess? Surely Lady Isabel did not—"

There was a silence. Grandmamma pleated the black folds of her mourning gown distractedly. Rachel waited, her thoughts in chaos.

"I can see I've distressed you terribly. If you don't want to tell me more, let it lie. Had it not been for Lady Isabel's illness, I should never have known, and better so."

"You have the right to know it all. There was a child. She miscarried. Simon knew it was not his. There could be no deceit. He'd been away from Glebe, in Fairfax's company."

"Dear God, how she must have suffered."

"He loved her, though she'd shamed him. He didn't denounce her. When you were born as you were, I think he considered your lameness a sign of the Lord's displeasure, and afterwards, when she died bearing Phoebe, he believed it to be the final punishment. He felt himself justified in wreaking vengeance on young Hetherington, the son of the man who'd tempted Dorcas to her own destruction. Phoebe is very like your mother. I think he can never look on either of you without remembering Dorcas's sin. If you have felt in the past an inability in your father to show you marks of affection, you can perhaps now understand the reason."

"Yet he made no objection to my marriage to a Hetherington."

"Yes, you'll recall I thought that strange at the time."

"And he never thought to marry again, until this last year."

"He has tortured himself continually with doubts about his own behavior. He considers he was weak, too easily forgiving. He had displeased his God and suffered for it."

Rachel looked bleakly out toward the moat below. How Lady Isabel had suffered. Had she ever forgiven William Hetherington? Those tortured words, uttered in delirium, had revealed the depths of her love for her husband. That terrible, silent venom directed at Dorcas Nashe's daughter had had its cause in that tragic affair so long ago. William Hetherington had died at Naseby. It was likely they had not had opportunity again to speak words of love or forgiveness to each other.

And Nicholas? Was he aware that his father's affair with Simon Nashe's wife had destroyed his mother's happiness and ruined the family's fortunes?

Grandmamma was weeping quietly and Rachel bent and kissed the gnarled hands clasped so pitifully on her knee.

"It's over," she said fiercely, "over long ago and we must now forget it. Those two are both dead and no one else must suffer for their weakness."

"But Phoebe and Christopher Hetherington . . . It goes on, Rachel, on and on. It happened there in Malkin Wood, probably in the same hut, for I doubt if there is another so near."

"Phoebe mustn't know. As for Kit Hetherington, he, too, is dead. All that matters now is Corinna. Nothing is going to spoil her chances of happiness."

When Nicholas rode in just before dinner, Phoebe was removing her coarse apron in the kitchen. She went out into the yard and waited until Gaston had taken his horse and he crossed to the door.

"Talbot was from home. I left him a message requesting that he call on us. There's been no word yet from your father?"

She shook her head. He made as if to speak, then thought better of it and hastened into the house. She went to her chamber and tidied herself for dinner. Toby had been sent over to Glebe with the news of their arrival. Her father would come here soon. How could she face his furious anger?

But then a sudden downpour that afternoon staved off the likelihood of a visit from Glebe. Nicholas shut himself away with estate accounts while Rachel and grandmamma took stock of the preserve cupboards.

Phoebe went into the drawing room to work on her embroidery. She was working a little cap for Corinna and was so engrossed in the work that when Tabitha knocked, she didn't, at first, hear her.

The girl knocked again more loudly and opened the door. "It's Mr. Talbot, from Barrow, calling, Mistress Nashe. He's asking to see Sir Nicholas."

Phoebe's heart missed several beats. She stabbed herself with her crewel needle and sucked at her finger, tears springing to her eyes—whether of pain or embarrassment at Roger's arrival, she wasn't sure.

"Isn't Sir Nicholas in his study?"

"No, Mistress Nashe. Shall I inform Lady Rachel?"

"Show Mr. Talbot in here first."

She was shaking when he entered. He stopped in the doorway, looking around for the company. His brown eyes passed over her slight form in her mourning gown and he bowed stiffly.

"Roger, please come to the fire. You should not have ridden over in this rain. I'll fetch Rachel. Nicholas seems to be out, in the stable probably, not far certainly, in this weather, but . . ." She knew she was gabbling away to try to cover her discomfiture.

"I came to see you, Phoebe, though Hetherington requested I speak with him first."

"I've treated you badly, Roger. I—"

He ignored that. "How are you—after the ordeal?"

"Gradually recovering my strength. Life was hard in London and . . . and I had a difficult labor."

"And the baby?"

"A daughter. We've called her Corinna. She is thriving. Rachel and Nicholas are to care for her. It will be all for the best."

"I see." He moved to the fireplace, waited courteously for her to seat herself, then sat down opposite. "You will be able to see her often, know she will be educated fittingly."

188

"Yes." The word was whispered. She looked down at her hands, twisting nervously in her lap.

"And young Hetherington? Have you seen him since . . .?"

"He—he was lost at sea. There was an engagement with a Dutch ship. His mother had the news from a friend on another vessel."

"Then your mourning is for him?"

"Yes, and for Lady Isabel. She suffered a heart attack and died in London. We thought at first it might be the plague, but we were spared that horror."

"I'm sorry. I must offer my condolences to Sir Nicholas." He looked beyond her into the fire. "Has your father driven over to see you?"

"Not yet." Her voice trembled. "I—I haven't seen him. He's written, of course, but his sentiments are always somewhat formal."

"He does not know, Phoebe. You can rest easy on that score."

"But how—what have you said to him of our betrothal?"

"Nothing. He thinks our marriage was delayed only because you were detained in the city by the imposed regulations against travel."

"But he will have to be informed that our marriage cannot take place. I—"

"I see no reason why it should not."

She looked up at him, startled. His grave expression showed no trace of anger. She gave a tearful little sob.

"I cannot hold you to it, Roger. If I am disgraced, then it must be. I—I am grateful for your forbearance."

"I love you, Phoebe. It seems you do not return that love; but I didn't expect you to, at once. Respect, consideration, these feelings we have for each other, and they are enough to build on. Now Hetherington is gone, you will need a protector."

She drew a hard breath. It was as if she had been

submerged in deep, muddy water and only now could see the sunlight piercing it. "You are sure, Roger? Rejection would be much easier to bear now than if we marry and you continue to hold this against me."

"I understand that. I'm asking you to marry me soon, Phoebe, quietly. That is only fitting, as I am only just out of mourning and the Hetheringtons cannot be seen to take part in open celebrations yet a while. Your father and Judith need never know that anything happened to alter our plans from the beginning."

"And you will not forbid me to visit Corinna? She will always be near us to remind you of the wrong I did you."

"It will be hard enough for you to bear, seeing her and not having the joy of acknowledging her."

"I have faced the thought of that since the day she was born."

"Then let me go to your father and name the day of our wedding."

He had risen and she hesitated. He reached out a hand to her. "Trust me, Phoebe."

Her eyes closed momentarily. A voice from the grave, laughing, teasing; a bittersweet memory of autumn bonfires and the damp smell of earth as she lay with Kit in the charcoal burner's hut. "Trust me, Phoebe."

She *had* trusted him and he'd betrayed her. He had said he loved her, perhaps had meant it at the time, yet only days later he had gone off to London in search of adventure and the nebulous wealth of the Indies. Even if Kit had lived and known of the child, he would not have stood by her. Rachel, grandmamma, even Lady Isabel had not had the courage to put what they knew into words, but she had read the ugly truth of it in Nicholas's look of pitying concern.

The joy of that hour had been so fleeting. She would cherish it always, knowing, instinctively, that few

190

women were fortunate enough to experience it. Now it must be laid aside.

Roger was offering her honorable marriage, a place at his side as mistress of the house at Barrow. She put her hand into his, diffidently. Their eyes met and he smiled encouragingly. He was a good man, if over-grave and stern. A commitment now to Roger and their children, this must replace her dreams of another life with a merry-eyed man whose touch had stirred her to undreamed of delights.

"I will marry you, Roger, and try to make you a good and dutiful wife, hoping you will, in time, forgive the wrong I did you in breaking my betrothal vows."

He drew her close, his kiss gentle and without passion, yet warm on her lips. As she drew away, she gave a little inward sigh for what might have been.

Chapter 13

The three families celebrated the Holy Season quietly at Glebe. Phoebe had married Roger in late November and taken grandmamma to Barrow to instruct her during the first tenuous months while she took over the household management. The weather had closed in early in the year and Rachel had seen little of either the Nashes or the Talbots. She had spent long days huddled before the fire in the drawing room, lonely for her grandmother's company, though her joy in Corinna comforted her considerably.

Early in March Sir Richard Summers had written to say he'd taken Magdelin and his young son, Lyonel, back to the capital:

"There seems now little chance of contacting the sickness. The plague pits and churchyards are being treated with fresh lime against contagion from the rotting corpses. The King returned to Whitehall on February 1st and, despite the icy weather, crowds lined the route to see him drive past. Normal business is being resumed and theaters reopening. Magdelin and the boy are both well, as I pray you and Rachel are also."

It had been some weeks since Rachel had seen her sister. Today it was chilly but dry, and the snow crackling powdery underfoot. Charley frisked across the courtyard, his nose buried in the snow, as she went to the stable. Toby's cheery whistle could be heard inside as he worked with Gaston cleaning the harness.

"Gaston, is it possible to drive to Barrow today or are the drifts very bad?"

"Non, madame, I hear the road is passable. I harness the bays, *oui?"*

"Yes, do that. I'll wrap up warmly and visit the nursery before I leave."

As Zillah did not come immediately to her call, she pushed open the door, her shocked gaze passing to the half-opened window where a watery sun and icy breeze fell onto the two cradles. Both babies lay unswaddled, their legs kicking delightedly free of their restricting bands.

"Zillah." Horrified, Rachel dashed to the window and drew to the casement. "Where are you? How can you leave the children uncovered in this weather?"

The gypsy came from the adjoining room.

"Lady Rachel?"

"Why is the window open and Corinna unswaddled?"

"The room was very stuffy. The fire is well made up and it's sunny out. The babies will take no harm."

"Take no harm? How can you allow Corinna to kick like that? She'll grow crooked."

"No, my lady. It's better far to give some freedom to move. See how she crows with delight. Those stinking bands are best off as often as can be."

"I don't care how you bring up Bart, Zillah. Your gypsy ways may well be right for him, but Corinna is gently born. Her legs . . . " Rachel knew her voice was shrill with anger, but her fear for the child was very real. Hadn't she suffered enough from her own disability? Corinna must not be affected so.

"Mistress Corinna's limbs will grow strong unfettered, Lady Rachel. Believe me, I know."

"You *don't* know, you only think you do. Swaddle her immediately. Obey me, Zillah, or I'll replace you as nurse."

"What is this?" Nicholas came up behind her. "Is something wrong, one of the babies ill?"

"They will be," Rachel snapped, "if they're left to lie in this icy room."

"I've explained, Sir Nicholas. My mother always taught me how good the air is for babies. It's pure like wine this morning. I'll do as my lady wishes if she's concerned, but—"

"You'll do as I wish always." Rachel's anger rose as Nicholas strode to the cradle where little Bart gurgled for attention. He lifted the child and it reached up chubby hands to grip his loosely falling fair curls. Nicholas laughed as he swung him high to the rafters.

"There's a beautiful boy. You show no signs of your mother's neglect."

They made a fine picture, the handsome fair man and the dark-skinned child. Over these last weeks Rachel's resentment of Nicholas's interest in the gypsy child had grown. He visited the nursery daily, and now that Bart was struggling up in his rocker, he was amused to see how the boy crowed with joy at the sight of him.

"Are my wishes to be countermanded in my own house?" Rachel said coldly. "I wish Corinna cared for according to my orders. If Zillah cannot obey me, I shall find another nurse who will."

Zillah's dark eyes flashed briefly, but she made no further attempt to excuse her conduct. Nicholas handed back the boy and drew Rachel from the room. His expression was thunderous.

"What fly stings you, pray? There's no call to treat the lass so discourteously. She's always served me loyally."

Rachel left him without a word, hastening down the worn spiral stair so that she almost tripped and fell. She snatched up her cloak from the riding chair in the hall. The coach was drawn up ready and Gaston sprang to open the door for her.

The carriage started off with a jerk and she leaned back against the new velvet squabs, knuckles pressed hard against her mouth.

She was furious with herself. How could she have berated Zillah so harshly? The gypsy could hardly be blamed for Nicholas's interest in her and her boy. She knew her anger sprang from her fear that Corinna might suffer as she had done. The doctors had assured her father that hers was not an inherited affliction, but what if they were wrong? She was also aware that her resentment of Zillah was intensified by her own childlessness. Zillah had borne a strong, healthy boy, and Nicholas made no secret of his pride in the child.

Phoebe welcomed Rachel joyfully and did not appear to notice her red-rimmed eyes.

"Oh, it's really good to see you. Roger is sitting on the bench today. Grandmamma and I will be very glad of your company. What a winter it's been. How is Corinna?"

"Very well, growing fast." Rachel divested herself of her cloak and handed it to a maid.

Grandmamma said, "You look pale, Rachel. Your hip isn't troubling you unduly, is it?"

"I always feel it badly in this cold, damp weather, but I'm well enough."

Phoebe looked from Rachel to her grandmother uncertainly. "I wondered if—"

"No, I'm not with child," Rachel returned shortly.

"I had thought you might be." Phoebe broke off, coloring. "Oh, I cannot keep it to myself much longer. I'm not completely sure, but I think I've conceived. I've not told Roger yet. He'd be so disappointed if I were mistaken, but it seems very likely."

Rachel felt the muscles of her face go taut. So soon. How unfair it seemed, that Phoebe could conceive a second child so easily, while she, Rachel, remained still barren after more than a year of marriage. She forced herself to congratulate her sister.

"Phoebe, I'm so glad for you. It will help soften the hurt of losing Corinna."

After dinner she asked that Gaston be called to drive her home. Once in the carriage she pushed clear the curtains and let the invigorating wind play on her face, breathing in the cold splendor of it. With all her heart she was glad that Phoebe was content, yet she could not dismiss her own smoldering anger at Nicholas's open approval of his gypsy mistress.

She was surprised to find they had a visitor to the manor. Nicholas came from the drawing room with their guest as she made for the stairs. Charley made a little rush at the man, barking shrilly.

She snatched him up and handed him to Sarah who came at her entrance.

"Rachel, you'll remember Sir Arthur Baxter, I believe. You met him at Whitehall."

Yes, she recalled seeing Baxter escorting the beautiful Lady Ryall. He bowed gallantly and she curtseyed. Baxter looked more prosperous than on the last occasion she'd seen him. His short jacket of green velvet was heavily trimmed with gold braiding and stylishly cut.

"Welcome to Leicestershire, Sir Arthur. Are you on business to the county, or perhaps you've come for the hunting."

"I've been visiting a friend, Sir Francis Maltravers. He has a country house at Belgrave, near the town. My stay has proved highly pleasurable, the more so now on seeing you again, Lady Rachel. I rejoice to see you so well after the tribulations you endured last summer in London."

Rachel extended her hand for him to kiss. "Thank you, Sir Arthur. You look in excellent health. I take it you spent the summer out of town, as Nicholas did." It was a barbed comment and she met her husband's frown coolly.

"I was fortunate to be traveling well clear of London for much of the time the sickness was rife."

"I have invited Sir Arthur to take supper with us."

"I am delighted, naturally." Rachel curtseyed and went upstairs.

If Baxter had called on Nicholas, was this an indication that her husband would soon be returning to Court?

Over the meal the men discussed the state of the capital and later fell to talking of more personal matters.

Baxter glanced approvingly around the dining room. "You appear to have done magnificent work in repairing the ravages. I noted the evidence of the disastrous fire as I rode in. Will you rebuild further?"

Nicholas shrugged. "That would take a small fortune, which I don't possess. My mother was obsessed

196

with the desire to see the great hall rise from the ashes, but that would seem to be impossible. Rachel is responsible for a great deal of restoration work."

Baxter bowed to her over his claret glass. "I'd guessed as much. What it is to have a a loving, practical wife, Nick. I envy you, man, and you'll soon have the hope of an heir."

Nicholas's blue eyes encountered Rachel's frosty ones. She fumbled with her wine glass.

"There's a great deal still to be done, Sir Arthur. Unfortunately, Sir Nicholas seems forced to spend much of his time away from the estate."

A little hiss escaped Nicholas's lips and Baxter raised one brow in surprised interrogation.

"You intend to leave for Whitehall soon then, Nick? Lettice and I spoke of you when we met a week ago, but she made no mention of the fact you were expected back in London."

Rachel's wine glass tilted and the wine made a scarlet trail on the cloth. Impatiently, Nicholas signaled to Sarah to deal with the stain.

"I've no such plans," he said stiffly.

"And how is Lady Lettice? Has she left her Suffolk home for Court now that fear of the pestilence is over?" Rachel's inquiry was over-polite.

"Yes, Lady Ryall has returned to Court."

"With many suitors dogging her steps, I imagine, so beautiful a widow."

Baxter's sensual, full mouth relaxed in a smile. He was clearly enjoying the verbal fencing between his host and hostess. "I think Lettice cherishes her freedom too much to surrender it, Lady Rachel. Sir George was elderly, though I understand Lettice had great affection for him. She now finds it pleasurable to hold court over a wealth of suitors. I confess I've laid siege to that particular bastion so many times without success that I'm forced to admit defeat."

Rachel played absentedly with the haft of her fruit knife. "Perhaps your circumstances render you unacceptable to the lady? The depth of a person's purse rather than his or her worth as an individual appears to dictate the gains in Court stakes, Sir Arthur. I would not be too downhearted as to the cause of your failure."

"You pinpoint my difficulty admirably, Lady Rachel." He laughed. "That may very well be the case, though Nick, here, is such a handsome devil he puts us all in the shade."

"You intrigue me, Sir Arthur. Am I to gather that my husband was once numbered amongst those unfortunate attackers?"

"Nick has won himself an inestimable prize, despite any earlier attempts in other encounters," Sir Arthur returned.

Rachel stole a glance at her husband beneath lowered lashes. His brows had twitched together in fury.

Changing the subject deliberately, he said, "So you've decided to investigate the possibility of investing in quarrying here in the country?"

"I've discussed it thoroughly with Frank. It seems he's already dismissed the idea of risking the layout of capital on his own property, but I'm impressed by the news that you've considered quarrying here at Hetherington, one of the reasons which brought me out here."

"My steward, Hawkins, appears to think such a scheme profitable. There's slate northeast of Malkin Wood. The problem, as with Maltravers, lies in acquiring substantial capital to begin the project. I've given Hawkins leave to investigate the cost of employing experienced workers from Mountsorrel, but it would be at least a year before we could hope to see any chance of profit."

"There's certainly call for quarried floors and roofing

198

in the newer houses, both in the country and in London," Baxter agreed. "These thin blue slates are far safer and more durable than thatch. Had you considered inviting a friend or relative to invest capital in the venture, your father-in-law, perhaps? I doubt if you could lose."

Nicholas pushed the wine decanter toward his guest. "We should discuss this in greater detail. I'm having all I can do at present to keep my head above water in the laying out of funds for necessary repairs. The estate cottages have been badly neglected over the years."

Rachel rose and curtseyed. "If you'll excuse me, gentlemen, I'll leave you to your business talk. I think the intense cold today has given me a headache. I trust we shall see you at Hetherington again soon, Sir Arthur."

At the door he kept her fingers imprisoned in his hold far longer than was necessary for propriety. She smiled at him graciously. Nicholas went with her into the hall. "I trust you are not too greatly afflicted. Get Zillah to brew you a tisane."

She glared at him as he bent to kiss her fingers. His lips were ice cold and she knew he was restraining his anger with difficulty.

What had possessed her to behave so challengingly? Once in her own chamber she sat down shakily. She'd succeeded in thoroughly rousing Nicholas by her baiting. Her barbs directed toward his relationship with Lettice Ryall and the implied criticism that he had deserted her in order to save his own skin during the plague crisis had not been lost on Baxter, she felt sure. It had seemed a fitting humiliation for the slight inflicted on her by his defense of Zillah Lee. Now she was not so sure of herself.

It was very late when he came to bed and she smelled brandy on his breath as he bent over the bed. He pulled impatiently at his cravat, tearing the lace.

"I trust Sir Arthur rides well armed," she said. "He leaves it very late to travel to Belgrave. Has he a groom with him? Attacks on the main Leicester highway have been happening more frequently lately, despite the bitter weather."

"Baxter is capable of defending himself well enough, with his tongue as well as with sword and pistols. I wonder at finding you so ready with yours, madam."

She swallowed hard. The candlelight revealed that his fair skin was unusually flushed, his breathing hard. He'd been drinking more heavily than she'd ever known him to do, and for the first time in their relationship, she was alarmed by his nearness.

"Sir?" she countered, jerking her chin in what she hoped was a gesture of unconcern.

She watched him as he continued to undress. His irritability showed itself in his impatience to pull off his clothes. She was at a loss as to how to placate him. Her heartbeat quickened as he approached the bed again.

"It seems I must instruct you in the art of entertaining, madam. You appear to be singularly inept."

Fear of him made her rush into a vituperative explosion of accusation. "Perhaps because I've not had experience of bandying quips with wastrels and harlots, however nobly born or clad in fine feathers. My inability to exchange scurrilous gossip and badinage shouldn't concern you, sir, since you'll soon be in more congenial company in London, though you may well miss your gypsy mistress and your bastard."

"I beg your pardon, madam?" He jerked back the bedcoverings, catching her arm and tightening his grip so cruelly that she was forced to bite her lip hard to prevent herself crying out. He shook her hard. "Answer me, what is the meaning of this nonsensical accusation?"

"Do you deny the child is yours? All the village believes it is, and understandably so, since you take such obvious pride in the boy, and countermand my orders in the woman's presence."

"Are you completely mad?" He struck her across the cheek so that tears sprang to her eyes. "Do you think I have so little sense of honor that I'd establish my mistress and her child under my own roof?"

Her teeth ached from the fierceness of the blow and even now his rage was not spent. "How dare you, madam, criticize me before my guest? If the thought of my seeking satisfaction outside my own bedchamber is distasteful to you, you might consider asking yourself the cause. I can see I've been too patient with you. I hold a maiden of ice in my arms and she charges me with neglect. Aren't my embraces passionate enough to satisfy you, madam, is that it?"

His eyes were blazing with that strange greenish light, and he thrust his face so close to her she recoiled, struggling from him to the far side of the bed. He was too quick for her; he sprang, his weight bearing her down, one hand ripping her nightgown from neck to hem. Sobbing, she tried to ward off the attack, explain, appeal for his mercy, but he was past hearing her. His kisses rained on her smarting cheek, her throat, fastening finally on her lips so hard that he bruised them against her teeth. She fought him doggedly, but he took her savagely so that she screamed and thrashed under his hold. Her fist pummeled helplessly against the hard wall of his chest, but he ignored the pain of the blows. At last she had the sense to cease fighting him further. Her guard broken down by sheer panic, she found her passion mounting to match his own.

Afterward she dragged herself away from him as he lay in a heavy stupor, his strong limbs sprawled against the torn sheets. She cowered back against the carved bed head, crying desperately, in an agony of fear that she would wake him. Her brain crawled with a sense of guilt and shame. He had used her as he would some doxy from a waterfront brothel and it was no consolation to know she had brought it upon herself. She had taxed him with neglect, adultery and, worse, by his book, cowardice. She knew now that her suspicions of Zillah were utterly groundless, that the gypsy's overt insolence did not spring from the knowledge that her master would support her against his wife whatever the provocation, but from her own inherited pride of race. Softly, Rachel climbed from the bed, careful not to disturb Nicholas. She crept to the chest and found herself a clean nightgown. Retrieving the ruined one Nicholas had flung across the room, she tore off a strip to form a pad, soaked it in the cold water from the ewer on her bedside table and bathed her bruised and smarting face.

As she turned back to the bed, she saw he'd awakened and was staring at her. She checked, one hand against her heart, restraining her panic by an effort of will.

"Come to me."

She hesitated and he half sat up. "Come back to me, I say."

She forced her leaden limbs to obey her. He reached up a hand and lightly traced the marks of his blows, already purpling in the greenish dawn light. "I hurt you badly?"

"I—I angered you, taunted you. You had the right."

"Perhaps. You touched my pride, and before Baxter, of all men. Come to bed. You'll take cold."

He drew her into bed and hard against him. She shivered and hoped he did not put it down to her fear. The heat of his flesh warmed her chilled body and she laid her head tiredly against his shoulder.

"I am sorry—about Zillah. I thought . . ."

"So it would seem. God's teeth, Bart is not mine. I cannot imagine where you should have got such an idea."

"You seem to take such an interest in the boy."

"Why not, he's a boy to be proud of."

Miserably, she considered her own failure to give him an heir.

"How should I know who fathered the boy, though I had my suspicions."

"Oh, someone in the village?"

He was silent for moments, then he said, 'I saw her in Leicester at the execution of that highwayman gibbeted later at Red Hill. Since Zillah is hardly the kind of woman who attends hangings for entertainment, it occurred to me that she had known the fellow well, very well."

"And she didn't seem distressed later?"

"You know Zillah. She never shows her anguish. You remember how it was with her after her mother's death. When I offered her employment, she told me honestly she was with child. I'm no hypocritical psalm singer. Why should I have denied her shelter for the sin of trusting to some man's empty promises? For all that, she must go if her presence here distresses you. I'll see she's compensated, give her sufficient to enable her to find work elsewhere, though it will mean finding a suitable substitute for Corinna."

"No, no. Zillah must stay. She is loyal and efficient. I would be churlish to dismiss her after all she did for Phoebe."

"As you wish." His arm tightened around her waist commandingly. "Now sleep."

He was dressed and staring out of the window when she stirred in the bed, wincing against the sudden pain of movement. He turned and looked down at her.

"You'd best keep to your bed today."

She reddened. "I—I couldn't. The servants—"

"God's blood, woman, when will you learn to disregard the gossip of underlings? I'll send Zillah to you.

She'll ask no questions." He frowned. "My own head's splitting. Baxter bade fair to drink me under the table last night."

It was the only reference he would make to his treatment of her and she accepted it ruefully as something of an apology. She moved her bruised limbs into a more comfortable position and sighed, knowing instinctively that she would be most unwise to anger him so again.

Zillah arrived within minutes. She took in the situation at once.

"I'll prepare you a hot tub, Lady Rachel, and make you comfortable in the bed."

Rachel was grateful to soak herself in the warm, aromatic-scented water, for Zillah had poured in the contents of a dark-colored phial. The bed linen was changed and Rachel sank back against the pillows while Zillah applied salve to her bruises. As she drew up the covering, Rachel caught at her hand.

"Zillah, I treated you badly and without just cause."

"Don't distress yourself, my lady. You're the mistress here."

"And if you truly believe Corinna would benefit from being free of the swaddling bands—I fear for her legs."

Her voice trembled and the gypsy regarded her gravely. "There's no deformity, Lady Rachel. The baby's perfectly formed and you mustn't frighten yourself about bearing a crippled child neither."

Color suffused Rachel's cheeks.

"I'll see that none of the girls disturb you. The marks'll soon fade. I'll bring you some drops in wine. If you sleep now, you'll be as right as rain later."

Rachel woke about six in the evening, feeling, as Zillah had promised, remarkably well. The gypsy answered her bell.

"I feel so much improved I'd like to go down to

204

supper, Zillah, it's just that—" She was peering uncertainly at the yellowish bruising of the cheekbone, already much fainter, but still noticeable.

"A touch of rouge applied with the haresfoot will soon cover that, Lady Rachel."

"I don't possess such a commodity, Zillah; you know that my father would have strongly disapproved."

"I can provide it, my lady. Let me help you into your gown."

A glance in the mirror reassured Rachel that her appearance would be unlikely to give rise to comment in the kitchens. Zillah had done well.

Disturbed by her husband's presence—she was clumsy at table, her hands shaking, but he behaved so normally that she soon calmed and they talked naturally enough of family affairs and of his plans for the quarry.

"I rode over to Glebe this afternoon, put Baxter's suggestion to your father. He seemed enthusiastic, so I'll call and see Baxter tomorrow. If something can be arranged between the three of us, I could be in business. God knows we need the money urgently."

"You think Sir Arthur will be willing to invest?"

"We discussed that thoroughly last night. It seemed likely."

"I would not have thought—" She broke off uncertainly.

"Go on. Did you take a dislike to the man?"

"Not exactly. He's courteous and attentive. Court flattery embarrasses me. It's not that. I hadn't thought he'd be in funds, certainly not sufficient to help finance your quarry venture. Last summer he appeared somewhat shabbily dressed."

"The thought has occurred to me. He's certainly come into ready gold unexpectedly." Nicholas shrugged. "It was always so in the old days in Paris. He'd turn up at our lodgings, the soles of his boots worn clear through, stay a while, disappear for weeks, then reappear extravagantly dressed, rolling in louis d'or and generous to excess."

"He's a gambler?"

"It would seem so." The hint of a frown drew Nicholas's fair brows together. "There were times when I thought he—however, that's all over long ago. He's not the business partner I would choose, but he's offered and I can't afford to be particular."

Inwardly, Rachel wondered at her husband's distrust of Baxter. Did it spring from the knowledge that Sir Arthur had once been a rival for Lettice Ryall's hand?

"Phoebe believes she is with child again," she said quietly.

"That should set Talbot's doubts to rest."

"She certainly seems to be contented."

Zillah was waiting in her bedchamber to help her undress. Rachel was thankful that the gypsy had kept the two girls from too close a scrutiny of her bruised face and body. She was shivering uncontrollably when Nicholas came to bed. He made no comment, lay for a while patiently, then drew her into his arms firmly.

"There's no call to be afraid," he said a trifle harshly. "There will be no repetition of yesterday's behavior." He was gentle with her and, at last, she slept, her head resting against his shoulder.

Both her father and Baxter came repeatedly to the manor over the next weeks. Eventually, Roger Talbot drew up the legal documents committing the three to furnish the capital for opening up the slate quarry near Malkin Wood.

One morning Rachel awoke early and was unaccountably sick. Nicholas was still sleeping when she returned, miserably, to bed. She lay still, her thoughts agitatedly considering the possibility. Her monthly course was late. She had no other signs, no tenderness of the breasts. Could it be true? Was she at last with child?

She waited several days before conferring with Zillah. Morning sickness had continued and her period of monthly bleeding did not arrive.

Zillah nodded. "I think we can assume you are with child, Lady Rachel. Sir Nicholas should be informed and Dr. Snell called in."

She chose to inform Nicholas that night, eyes lowered shyly, fingers toying nervously with the lace of her nightgown. At last she stole a glance at him. There was a dark flush of excitement on his cheeks.

He lifted her clear off her feet, his kiss hard on her lips.

"This is joyful news, indeed, the hope of an heir for Hetherington."

"We cannot be sure. It's full early yet. You mustn't be angry if—"

His mouth became suddenly tender and he touched her cheek lightly. "How could I be angry if this time we are disappointed? But we must take great care of you from now on—no riding about the estate."

As she lay beside him, her mind went back to the night of Baxter's first visit. She could not be unaware of the embarrassing likelihood that, in the frenzy of fear and passion, she had at last conceived.

Chapter 14

Rachel's pregnancy advanced normally. The first months she was miserable and uncomfortably sick as she'd expected, but once her early morning sickness was over, she felt extraordinarily well.

Zillah encouraged her to take exercise, but riding was forbidden. Nicholas expressed himself forcibly on that score.

"I'll not have you take risks, Rachel. The carriage is at your disposal. Get Gaston to drive you to Glebe or Barrow whenever you wish."

May came in with a burst of warm sun and fresh showers. The countryside was looking its best; hedgerows festive with May blossom, cow parsley already growing thick and green in the ditches. On one such fine morning Rachel ordered Gaston to drive to Barrow to call on Phoebe.

"Come to the village with me. Alice Newby is ill and, though I dislike the woman, especially since her vicious accusations about Zillah, I feel I ought to go and see her. I'd feel less embarrassed if you were with me."

"I shall be delighted. It's such a beautiful day. Grandmamma is resting, but I'll be glad of the outing."

Mistress Newby received Rachel's basket of delicacies gratefully, but with some restraint. After leaving her cottage, Rachel and Phoebe walked the short distance to The Sun, where Gaston had been sent to wait for them. The innkeeper greeted them obsequiously and escorted them to his private parlor. Rachel had always loved the cozy brightness of this room, with its scrubbed tables, pots of geraniums and the dull glint of pewter on the shelves. Phoebe sank thankfully onto the window seat and fanned herself with her kerchief.

"Mistress Nashe?"

Rachel swung around, startled, unaware that anyone else was in the parlor with them. The stranger rose from a seat in a shaded corner, moving into direct sunlight.

Phoebe gave a half-choked gasp.

Rachel stared at the man incredulously. His sturdy frame was wasted as if by long illness, his pallor ivory yellow, the skin stretched taut over hollowed cheekbones.

"It's . . . it's not possible."

"I'm not surprised you look at me as if I were a revenant." His lips twisted into a bitter smile. "My friends, not to mention my mirror, tell me I'm vastly changed."

Rachel bent instinctively to catch at her sister's hand as he sketched them both a gallant bow.

"Kit Hetherington. I cannot believe . . ." Phoebe's eyes brimmed with tears of wonder and joy. "We—we thought you lost. We heard that your ship was sunk many months ago—" She held out her hand to him, laughing shakily. "This is like a miracle. I have to touch you to realize the truth of it."

He laughed as he bent to kiss her hand, a harsh, dry little sound, a travesty of his former boyish one.

"Faith, sometimes I need to pinch myself to be sure of it, too, Mistress Phoebe."

Phoebe surrendered her fingers to his salute and Rachel could see how they were trembling in his hold. Her own thoughts raced wildly. Miraculous as this was to have Kit restored to them, she could not dismiss the thought that his reappearance would put a severe strain upon Phoebe's relationship with her husband, and now, with the child on the way . . .

The chambermaid came in with their wine. Rachel noted how Phoebe's hand was trembling as she raised her glass to her lips. Kit was chatting, naturally, easily, as if he had not come back to them from the other side of the grave.

Kit explained. "I was picked up by a Dutch ship, confined in a stinking prison in Leyden until three weeks ago. London seemed deserted. I was informed my mother had left Somerset House. I take it she is with Nicholas at the manor."

Rachel and Phoebe exchanged glances. In her sister's eyes Rachel read her agonized bewilderment. The man she had loved so dearly had come back, yet was now so cruelly lost to her. She struggled to find the words to tell Kit of his mother's death. It could not be left to Nicholas. The sooner Kit was informed of his loss, the easier it would be for him to accept it. It would be hard, indeed, for him to ride for Hetherington in hopes of seeing her there.

Rachel swallowed hard. "Lady Isabel died," she said quietly, "last July, in London."

"Of the plague?"

She shook her head. "No. Her heart failed. Apparently, she had known of her condition for some time."

"Ah." His mouth tightened. "I should have guessed. She was so anxious to see Hetherington again that Christmas." He rose abruptly. "Excuse me, ladies, I must get off to the manor. Thank you, Mistress Nashe, for preparing me."

What was she to say, how explain to him the changes that had come about since his absence, that she was Nicholas's wife, the new mistress of Hetherington? He looked so ill. How had he managed to ride alone from London and stay in the saddle?

Her dilemma was settled by the respectful arrival of Gaston in the parlor doorway.

"Madame, the horses are ready . . ." He stood, stock-still, mouth agape like a landed fish.

Kit swung around on Rachel, *"Madame?"*

"I—" she floundered somewhat helplessly. "Sir Nicholas and I were married last winter and my sister married Mr. Roger Talbot. You will remember—"

"Yes, of course. I attended your betrothal, Mistress Phoebe. My felicitations but, Mistress Rachel, I find this joyous news indeed." He turned laughingly to the stunned Gaston. "Come, man, it's me you see, no ghost, though I somewhat resemble one at present."

"Monsieur Kit, praise *le bon Dieu.*" Tears had started to the Frenchman's eyes in the suddenness of his discovery. *"Monsieur le Chevalier,* he will . . ."

"Jump out of his skin in his amazement, no doubt, but I hope he will see the prodigal returned with some delight."

He stumbled awkwardly, catching at the tabletop for support. Rachel waved to Gaston to help him.

"You are over-wearied. The carriage is outside. Let Gaston help you to it, Kit, please."

"Willingly." Kit smiled. "It's been a hard ride north, but I was anxious . . ." he shrugged, "to see my mother. Tom Spicer wanted me to wait till he could accompany me, but he'd business in the city. I managed."

Rachel guessed how bad it had been for him, resting up briefly in the inns along the way, alarmed by the possibility that his mother might not have survived the plague, driven on in hope, only to have that dashed by her news.

He insisted on Rachel and Phoebe taking their places in the carriage before him, then he allowed Gaston to help him up.

"Pardon, monsieur, I go first to arrange for your

mount to be attended. Our stableboy, Jem Paskell, can collect it later."

Kit nodded. He sank back against the leather squabs and Rachel saw how Phoebe's concerned gaze took in that bloodless, pinched look. He had suffered horribly in that Dutch prison. Twice he gave a harsh, barking cough which seemed to pain him, for he was unable to conceal from them the sudden spasm which contorted his features.

At Hetherington Gaston helped him down, and Rachel's alarm grew as she saw how he leaned heavily on the Frenchman's arm.

"Phoebe, will you dine with us and Gaston can take you over to Barrow this afternoon?"

Phoebe's tortured gaze followed Kit's unsteady progress into the house. "Rachel, how terribly ill he looks. You do not think that he may die, even now?"

"No, no, the journey has been too much for his strength. He will need to lie up, recover slowly. I would guess he caught jail fever in Holland." She looked around a trifle distractedly for a messenger to send to the quarry, for Jem had informed them that the master was there.

"I think Gaston should go for Nicholas. He will know best how to break the news, but first we must get Kit to bed."

"I'll find Zillah." Phoebe nodded. "You go ahead and arrange for a room to be prepared."

Rachel hastened to Kit in the hall.

"You should go straight to your room," she said firmly. "Eat and then sleep for a while."

"For a month, at least," he said wryly. "Faith, Rachel, it's all I'm good for these days, that and brief returns to consciousness to eat. God knows you'll see a change even in that. My appetite shrank in that rat-infested cell."

Gaston assisted him to the chamber Phoebe and grandmamma had formerly shared. He sank tiredly onto the bed, gazing around at the newly furnished room appreciatively.

"I can see the house has been put in fair order. I'll have to mind my manners, now Hetherington has so excellent a chatelaine."

"Indeed, you will, sir."

Gaston removed Kit's dust-stained riding boots and he lay back against the pillows at Rachel's insistence.

"Gaston, will you go to the quarry to Sir Nicholas?"

The Frenchman cast her a meaningful glance. Sir Nicholas must be prepared, not only for the incredible joy of reunion, but also for the pitiful change he would find in his brother.

He bowed. *"Oui,* madame, at once."

Zillah came to the door, ordering Tabitha to bring up a jug of warm water and fresh towels for the young master's comfort. Kit gave an amused yelp of laughter at seeing her calm acceptance of his return.

"So you aren't so amazed, my lovely gypsy. Did you read the possibility of the wanderer's safe return in the runes or whatever else you consult? I'll need some of your magical potions to restore me fully to life, Zillah."

She advanced to the bed, smiling that elusive, secretive smile Rachel always found so disquieting.

"That is very simply done, sir. I will see him comfortably settled, Lady Rachel, and prepare a light meal for him."

"Not too light. I'll eat no pap. I've existed on garbage too long. I dreamed of good food in that stinking straw, drooled at the thought of it."

"It is the first rule of magic, sir. Trust and obey your magician implicitly."

He reached for Zillah's hand and squeezed it, the old, impish mischief revealing itself briefly.

"So they were right about you, on that October day, my lovely enchantress. I was thinking of a different kind of magic, which you alone can supply."

He was irrepressible, Rachel thought, as she left him in Zillah's care. Not two minutes in the house and sick to boot, and he was attempting to seduce her servants.

Phoebe was peering anxiously up from the hall.

"How is he?"

"Utterly exhausted. Zillah has taken charge." Rachel drew her sister into the drawing room, well away from the prying eyes of the gaping serving wenches. "He will get well, Phoebe. Don't torture yourself."

"Oh, Rachel, I thought I was dreaming, imagining it. There he stood, so terribly changed, yet how could I fail to know him, ever?" She sank down on the settle, tears dripping heedlessly through the fingers which covered her face. "I—I don't know why I'm crying like this. I'm so distraught, it's just—just seeing him again when I thought him lost."

"We have all had a shock," Rachel said soberly. "It will take a while to sink in. Kit's return is marvelous, God-given, but we have to recognize that it poses certain problems."

"You—you mean Roger?"

"Roger must be told, certainly, and then there is Corinna."

Phoebe blinked away tears doubtfully. "You mean we must consider what to tell Kit?"

"Yes." Rachel drew a hard breath. "I think it would be better if Kit is kept in ignorance about Corinna's parentage, better for the child, far better for Roger."

Phoebe was silent, her face a mask of suffering. At last she said tremulously, "You wish me to keep silent, never to tell him that our love culminated in Corinna's birth?"

"How can it help, now?" Rachel said, knowing the words were brutal, yet unable to soften them. "You are married, Phoebe. There is the coming child to consider. Roger's child. If Kit were to know the truth, he might act indiscreetly. Kit is . . ." she struggled for the right words to express her doubts, ". . . irresponsible. It has to be faced. He left you, not caring if the result of your lovemaking could bear fruit and destroy you. He left his mother, fearing she might be ill—he confessed that to us just now—to risk life and limb on the high seas. The shock of his supposed death could well have hastened her own death. Kit is young, unthinking, he is not to be blamed for the heedlessness of his upbringing, but he cannot be trusted, either. He should never be allowed to interfere in Corinna's life. You entrusted her to me. You owe it to your daughter to keep your secret, Phoebe, however hard that is for you to bear."

She waited while Phoebe gazed bleakly ahead of her.

"Just now, while we were all sitting in the carriage, I was thinking, how can I blurt it out, tell him, you have a daughter and I nearly died in giving her birth."

Rachel drew her sister close into her arms. "I know, I know, my dear, but you must be brave now, as you were then. Promise me you will be sensible, do nothing to endanger your future with Roger."

"But if Kit seeks me out?"

Rachel averted her eyes. How could she tell Phoebe that in her opinion the affair had meant nothing to Kit, a pleasant interlude in an otherwise dull duty visit to the country?

"Then you must be strong. Keep your distance. If possible, do not give yourself opportunity to speak with him alone. Roger forgave your lapse. He has a right to your loyalty."

She rose hurriedly as Nicholas thrust open the door.

"Where is he?" His blue eyes blazed in a pale, incredulous face.

"In the second bedchamber."

"Gaston tells me he is ill."

"He looks extremely ill, has been in jail in Leyden, he says. Zillah is caring for him. I do not think he should have made the journey from London so soon. He was impatient—to—to see your mother."

"Does he know?"

She nodded. "I thought it best to tell him at once."

"How did he take it?"

"Stoically, but I think it was a terrible blow to him."

"I'll go up." He glanced impatiently at Phoebe, inclining his head in greeting, then they heard him taking the spiral stairs at a run.

Phoebe had striven to master herself.

"I should go, Rachel. I do not think I should try to talk to Nicholas now. I need time to think about what I shall say to Roger."

"Yes, I'll call for the carriage. You will consider carefully what I said? Kit should not be told he is Corinna's father, nor that she is your child."

A spasm of pain crossed Phoebe's lovely face, then she inclined her chin briefly. "I know you are right. Trust me, Rachel. I shall be—sensible. I must be, for all our sakes."

Nicholas came downstairs looking concerned. Finding Rachel alone, he said, "He looked so drained and exhausted, I forbade him to speak. I see Phoebe has gone. Did you speak with her about what our attitude is to be about the child?"

"Yes, I think I've convinced her that it will be in Corinna's best interests that Kit should not know she is his daughter."

"Far better so. It could only complicate matters further. Your father could discover the truth and Roger's position would become intolerable."

Despite Nicholas's objections, Kit insisted on rising and taking supper with them. Already he looked much better, though he ate little, toying with the food on his plate and drinking more claret than Rachel thought was

216

wise. His story came in short, bald snatches, while he played absently with his knife hilt, then ran one finger around the rim of his wine goblet.

"Tom Spicer got me out of that pest-ridden hole in Leyden, bribed my jailor. I don't know just how it was managed. I was more dead than alive—fever. He got me to Paris, nursed me for a week or more, then we took the Dover packet for home. I went immediately to Somerset House, only to discover that the Queen had left for France. They told me my mother had gone to your townhouse in Russell Street, but I found the house shuttered and boarded up. Naturally, I hoped that—she was with you at Hetherington."

"She was a tower of strength to us all," Rachel explained gently. "She is buried in the graveyard of the Covent Garden Church."

"How did you manage to escape the sinking ship?" Nicholas asked. "Were you injured in the fighting?"

"I don't remember much of what happened. Tom told you I was on board *The Royal Stuart*. I was in the cabin, heard trumpet and drum summoning all hands. I think I must have been struck by some part of the falling rigging, for I found myself numbed and bewildered in the water with the burning ship behind me. I was hauled out and spent the remainder of the voyage to Holland in the brig. When we docked, all prisoners were transferred from Rotterdam to Leyden." He smiled tiredly. "The weeks in the jail were mainly uneventful. Many of my companions died of the fever. The days and nights seemed to merge into each other, then I caught a fever. It left me with this wracking cough. I feel so cursed weary all the time. I'll mend."

"I think you've talked enough and should go back to your bed," Nicholas said, "We must get you well."

Once on his feet again Kit betrayed signs of the weakness which had so distressed Phoebe.

"I'll come up with you," Nicholas said firmly.

As the men mounted the stairs, a sudden wail came from the nursery. Rachel halted in the hall; then, at a quick look from Nicholas, came up behind them. Kit made for the room and stood in the doorway a trifle bemused. He looked inquiringly from the happily crowing Bart, whose wails turned to coos of delight at the sight of Nicholas, to Corinna, as usual sleeping contentedly, her thumb thrust deep into her mouth.

"Zillah's boy," Nicholas said quietly, and then, as Kit gazed down at the fair-haired child, "this is our adopted daughter, Corinna. She had been left in mother's care; it was incumbent on us to bring her to Hetherington."

Kit glanced up at his brother frowning, avoiding Rachel's eye.

"Yes, I see that. She is a beautiful child."

"She is." Nicholas's expression remained inscrutable and Kit nodded and moved softly out of the room.

Phoebe faced Roger and grandmamma across the heavy oak table, while Alice Mayhew grimly supervised the maids as they served the meal. Roger solemnly said grace and they ate in silence. Afterward they repaired to the parlor, where Phoebe took up the baby cap she was embroidering, largely to have her hands occupied and her eyes lowered while she strove to find the right moment for giving Roger her news. She watched him covertly as he carried his wine glass to the window to survey the garden. He was a handsome enough man, if rather serious in repose, sturdy, well proportioned. Her eyes brimmed with tears, despite herself. Roger loved her, why could she not return that love? She admired him, respected his gentleness and consideration for her needs and failings, but she could not hide from herself the ache of longing for Kit Hetherington. How could she continue to exist here quietly with Roger when she would now see Kit, perhaps daily, behave decorously in company, conceal her tumultuous joy at his nearness?

Phoebe stabbed herself with her crewel needle and sucked at the wound. She looked up at Roger doubtfully.

"I thought it best to wait till the servants were dismissed before telling you. Kit—Mr. Hetherington, has come safely home from Holland."

Roger's mouth parted in a little silent gasp. She saw him struggle to come to terms with his emotions.

"Praise the Lord," he said at last, fervently. "You saw him? Is he well?"

She shook her head. "No, far from it. He was imprisoned for months, has had jail fever and he coughs a great deal. He's greatly changed. Rachel and I saw him first at The Sun. I imagine he stopped there because he was too wearied to go on to the manor. We hardly recognized him, you can imagine how it was, he looked so thin and wasted, but Zillah is hopeful that with rest and care he'll recover fully."

"I must ride over, express my delight to Nicholas."

"I should wait a while," Phoebe said hastily, "the house is in utter confusion. Rachel packed him off to bed immediately."

"You're right. We must give the man time to rest and recuperate. Jail fever, you say? That's bad. Let us hope there are no permanent ill effects." He drained his glass and stood for moments staring into space.

Phoebe whispered, glancing meaningly at grandmamma, "We thought it best he—he should not know about Corinna."

A light blazed suddenly behind Roger's brown eyes and his mouth tightened.

"Certainly, nothing could be gained by his discovering that he is the child's father. I imagine he will accept Nicholas's explanation of how Corinna came into his care; it will be expedient to do so. If you will excuse me,

I have some reading to do in my study." He stooped and kissed her gently.

She drew a hard breath as he left her, then bent her head over her embroidery again, shaking her lashes to clear the misting of tears.

Over the next few days Roger had made no further comment about Kit's miraculous reappearance, but had dispatched a groom to Hetherington with his congratulations. Phoebe was grateful that her advanced state of pregnancy now made it convenient for Roger to sleep apart from her. It would have proved almost impossible for her to hide her lack of response had she been required to fulfill her wifely duties. Her whole being throbbed to feel Kit's arms around her and she despised the advancing heaviness which would render her ugly in his eyes when next they met.

By the following Wednesday her need to see him urged her into declaring her intention to visit Rachel. Grandmamma insisted gently but firmly on accompanying her, so there was no need for them to be attended by a groom.

Tabitha received them and ushered them into the drawing room.

"Oh, Mistress Talbot, I'm that sorry, but the mistress has gone to Glebe. I'm expecting her back very soon, though. Shall I bring you both wine or ale?"

"Ale, please, Tabitha. It's too hot for wine." Grandmamma sank contentedly onto the cane daybed while Phoebe paced restlessly to the window. "Is Sir Nicholas with Lady Rachel and—and Mr. Hetherington?"

"Yes, Sir Nicholas is at Glebe. There's a quarry meeting, I believe, with the colonel and Sir Arthur Baxter. Mr. Kit is in his chamber. He's mortal poorly still. He comes down to dinner, though."

"Thank you, Tabitha. I'll go up to see the baby. You need not come up. Zillah will be near the nursery, I imagine. If I want anything, I'll call her."

"Yes, mistress, she went up to feed the babies about an hour ago, has found some sewing up there, I guess."

Phoebe took the awkward stairs slowly, a further, hateful sign of her condition. She needed to hold Corinna, Kit's child, to her heart. Why, oh, why had she become pregnant again so soon after her marriage to Roger? At first she had rejoiced, knowing how the news had pleased and reassured her husband. Now she thought only that her condition would impede her in any possibility of meeting Kit in secret. Her heart quickened guiltily at the suggestion. It was wicked to encourage such longings, even to her secret self, yet already she was dreaming of engaging in an illicit relationship, which, if discovered, would ruin any chance of future happiness for herself or the child she was carrying. She had fought a battle with her own desires, lying sleepless, apart from Roger, but she was helpless to resist temptation and she knew it.

Corinna was lying contentedly in her crib, fingers reaching eagerly to capture a sunbeam which was dancing above her. Phoebe bent to kiss the golden head. How lovely she was, so like the Hetheringtons. The baby chuckled delightedly and Phoebe's heart stirred, as she remembered Kit's laugh, his glorious love of every facet of life and beauty. If only they could have been together now, the three of them. She was rising to her feet when she heard the sound that froze her where she stood.

A laugh, soft but deep in the throat, Zillah's laugh, followed by an amused chuckle—Kit's.

"I must go now, sir. I'm wanted in the kitchens."

"Wanted, not needed."

"I'm wanted here, not needed," the gypsy teased.

Phoebe remained stock-still, her lips compressed to prevent herself crying out in shocked pain.

"Aye, you are always wanted here, witch, enchantress. You hold me in thrall." Kit's voice was slurred with desire. "Your hair, the olive smoothness of your belly and thighs, the scent of you, like grass and spring flowers after rain. You make me whole again. Don't leave me yet."

There was a little silence. Phoebe tortured herself with the vivid picture of the gypsy sprawled in Kit's arms, dark hair spread like a silken web across the pillow, lips red and swollen from passionate kisses, eyes bright with the ecstasy of their mating. Phoebe gave a small sob of anguish.

There was a sound of movement within Zillah's room. A soft scuffling, a muffled laugh, as she dressed hurriedly, a whispered entreaty, as Kit attempted to keep her with him.

"The child. I must go to her."

Suddenly, she appeared in the doorway, lacing her bodice. Her wild hair flowed free to her shoulders. She stopped, dark eyes widening at the sight of Phoebe.

Zillah gave her a faintly mocking smile, which so infuriated Phoebe that she could have struck her.

"Mistress Talbot, I did not hear you come up."

Angrily, Phoebe said through gritted teeth, "I imagine you were over-busied, Zillah."

"Yes." The slow smile revealed that Zillah fully recognized the cause of Phoebe's anger.

Kit did not emerge from Zillah's room. Doubtless he had heard their voices and thought Rachel was back. Phoebe blinked away smarting tears. She could not have borne to see him at this moment.

"I'll go down and wait for Lady Rachel."

She was in such a blind rush that she lurched heavily against one curve of the spiral stair, stopped and forced herself to breathe steadily, take more care. What could it avail her now if she lost Roger's child?

When Nicholas and Rachel returned, no one seemed to note Phoebe's agitation and she fought to master her distress.

Her heart threatened to burst from her breast when Kit soon joined them. He was elegantly, if not foppishly, dressed in olive-green velvet which did nothing to enhance the waxen cast to his complexion. He was still appallingly thin, but walked more jauntily than he had at The Sun. His merry brown eyes laughed at her out of a face lined by much suffering.

He stooped to brush her hand gallantly with his lips. His touch scorched her fingers. Was he aware that only moments ago she had overheard his love play with Zillah? If he did know of it, he gave no sign of embarrassment.

"Mistress Phoebe, how good it is to see you again. I was not feeling my best when last we met."

"No," she faltered, swallowing the hard knot of anguish which had formed in her throat. "I'm glad to see you are recovering, Mr. Hetherington."

"Snell expresses himself delighted with my progress and Rachel has so improved the quality of life here I almost hate to consider leaving again."

Her heart lurched. She looked beyond him to where Rachel and grandmamma were engaged in talk. Nicholas had already excused himself. She strove to keep her voice level.

"You are already thinking of going from us?"

"Yes, indeed, I'm no country squire."

"You'll return to Court?"

"Not for long. I'm off to the Indies as soon as my plans are complete. Tom Spicer and I own half shares in *The Yorkshire Rose*. We shall sail for Barbados shortly. I've a mind to put my prize money to the purchase of a sugar plantation. There are fortunes to be made in the Antilles."

He prattled on and her future life assumed a sudden bleakness. Despite her revulsion, her eyes would always continue to long for the sight of him. He would so soon put half a world between them. She came to herself with a start as he said pleasantly, "I see you are to bless Mr. Talbot with the gift of a child soon. I am very glad for you."

"In September," she heard herself telling him quietly. She sought his features for any sign of special affection for her, longing to scream to him of Corinna's birth.

"Your child and Rachel's will be playmates and they will share the nursery with Nicholas's little adopted daughter. Is she not a beautiful child? I do not expect to leave England until late autumn, so, God willing, I'll have news of the children, and possibly act as godfather."

He chatted on, flattering her in courtly gallantry so insincere that she writhed inwardly.

"You know, Mistress Phoebe, whenever I was closest to despair in that dreary prison in Holland, I conjured up the sights and sounds of an autumn day at Hetherington—our rides together, your innocent beauty—and was comforted."

The reference to autumn. Her lips curled in shame. He called her "innocent." Had he forgotten so soon the spell of that magical day, how she had lain trustingly within his arms in the charcoal burners' hut, surrendered her "innocence," risked her very soul for love of him? It seemed he did not recall the incident, or if he did, it took its place with a score of other, pleasant interludes.

Grandmamma had called Kit to her. She was eager to hear the full story of his rescue from the burning ship and later, the prison.

"Come into the herb garden, Phoebe," Rachel said. "I'm so proud of it, and determined to show it off." Phoebe followed her sister dutifully.

"You look pale," Rachel commented as she stooped to examine a leaf.

"I heard Kit with Zillah," Phoebe said abruptly. "I

could be left in no doubt that they had been making love."

Rachel's face blanched. How could she tell Phoebe that Kit's manner on his return had been over-familiar with Zillah, amiably possessive.

"I'm sorry, Phoebe, I'd hoped you would not hear of this, be wounded by it."

"I love him so, Rachel. And now I realize he never loved me. It should make me free of all the ache and longing for him. It doesn't. I wish he had never come home. Is that so dreadful?"

"No, it is not. We all wish to keep our youthful dreams intact."

Rachel was in that pleasant state, wrapped up in herself and her changing body, which grandmamma had told her often accompanied pregnancy. She sat for hours in the pleasance stitching her baby clothes, leaving more and more of the household management to Zillah.

Kit was now almost completely recovered and rode out frequently with Nicholas about the estate and to the quarry. They were together there one fine May morning when Rachel decided to stroll within distance of Malkin Wood. She'd become lazy recently and Zillah had stressed the advisability of gentle exercise. Rachel called Toby to bring Charley's leash and the boy fell into step behind her. Charley joyfully chased white butterflies. The air was warm and Rachel reveled in the sight of buttercups and clover decking the meadowland.

They were just within sight of the wood when a shot rang out. Charley stopped dead, belly cringing to the ground in abject terror. Toby drew in close in a vain effort to protect her as two horsemen topped the rise. Horrified, Rachel recognized them, her husband and Kit. She screamed a warning as a second shot followed and both men leaned low in the saddle.

From the far side of the wood a third horseman appeared and men came running from the quarry. A matchlock musket was raised and fired. The men halted before the entrance to the wood and the horsemen dismounted. Nicholas was pointing, directing his men to scatter and search the copse. He turned as Rachel panted up to him.

"What are you doing here?"

"I was just walking. Nicholas, you are not hurt?"

"No, no one is."

"You were fired on deliberately."

"It seems likely." His tone was grim.

"A poacher?"

"Possibly." He frowned. "You should not have been running."

Rachel identified the third horseman as Roger Talbot. He was talking urgently to Kit. Both men swung around as Nicholas led Rachel to them. She was still visibly shaken.

"There were two shots. Whoever it was saw you all close, recognized you."

Nicholas beckoned to Toby, who was holding Charley tightly.

"Lead my horse back. I'll walk Lady Hetherington home."

"Yes, Sir Nicholas."

The quarrymen came back to report, shaking their heads.

"No signs of poachers, Sir Nicholas, they must have got clean away."

He nodded curtly. "Likely enough one of the villagers fired at a rabbit, got scared by the commotion and made himself scarce. Keep a watch, the rest of you get back to work."

"Aye, Sir Nicholas." The foreman took charge and Nicholas took Rachel's arm.

Kit said, "I'll stay with the men and . . ."

226

"No!" Nicholas snapped. "Ride on to the manor and alert Caleb. Tell him to have a search made of the grounds, but you stay in the manor."

At supper Nicholas had nothing to report.

"The park was well scoured for intruders, though it's unlikely any further attack would be made here. I'm taller than Kit, and much fairer and I wasn't wearing my beaver. The shot was aimed at Kit, not me. It whistled by his shoulder and damned near winged him."

She stared at him blankly. "Why should anyone wish to kill Kit? It makes no sense."

Nicholas poured himself more wine. "Kit might have been mistaken for someone else, someone who could have been expected to be with me at the quarry."

"You mean Sir Arthur Baxter—or my father?" She blinked unhappily. "Both men are square-built like Kit and Baxter is brown-haired, but, why, Nicholas?"

"I don't know. On the other hand we could be right in the first assumption that the assailant recognized Kit and meant to kill him."

"But Kit has no real connection with the quarry and—" She went suddenly cold. "You cannot believe that Roger . . . It isn't possible, Nicholas. Not Roger."

"My opinion of the man matches yours. Obviously, he's not pleased by Kit's reappearance at Hetherington, but is hardly likely to resort to murder and yet he appeared so conveniently from the far side of the wood. It remains a mystery. Kit is talking of leaving for London and I think it's better he do so at once. I'll ride south with him. There are legal matters to be settled, my mother's will. I shall be back within the month. The work at the quarry is proceeding to plan. My foreman's a good man and he'll take precautions to protect his workmen. It might be just as well if your father doesn't ride over there for a day or two unless some emergency arises. I'll call at Glebe and put him in the picture.

Baxter's out of the county for the moment, so he'll be safe enough. Certainly, you are to keep well clear of the place."

"Of course you should ride with Kit. There may be footpads on the road, and he's still not completely recovered. I shall be well occupied and I have father and Roger to call on if there's need."

As Nicholas went out to give orders concerning the journey, thoughts chased each other with bewildering speed through her brain. Roger Talbot could not be responsible for such a cowardly attack on Kit. But for whom had the shot been meant?

She jumped, startled, as Kit spoke her name softly.

"Rachel. I'm sorry, I frightened you."

"No, no, I'm still concerned about the shooting incident."

"Nicholas has told you I intend to leave tomorrow?"

"Yes."

He sauntered to the court cupboard and poured himself wine.

"I wonder if you would speak to Zillah for me."

"Zillah?"

He grimaced comically over the rim of his glass. "Oh, Rachel, you're no hypocrite. You must be aware I have some fondness for Zillah."

Rachel nodded stiffly.

"I want her to go with me, regularize our relationship."

"That is for Zillah to decide. I would not try to keep her here."

"She feels she has responsibilities, duties, which prevent her leaving."

"She is fond of Corinna, but I could make other arrangements if necessary. I should miss Zillah." She hesitated. "I always feel it is my duty to try and ensure her welfare."

"You need have no fears on that score."

Rachel sighed. "So be it. I'll have a word with her tonight."

She broached the subject as Zillah was preparing her for bed.

"Mr. Hetherington has asked you to go with him—to the Indies?"

"Yes, Lady Rachel."

"You have refused?"

"Yes, Lady Rachel. I stay here at Hetherington." The sloe-black eyes regarded her unblinkingly. "I shall be needed here."

"You know I would prefer you to stay with us, but—I think Mr. Hetherington would deal generously with you, Zillah. It could be in your best interests to go."

"No, Lady Rachel."

"You are thinking of Bart."

"Yes, the child's needs must come first."

"Would he not agree to your taking the boy?"

"Oh, yes, Lady Rachel, it has been made clear to me that my son would be amply provided for, but I wish him to be brought up here, at Hetherington."

Rachel was about to question Zillah about her depths of feeling for Kit, then thought it an impertinence. The gypsy had that effect on her. Despite their relationship, Rachel had the strangest feeling that Zillah regarded her as an equal rather than a mistress.

"I think you have made the right decision, Zillah," she said quietly. "I hope you will continue to be happy here at Hetherington."

Zillah's lips parted in a little smile, then she turned to prepare Rachel's bed.

Chapter 15

Judith Nashe turned impatiently as Dinah came to the door of the dairy. The maid eyed her uncertainly.

"I'm right sorry to bother you, mistress, but it's Sir Arthur, he says he 'as to see you."

Judith's dark eyes flashed imperiously and the little maid drew back nervously. The mistress had been more than a whit short-tempered these last weeks and she'd felt the sting of those beringed fingers across her cheek. The master seemed rare worried, kept to his study most of the time, hardly eating enough to keep a bird alive, then those men had come and upset him, and the letter! Dinah had seen him sit with it in his hands, whey-faced, then he'd torn it to shreds like it 'ud done him some harm and burnt it, pushing it down with the poker and leaning over it as if it was some foul cloth that could give him a fever from the touch of it.

Now *he'd* come again, Sir Arthur Baxter, and whenever he was here, the mistress got all jumpy and sharp-eyed, finding them all extra work to do.

"I took him to the drawing room, mistress, and Mistress Ashley's giving him wine."

"Very well. Come up and help me change my gown. Is the master still out?"

"Yes, mistress. He told Job he was off to the quarry and would likely take a bite to eat at The Sun."

Judith stared at her reflection irritably. She was not looking her best. Purple shadows ringed her eyes and she could see a deepening of the network of little lines around her nostrils and mouth. Was her condition apparent yet? That drawn look to her features? Was her pregnancy responsible for that or the incessant fear that nagged at her consciousness since Arthur Baxter had first come to Hetherington? She must tell Simon about the child soon. In the first year of their marriage she had longed to find herself with child, especially since her stepdaughters had both become pregnant. She was not so old, thirty-four, and still attractive; but now she dreaded the birth pangs and the months of waiting which would make her ugly and undesirable.

Arthur Baxter! Her heart pounded guiltily. She had tried so hard to fight the waves of hot desire which washed over her in his presence.

She was fond of Simon. She had burned to become a true wife to him, as she had never been to the sick old man her parents had pushed her to accept, bear him sons. Simon Nashe was still a handsome man and well enough when his cough did not trouble him. She admired his uprightness of spirit. And he had wanted her, and the early days of their marriage had been everything she'd yearned for. He had taken her passionately and she was fulfilled at last, a whole, complete woman.

Then it seemed that some cloud of doubt, stirrings of conscience, had overcome him. He'd become restrained, his eyes had slid from her naked body on their bed, as if he were ashamed to look on her, his taking of her mechanical, no longer joyful. She'd seen his burning glance pass over her and become cold, distant. She'd searched her innermost thoughts to find the cause. She had failed him in those early months by not conceiving, but he had assured her he was not unduly grieved by that. No, it was as if he castigated himself for his own sinful need of her. They had become strangers, living close, touching, but sharing nothing of their true feelings and longings.

And then Arthur Baxter had come to Leicestershire. His bold eyes had raked over her, his handsome, sensual mouth curled in amusement, as if he had instantly recognized the reason for her discontent. He had laid siege to her as if she had been an enemy fortress, determinedly but with infinite patience. His touch had been feather-light on her arm, courteous, assiduous, until it had seared through her being. She read in his mocking gaze his acceptance of her rigidly controlled desire and she had raged inwardly against her own weakness.

Simon had appeared oblivious of Baxter's obvious attentions, especially since the visit of those former companions of his, Master Hayward and Master Grant. Indeed, sometimes Judith thought resentfully, he seemed almost unaware of her presence at Glebe. Recently, he had taken to sleeping in another chamber, pleading that his constant coughing would disturb her; but even before that he had slept by her side as if a naked sword had been placed between them.

Could she be blamed if she had found reassurance in the glances of admiration Baxter openly bestowed on her?

She snapped at Dinah. "Get Leah to help you with the butter-making, and the cheese presses need tightening."

"Yes, mistress." The girl scuttled nervously from her chamber.

Judith pinched some color into her pale cheeks, smoothed her dark hair, on impulse removed her cap, then descended the stairs.

Baxter sprawled on the settle, a wine glass in his hand. He rose immediately, made her an over-elaborate bow and lifted her hand to his lips. She pushed him from her as his hot, lax mouth moved caressingly to her wrist beneath the tight buttoning of her sleeve.

"How lovely you are, Judith. Few women could wear that olive-green, my dear, without their complexions appearing muddied and sallowed in the process."

"Perhaps that's because I don't ruin my skin by the application of rouges and fards," she said sharply. "Release my hand, Sir Arthur, please," then, as he complied, smiling at her tolerantly, "what do you want? Simon is at the quarry."

He shrugged expansively. "I know he is."

"Then you shouldn't be here."

He moved closer as she turned her back on him. She trembled as his hand fell lightly, teasingly, on her shoulder, moving lazily upward to stroke the soft skin of her throat and cheek.

"Are you telling me you don't want me here?"

"Yes." Her reply was muffled.

"Truly?"

Savagely, she turned on him. "Leah Ashley is no fool, even if Dinah is one. She will know—and find the means to inform Simon."

"And that frightens you?"

"It worries me, certainly."

"He is a hard spouse then, our Master Simon?"

"He is a good man, stern, self-righteous, perhaps, but I respect his worth."

"And mine you find of little account?"

Tears glimmered on her thick dark lashes. "I—I find you attractive, Arthur. I cannot deny that. What woman would not; you are gallant, attentive and—dangerous."

"Dangerous?" His amusement deepened. "You flatter me, indeed, my dear Judith. Few women find me anything more than a divertissement—or some, unfortunately, a nuisance."

"*They* are the fools then," she said. "I've sense

233

enough to know that your interest in me stems from a need to acquire more than—momentary gratification, shall we say?"

"You belittle your own charms, Judith," he replied blandly.

"I gave in to you," she whispered hoarsely, "once. I shall not allow myself such a weakness again. Leave Leicestershire, Sir Arthur. What can you hope to gain here if I remain obdurate?"

"The hope perhaps that I shall persuade you to succumb to temptation a second or even a third or fourth time."

"That will not happen. I am with child."

"Ah." He tilted her chin, chuckling. "Mine?"

"Of course not."

"Are you so sure?"

"I am sure." Her voice sounded breathless even in her own ears.

He did not press the point, but seated himself on the settle again. "I hear there has been trouble at the quarry."

"Poachers," Judith said stiffly, seating herself as far from him as the furnishing of the room would allow. "Some shots were fired, almost hit Kit Hetherington."

"H'm." He regarded his well-tended hands appreciatively. "I thought Simon appeared over-preoccupied when I saw him today."

"Then you've been to the quarry?"

"How else would I have known it was safe to call here?"

Her complexion darkened in guilty shame.

"He knows—about the child?"

"Not yet." Her gaze slid away from his. "I was awaiting my opportunity to tell him."

"He'll be delighted, naturally." Baxter's voice was heavy with irony.

"Why should he not be?" she retorted sharply.

"As you say, my dear, why should he not be? Yet why is he so preoccupied? Quarry business?"

"I hardly think so. Sir Nicholas appears to have matters well in hand. No, I think something else troubles him."

"And he's soon to become a father again. A pity his peace is disturbed at such a time."

She frowned at the silky note of sarcasm. "I wish he would not concern himself over troubles long past. The War is over and done with."

"So, his old comrades of Fairfax's company have been here again?"

"No, but he has had letters—"

"From them?"

She moved fretfully at the blatant curiosity of his tone.

"How should I know? He doesn't see fit to inform me."

"Judith," Baxter said softly, "let me show you how much better I appreciate your worth than Simon appears to do."

"No." It was a fierce, husky whisper.

"Am I so inadequate a lover?"

"I have no complaint." He'd risen and come behind her chair. His wine-laden breath fanned the soft hairs on her neck. She gripped her hands into tight balls. "It was a betrayal of all I hold sacred."

"Afraid of the consequences?"

His lips touched the top of her head lightly, yet her pulses raced madly.

"Yes—no. It doesn't matter. I was foolishly weak. I—I wanted you, needed you."

"And still do. Am I wrong, Judith?"

"I am a Godfearing woman. I pray nightly, almost hourly, that I will be forgiven for this lapse. I would be publicly shamed and I should deserve it. I mean nothing to you, Arthur Baxter."

She rose abruptly, standing well clear of him. "You must go. Don't come here again."

"You fear for the child should Simon suspect you betrayed him?"

"I fear for myself," she said pleadingly. "Arthur, please don't come near me again. We have a chance of happiness now—the child. Be generous. Let me go."

"My lovely firefly, I'm no spider," he said laughingly. "I'll not eat you alive while you're caught in my net. If you wish it, I'll stay clear for the present. I have business in the capital over the next few months. This visit was really to pay my respects before leaving the county."

A faint murmur of regret escaped her. She would miss the mingled delight and pain of their meetings. On only one occasion had they been alone together. She had been attended by Prue in Leicester. Baxter had come upon them in the High Street. The dull ache of her longing for Simon's lovemaking had sharpened to breaking point. Baxter had paid her such ardent attentions. She'd dismissed Prue on an errand and gone with him to The Angel. They'd dined together in his chamber. Replete with good food and wine she'd succumbed to his fascination. Now the terrible fear that Prue would blurt out her suspicions was ever-present.

She'd been sharp with the girl, goaded by self-disgust and guilt. Feeling those frankly curious eyes fixed on her frequently since, she'd taken Prue to task repeatedly and, in the end, the girl had stormed out of the house in a temper.

He came closer, seeking a response to his nearness. He put up both hands to lift her face for his kiss. She struggled as his tongue probed between her lips and she felt herself frighteningly aroused. Shuddering, she put up the palms of her hands to thrust him from her.

"When I come back," he said thickly, "I'll test your resolve."

She pulled impatiently at the bell pull. Sickness rose in her throat like burning bile as she recalled her betrayal of her husband with this man. It seemed an age before Leah's slow steps answered her summons.

"Sir Arthur is ready to leave. Have his horse brought around."

Leah withdrew and Judith found herself agreeing to accompany him into the courtyard. He made pleasant conversation as she paced by his side.

Simon Nashe rode abruptly into the yard as they neared the stable.

Tragedy struck with incredible suddenness.

Simon pulled in his mount and made to dismount as Job came forward to hold his horse steady. Baxter called a greeting and he turned sharply in the saddle and stared at them intently. His eyes held a strange glitter and his gaze was so fixed that Judith gasped. Her husband made to put up his hand, choked horribly and toppled from the saddle.

Job turned his master gently onto his back.

Judith stifled a scream as she saw how her husband's features were twisted unnaturally into a harsh grimace.

"It's a seizure." Job looked up at her, awkwardly embarrassed by her distress. "Leastways, it do look like it, but he's breathing right enough. It's most sudden and peculiar like—"

Baxter took charge. "Get a hurdle or pallet, man, and move him to the house. Summon a doctor."

Judith could not bring herself to touch her husband. It seemed that in that one pathetic gesture before he'd fallen from his horse, he had been making an effort to point an accusing finger at her. She stood rigid, unable to cry or scream. Baxter took her urgently by the arm.

"Let me help you in, fetch your woman."

She shook him off, waiting mutely until Barnaby ran

back with Diggory Whatsize. They carried Simon carefully into the house on a hurdle. He appeared to be completely unconscious. Leah led her into the drawing room and sat her down in a chair. The old woman's experienced eyes passed over her.

"Now don't you upset yourself too much. Dinah must go for Lady Rachel," she said briskly.

Voices by the door, Baxter's and Leah Ashley's, then Dinah's, frightened, excited. Leah could be heard climbing the stairs heavily. Baxter came back to Judith's side.

"It's best I go now. He's in good hands. Let me know how he does."

Her eyes, huge with bewilderment and unease, searched his distractedly.

"He couldn't know," he assured her. "We were walking naturally, hostess and guest in courteous talk, not touching. All will be well. Simon's attack is an unfortunate coincidence, nothing to do with us."

She found her voice at last, though it sounded unlike her own.

"He—he was looking straight at me. So oddly—accusing."

"He's ill," he sighed. "He's not a young man, Judith. Don't torture yourself. I must leave. The house will soon be full of his relatives. The doctor will call." Embarrassed, he added, "Take care of yourself. Leave the nursing to the servants."

She stared after him as he stalked out. He was implying that she, too, was no longer young. She swallowed hard and found the strength to move. Rachel would soon be here. There would be questions, demands made on her. She forced herself to go to his chamber.

Simon lay like a log in the huge bed, his face contorted. Leah fussed round him. The old woman looked up and her eyes met Judith's challengingly.

Judith put a hand to her mouth to choke back a sob. She knew the signs. Simon could lie like this for weeks, months. He might never recover, if he did not die very soon now.

She could not bear it again, not after all those endless, vain years of tending Josiah.

She gave a little choked cry and fled to her chamber.

Leah hastened down the steps to greet Rachel.

"How is he? Will Judith mind if I go straight in?"

"I shouldn't think so," Leah commented grimly. "She's locked herself in her chamber and hasn't been to see him since we first carried him in. His condition is unchanged. He can't move or speak. It's a seizure right enough. I've seen too many of them to be mistaken." Her eyes met those of Zillah, who'd come with her mistress. The gypsy inclined her head.

Rachel halted on the landing, striving to read Leah's expression in the dim light from the upper window. "Her chamber? I don't understand. Isn't she sharing my father's room?"

"He moved out some time ago. He'd been having disturbed nights. His cough has been bad."

Rachel stooped her head to enter her father's room. It was pitiful how his eyes appealed though he could not so much as turn his head to look at her. He was fully conscious, and recognized her.

"Phoebe will soon be here, father, and Dr. Snell is on his way."

His mouth was twisted downwards on the right and a dribble of saliva escaped from his slack mouth. She remained by the bedside holding his chilled hand until the doctor's trap had driven into the courtyard and she went down to speak with him, pausing on the way to tap on Judith's door.

"The doctor is here, Judith. He'll want to talk to you."

There was no answer and she'd descended and stayed with the doctor, then went up with him and Leah while he made his examination.

"It is as I feared, Lady Rachel: a seizure, a bad one. It's taken him worse down the right side. There's a tremor of movement in his left hand. It's fortunate it's not the heart side."

"Will he recover?" She knew the question foolish, for common sense told her the doctor could not give a reliable answer.

He pursed his lips. "He's a relatively young man and his heart's sound. I can't say yet how badly he'll be affected and, of course, there's always the possibility of further attacks. He must be kept very quiet, not only now, while he's laid low, but afterwards." He looked around doubtfully as if suddenly aware that the mistress had not put in an appearance. "Is Mistress Nashe away?"

"She was so alarmed she fainted, and I thought it best to have her keep to her chamber."

"Sensible." He consulted his watch. "I'll send my groom over with a sleeping posset and I'll call tomorrow, early. Send at once if there's any change in his condition."

"Will he—will he be able to speak soon?"

He avoided her eyes. "That's hard to say, Lady Rachel." He glanced at her, mildly reproving. "Try not to get yourself into a state. Will you stay here?"

"I think it best, but Leah and Zillah will see that I behave sensibly."

"Good."

She sank back in her chair, fingertips gripping the arms tightly. It was not going to be easy. How could she wield authority here at Glebe, with Judith still under its roof, yet, undoubtedly, her stepmother was behaving very oddly. Rachel breathed a sigh of relief as Judith came into the room. She rose respectfully.

"Judith, are you feeling better? You've just missed the doctor."

"Is Simon going to be paralyzed?" The words were diamond-hard.

"We don't know yet. Dr. Snell offers hopes of recovery. You should go to him, Judith, he will need you."

A shudder ran through her stepmother's body. "I—can't. I am going back to Mountsorrel for a while."

The statement, so baldly uttered, took Rachel's breath away.

"Judith, you can't. That would be too cruel."

"Why can't I? I kept the house on. A mercy it was never sold. I'm with child at last. That must be my first consideration. Simon would wish me to take great care." She turned away. "I can't do it, Rachel, so there's no point in you chiding me. That constant stink of sickness. I endured it for years on end. I'll not do it again."

Rachel blinked. "I see. Father will understand and be relieved you will be well away from here where you won't run the risk of exhausting yourself."

Judith's dark eyes darted a glance at Rachel, half curious, half suspicious.

"I shall move in here. Phoebe will come often, though she is very near her time, and Leah is a treasure. I'll send Dinah up to help you pack."

Judith hesitated. Rachel guessed she was engaged in struggling with her conscience. Something more than her father's sickness was troubling Judith. She was sure of it.

"I'll keep you informed of my father's condition, naturally."

Judith nodded and left in a swish of green taffeta.

Rachel found it hard to explain the situation to Phoebe and grandmamma when they arrived. She had taken her sister up to see their father, but he had

241

already dozed off. Downstairs in the drawing room Phoebe was bitter concerning Judith's decision.

"How could she desert him like that when he needs her most?" she said hotly.

Rachel shook her head. "I don't think it was easy. She looked almost—guilty. I had the uncomfortable feeling that she blamed herself for his attack, though I don't see how that could be possible."

"You don't think they are happy together?"

"Leah says he's moved out of their chamber." Rachel sighed. "I thought him content with the match. Now, I don't know." Uneasily, she recalled the betrayal of her father by her own mother. Surely this had not happened again? She had noticed on more than one occasion that Sir Arthur Baxter had paid her stepmother marked attentions, but she surmised that was his way. Suddenly, the full weight of the tragedy took hold. Tears pricked at her lashes. Her father was a stern, unyielding man, but he did not deserve this.

Phoebe was anxious for her. "You look white and shocked. How will you manage?"

"I shall stay. Zillah can move here with the children and Leah is utterly reliable."

"Grandmamma, perhaps you should stay with Rachel?"

"No, you need companionship." Rachel forced a confident smile. "I can send to Barrow if I need grandmamma. I'll dispatch a groom to London to inform Nicholas, although he may already be on his way home."

Phoebe went up again to see her father, but as he was still sleeping, allowed herself to be driven off to Barrow.

There was little change in Simon Nashe's condition over the next three days. His eyes flashed at the mention of Judith and again Rachel was aware that there was more between her father and stepmother than her callous decision to desert him on his sickbed.

Did he know of Judith's condition? She had discussed the matter cautiously with Leah. The old woman was wary.

"She never told me, but I know."

"But does my father know?"

"I don't think he does." Their eyes met and Rachel shook her head in bewilderment. She could not broach the matter of Sir Arthur Baxter's visits here, not even to a servant as fiercely loyal as Leah.

On the fourth day strangers from London arrived.

A scared-looking Dinah conducted them into the drawing room.

"These gentlemen insist on seeing the master, Lady Rachel. I keep telling them he's poorly and—"

"Thank you, Dinah. You can go. I'll explain. What can I do for you, gentlemen? I am Colonel Nashe's daughter, Lady Rachel Hetherington."

The older man she judged to be about her father's age. He was dressed soberly in a plain-cut, almost Puritanical coat of bottle-green fine worsted. He introduced himself gravely and courteously.

"I am Master Thomas Wright, at your service, my lady. My colleague is Mr. William Clevedon. We are on the King's business and have a warrant." He placed before her on the table a heavy parchment, its blood-red seal oddly menacing. "I require access to Mr. Nashe's study, his drawers, desk, papers and bedchamber."

Rachel went deathly cold. She was trembling with an unnamed fear, but she faced them fiercely.

"As my maid explained, sir, my father has been taken gravely ill. It is impossible that you should invade his chamber. Our physician has warned us against exciting him."

"Unfortunately," the younger man interposed, "it is imperative that we question him."

"At present my father has not the power of speech," Rachel replied tartly. "Dr. Snell has no notion when that will return to him, if ever. You behave, sirs, as if he were guilty of some crime."

"Mr. Nashe was, I believe, a former colonel in Fairfax's company, well known to the tyrant, Cromwell." Mr. Clevedon was taking the initiative once more and he checked her before she could add further objections.

"He was, but is now totally loyal to His Majesty. My husband, who is gentleman of the bedchamber, will attest to the truth—"

"Lady Rachel, we are aware of Sir Nicholas Hetherington's standing at Court and of his former loyal service above and beyond the call of duty—and the cost he paid for it. We mean you no discourtesy but merely request that, since your father is too sick to do so, you place at our disposal the means of concluding our business."

She stared numbly from one to the other. Mr. Wright was smiling, Clevedon impassive. She rose and led the way to her father's study, taking from the chatelaine at her waist the keys to the room and desk.

"I do not know if these will open all the drawers in the room. I prefer that you complete your search before disturbing my father. If necessary, you must force the locks. I'll inform my brother-in-law, Mr. Talbot of Barrow, of your presence here. He is a magistrate and will best know how to advise me in my husband's absence."

Wright bowed. "Thank you, Lady Hetherington. We will cause your household as little disruption as possible. Is your father able to communicate in any way whatever?"

"I cannot allow you to hector him, sir. I believe he understands what we say, but he cannot, as yet, nod or move his hands."

"Then it would be cruel and useless to force our attentions on him."

Rachel compressed her lips angrily as Clevedon deliberately drew to the study door, excluding her. Heart pounding, she retraced her steps to the drawing room to write a note to Roger, then hastened down to the stables to call Job.

"Go to Barrow and give this to Mr. Talbot. If he is out, wait till he returns. Impress on him how urgent my business is."

"Aye, Lady Rachel." The old man shook his head doubtfully, saddled a mare and was off within minutes.

Rachel avoided the eyes of the avidly curious servants. Dinah was sniveling nervously. Rachel hurried up to her father's chamber.

She sat close to the bed and took her father's left hand in hers. Once she had detected in it some tremor or movement. Perhaps, in dire need, he might find the means of making her understand his fears and wishes. She told him, as quietly and calmly as possible, the identity of the two officials and of the conversation she'd had with them.

"Squeeze my hand if you can, to indicate yes. Is there anything I can do to restrain them from searching?"

He struggled pitifully to answer her.

"We've no reason to fear, father. This must be a mistake."

His tortured eyes beseeched her to understand him and she felt the faintest movement of the fingers imprisoned in her grasp.

"This mention of Cromwell? This is connected with some incident which happened during the last War?"

Again a definite faint movement.

"But it is over so long ago, surely you've nothing to keep hidden now?"

The answering squeeze was stronger now. She felt sick with a nameless terror. The King had pardoned all those who had taken up arms against him except—her eyes blurred suddenly as she saw those decayed heads she'd viewed with Nicholas above the Tower on her visit to London. "The Regicides." Only those men who had assented to and facilitated the execution of the King's father had suffered. Rachel's father had been shocked to hear of the arrest in October 1666 of Major General Harrison who had been subsequently hanged and quartered at Charing Cross, dying bravely as a soldier should. On the anniversary of the martyred King's death the bodies of Cromwell, Ireton and Bradshaw had been exhumed from their tombs in the Abbey and hung on a common gallows at Tyburn. But her father had not been involved with the greatest in the realm. He had not put his name to that fatal death warrant.

Rachel stared down at him distractedly. She suspected that it was this terrible event in the past he feared. Had he been approached by Cromwell by letter, testing out his opinion on this far-reaching decision? She bent close and mouthed the words.

"Was there a letter from Cromwell concerning the death of the King?"

Wonderingly, she saw a writhing of his lips and the first syllable uttered since he'd fallen from his saddle. "Yes."

She closed her eyes in sick horror. Why had he been so foolish as to keep a letter so damning, once the King ascended the throne again? He had venerated the Lord

Protector as the country's savior, the victor of Marston Moor and Naseby, but surely he had kept those mementoes safe hidden? If so, who could have betrayed him so long after the event? Who could have known of their existence?

"Can I get the letter, destroy it?"

"Study—" Grimly, he forced out the words. "They'll—tear—the panels—find it."

"I don't understand this, after all this time. Even if it is discovered, how could it harm you?"

"Old companions—came—weeks ago—tried to implicate . . ." Spittle formed at the corners of his mouth and he struggled on gamely. "If—the letter is found—I could be—questioned—forced to—divulge names—doom them—and me."

"A plot—on the King's life?" Her horrified whisper seemed to echo in the room.

He nodded exhaustedly.

So that was what had been preying on his mind these last weeks. He had seemed unnaturally depressed. She had believed him concerned for the success of the quarry and alarmed by the attacks made on Nicholas and Kit.

The stultifying truth hit her like a physical blow. Had this dread been the cause of him being stricken down, not his suspicions of Judith's interest in Baxter—for that had not been lost on Rachel. Then why had Judith fled so desperately from Glebe? Another possibility occurred to her as one thought chased another hurriedly through her brain. Had the unknown assailant at the quarry mistaken Kit for her father? At the time Nicholas had been taken up with that idea. Now all seemed to fall into place and her father was in grave peril of his life. What was to be done?

She forced a smile. "Our one hope is Nicholas. He will go to the King, plead for you. Be of good heart."

She went outside, leaning, exhausted, against the door. Those fools, attempting to persuade her father to an act of treason. Hayward and Grant! She remembered now that Judith had spoken of the visit of her father's two companion officers that night when they had first entertained Baxter at Hetherington. Baxter? Had Judith wittingly or unwittingly spoken too plainly of her husband's affairs to her constant admirer, for the man had made no secret of his interest in her stepmother. How much had Judith known, blurted out? Rachel searched her tired mind for any reference to Baxter which could point to such a chilling possibility. Though he had accepted the man as his partner, Rachel was sure her husband distrusted him. He was always in funds, he'd said. Was he a paid spy? She shivered, chilled with fear.

Fortunately, Job had found Roger at home and he rode over immediately. He listened without interruption and she could see by his expression that he was as bewildered and concerned as she was.

"Where are they now?"

"Still in father's study. Roger, could they arrest him, carry him off to prison? He'd not survive."

"That's unlikely. They'll need hard evidence to indict." He forced a confident smile. "It has been so long since any regicide was tried and executed, I cannot imagine the King would order his officers to proceed against your father now."

"But there's the matter of this plot. Though father will have refused to countenance any part in it, he will be most anxious to avoid revealing information which could damn his friends. If father is indicted, he'd die in jail. Roger, I must go to London to Nicholas."

"But he could be well on his way home by now. He should have been informed of your father's illness. You could miss each other on the journey."

"I know, but time is vital now. If necessary, I will plead with His Majesty myself for my father's pardon. He received me kindly when I went to Court, made me a gift of Charley."

"You should not travel in your condition. The roads will be hard-rutted. The journey will be acutely uncomfortable, if not downright dangerous, to you and the child."

"I have to go, Roger. I think . . . " Her eyes blurred with sudden tears. "I think Nicholas would do this for me. He might refuse anyone else. Father *did* order the destruction of his property. It must rankle. I'm carrying his heir. That must count for something. I must be there to beg him to intervene."

He nodded soberly. "Then I must escort you."

"Phoebe will need you here when her time comes."

"Phoebe loves her father. She'll see the need. I can't let you go alone, subject to insults along the way and at Whitehall if by any chance Nicholas should be away from his lodging."

There was a curt command from the courtyard. The two officials were preparing to ride out. Wright paused in the act of mounting, removed his foot from the stirrup and crossed to her side.

"I regret that I've been forced to trouble you at such a time, Lady Hetherington. We have not found it necessary to intrude on Mr. Nashe. I hope he will soon be sufficiently recovered to sit out in his own gardens in this fine weather. Good day to you."

She suffered his kiss on her fingertips, nodded, and clutched at the gatepost as, with a flurry of dust, the two men swept out of the yard. Roger touched her imperatively on the arm.

"The study, let's see what's been done."

She stopped short in the doorway, her limbs turning to water beneath her. The paneling had been forced from the wall though, typical of the correctness of their visitors, the sections had been stood down neatly. Even the drawers and chests had been scrupulously tidied and their contents replaced. She gave a little hopeless sob. "They found what they were looking for and without too much trouble, it seems. I'm frightened, Roger. They seemed so chillingly efficient."

"I'll get back to Barrow and pack a valise. Grandmamma should be here with your father."

"He's better, I think, he even managed to speak to me, but this business is likely to cause a relapse. Phoebe shouldn't be left."

"Then both must come over. Get your maid to pack necessities. We must leave as soon as possible. We can make two or three hours journeying before dark. Is the coach here or at Hetherington?"

"Here."

"Then order Gaston to make ready. Best take that London urchin of yours. He knows the capital and may prove invaluable to send on errands."

"Yes, he can take care of the dog."

His incredulous expression brought the ghost of a smile to her lips. "You can have no idea how Charles dotes on his darlings. Charley could soften his heart toward me."

"In that case . . . " He lifted his shoulders in a bewildered little gesture and let them fall. "A reliable maid?"

"Sarah. Zillah must stay with the babies."

She went to the stables to find Gaston after sending one of the stablehands to give her instructions to Sarah. Toby was sent to bring the spaniel from Hetherington. Gaston received her news with his usual calm.

"We may pass Sir Nicholas on the road, but we must risk that. Mr. Talbot thinks we should go well armed."

"Certainement, madame."

Her father was conscious when she went up and his eyes spoke to her of his desperation.

"They've gone. The paneling was forced, so we must assume they have what they came for. I'm going to London at once."

"No." His eyes were anxious.

"I must, father. I'll take care and Roger is going with me." She stooped and kissed him. Two slow tears squeezed from beneath his sparse lashes, but he nodded slowly.

There was no more time to despair.

Zillah came to the carriage door. "We've seen to it there are ample cushions to protect you against jolts, but take all possible care, my lady."

Roger had returned hastily with Phoebe and grandmamma. They embraced tearfully before Rachel took her place in the coach, holding tightly to Charley, an excited Sarah opposite, Gaston and Toby on the box, Roger on horseback.

As the vehicle swept onto the main Leicester road, she reflected that neither of the officials had seemed surprised that Mistress Nashe was not present in her own house to tend her husband. Was that fact significant?

Chapter 16

A young lackey answered Gaston's knock. Roger assisted Rachel out of the carriage. She could hardly walk, she was so stiff, and her hip caused extreme discomfort. But all the misery of the journey was forgotten now that she would soon be able to call on Nicholas's assistance.

The young servant's face expressed utter incredulity at the sight of her. Hastily, he tidied his hair and ran a nervous finger around his grubby collar.

"Sir Nicholas Hetherington, is he at home?" Roger snapped. "Come, man, this is your mistress, Lady Rachel. Admit her at once."

"Please, my lady, this way." The lackey pulled his forelock respectfully and led the way into the cramped quarters Nicholas had inhabited before his return to Hetherington. He had written to tell her soon after his arrival in London with Kit that he had taken up his old rooms.

The lackey assiduously dusted a chair for her and Rachel sank down stiffly, wincing against the pain of the cramped limb.

"Sir Nicholas left London over a week ago, my lady."

"On his way back to Leicestershire? But, surely . . ."

"No, my lady. I understand Sir Nicholas was off on some errand for His Majesty. I packed his valise and a coach called for him. Last Wednesday, it must have been."

Rachel compressed her lips. So Nicholas had again accompanied Lady Ryall to her Suffolk home. It was hardly to be expected that he would return quickly to Hetherington, where his wife was pregnant and the summer months would prove boring in the extreme without even the excitement of the hunt to make life pleasurable.

"Then would you inform Mr. Hetherington of my arrival? Is he from home, at Court, perhaps?"

"Mr. Kit's not here, neither, my lady. He's in the north with Mr. Spicer, waiting attendance on the Duke of York. Is there anything I can get your ladyship?"

Rachel was close to tears. Both men away when she had most urgent need of them!

"You've no idea when either gentleman is expected?"

"No, my lady."

"What is your name? I take it you are Mr. Hetherington's manservant?"

"Yes, my lady, Petts. I comes up from Kent with Mr. Spicer. Will you want to put up here, my lady?" He looked at her doubtfully. "There's but the one bedroom and this room—"

"No, obviously I shall have to go to an inn."

"I put up last year at The Crown in Fetter Lane," Roger said. "Mistress Weaver, the innwife, seemed a respectable, motherly woman. She might be able to recommend suitable apartments."

"A public inn is scarcely suitable," Rachel agreed. "And my business could take some time."

Roger rode off to Fetter Lane, leaving her to rest. Petts put himself out to provide her and Sarah with a cold collation after Gaston and Toby had been dismissed to a nearby tavern. Roger returned quickly.

"We are fortunate. Mistress Weaver's son-in-law has an apothecary's shop a few doors from The Crown. He's willing to rent us the furnished accommodation above. I've looked it over—a trifle cramped, but it would serve for us and we shall be near enough The Crown to eat there or have meals sent in to us."

Thankfully, Rachel allowed herself to be driven there and found the quarters clean and comfortable, though somewhat noisy.

Rachel rose early and, though impatient to set off for the Palace, dressed with extreme care. She chose her gown of apricot silk, for the day promised to be oppressive. Sarah was clumsily awkward with the heated tongs, but finally managed to achieve a profusion of curls to frame her mistress's face. It was impossible now to hide her condition and she knew she would be open to impertinent stares from both Court officials and petitioners.

Gaston had stabled the horses and established the vehicle in the courtyard of The Crown. He drove around early and they set out immediately for Whitehall.

As she had feared, the anterooms of Whitehall Palace were crowded, the atmosphere over-scented and oppressive. She was not admitted to the Privy Chamber, since she was not accompanied by Nicholas as on the former occasion.

A bored major domo, resplendent in purple velvet, his coat and fine red-heeled shoes festooned with white satin loops, demanded her name and business. She hesitated, then gave her name and rank.

"My husband is gentleman-in-waiting to His Majesty," she said haughtily, as the man yawned at her behind his hand. "The King received me graciously last year and did me the honor of making me a present of one of the royal spaniels. My business is private, of a family nature."

He made no promises, but he did straighten up more respectfully at her announcement, gazing hastily at the dog and back to Roger in his sober gray coat. He sauntered off, swinging his silver-topped cane of office foppishly, and Rachel sank down on a window seat while Roger prowled the room impatiently.

At their entrance the talking and laughter had ceased momentarily, and she found herself the target of several pairs of hostile eyes. She jerked up her chin determinedly and looked down over the bowling green and cockpit below.

Time passed slowly and Roger took Charley out to be walked by Toby. Rachel found herself regarding her fellow petitioners curiously. Most were richly dressed, but she could see that the flamboyant velvets and satins were sadly rubbed. So these men were of the sad company of former Cavaliers who had lost everything in the King's service and now haunted the antechambers in the hope that he would refurbish their empty coffers.

All eyes were fixed eagerly on the double doors through which successful petitioners were admitted, as a man stepped through them. He was tall, holding himself superbly. Rachel judged him to be about thirty-six or -seven years old. His eyes were glassily indifferent to the avid curiosity of the watching company and he stalked toward a woman who half rose at his entrance.

They whispered together anxiously and Rachel caught the name "Castlemaine" angrily and contemptuously uttered. The woman pleaded with him tearfully to stay, but he shook her off and she followed him unwillingly as his red-heeled shoes beat an irritated tattoo on the black and white tiled floor.

Rachel's heart sank lower and lower as the day advanced. Roger could not persuade her to leave when, at any moment, she might be called into the royal presence. Few names were called by the returning supercilious major domo, and those who were fortunate jumped up eagerly and almost tripped over their own feet in their haste to pass through to the inner sanctum.

Gradually, the anteroom emptied as the light faded. Rachel rose and stretched her painfully cramped limbs. Liveried footmen carried in tapers to light the tall wax candles, adding to the fetid atmosphere of the room. There would be no more audiences granted today. Roger shook his head regretfully and she rose and left with him.

Day after day they returned to Whitehall to wait through the long hours without sign that their patience would ever be rewarded. Each morning her name was taken by the major domo with his irritatingly supercilious air. Roger did not voice what she felt he must be thinking. Soon it would be too late to save her father from the ordeal of imprisonment and trial and her mouth became dry as she thought of what he might be forced to divulge. He would not be able to convince his judges that he had had no intention of allying himself with the plotters.

They were now in the third week of August and the heat within the city was almost unbearable. Roger was completely out of his depth, longing to return to Leicestershire to be by his wife's side when his first child was born, but staunchly determined to remain by Rachel's side while she needed him. Over the appallingly long hours she was grateful for his reassuringly sturdy presence to protect her from insult.

She was sunk in an apathetic lethargy one interminable afternoon. Roger had left her for moments to walk Charley in the courtyard. She heard her name called sharply.

"Rachel?"

She looked up, startled, to find Sir Richard Summers staring down at her.

"It *is* you. Whatever are you doing here? Is Kit not with you?"

She rose, offering her hand in a rush of eagerness. It was wonderful to glimpse the one man in all this press of courtiers she would most welcome.

"Oh, Richard, how good it is to see you. How is Magdelin?"

"In excellent health, and the boy, too, thank God. We arrived in town only yesterday. Are you without a protector here?"

"No, my brother-in-law, Mr. Roger Talbot, is with me. We are staying in Fetter Lane, but Kit is away, I don't know where; in attendance on the Duke of York, I understand."

"Ah, yes, Talbot. I remember. That *is* a mercy. Court is no place for a woman alone."

"I—" She hesitated, wondering how much she dared reveal to him and decided very little, certainly not in this crowded thoroughfare. "I have requested an audience, but Nicholas is from home and no one appears to heed me, or His Majesty is unwilling to receive me."

"I imagine Charles has no idea you are here," he said bluntly. "Did you bribe the major domo?"

"No, I didn't think . . ."

"Just so. I'll see what I can do. Is there some need, money, perhaps?"

"No, no." She colored. "Not that. I need His Majesty's help for—for someone in danger."

"Oh?" That comically lugubrious face became strangely sensitive to her need. "And Nick is liable to be away some days yet?"

"You know where he is?"

It was his turn to appear discomfited. "I—I understood . . ." He shrugged. "On the King's business, I am informed."

Rachel's mouth hardened. Richard would naturally cover for his companion. She would not press him to divulge a confidence.

Dick's eyes passed over her figure. She reddened. Her condition had made her sensitive to the inquiring glances she was constantly receiving.

"You should be taking things more easily now, Rachel. We are lodged in Chancery Lane. Can't you move to us under Magdelin's care?"

"That is most kind of you, Dick, but I have Roger Talbot in attendance and—" She was relieved to see Roger hastening back to her side.

The two men exchanged bows.

"I'm sorry to hear, Mr. Talbot, that you have been kept kicking your heels here. I have some influence and will try to get an audience for Lady Rachel within the next few days. In the meantime I suggest that she waits quietly at her lodgings for my summons. May I escort you to your coach?"

Rachel rose gratefully, thankful to leave affairs in his hands. As they crossed Palace Yard, she glanced quickly at Roger. He shrugged, indicating that he left it to her own discretion whether to confide in Dick Summers or remain silent. She decided she must trust Nicholas's good friend and, since no one was in earshot, as they walked she informed him of the visit of the King's officials to Glebe and her very real fears for her father. His brows drew together, but he did not interrupt her.

"I am desperate for Nicholas's help and advice. Even now my father could be in custody. He has been so ill. If this happens, Dick, I fear for his recovery."

He stopped near the coach, his fingers gripping hers consolingly. "Trust me, I see the need for urgency."

"If you can contact Nicholas tell him—tell him he must help me now." Her lip trembled and she turned from him, determined that he should not witness the full extent of her distress.

"I'll do what I can, you know that." He handed her into the vehicle, bowing deeply. She sank back thankfully. Roger stared moodily ahead as the coach lumbered off.

"You think that Summers is in touch with Nicholas? This Ryall woman is known then to both of them."

"Lady Lettice is well known at Court," Rachel replied somewhat stiffly.

Magdelin called the following day. She chided Rachel for taking risks.

"Why didn't you send immediately to Dick to handle this affair for you? You are in no condition to make the journey so near your time, let alone wait day after day, hour after hour, in that dreadful anteroom. I can imagine what insulting glances have been cast your way."

"There was no time, Magdelin. I just packed a valise and came. Phoebe and my grandmother were helping to care for my father. She should be delivered any day now. Roger is anxious to get back to her, but he loyally stays with me while I need him."

In obedience to Dick's instructions, Rachel did not again present herself at Whitehall, but the waiting over the next three days was pure purgatory.

On the third day Barnaby Paskell rode into the court behind the shop, dusty, travel-stained and bursting to impart his news. Fortunately, Roger was present.

"It's Mistress Phoebe, sir, borne you a fine son early on June 16th. He's nigh on eight pounds, Zillah says, and the mistress is recovering well." He grinned delightedly. "He yells fair to lift the roof, got a right good pair of lungs and the master has taken heart at sight of him and seems a lot stronger."

Rachel said fervently, "Oh, Roger, I'm so pleased for you. Shouldn't you go home to her? I can rely on Sir Richard and Lady Summers, and Barnaby can stay with me until Gaston returns and—Sir Nicholas."

He shook his head. "Soon now. I want to see you safe through this and it seems they are managing well at Glebe without us." His face was flushed and his eyes gleaming with pleasure. Rachel knew only too well how much it must mean to him that Phoebe had given him a child of his own. He questioned Barnaby more closely.

"Have there been any further developments? Any more strangers at the house?"

"No, sir, only the Stones called to congratulate the mistress and gifts have been arriving, though I didn't wait for much. When Leah was sure the mistress was doing well, and the babe, she dispatched me straight away."

"And Mistress Nashe," Rachel said cautiously, "has she seen the baby?"

"No, my lady. The mistress is still at Mountsorrel. They're saying she's not well. I think the news was sent to her."

"Thank you, Barnaby. It is wonderful to have you here with such welcome tidings. Now get Sarah to provide you with a meal. Toby will show you where to sleep. Stay in town some days. You'll want to explore."

"When you can spare me, my lady. I never expected to see London, not in the whole of my life."

"Well, you can now."

When Dick Summers called next day, he clapped the bashful Roger on the back heartily and carried him off that evening, despite his objections, to celebrate. Rachel added her inducements to Dick's.

"Of course you must take some pleasure in the birth of your son. I have Barnaby and Toby as well as the servants to protect me. Go, and don't get too drunk, either of you."

"I can't speak for Talbot," Dick said genially. "An occasion like this is the perfect excuse to get roaring drunk, but don't worry. I'll guard him from rufflers and pickpockets."

"I hope so," she said laughingly as they departed.

Despite her brave words to Roger she was somewhat alarmed when there was a knocking on her door some minutes after eleven. She had gone up to her room and was about to undress. She waited nervously until Sarah raced back to her breathlessly.

"A gentleman, my lady, asking to see you. He won't give his name and he's all muffled up in a drab cloak in spite of it still being so warm."

"I don't understand. Is he one of the men from Sir Richard Summers's house in Chancery Lane?"

"He's no ordinary servant, my lady, he's soft-tongued like a gentleman."

260

Who could it be, since Richard was out roistering with Roger? Rachel's heart leapt in panic as she thought some further harm threatened her father—yet how could the King's men know where she was lodged? She summoned her failing courage and waited while Sarah fixed her hair, then descended to speak with the stranger.

He was strangely wrapped up for such an oppressive night, and turned from her, gazing down from the window into the darkened street below.

"If you will dismiss your maid, Lady Hetherington, I'll state my business."

"Leave me, Sarah, *leave* me," she repeated as the maid seemed inclined to argue, then, as the door closed on the girl, "Sir?"

He turned and let his cloak slip and she saw he was a small man in early middle age with a pleasant, almost droll countenance. He was a complete stranger to her.

"Forgive the theatrical manner of my arrival, Lady Hetherington, but I have strict instructions to keep our business utterly private. Allow me to introduce myself. I am Will Chiffinch."

No one within the city could be unaware of the identity of the King's most trusted groom of the bedchamber, or of the nature of his many services to his sovereign.

He stooped and kissed her fingers. "I am asked to convey you to His Majesty, tonight, without your maid, if you will trust yourself to me."

He smiled at her encouragingly. "His Majesty further requests that you bring with you the little spaniel he gave to you a year ago. It would give him great pleasure to see it fully grown."

"Oh, yes, Charley. I will ring for my maid. Our coach must be made ready."

"I have a vehicle waiting in the street."

She stared back at him. It was clear that she was not

to be allowed to reveal to Roger where she was gone. He would be frantic with worry.

She hurried to Sarah in the kitchen and took charge of Charley. The girl was tearful. "You shouldn't be going, my lady, not without me. Whatever am I to tell Mr. Talbot when he gets back?"

"Tell him that I am unexpectedly called to a private meeting, that he is not to be unduly alarmed and that I am suitably escorted."

She took a gray silk cloak to cover her gown and returned to Mr. Chiffinch. He nodded approvingly and stood back to allow her to pass before him into the street. A closed vehicle, leather curtains pulled tightly across the window apertures, was drawn up ready. Rachel was handed in and the dog scrambled onto her knee. Mr. Chiffinch seated himself opposite.

"The distance is very short. We proceed by boat from Somerset House steps."

Rachel wondered how many women Chiffinch had escorted to similar assignations as she stepped down gingerly into the small rowing boat which was steadied for her by an attentive boatman. Chiffinch followed holding the dog and the man pushed off into midstream. Though small, the boat was luxuriously furnished, for Rachel felt the soft plush of rich velvet cushions as she sank back against the thwarts.

The palace of Whitehall loomed even larger and blacker than usual out of the darkness, for there was little moon and the men were especially protective as they assisted her onto the landing stage. Chiffinch, with Charley tucked somewhat unceremoniously under his arm, took Rachel's hand to lead her forward.

She did not recognize the door through which they entered the Palace, nor any of the dimly lit corridors. They climbed a steep, narrow staircase, carpeted thickly to soften the noise of arrivals and departures, she concluded, and Chiffinch halted within a small, well-appointed chamber and tapped respectfully on a door which appeared to open out from it.

A man's voice called for them to enter and the groom of the bedchamber nodded to Rachel, opened the door wide and ushered her through into the adjoining chamber. She blinked in the sudden glare of many candles and looked up into the gently sardonic features of Charles II of England.

He bowed to her courteously. "Thank you for accepting my somewhat unconventional invitation, Lady Rachel. No, please do not curtsey. Sit in this comfortable chair. Thank you, Will,"—this to Chiffinch—"I'll take the dog."

A brown and white spaniel bitch burst abruptly from her velvet-padded basket against the far wall and the King quelled her shrill barks with an upraised finger. "Quiet, Petronelle. Don't you recognize your own son?" He chuckled as he lifted Charley high and the little dog licked at him in an ecstasy of delight, welcoming a new admirer. The King seated himself in an armchair opposite to the one in which he had placed Rachel, the dog comfortably settled on his knee, one hand gently pulling at its ears. Petronelle jumped up, too, sniffing suspiciously at the newcomer, then cuddled down against her returned offspring.

The King was dressed in a blue and gold brocaded bedgown, more colorful attire than anything Rachel had previously seen him wear.

"Please put back your cloak, Lady Rachel. It is still astonishingly hot and the air very still tonight. Don't be alarmed. I mean you no discourtesy. Faith, if I did, Nick would spit me living on that appallingly long rapier of his. It was essential that we talk in utter privacy. This seemed the best time and place for it."

Rachel's fingers trembled as she undid the cloak

263

clasp. She watched the King covertly as he petted the dogs, her fears for her father sharpened to breaking point.

He teased Charley's silky coat. "This one *has* become a beauty, and spoiled, I fear, like Petronelle, here. What was it you called him?"

Embarrassed, she whispered, "Charley, Your Majesty."

His lips twitched. "Ah, yes, Nick did tell me. I hope he has not proved a burden to you."

"He is deeply loved by us all, Your Majesty."

"I saw in you a like passion to my own where dogs are concerned, Lady Rachel. No other creature gives such unquestioning devotion, I'm sure you'll agree. Now, Dick Summers tells me you are anxious about your husband." She gave a little gasp and he leaned toward her. "Nick is in France. I expect him home soon, possibly tomorrow. He was unable to inform you of his destination, for, at my request, he undertook a mission of particular delicacy. He didn't desert you last year without due reason. He was then on a similar mission. I can explain something of its nature, but details I cannot reveal. You understand?"

She nodded dumbly.

"I feel I must give you some explanation for Nick's sake. I'd not have you think he abandoned you in town during the plague months in order to protect his own hide. Lady Lettice Ryall was formerly lady-in-waiting to my sister, therefore it seemed practical that my messenger should accompany that lady on a visit to the Duchess of Orleans. Few questions would be posed regarding a visit of so private a nature. You are aware that my cousin, King Louis, is the ally of the Dutch. Any overtures made by me to the French King, as I am sure you will appreciate, would be regarded with extreme suspicion and disfavor by some members of my own privy council; therefore any such moves must be tentative, handled with particular care. Sir Nicholas is also well known to the Duchess of Orleans, and, by her good offices, may well be granted the ear of King Louis. I need say no more?"

"No, Your Majesty." Rachel was close to tears.

The King thrust his hand into the deep pocket of his bedgown and withdrew a small package. "I see Nick is blessed with a lady of loyalty and courage, which pleases me. I saw to it that this was delivered to me this morning. I suggest that you consign it to the flames, Lady Rachel. Such mementoes of the Protectorate could prove dangerous to anyone holding such in his possession."

She clutched the package tightly, a lump forming in her throat, inhibiting speech.

"I do not know how to thank Your Majesty for your understanding and kindness. I—I cannot excuse my father's political views, they are his own and not mine to oppose or defend, but he is a sick man now and could not prove any threat to Your Majesty, nor, I think, would he willingly plot to harm you."

"Dick Summers explained the situation." He gave a little sigh, his hand playing with the ornamental studs on Charley's velvet collar. "On the subject of my father's murder, I am not, alas, my usual tolerant self; however, it is all so long ago and those responsible are gone from us. Your husband's services to the Crown far outweigh any consequences of the late wars. I have given commands. You will not be troubled further at Glebe. You have my royal word on it."

She knelt and kissed his fingers and he laughingly offered her a lace-trimmed kerchief on which to dry her eyes.

"A glass of wine before I summon Chiffinch to return you to your lodgings. If I did not expect Nick home very shortly, I'd send you home to Leicestershire under escort at once. Don't you know how anxiously he looks for an heir?" She saw a sudden shadow cross that dark face and felt for him. So many bastards and no legal heir for the Kingdom.

Moments later Will Chiffinch arrived to conduct her downstairs, through the silent passages and across Palace Yard to the water steps where the King's private boat was waiting.

Chapter 17

Kit Hetherington rubbed his hand tiredly over eyes smarting from the blue haze of tobacco smoke which was obscuring his vision and irritating a throat already roughened by too much laughing. Locket's Tavern in Charing Cross was packed to the doors and just as rowdy. Tom Spicer had insisted they come on here from the theater, but Kit would rather have made for his lodgings in Pall Mall. The wench on his knee giggled to draw his attention, her arm tightening enticingly around his neck.

Kit looked for Tom, partially hidden from him by one of the tall wooden screens Locket's provided for the comfort and convenience of its patrons. From the sounds of slaps, chuckles and shrill, stifled screams of mirth proceeding from the alcove, his friend was thoroughly enjoying his first night back in the capital.

Kit slapped the buttocks of the girl on his knee playfully.

"Off with you, my lass. I'm for my bed." Kit drained his wine glass and stretched. If Tom didn't emerge within the next half hour, he'd hire a hackney and get off to Pall Mall alone.

"Hetherington, you here? I thought you still in the north with the Duke."

Kit looked up sharply as the speaker seated himself opposite and puffed contentedly at his long clay pipe: Will Grantley, a dandified puppy, newly come to Court, a hanger on the heels of Lady Castlemaine.

"We arrived back in town about midday," Kit said curtly. He distrusted the man, knowing his habit of listening at keyholes and absorbing malicious tittle-tattle, so prevalent at Court.

"H'm." Grantley leaned back and lazily regarded the pink satin rosettes on his shoes as he crossed one leg over the other. "I thought you could not be aware of what was going on. Nick's wife, I mean, newly come again to town."

Kit forced his befuddled brain to take in this tidbit of information.

"Rachel," he said guardedly, "in London? Impossible."

Grantley sniggered. "Saw her in Palace Yard with Dick Summers and some puritanically dressed fellow whose disapproving frown would turn cream sour."

"You must be mistaken." Kit's tone was sharp.

"No doubt, my dear fellow, not possible." Grantley coughed delicately, but his black eyes glittered with malicious intent. "Summers handed her into the Hetherington carriage. She was clearly being squired by the clerkly gentleman. And Nick away with Lady Ryall, I hear. Most unfortunate. Has his lady taken umbrage and determined to have her revenge?"

The wine fumes had cleared slightly and Kit leaned across the table, one hand tightening and twisting Grantley's lace cravat. "You impugn my brother's honor, Mr. Grantley. You have me to answer to." The voice was as hard as tempered steel, and as menacing.

"Strap me, Hetherington," the other choked, "I mean no harm. Since you returned from that Dutch hellhole, you've grown uncommon quarrelsome."

Kit's grasp slackened and he leaned back again in his seat. His mouth curved in a sneer. "Take yourself out of my sight, Grantley. If it comes to my ears that my sister-in-law's name has again crossed your lips, I'll send my seconds to call on you."

Grantley climbed readily to his feet. His fingers shook as he straightened his cravat. His clay pipe had fallen and the bowl smashed on the wine-stained table. He bowed stiffly.

"As you will, sir, but if Lady Hetherington is not to encourage further gossip concerning her own or Nick's affairs, she'd be best to keep from Whitehall with her escort, considering her delicate state of health."

Noting Kit's lips harden, he backed from the table and, turning awkwardly, let out a surprised oath.

"Odds blood, if it isn't the fellow now with Summers."

Kit stiffened as his eyes followed Grantley's gaze. Dick Summers was steering a reluctant Roger Talbot to a table near the door. Kit leaped to his feet and confronted them as Grantley scuttled for the street door.

"Kit?" Dick's eyes lit up at the sight of him. "Well met, man. I've been hoping you'd be back in town soon."

Kit's eyes were hard as granite pebbles.

"From what I hear, my presence is the last thing Talbot here would wish to be aware of."

"What?" Dick gazed blankly from one man to the other. It was obvious there was bad blood between them, for Talbot's face had mottled with angry color at Kit's openly abusive manner.

"I don't like your tone, Hetherington," he snapped.

268

"I don't pretend to understand your meaning, but you are offensive, sir."

"And drunk, to boot," Dick said bluntly. He seized Kit by the edge of his velvet coat as he lunged toward Talbot. "See here, boy, cool down. You've had more than enough to drink for one day. You'll come with me to Fetter Lane to Rachel's lodging and, on the way, I'll make some attempt to get through your thick skull the reason why she's here."

Dick hustled the two men out and summoned a hackney. He instructed the driver to drive to Fetter Lane. Inside he briefly explained the reason for Rachel's hasty arrival in the capital. Roger sat slumped in angry silence.

"God's teeth, Dick, if she loses the child, Nick will half kill her. Surely this affair over Simon Nashe could have been handled from Hetherington."

"Do you think Rachel is risking her life and that of the child's needlessly?" Roger said through gritted teeth. "If your brother had stayed by her side, where his duty lay at this time, she would not have been forced into such a predicament. It seems that when either or both of you is needed, you've a way of deserting your responsibilities."

"I haven't the devil of a notion what you are implying, Talbot . . ."

They were squaring up to each other like two turkey cocks and Dick was thankful when the hackney drew up outside the apothecary's shop in Fetter Lane.

It was nearly two o'clock when Chiffinch set Rachel down outside her lodgings. The watchman was just moving off into the Fleet, his lantern bobbing, his resonant voice beginning to fade into the distance.

"I'm grateful for your care of me, Mr. Chiffinch," she said as he stooped to kiss her hand.

269

He lingered until Sarah hurried down to admit her. The girl looked unduly flushed and agitated.

"Sir Richard Summers is here, my lady, with Mr. Talbot and young Mr. Hetherington. They all seem upset and concerned."

"Sarah, you get straight to bed. I can manage."

"Yes, my lady." Sarah scuttled off as Dick came down the stairs into the hall.

"I'm glad you're back safely." He looked at her keenly. "Were you summoned to the Palace?"

"Yes, all is well. Thank you, Dick, for all you did. I could not have managed without you."

"Good." He glanced briefly up the stairway. "I'm afraid you've trouble up there. Kit has imbibed too freely and appears to be in a singularly aggressive mood. He's furious that you made the journey at all."

She sighed. The last thing she wanted now was a scene with Nicholas's brother. "Does he know? About my father?"

"I didn't give details, simply stressed the urgency of your need. He had no notion Nicholas was out of town."

She nodded and he went with her above stairs.

Kit was frowning as he came toward her. "Where in God's name have you been at this hour?"

"I was summoned to the Palace to a private audience," she said tiredly. "Mr. Chiffinch was my escort."

"Chiffinch?" He looked at her in angry bewilderment. "Do you know the fellow's reputation? He's a procurer to His Majesty."

"I'm well aware of that, Kit," she said tartly. "I trusted Mr. Chiffinch and he treated me to no discourtesy, which is more than I can say about your greeting, sir."

Kit drew back, abashed. His head was throbbing and he was beginning to feel more than a little ridiculous.

Roger said quietly, "I should have been with you. I should not have left you alone."

"I was quite safe." She sank down into a chair. She was feeling trembly now that the ordeal was over. "The King was most kind and sensitive to my need." She turned to Kit, who hovered near the door with Dick. "I'm tired now and in no mood for recriminations. Will you call on me after noon tomorrow? I'll sleep late. I'll explain further then."

He nodded, bowed a trifle stiffly to Roger, kissed her hand and Dick hustled him out.

"Now get some rest, Rachel, and take good care of yourself. Magdelin will be anxious."

Roger poured wine for her. "I'm sorry about young Hetherington. I'd no right to make trouble. The man infuriates me. It seems he heard some stupid, vapid gossip about you and me being seen together. Dick was furious with him. I don't know how we both managed to keep our tempers."

She sipped the wine thankfully. "I expect Nicholas home soon."

His eyebrows rose in a question.

"He has been on a mission for the King. I'm unable to say more. You must leave tomorrow, now Kit is here to squire me. No," she said, laughing, as he was about to argue. "Never fear, I'll manage Kit. I would like to wait for Nicholas now."

He nodded. "Was the audience difficult?"

"No, as I said, the King was understanding and gracious."

"The letter?"

"I have it. We'll destroy it. No more inquiries will be made. The King assured me my father will be safe."

He brought the candle close and she took the folded package from her glove, hesitated, then thrust it into the flame.

That night Rachel slipped off easily to sleep for the first time in weeks.

Roger left in the morning just before Magdelin and Kit arrived to call on Rachel. Kit was sober and apologetic.

"I can see you had better stay where you are for a while," Magdelin said. "Send to Chancery Lane, Kit, if you've need of me."

Kit looked anxious and Rachel laughed at his dismay. "I'm not going to have my child yet a while. Thank Dick for all he did."

"Everything is well with you?"

"Everything."

She felt better later and Kit stayed to supper. She told him of the officials from Whitehall and the letter, but thought it wise to make no mention of the plotters.

"Faith," Kit said, frowning, "someone wishes your father no good. I'm grateful Summers was on hand to take your part at Court. Where *is* Nick, do you know?"

"On the King's business," she said quietly.

Sarah appeared in the doorway. "It's Gaston, back from Southwold, my lady. He's very anxious to see you."

"Send him up."

The Frenchman looked agitated, but was obviously relieved to find Kit present.

"Madame, *le maître* is not at Southwold, the servants, they insist, he has not been there and I—"

"Yes, I know, Gaston. There's no need for concern."

"Madame Ryall, she is not at home and . . ."

Kit frowned darkly and Rachel flushed. "Yes, I know. Go and eat, Gaston, then rest. I imagine you've half killed your horse."

"She went lame, madame, and . . ."

"I understand. Mr. Talbot has returned to Glebe. Everything is well now. Get some rest."

Kit said angrily after the Frenchman had gone, "Nick had no damned business to flaunt—"

"I understand the situation, Kit. It's not entirely as you think."

She felt unaccountably dizzy the next morning as she began to dress, so that she was forced to sit down abruptly again on the bed. Sarah was alarmed and Rachel had to be curt in stopping her instantly rushing downstairs and sending for Lady Summers.

"I'll go back to bed for an hour. I shall be all right," she snapped, gritting her teeth. "My time isn't here yet a while."

While resting she felt better, but longed for the comforting presence of Zillah and grandmamma.

Her malaise reappeared when she tried to get up for supper and, reluctantly, she sent Toby for Magdelin Summers. Pains were shooting up her back and thighs so that she gasped uncertainly. She couldn't restrain the slow tears which coursed down her cheeks. Not now. She mustn't lose Nicholas's child. She mustn't. He would be so angry.

Magdelin was reassuring but advised her to send for a noted accoucheur. "I don't think labor has started yet, but we'd be wise to take precautions."

Rachel gasped as another pain shot through her. "Magdelin, do . . . do you think I'm about to give birth? Be truthful."

Magdelin hesitated. "I've heard of women having symptoms like this before time and pains subsiding, but it looks as if your baby is coming, Rachel."

"But it's much too early. The child will die."

"Small babies *can* survive. Try not to fret."

Dr. Devaux arrived within the hour, fashionably dressed and affected in speech and manner, quite unlike any doctor Rachel had ever met. He examined her.

273

"I understand my lady has been overtiring herself of late. At such a stage in pregnancy she was ill-advised to travel."

"Is she in labor?" Magdelin demanded.

"It seems so. There is no undue cause for alarm."

"But six or seven weeks premature?"

He nodded gravely. "It will be some hours yet. I'll return early tomorrow morning."

Magdelin went back to the bedside.

Rachel's fingers clawed at Magdelin's hand. "The child, Magdelin—it mustn't die, dear God, it mustn't."

"And it won't." Magdelin bent and kissed her gently. "Trust us, Rachel. Devaux is a good man and I shan't leave you. He assures me everything is going well. Take your rest or you'll exhaust yourself before time. It will be hours yet before I put your child in your arms."

Even before Nicholas reached The George in Southwark, he was aware of the strange red glow in the sky.

"You'll not have heard about the fire then, sir?" the stableman at The George asked. "From Kent, are you?"

"Blackheath, this morning. See my horse is fed and watered. I'll take ale in the taproom. What's this about a fire?"

"In the city, sir, started last night in Pudding Lane near the river, so they say. You can see it from here." He pointed to the ominous red stain in the distance. "Travelers passing through say it's already taken hold of Thames Street."

Nicholas caught the man by his smock. "Wait. Tell me all you know. Near the river you say, then Whitehall's in no danger?"

"Couldn't say, sir. We had a chapman here a couple of hours ago. He said the wharves had gone up in sheets of flame, well, they would, sir, being packed tight with oil, pitch and tar as well as brandy wine."

"Good God, man, the bridge will be endangered. Those houses must be tinder-dry after all this hot weather. I need another horse. Find me one."

"Well, sir, I don't know as how I can . . ."

Nicholas flashed two gold pieces before the stableman's startled gaze. "Now. I must ride on, at once."

"Yes, sir, certainly sir, if you say so, but if the bridge is burning, you'll have a rare job getting across. Wouldn't your honor be wiser to stay here for the night?"

"A horse, man, immediately." Nicholas impatiently summoned a pot boy and swallowed a tankard of ale. His bones ached with weariness, but he could waste no time now to rest inside the inn.

Nearer to the river he saw, to his horror, that crossing would not be easy. The main roads were choked with nervous householders from the north bank who'd had the foresight to get their most cherished goods into boats and have themselves and their families rowed across. Frantic women struggled with bundles and jewel boxes, men shouted at the ferrymen, bargaining, ordering, wrestling with refractory animals.

Nicholas dismounted and tethered his horse to a ring on the wharf. He started, aghast, at the inferno which faced him across the river.

The northern end of the bridge was one mass of flames, sparks shooting upward high into the dark pall ahead, which was the sky directly above the inner city. Even from this distance he could hear the crackling and terrible hiss of steam as the houses and shops built over the bridge disintegrated, throwing beams and thatch into the steaming water. The bridge was impassable. He turned to gauge the river traffic. He must get a boat and quickly.

Nicholas's arm was caught urgently by a young man who pointed imperatively to his horse.

"You intend to leave the brute here, sir?"

"Yes, I have to cross by boat."

"I'll buy your horse, sir, no time to haggle. I was forced to leave my own horse by the Tower."

"Yes, take him." Nicholas scanned the river impatiently. "I need a boat."

The man swung himself into the saddle and edged the snorting, frightened horse through the crowd. Nicholas cupped his hands and yelled to a boatman who was just coming in to the wharf with two women, both frantically clutching at children.

"Over here, man."

While the family disembarked, Nicholas bargained for passage.

"Take me to Whitehall steps. I've urgent business at the Palace."

The man hesitated. He looked utterly exhausted. Nicholas sprang down. "Come, man, I'll help you row and make it well worth your while."

The boatman was young, broad-shouldered and brawny, but he was clearly feeling the strain.

"Just you, sir, no heavy baggage?"

"Nothing. I tell you, I'm a King's messenger."

"Right, sir." The man wiped a grimy forearm over his sweat-streaked forehead and pulled out.

The water was stained scarlet and gold by the reflected light of the fire glow as the boatman and Nicholas pulled out.

Whitehall Palace was crowded, but since this was the usual state of affairs, Nicholas thrust his way through the packed anterooms to the Privy Chamber and made himself known to the major domo. The man glanced at him hurriedly as he mentioned Will Chiffinch's name, bowed and left him. Nicholas paced to an open window and looked out onto the Queen's Privy Garden. He wondered if Kit were present in the Palace or down in the city, viewing the fearsome spectacle of the fire.

"Nick, thank God you're here, man."

Nicholas turned as Dick Summers pushed his way through to him.

"You know Rachel is in town?"

"What?" Nicholas stared at his friend, stupefied. "That's impossible."

"I know, I know. She's been here several weeks. I only came back myself a few days ago. There was some trouble at home. Best if she tells you, but you should be with her, man, right now."

"Where is she, at Kit's lodgings?"

"No, Fetter Lane, apartments above the apothecary. Magdelin's with her."

"God in Heaven, man, the fire could be moving that way. Why didn't you bundle them both to St. James's or get them right out of town?"

"Sir Nicholas Hetherington?" The major domo bore down on him majestically.

Nicholas turned to go, tight-lipped, and Dick called after him. "Rachel's safe with Magdelin. I'll explain later."

The King received Nicholas graciously and turned from him to read his royal cousin's letter. Little grunts of evident satisfaction convinced Nicholas that his mission had proved entirely successful.

"You had no trouble?"

"None at all, Your Majesty. The presence of Lady Ryall smoothed out all difficulties. What more natural than that she should call on the Princess Henriette, who was overjoyed to see her former lady-in-waiting?"

"Good, you've done well. You will find me suitably grateful, Sir Nicholas."

"I am honored to serve Your Majesty, as always. I pray you excuse any discourtesy in requesting an immediate dismissal. My wife is in London and I'm concerned about her safety."

"Certainly, man, go at once. I had thought the lady gone to Leicestershire by now."

"You knew she was here, sir?"

"Dick Summers requested an audience on her behalf. Let me recollect . . . Friday, yes, late Friday night. Will Chiffinch brought her to me."

As Nicholas gave an astounded gasp, the King added, "She seemed well, but anxious. Her father was in some danger of harassment from my over-zealous officials. Don't alarm yourself, Nick, the business is already concluded. Lady Rachel need have no further anxiety on that score, but you must get off to her at once." The King shrugged expressively. "You'll want her out of the bustle and confusion of the city."

Nicholas bowed and took his leave. Dick joined him outside.

"I'll come with you to Fetter Lane. There's little I can do here. The river's crowded with people evacuating property. We'd be best to proceed on foot."

Nicholas nodded grimly. "We must get the women clear today."

"That won't be possible, Nick." Dick nodded gravely as Nicholas checked his stride and gazed at him. "Rachel's in early labor. She's in good hands, Magdelin won't leave her and she's called in Devaux. He's highly thought of in Court circles."

Nicholas made to speak, then abruptly turned and moved off so fast that even Dick's long limbs had some difficulty in matching his stride.

In Fleet Street the two jerked to a halt, mouths agape, as flames engulfed church spires beyond Ludgate Hill like some Popish illustration of Hell. The very copper and lead on the church roofs were melting under the intense heat and pouring down the guttering and walls.

"At this rate half of the city will burn," Dick muttered through tight lips.

Through the haze of pain and fear Rachel was aware of excitement and noise below her bedchamber. The air in the room was stifling and strangely acrid.

The accoucheur had returned soon after dawn. Magdelin had dispatched Gaston to fetch him.

"What is it?" Rachel clawed at her friend's hands as she came back to the bedside.

"Be easy. It's nothing to worry you, Rachel. Mr. Sewell, the apothecary, and his family are moving out."

"I don't understand." Rachel thrust back her sweat-soaked hair impatiently.

Magdelin and the doctor exchanged glances.

He pushed Rachel gently back against the pillows. "Rest, Lady Rachel."

"But there *is* something wrong. All night there have been people in the streets, carts, running feet, much more confusion than usual."

"There's a fire in the city, Lady Rachel. This drought and a high wind has fanned the flames. The blaze has been spreading and some townsfolk have panicked. It will soon be under control. Do not be alarmed."

"A fire?" Rachel peered at Magdelin unbelievingly. "So bad that our neighbors are abandoning their homes? Magdelin, are we in danger? You should leave me."

"Rachel, don't be foolish. Of course we are in no real danger. The fire began near the wharves and it's fierce. You could see the red glow of it from the window all through the night. That's why I pulled the curtains earlier and kept the casement tight closed, but it's still a good way off. We've time yet."

"Dick and Kit—they came earlier . . ."

"Yes, but they've both gone to Whitehall to offer their services. There is some panic in the streets and property must be destroyed to create fire gaps. The poor folk are making for the river. That's natural

279

enough. They hope to save at least some of their household possessions. Churches are being used to store goods. Stone will stand up against the fire much better than the wood and plaster lath of their houses."

"But what of *your* lodgings? Little Lyonel, what of him? Magdelin—"

"Dick has packed Lyonel off to The Swan in Barnet with his nurse and one of our grooms. She's a sensible girl and very attached to Lyonel. I trust her. I've given Sarah instructions to pack your belongings, just in case, and Gaston is guarding the coach and the horses. People will steal any form of transport they can lay their hands on."

"If it proves absolutely necessary, we'll move you," the doctor said quietly, "but there's ample time. Leave these problems to us, Lady Rachel."

"Sarah must be terrified—"

"She's a good girl, keeping herself well under control."

Rachel nodded, biting her lip.

They'd assured her the birth was progressing well, but it was too soon—much too soon. What if her child was stillborn? Helpless tears streamed down her cheeks unchecked as she thought of Nicholas's anger.

It had been part of the bargain. Her dowry and an heir for Hetherington. Yet how could she have stayed safely in Leicestershire while her father was so terribly threatened?

Magdelin's face hovered over her, then she was thrust aside and, for one split second of time, Rachel glimpsed Nicholas's face, grim, angry. She let out a little anguished wail. He must understand, he must, and forgive . . .

Dr. Devaux was giving urgent instructions. The room seemed to recede. She heard his voice as from a distance, measured, firm, and she brought all her failing strength and determination to obey him. It was a grim struggle, then she heard a thin, mewling sound like a kitten's and knew that her child was born.

She fought the blackness which was waiting to engulf her, concentrating desperately. Her child was alive; she had heard it cry.

They came to her bedside. Magdelin was smiling.

"You've a son, Rachel, a fine little boy. Hold him for just a moment." She placed the swathed bundle into the crook of his mother's arm.

Rachel looked down at the unbelievably tiny wrinkled face of her child, her voice choked with sudden tears.

"Doctor, is he—will he live?"

"He is very small, Lady Rachel, as we expected, but he is breathing well and, fortunately, the weather is warm. The extreme cold is the deadliest enemy to early babies born in the winter. He has an excellent chance of survival." He signaled to Magdelin to take the baby. "My concern is now for you, Lady Rachel. You must rest. It may prove necessary to move you to a place of greater safety soon."

Rachel's eyes closed wearily. She was content.

She woke suddenly to a gentle but imperative shaking of her shoulder. Magdelin was looking down at her anxiously.

"How do you feel, rested?"

"Yes, much better." Rachel moved awkwardly. She felt leaden. "What time is it? The baby . . ."

"He's sleeping contentedly. There's nothing to fear, but Devaux is expected and, if he gives the word, we must move you."

Rachel struggled up frantically in the bed. "The fire? It's still raging?"

"I'm afraid so. Dick reports that St. Paul's is engulfed and the Guildhall. Nicholas thinks we can wait no longer."

"Nicholas?" The blood drained from Rachel's face. She felt suddenly cold and deadly sick. "He's here—he knows?"

"He arrived last night, came in to see you. Don't you remember? He insisted, then Devaux ordered him out as the actual birth was imminent."

Rachel swallowed painfully. "Has—has he seen the child?"

"Yes, of course. I'll bring the baby in to you now and Nicholas is impatient to see you again."

"Magdelin, is he *very* angry?"

"Angry? Why should he be? He has a son. He's concerned, alarmed for the safety of you both."

Rachel waited anxiously until her swaddled son was placed in her arms. She hugged him very close. His eyes opened. They were deep blue and he gazed at her mistily. There was a soft fuzz of fair down on his perfectly shaped head. He would be like Nicholas.

There was a click of the latch and she looked up to see Nicholas in the doorway. He crossed to the bedside and put out a hand to touch her disordered hair.

"How are you?"

"I'm well, tired, but that is natural." She moved the covering from the child's sleeping face. "He's quite beautiful, but, oh, Nicholas, so tiny. I'm afraid—"

She could not read his expression. He looked tense and grim and she realized he too was exhausted after the journey and the alarms of the last hours.

"Devaux says he has a good chance of survival." His voice was harsh.

"Nicholas, forgive me. I had to come. My father . . ."

"We'll talk of that later. The King informed me of your audience with him. Now we must think of your safety. The fire is advancing in spite of every attempt to contain the blaze and there is looting and rioting in the streets. Fools are blaming the Dutch, even our own

Papists, for starting the fire. Kit is at Whitehall. York's troops have been called into service to prevent further rioting, but we cannot rely too much on them. The city will be in a ferment. Drunken revelers have not improved the situation. Last night they were gathering by the river to watch the spectacle. Try to eat some breakfast while Gaston brings around the coach in readiness."

"Nicholas," she said hesitantly, "will you wish him named for your father, William?"

He touched the soft down on his son's head.

"Edward, for Ned Hesketh, my dear friend, who died in my arms after Worcester."

He bent and kissed her fingers in gallant homage, then left her. She lay back.

Dr. Devaux called soon after Rachel had managed to swallow a little gruel and a cup of hot chocolate. He examined her and nodded to Magdelin, satisfied.

"Lady Rachel is making excellent progress and the child is doing well."

Nicholas came into the room behind him.

"Can I move my wife and child now?"

"You've no choice, Sir Nicholas. I intend to leave the city today. There will be further disruption and looting, if I'm any judge. You'll keep her as still as you can in the vehicle? I want no possibility of hemorrhage."

"Naturally."

"And I advise you all to go well armed."

"Doctor," Rachel called him back as he prepared to leave. "The baby—is he well formed?"

"Yes, Lady Rachel, perfectly formed. You've nothing to fear, provided he survives these early days. I'm confident he will do so. He's strong, though very small."

Under the veneer of affected foppishness Devaux was both competent and courageous. He had remained with her throughout the long hours, when many would

283

have panicked and left her to her fate. Softly, she whispered her gratitude as he took his leave.

Nicholas lifted Rachel into his arms and carried her below stairs. Magdelin followed with the child. Rachel wrinkled her nose against the acrid stink of burning. The sky was black with billows of smoke.

The quiet of the deserted street was suddenly invaded by a gaggle of apprentice lads, bellowing threats against the "Frenchy spies" and "lily-livered Papists." Most of the householders had abandoned their property and the boys smashed down doors, tore shutters apart and dived into shops to emerge triumphantly laden with spoils.

As Toby scrambled up to his seat by Gaston, Charley, excited by the general confusion, tore himself free from the boy's arms, jumped down and launched himself at the gang of lads, barking hysterically and snapping at their heels.

"Drive on," Nicholas ordered Gaston.

"Charley." Rachel's hands gripped the window sill agitatedly. "We can't leave him. Please—"

"Stay where you are," Nicholas shouted at Toby as the boy was about to jump down. "Gaston, do you hear me, get the coach clear. Dick, stay with the women. I'll go after that confounded dog."

As the vehicle lumbered ponderously by him, he caught sight of Rachel's face, white, imploring.

He whistled and called, to no avail. One of the apprentice lads swiped viciously at the dog with his heavy wooden rattle. Nicholas rode full-tilt at the group, which parted under his onslaught. Leaning low in the saddle, he snatched at Charley's infuriated, snapping form. The dog turned on him, then, astonishingly recognizing his master, quietened in his hold. Swearing, Nicholas clutched him tightly by the scruff of the neck, bent low in the saddle and urged his horse on. The boys screamed abuse after him. Something sharp whistled close by his ear and Charley squealed shrilly. Then he was through and catching up to the coach.

As he drew level, he pushed the squirming bundle of silky fur onto Rachel's lap and sucked at the injured thumb where Charley had bitten him in his first frenzy. Dick grinned at him and the two men closed in on either side of the carriage.

Chapter 18

October came in cold and blustery at Hetherington and Rachel was content to sit near the fire in the drawing room with her foot on Ned's rocker.

Little Ned had made steady progress, and Rachel felt some relief after two weeks of secret dread that his obstinate hold on life could, at any time, be abruptly terminated.

Kit had come to them days later with news from the city.

"It's all over, at least there is little danger of new outbreaks, though, in places, the rubble is still smoldering. Most buildings within the city perimeter have gone. The King was wonderful, riding with York through the streets, encouraging the fire-fighters, distributing coin to the needy, standing ankle-deep in water, filthy, smoke-grimed, handing on buckets in the chains. We used explosives to create fire breaks, but nothing seemed to check the fire till, suddenly, it began to die down of its own volition. The walls of St. Dunstans and the Temple held and contained it in the west, but they were still fighting desperately to save the Tower. Further panic was caused by the King's order to blow up the houses in Tower Street, but that did save the day."

He was relieved to hear that neither Rachel nor the child appeared to have taken great harm by their hasty removal from Fetter Lane.

"I'll stay a night here, then I must get back. The Duke will need every loyal man. The poor have suffered enough. They'll be in no easy mood to handle."

"When do you plan to sail?"

"I don't know, Nick. I think it unlikely before the New Year. Tom's busy assembling a crew for *The Yorkshire Rose*. I hope to come to Hetherington again before we leave."

Rachel wondered if he still wished to try to persuade Zillah to go with him.

So they had come home at last. Zillah came into the courtyard holding Corinna, and the child threw up her arms in delight at the sight of Rachel. Inside the house Rachel looked around at the heavy, outmoded furniture and worn hangings and uttered a silent prayer of gratitude to be back safely where she belonged.

They had stopped at Glebe before driving on. Rachel had found her father half dozing in the garden, sheltered by the old brick wall, apples ripening on their espaliered branches.

Nicholas had gone into the house with Phoebe and Roger, leaving them alone together.

"Rachel?" His voice was much stronger and more confident. "I was concerned for you and the child. How are you both?"

"Well, father." She signaled for Sarah to bring the child close. He took little Ned in his arms briefly, then Rachel nodded to the girl to return him to the shelter of the carriage.

"He is gaining weight steadily. He came too early but, God be thanked, he is thriving."

He looked at her questioningly and she leaned closer. "You should be perfectly safe now. The King received me graciously. He returned Cromwell's letter." She hesitated. "I burned it. I thought it best. His Majesty promised me that no further action would be taken against you."

She had felt unwilling to mention Judith, but the question had to be put. "Has Judith come home?"

"No." He'd averted his eyes from her, but she'd read his suffering in the rigidity of jaw and mouth muscles. "Go and see Phoebe's son. Roger is besotted with him." His mouth twitched grimly. "They've called him Oliver."

He stood up without support and tears of joy sprang to her eyes.

"I can't walk far yet, but my speech is fully restored and it won't be long now before I can sit my horse again."

Nicholas was courteous and considerate toward her, loving and demonstrative with the children. Once, when she came upon him in the nursery with little Ned in his arms, she glimpsed his pride in his son, and the child was thriving daily under Zillah's skilled care.

Rachel found herself watching Nicholas longingly, her eyes drawn irresistibly to the fine-drawn facial bones, the way his thick fair hair swept forward in heavy waves to obscure his features from her when she had most need of reading his expression. He was arrogant, demanding, driving the servants and quarrymen hard, at times to the point of exhaustion, and himself equally so.

Every day he spent riding about the estate and manor lands or conferring with his quarry foreman. She came to wonder if he were deliberately avoiding her, she saw him so infrequently. The responsibility for the success of the quarry project now lay entirely with him, since Baxter remained absent from the neighborhood and her father was still too ill to do more than talk over plans and look at accounts.

Nicholas did not yet share Rachel's bed. At first she was relieved, for she needed to recover her strength, but she could not hide from herself her sinful desire to lie with him, feel his arm tighten possessively around her waist, his lips linger enticingly on her throat, breast and belly.

She was delighted when her father was well enough to come to the manor. Barnaby drove him and he was still walking with the aid of a stout cane, but he was much improved. They sat together in the drawing room.

Suddenly, he gave that familiar clearing of the throat which she knew heralded some statement of particular importance and one which embarrassed him in the telling.

"Have you heard that Judith was delivered of a son on November 3rd?"

She looked up, startled. "No, I had not. Have you also heard she is recovering well?"

"My informant tells me so." Simon Nashe looked into the fire moodily. "She has not seen fit to contact me."

There was a silence. Rachel knew she must choose her words with care. "Father, I never knew the reason why she . . . Did you quarrel?" She blushed hotly. "Surely you have no cause to think the child is not yours."

"I have every cause to believe he *is* mine. I've been considering what steps to take in this matter."

"Should you not—ask her to return to Glebe, for the boy's sake?"

He looked beyond her bleakly.

"Yes," he said sternly, "my son's place is at Glebe, certainly."

Judith was astounded when her maid, Hannah, announced in a voice breathless with nervous excitement that Mr. Nashe was demanding to see her.

Judith found her legs trembling when she tried to rise. She stiffened her spine determinedly.

"Show him in here, Hannah. Is—is he alone?"

"He's got that housekeeper of his with him, but she's waiting in the carriage."

"Mistress Ashley? Are you sure?"

"Yes, mistress. I saw him turn to talk to her before coming to our door."

"And he is walking—without assistance?"

"Yes, mistress, slowly like, but steady enough on his legs."

Judith was conscious that she must look drawn and pale. It had been a hard birth, taking a great toll of her strength. She waited in trepidation for her husband's greeting.

He stood stiffly in the doorway and she curtseyed, hiding her face from that cold, impersonal stare.

"Please come in, sir, and be seated." She nodded to Hannah. "Leave us, or will you take wine—Simon?" There was the slightest hesitation before she used his given name, as if she felt she no longer had the right to do so.

He sank down heavily in the proffered chair, waving the maid away. "Nothing, thank you."

Judith seated herself opposite, deliberately arranging her skirts, giving herself time to face his anger.

"It is a considerable time since we talked together." It came at last, the opening gambit, stern, coldly stated.

"Yes." Her voice was very low, whispered. "I see you are greatly improved. I thank God for it."

"And you, madam, are you well, and the child?"

She met his gaze as calmly as she could. "I am recovering. And Saul is a fine, strong baby."

"So you wish to name him Saul?"

"I had thought—I should have consulted you, but—"

"You should indeed, madam. The naming of my son is of vital concern to me. However, I have to agree. The name is eminently suitable."

She drew a hard breath. He had no intention, then, of repudiating little Saul.

"You will wish to see him?"

He inclined his head.

She pulled the bell cord and Hannah appeared so quickly she must have been listening outside the door in the hallway.

"Fetch Master Saul from the nursery."

"Yes, mistress." The girl bobbed a curtsey and hurried out.

"He is like me, they say," Judith said hastily, "dark-eyed, but it is too soon to tell yet . . ."

Hannah edged by the unyielding man in the high-backed chair and approached her mistress, the baby clutched tightly in her arms.

Simon Nashe said coldly, "Take the boy out to the carriage to Mistress Ashley. See he is well wrapped against the cold."

Judith stumbled to her feet as Hannah regarded her open-mouthed with astonishment and distress.

"Simon—what—what do you mean? Saul . . ."

"Is my son. His rightful place is at Glebe. I intend to take him there immediately."

Judith's whole body went icy with fear, the blood draining from her face and throat. "You would not—cannot take him from me, Simon."

He stood up, his expression impassive. "Where you decide to live, madam, is a matter of no importance to

290

me. You may go to Glebe with the child or remain here, just as it pleases you." He turned on the maid, "Did you hear me, girl? Take the child to Mistress Ashley."

"Mistress—" Hannah was fast dissolving into sobs.

"Obey Mr. Nashe, Hannah." Judith's voice was toneless.

She waited until the door closed on the maid. "He is your son, Simon. I swear it on everything I hold sacred."

"I believe you."

"I betrayed you with Arthur Baxter—once. The child cannot be his, I know it."

As he remained silent, she said despairingly, "I left you because—because I felt besmirched. You looked at us so accusingly, so terribly. I was afraid. Then you were so unaccountably stricken. It seemed like a judgment on me, and there was the child coming—I dared not come back to Glebe. I wanted to, needed to. Try to understand."

"I understand, Judith. You had no desire to nurse another sick, aging man. Natural enough."

"I am—was—ashamed, Simon."

"That, too, I understand."

"Then do not punish me so hardly and take my son from me."

"I have already said, Judith, that it is for you to decide whether you will return to Glebe."

"You would take me back?"

"I will accept you within my household. You are my wife, the mother of my son."

"But I am not to be forgiven?"

Those chilling gray eyes regarded her dispassionately. "It is my Christian duty to accept you back. You have confessed your faults, are contrite. I must pray to the Almighty that He will grant me the benison of forgiveness."

She gave a great sob of despair, turning from him.

"I loved you, Simon, truly loved you. You were ashamed to love me."

Stiffly, she moved past him to the door. "If you will wait, sir, I will get Hannah to pack necessities for us. I may bring my maid to Glebe?"

Again he inclined his head as she half stumbled by him to the stair.

Christmas threatened to be a cheerless season at Glebe. Judith took up the reins of household management as if she had never been away. Simon made an almost complete recovery, though his gait was somewhat stiff and slow, but he could now sit his horse again. He kept strictly to his own bedchamber, rarely engaging Judith in conversation, even at meals.

She was uneasy in the presence of her stepdaughters. Rachel had gone to some pains to make her feel welcome at the baptism of baby Edward, but Phoebe remained openly hostile and resentful. Saul's baptism was a quiet ceremony immediately following matins, and Simon had encouraged only family members to attend—nor were they invited to any celebration at Glebe afterwards. When Judith tried to broach the matter of her desertion to Mountsorrel, Simon told her curtly that the subject was closed. Outwardly, she had been received back into his home, restored to her rightful place as wife and mother, but she was not for one moment allowed to forget her sin.

And then Sir Arthur Baxter returned to Leicestershire.

Sir Nicholas informed his father-in-law after a morning discussing quarry affairs.

"He called on me this morning early, told me frankly he'd a mind to pull out of this venture. I'm by no means loath to oblige him. I'd feel easier in my mind if he were no longer concerned in the partnership and I imagine you are in agreement with me."

"Nothing would please me more." Simon's eyes avoided those of his wife. "I take it we are in sufficient funds to buy him out?"

"It would seem so. I'll leave the matter in Talbot's hands. In the meantime Baxter has my permission to examine the quarry accounts and discuss progress with the foreman. I understand he has taken himself off there today to do just that." Sir Nicholas's blue eyes flashed greenish lights and Judith knew he was warning his father-in-law deliberately of Baxter's presence at the quarry. Judith toyed with the food on her plate. So Nicholas Hetherington had his own suspicions about her affair with Sir Arthur Baxter.

After Sir Nicholas left, Simon withdrew to his study while Judith occupied herself with the repair of some household linen.

She was surprised to hear a second visitor ride into the courtyard. She folded away her sewing restlessly and went to inquire about the visitor.

As Judith descended the stair, Simon's visitor was coming from the study, her husband close on his heels. Judith saw that it was Colonel Hayward's manservant. Simon's features were set and pale with fury, though his tone was mild enough.

"Get yourself to the stables. My grooms will see you bedded down for the night. You'll need to lie low for a while."

"Aye, Colonel, I'll do that, and thank'ee." The man looked back at him almost conspiratorially. "You'll not need to fret, sir. I'll be gone first thing in the morning. I'll not endanger you further. My colonel wouldn't have wanted that. The Lord bring him to salvation."

"Amen."

The doorlatch clicked and Simon turned to go back

into the study. Catching up her skirts, Judith ran down to join him. As he made to avoid her, she caught urgently at his sleeve.

"What is it? The man spoke of danger—to you!"

"This doesn't concern you—now." The last word was added pointedly.

Determinedly, she followed him into the study before he could bar the door against her.

"Simon, I demand to know why that man came here. I am your wife. I have that right."

"So you now wish to claim the right which months ago you were so anxious to deny."

She winced at the coldness of his tone. This steellike fury, held in tight check, was not for her betrayal and desertion, much as they had meant to him. This was something else, infinitely more terrible.

"The fellow who left. He is Colonel Hayward's man. Then why is he here?"

"*Was* George Hayward's man."

"He is dead? Your friend?"

"He took a pistol ball in the back running from the King's men who arrived to arrest him. Grant was less fortunate. He was taken alive."

His eyes bored accusingly into hers. "You must have had some inclination why they came here last summer. They were formerly Fairfax's men, loyal to the inspired hope of a realm governed by a Godfearing ruler chosen freely by the people. They abhorred the conception of a dissolute monarch seated in St. Edward's chair surrounded by a bevy of painted whores."

"There was a plot—to murder the King?" She mouthed the words incredulously. "You—you supported them?"

"I'd have no hand in the murder of the Lord's anointed. I refused to have any truck with this business, as I refused to give either my hand or my voice to the execution and trial of the late King. Yet they were my friends. I counseled them against this folly. I would do nothing to put them in the hands of their enemies. That, your lover did for them."

She rocked on her feet at the full disclosure of how she had been used.

"I did not know, *couldn't* know. They said, in the village, your house was searched, but I did not understand the reason. Simon, how, why?"

"You talked to Baxter of Hayward's visit? Mentioned Grant by name?"

"Yes, but innocently. I was concerned for the effect their arrival had on you. Afterward you were singularly depressed. I thought perhaps you owed one or both of them a heavy debt."

"I detested the man for his fawning gallantry, yet I judged him nothing but a Court fop, harmless. I should have known him for what he was. Baxter and men of his ilk cared nothing for which side they spied, providing they were paid enough. Well, he put me in dire peril. To save me Rachel went to London to the King, risked the child she was carrying. Now Baxter has taken the lives of comrades who fought bravely beside me at Naseby, aye, and many more skirmishes. That I cannot ignore."

He pushed past her to the door and called up the passage.

"Barnaby, Job, are either of you in the kitchen?"

The door jerked open at the end of the passage and Barnaby came at a run.

"Master?"

"You've been at the quarry today. Did you see Sir Arthur Baxter there?"

"That I did, sir. He was inspecting the site."

"What time was that? Had he left when you came away?"

295

"No, sir. He went into the hut, to look at the books, I think. I saw a lantern lit. Let me see. That'd be about an hour and a half ago."

"And the men are still working?"

"They'll go on while the light holds, but it's closing in fast now, sir."

"Right, you can go."

"Do you want me to take a message to Sir Arthur?"

"No." Simon's smile became almost a death's-head grin. "If I have any message for Sir Arthur, I'll deliver it myself."

He went immediately to the carved oak chest where he kept his riding clothes, army buff coat, uniform sashes. Swiftly, he donned coat and riding boots. Judith watched fascinated as he drew a leather-covered case out of the chest and snapped it open. A pair of wheellock pistols glinted dully in the light from the window. Powder bag and pouch containing shot were thrust deep into his sash; then, deliberately, he drew out baldric and sword sheath and buckled them on.

"You cannot mean to challenge Sir Arthur," she said at last, swallowing back the hard lump of panic forming in her throat. "He is considerably younger, more than likely a good shot, particularly if he is what you say he is, a trained spy, and you are still not completely fit, Simon." Her voice rose hysterically. "It would be murder, without seconds and the correct preliminaries. Listen to me, please." Tears were raining unchecked down her cheeks. "You must not do this, Simon. You will be throwing your life away to no purpose. You cannot save Grant now and your other friend is dead. Simon, I love you—love you."

He shook her off impatiently as she clawed at his arm. "This is none of your concern, madame. I order you to remain here. Keep silent. Do not alert my servants."

"You are condemning yourself uselessly. Your friends were brave, but foolish. You told them that yourself. What good can you do them now?"

"I can avenge them." His face was savage in the flickering firelight, deadly pale, fanatical.

"You've no proof that it was Baxter who laid information against them. They were indiscreet to come here. You were known to be an adherent of Cromwell—"

"I *had* proof. Hayward supplied it. That day I rode in and saw you with Baxter, Hayward had warned me I was suspect."

"Dear God, all the time he was making me pretty speeches, he was watching and waiting to pounce. Simon!"

He took her cruelly by the shoulders. "This is no time for self-pity or recriminations. You will obey me."

He shook her briefly and released her so that she stumbled backward, catching her trailing hem in the turned-back edge of the carpet. By the time she had risen, he had gone. She heard his spurs ring against the corridor flagstones, then his voice calling to Barnaby to bring his horse around.

Shakily, she wiped away her tears, glancing up at the clock. It was a little past three. The quarrymen would still be working. He could not outface Baxter before witnesses. He would have to wait. A single hope flared. Arthur Baxter might already have left. Would Simon attempt to waylay him on the Leicester road, or even follow him into the town? She dared not make a move to alarm Barnaby or Job. If Baxter were to die, Simon could well be accused of his murder. She drew steady, calming breaths, then moved as unhurriedly as she could to the kitchen.

Hannah sat there alone, warming her toes by the hearth.

"Where is Mistress Ashley?"

"In the village. She'd permission from the master. She's gone to see—"

"And the other girls?"

"Two are out. Martha's in the dairy."

"Now listen, Hannah. I am going out for a while, alone. No, don't interrupt. I *must* go alone. If I am not back by full dark, you are to go to Hetherington. Take little Saul if Mistress Ashley is not back. Don't leave him to Moll. Tell Lady Rachel I have gone to the quarry."

"The quarry, but, mistress, it will soon be dark—"

"The master is there, too, on important business. You are not to speak of this to the other girls. He would be angry but"—her voice shook slightly—"should either or both of us not return, do exactly what I asked. Don't fail me, Hannah. Make sure that the manor servants do not prevent you from seeing Lady Rachel. She will know what to do."

"Shall I have your mare brought around?" Hannah's eyes were rounded like gooseberries.

"No, I shall walk. It will excite less comment. I'm going up to change into a warmer gown, cloak and stout shoes, then I want you to watch that the hall is clear for me."

"Yes, mistress."

Hannah was devoted to Judith, who had engaged her from the poorhouse soon after reaching Mountsorrel. The maid had been pathetically grateful for her change of circumstances. Now Judith knew she could rely on Hannah as she could none of the Glebe servants.

Simon would be forced to wait within the shelter of Malkin Copse until after the workmen had left the quarry. Only then could he confront Baxter. If she moved quickly, she could still overtake him by going across Hetherington Park. Since she could not appeal to Simon, she must make an effort to warn Baxter. It

298

was her only hope. If she failed, then it was likely that either Baxter or Simon would die, and even should Simon be the victor in a duel, he would surely hang for the murder of his adversary.

Rachel and Nicholas were at supper and suddenly made conscious of an undignified scuffling and sounds of raised voices from the hall. Sarah came in, clearly agitated.

"It's Mistress Nashe's maid from Glebe, Lady Rachel. She's in a rare state, out of breath, been running hard and she has the baby with her. She begs you to see her, but she won't tell us what's wrong."

Nicholas thrust back his chair with a sickening scrape across the highly polished boards.

"Send her in here, Sarah, at once."

Rachel half rose as Hannah flew in, hair streaming wildly from her cap. She stood staring helplessly from Sir Nicholas to his lady. Little Saul wailed unhappily; he had been snatched from his warm nest in the nursery. Rachel took him and rocked him into silence. Nicholas poured Hannah wine and stood over her while she protested until she had finally swallowed it.

"Come, girl, drink it, get your breath, then let us have your story."

Hannah gulped, choked and finally, in tearful, incoherent phrases told of her mistress's direct and implicit order not to involve the Glebe servants.

"I couldn't leave the baby, my lady. Mistress Ashley's still not back and that Moll's not to be trusted, she drinks if she gets the chance."

"Take Master Saul to Zillah. Sarah will show you the way. You had better stay with him, Hannah."

"But, my lady, the mistress! She seemed rare troubled and so particular I wasn't to tell nobody. She's been gone hours now, *and* the master."

"He was riding?"

"Yes, Sir Nicholas. I 'eard him call for his horse, but he's not properly well yet. He couldn't ride for long. I just don't know why he's not back."

"I'll deal with it, Hannah. Do as Lady Rachel orders. Stay in our nursery with the children."

Wistfully, she said as she backed and bobbed a curtsey, "She will be safe, sir, won't she, the mistress? I'm rare fond of Mistress Nashe."

"We'll find her," he promised. "Sarah, tell Gaston and Jem, yes, and Toby, too, to saddle horses. They're to bring lanterns, and don't gossip of this in the kitchens."

"No, Sir Nicholas."

"You're going to the quarry?"

"Yes, Rachel, I must."

"Let me come."

"That would be pointless. Best if you stay here. Judith may arrive and need help."

"You think my father has challenged Baxter? He could be lying dead out there." She shivered.

"Or a fugitive, if he's killed Baxter."

That sobered her. She turned wide, frightened eyes on him. "What can we do if—"

"I don't know. The fool," he ground out. "I warned him Baxter would be at the quarry, so he could avoid meeting the man. It didn't occur to me he'd seize the opportunity to confront him. It should have."

"Judith is back at Glebe. My father would not kill a man over . . ." Rachel's voice trailed off. Simon Nashe had destroyed Hetherington in revenge for the dishonoring of his name and that of her mother.

"I think there's more to this business than that."

"Then you believe, as I do, that Baxter was involved in the investigation from Whitehall and that my father knows it?"

"He arrived opportunely and courted Judith with singleness of purpose."

"He was sent deliberately to spy by his masters at Whitehall? Then my father was suspected from the beginning?"

"It would seem so. Both men are desperate. There'll be no quarter and less fear of the consequences. Judith was aware of that. That's why she didn't organize a search from Glebe."

Gaston hurried in with Sir Nicholas's boots and his scarlet velvet cloak. He glanced pointedly at his velvet coat. "Will you change, monsieur?"

"No time. Lanterns? Ropes?"

"*Oui*, monsieur."

Nicholas bowed over Rachel's hand. "Your task is the hardest, to wait in patience. We'll not involve Talbot—yet."

Malkin Copse was palled in velvet blackness as the men rode up to the quarry. Sir Nicholas dismounted at the hut. There was no lantern glow to be seen and the place seemed deserted. Gaston held his horn lantern high as Nicholas checked the interior.

"No one." He cupped his hands to his mouth and called. "Colonel Nashe? Baxter?"

His voice smote the uncanny silence and the disturbance caused rustling and scuttering from the creatures in the undergrowth. Gaston's features appeared jaundiced in the yellow lantern light.

"Monsieur, this place it is bad at this time."

Nicholas grunted mirthlessly. "Don't tell me you fear witches, Gaston."

"*Les beldames? Non*, monsieur, but the old one, she was dragged from here to die."

"I remember." He turned and called out, "Jem, Toby."

"Sir," they responded in unison.

"Check around the rear of the hut and the road. We should know if men rode away. The quarry workers were all on foot. Gaston, come with me; we'll penetrate the copse some distance, *mon ami,* unless you fear the curse of Salome Lee."

Gaston was about to answer when Toby's voice came, high, excited.

"A horse, Sir Nicholas, tethered."

Nicholas hastened to the boy's side, his eyes quickly identifying the bay mare.

"Baxter's. So he didn't leave the area. Then where, in God's name, is Nashe?"

Gaston informed him in a concerned whisper. "Here, monsieur. Tread carefully to your left. Monsieur Nashe is lying near the oak tree."

The Frenchman was holding up his lantern to examine the slumped form. Nicholas cursed below his breath as he saw the telltale stain on the leather buff coat.

"He took a ball in the chest. Is he dead, Gaston?"

"No, monsieur, he breathes, but he has lost much blood." He tore off his linen cravat, nodding as Sir Nicholas added his own to the pad the Frenchman was fashioning. Nicholas narrowed his eyes as he looked from the injured man to the horses.

"We need a hurdle, Gaston. Stay with him. I'll see if I can find something suitable in the hut, shoring for the quarry. We can make a bier by stretching our coats between. He must be carried carefully."

"*Oui,* monsieur. If he bleeds inside . . ." The Frenchman shrugged regretfully.

Nicholas rose from his knees and turned back to the hut. Toby padded softly to his side.

"Sir, there's been a fall of slate a bit further on. The wooden railings—collapsed."

Nicholas checked and stared at the boy. "Are you sure?"

"Yes, sir." Toby swallowed. "Looks like somebody went over. We held up our lanterns, but there's nothing to see but loose scree and slate."

Nicholas strode to the section of broken fencing where Jem was peering below into the black depths of the quarry.

"Here, Sir Nicholas."

"No sounds, cries or moans?"

Jem shook his head. "Nothing, sir, and if I'm any judge, no likelihood of them. Nobody who fell down there could hope to survive. It looks like there's been a proper landslide."

"You're right, of course. We can do nothing now. We must wait till it's light and set the men to dig."

"So you've found Colonel Nashe, sir?"

"Yes, badly injured. We'll get him back to the manor. Toby, you mount up and go for Dr. Snell. While you are in Mountsorrel, get hold of Jones, the quarry foreman."

"Yes, Sir Nicholas."

The boy was off in a clatter of hoofs on the flint road. Nicholas gestured to Jem to accompany him into the hut to forage for shoring timber. So far he had found no sign of Nashe's horse—nor of Judith Nashe.

Rachel watched, dry-eyed, when they carried her father in. Her legs shook beneath her, but she gestured the men toward the stairs, her eyes looking to Nicholas for guidance.

"Take him into my bedchamber," he instructed.

He stood aside as the men made their careful climb. Zillah had appeared as if by some pre-knowledge of disaster before Rachel had sent for her. She pattered up behind the men, ready to help as soon as the sick man had been laid on the bed.

"Is he . . . ?"

"No, Rachel, but I think you must prepare yourself for the worst. He took a pistol ball in the chest and he's bleeding badly. There's a head wound and he's unconscious. He may have injured himself when he fell, struck himself against a boulder, perhaps, but he was face down when Gaston found him."

She put up a hand as if to forcibly prevent her lips from trembling as he helped her up the stairs.

"I sent Toby for Snell. He should be here very soon. Until then I suggest we disturb your father as little as possible."

Simon Nashe looked waxen pale, already shrunken, his eyes tightly closed. Rachel reached for his hand and found it ice-cold. Zillah had checked that the wound pad was still in place.

Rachel drew aside to the window as the men moved out, awkwardly quiet. Nicholas said softly, "Gaston, send a groom to Mr. Talbot at Barrow."

"Then they fought? Did Baxter ride off, do you think?"

Nicholas hesitated then said grimly, "I doubt it. I think he went over the edge of the quarry. His horse was still tethered around the back of the hut."

Rachel turned tortured eyes toward the man on the bed. "But my father would not have done that; he would not have tried to cover up, and he's too gravely hurt."

"No, that's patently obvious. Baxter must have fired and hit your father." Nicholas shrugged uncomfortably. "It's likely he had no choice, he was forced to defend himself. Perhaps there was a struggle and he fell. The railing is broken."

"He could be lying hurt, dying—"

"No one could be alive down there. The fall of slate was tremendous. The edge of the quarry collapsed. We always feared it there, that's why I ordered the men to put up the rough fencing."

She shuddered. "Judith?"

"I don't know. We saw no sign of her."

He saw his own fear mirrored in her eyes and put a strong brown hand over hers. "Take heart. We cannot know that. Simon may have ordered her away, sent her with one of the workmen."

"But she would have gone straight home to Saul."

He nodded, and was saved from the necessity of replying by the arrival of Dr. Snell.

The little physician pursed his lips doubtfully as he bent his ear to Simon Nashe's chest.

"Take your lady below while I make my examination, if you please, Sir Nicholas. Zillah will help me here."

Rachel would have protested, but Nicholas drew her firmly outside.

"He knows what he's about. You can do nothing. You're shaking. Come down to the drawing room and take some wine."

Nicholas insisted she drink some brandy. The fiery liquid coursed through her, making her choke and cough.

"What—what are you going to do about—about finding Baxter's body?" she said shakily.

"I told Toby to knock on the foreman's door. He'll rouse the men. They'll start digging at first light." He pulled back the window curtains, staring out into the blackness. "It's not possible to do anything yet. It would be hazardous to send anyone down there without light."

Dr. Snell came softly down the stairs. His eyes met those of Nicholas and he shook his head. Rachel choked back a sob.

"You can do nothing, nothing at all?"

"Lady Rachel, it would only give him needless pain to attempt to dislodge the ball. He's bleeding internally. It is merely a matter of time. He is conscious now. Go up to him. He's asked for you."

"Is he in great pain?"

"I've administered a mild infusion of poppy. He needs to talk to you. I suggest you send for the rector, though I doubt if he can arrive in time." He smiled

305

wanly at Sir Nicholas. "I'll stay in case I'm needed—at the end."

As Rachel entered the room, Zillah rose from her chair near the bed. They had sat Simon up against the pillows, and he smiled as Rachel entered.

"I'll be right outside, my lady, should you need me." Rachel nodded to Zillah. She seated herself very close to her Father and gripped his hand as he reached for hers. She was crying now, aware of the wetness running down her cheeks.

"Don't try to talk. Rest. You're not in pain, are you? Dr. Snell . . ."

"No, the pain is not bad. I have to talk, Rachel." His voice was weak, but firmer than she could have dared to hope. She bent and kissed the chilled fingers.

"We've sent for Phoebe. Don't fret."

"She—will need you. She's—like her mother, Phoebe. She wan—wanted demonstrative love. Poor Dorcas. I—I failed her as I failed Judith."

"No, father."

"Yes, Rachel. Judith—loved me and I her." His eyes closed as he strove to garner his strength. "I was ashamed to—to pleasure her. Conscious of my great sin in—desiring her."

Rachel waited, biting back her sobs, and his eyes flickered open again.

"She came out of the wood like some wild spirit, cloak flying, hair streaming and she ran at him, clawing and biting."

"At Baxter?"

He jerked his chin slightly. "I faced him—when the men had gone—challenged him, said if he wouldn't fight I'd—I'd draw on him and cut him down—deserved it—no honor in a spy."

Rachel reached for a dampened cloth and wiped his brow. "It doesn't matter. Don't talk."

306

"You have to know—just—how it was. He took—took me seriously then and—and we paced out the ground and turned—then—then she came, screaming at him. They struggled. I couldn't fire for fear of hurting her—" He gave a terrible, convulsive shudder and blood specks appeared in the spittle frothing his lips. Feeling a steadying hand on her shoulder, Rachel turned to find Nicholas behind her.

"There—there was a sudden report and—and I went down, sickening blow to my chest—white-hot pain. I heard—heard her scream again and they fell—splintering wood—showers of scree and slate and then—then, utter stillness. I tried to crawl to the edge to listen, know if she were crying out, down there. I couldn't reach her—"

He coughed weakly and choked, blood bubbling horribly to his lips as Nicholas sprang to support him.

"Saul, my son . . ."

"We'll care for Saul, I promise, father, promise . . ."

"Loved—loved Judith . . ."

His voice choked off again and there was a heart-rending wheezing and rattling as he fought for breath. Rachel turned away, furious at her own fear and horror, then it was over. The hand slackened in her grasp and she laid it gently onto the coverlet.

She was aware of Nicholas moving from the bed head, drawing her to her feet. She struggled stubbornly.

"I want to stay with him."

"No, Rachel. Zillah will do what is needed and Leah Ashley can be sent for to help. Come down with me now. Your sister will need you."

She was numbed. She went downstairs unresistingly and he seated her on the settle. Sarah bustled in quietly to make up the fire and wrap a warm rug around her knees. Would it never be day?

307

Wheels clattered over the cobbles of the yard and Nicholas left her to meet Phoebe and Roger, prepare them. Her sister ran to her, kneeling before her on the hearth, sobbing bitterly. They clung together while the men drew apart. As she held Phoebe tightly, Rachel could hear her husband's voice, quiet, authoritative, fully in command of the situation. There would be formalities to attend to, the other magistrates must be informed, the coroner; but first the bodies of Judith Nashe and Arthur Baxter would need to be unearthened from the quarry.

"Why was he fool enough to be taken in by that woman?" Phoebe spat viciously. "She brought him to this, and now she's run off with her lover, deserted her child—"

"Hush, Phoebe," Rachel said softly, "Judith is dead. She gave her life in an attempt to save father. She loved him."

Phoebe drew away from her, staring in blank astonishment.

"She fell to her death struggling with Baxter as he was about to fire. Father was just able to tell us."

"Dear God, how horrible. Have they—have they found them?"

"Not yet. Nicholas says the men must wait until it's light."

Grandmamma had been persuaded to wait at Barrow. Roger explained she had a chill and he'd thought it pointless to expose her to the raw night air. He took the weeping Phoebe to pay her last respects to her father. Rachel sat on alone. Nicholas had left her to change and go back to the quarry.

Dawn came slowly, the first gray light shedding ghostly fingers over the room and, in spite of the fire now blazing on the hearth, Rachel shivered uncontrollably.

It was when they brought the bodies of Judith Nashe and Arthur Baxter to the manor that Rachel finally broke down. The quarrymen carried them in reverently on roughly constructed biers, covered with holland sheets conveyed to the quarry for the purpose. Their embarrassed sympathy for the bereaved family was painfully touching. Nicholas thanked them, dismissing them for the rest of the day.

"Go to your homes, lads. There will have to be a thorough examination of the site before we risk further working. Thank you for what you've done. It has been neither easy nor pleasant."

Rachel could not bring herself to look at Baxter, but she resolutely turned back the sheet and gazed down at Judith. Her stepmother's face appeared dignified and peaceful in death, one livid bruise standing out starkly on the waxen-pale features. She replaced the sheet, ran up to her chamber and burst into a storm of weeping.

It was all such a waste, of life, of beauty, of hope.

Her father's last thoughts had been for Judith and the child. He'd finally confessed his inability to show his wife the affection she craved. And it had been the same with Rachel's mother. So many lives ruined because Simon Nashe had believed that the warmth and ecstasy of love were forbidden to one whose devotion was dedicated to the Lord God alone. Desire must be fought and subdued, a weakness to be steadfastly abhorred. He had rigidly controlled his passion for Judith, and at what a cost? She had turned to Arthur Baxter for consolation and he had known, only too well, how to turn that desperate need to his own avaricious use.

In the depth of her sorrow Rachel saw clearly the futility of that tragedy at the quarry.

And her father's rigid teaching threatened her own happiness! She recognized that, too, starkly. She loved

Nicholas with every fiber of her being, burned to surrender herself completely to the wild delight he was capable of arousing in her, yet she had held herself back, doubtful of her own longings and the tender warmth of her feelings for him. Happiness was within her grasp, yet she was afraid to reach out and take it.

The door clicked open behind her. She lay huddled on the bed, face hidden, her fingers grasping the fine lace of the pillows. She did not dare turn or lift her head.

She was abruptly drawn close into his arms, smelled the sweetly familiar masculine odors of leather and hair pomade. Nicholas was still dressed in his leather riding coat. She tried to avoid his gaze. Her face was blotched and hideous with weeping, her eyes red-rimmed and swollen.

His lips pressed close to her hair, for once comforting, tender.

"You've nothing to fear from the authorities. There will be few questions to answer. Legal formalities will be cut to a minimum. I've some control over the petty restrictions of county affairs."

He put her at arm's length, gazing deep into her eyes.

"This nightmare will soon be over. I've no doubt that you can face this with true courage, Rachel, as you have proved to me so often in the past."

She choked back her tears and rose from the bed, putting up a trembling hand to straighten her disordered hair. "There will be ugly gossip . . ."

"Ignore it. Remember, you are the squire's lady, mistress of Hetherington. How can the spiteful talk of farm workers and inn servants touch you in the slightest?"

She forced a smile. Imperious as ever. Hetheringtons were bred to believe they trod a different world from lesser mortals. He was right, of course. No one would dare to utter one word of scurrilous doubt in her hearing.

She crossed to her mirror and stared at her reflection. She must prepare herself to face them all.

He came up behind her. His hand reached out and took her hairbrush.

"Shall I send for Zillah or shall I act as lady's maid?" His voice was soft, husky with desire, and she blinked back the tears at the sight of herself, ugly, despairing. She should always be beautiful for him.

Then suddenly, for the first time, she recognized the truth. In his eyes she was lovely. She saw that his blue-green eyes had softened as his fingers touched her dark lashes, spiked with salt tears. He stooped and kissed the top of her head and, impulsively, she caught his hand and kissed it.

"No, don't summon Zillah, not now."

This arrogant man with his courtly airs and handsome face had chosen her, Rachel Nashe, crippled, unworldly, as mistress of Hetherington, mother of his children.

If Lettice Ryall had meant so much to him, why had he not married her long ago? Lady Ryall had wealth enough to match Rachel's dowry.

She loved him and she would fight to keep him. She would not fail to hold him as her father had failed to hold Judith or Dorcas, her own mother. Nicholas Hetherington needed, demanded a mate spirited enough to match his own passionate ardor.

As if he read the sudden resolution in her gaze, he laughed and pulled her to her feet and around to face him, running his fingers caressingly through the loosened masses of her hair. She surrendered to his kiss, her own being melting, fusing into his. She would draw the courage to face what lay ahead from him.

She gave a little sigh of contentment, then resolutely

drew herself free from his embrace. There was still much to be done. Nicholas needed her. His needs would be met and satisfied—but later.

Now, at last, she felt free, able to give herself completely, without restraint. His blue-green eyes flashed fire just once, then his mouth broke into a slow smile. He kissed her fiercely on the lips, just once, and then he released her. There would be so much time for their love during the long years ahead.